Holcum's Dynasty:
# The Grandmothers

# Farley Dunn

THREE SKILLET

HOLCUM'S DYNASTY: THE GRANDMOTHERS, Dunn, Farley

First Edition

THE SE'YAN'T CHRONICLES, Book 4

 THREE SKILLET

www.ThreeSkilletPublishing.com

Cover design by Farley L Dunn

ISBN: 978-1-943189-38-0

# Holcum's Dynasty:
# The Grandmothers

# —Chapter 1—

*Cry your tears, my child.*
*The day is almost done.*
*Your pain will be wiped away*
*In the setting of the sun.*

*—Child's bedtime song*

"ONE HUNDRED YEARS." The old invalid's crippled and pal-sied hand shook, holding an old-fashioned ID card wrapped in gnarled fingers.

"What, Grandmother? What about one hundred years?"

The ancient woman rasped, her words sandpaper on stone, "Dead, one hundred years, and he would have loved me." Her hand was barely under her control, her deteriorated muscles too old and worn to care any longer what her mind might tell them to do. She thrust the ID card at her granddaughter, drumming it in a desperate beat against her arm. "Rom'n."

The old woman's body jerked in a violent fit of coughing, her pain written across her tortured features.

"Grandmother!" The beautiful young granddaughter looked to the man standing across the bed from her, desperately search-ing for relief from her grandmother's pain. "Gregor, what should I do?"

Gregoirini Abbadelli consoled her in a tender voice, "My own grandmother, when she died, her hand, I held. Sometimes, to do, that be all we can. Knowing they be held in love when they need us the most be the best anyone can offer." With the tears of his own memories moistening his eyes, he gave his wisest advice to the old woman's most loyal protector. "Love her, Innocetta. So she knows, hold her. Hold her, now."

Innocetta Verona reached to place her arms around the old woman, the coughing shaking them both. Feeling the hand with the ID card pressing them apart, she released her grandmother. In a quivering parody of an old-fashioned dance, the gnarled hand placed the ancient card into Innocetta's hand. Innocetta leaned in closely, pleading, "What is it, Grandmother?"

"He could have been mine."

Innocetta turned her tear-filled eyes to Gregoirini. "What does she mean, Gregor?"

"Listen, be all you can do." He placed a gentle hand on her shoulder.

She leaned over her grandmother, her ear pressed close to pick up her final whispered words. "He would have loved me. Now, he's yours."

Those were the last sounds Innocetta heard her grandmother speak. Rising to look at Gregoirini standing across from her, letting her tears wash her face, a sudden odor of urine permeated the room. A numbness came over them. When they looked down, they could tell.

The grandmother was dead.

# —Chapter 2—

*Rain.*
*The sweet smell*
*Of the summer rains beckons.*
*Yet, the rains are a fierce two-edged sword.*
*They tempt the smallest of the seeds to produce the harvest.*
*They flood the valleys, destroying all within their reach.*
*We cannot live without the rains.*
*Baby Johanaston lies here,*
*Drowned in the*
*Summer*
*Rains.*

*7-3-2207 to 7-12-2207*

*—From an old-Earth tombstone*

REGGEANTE SELVAGGIO, tall and slender, with thick, dark hair not quite under anyone's control, walked across the room to a screaming control panel. His eyes, brilliantly green, flashed as he pursed his full lips. Reaching to the blinking warning light, he slapped the alarm off. His duty partner across the room was oblivious as far as he could tell, and that irritated him.

"Carli," he called, with more than a hint of ire, "since we

came on duty, it be the third time, gone off, this alarm has. Be it malfunctioning, you think?" He focused for a moment on the displays, then hit a few keystrokes on an old-fashioned keyboard. "Upgrade this system, you think they would. Use this very one, my grandfather did." He shook his head at the letter he knew he always had to hit twice to make work. He struck it a second time, hard, before it gave him what he wanted.

"Complain too much, you do, Regge, my friend. Be satisfied that the guidance systems of the latest design be, even if all else be ancient." Carlan'te Fausti was Regge's good friend, but not too good a friend when the man complained excessively. He spread his hands to indicate the consoles. "Warning systems, only, these be. And of it, think, my friend." He sat back and laughed, his round face and plentiful girth fitting his ebullient mood. "Would this harsh, unvisited world be a place of choice riches for thieves to steal? Ah, lands they wish to raid, fertile and green? Here? Thinking that, you be, huh, Regge?"

"Not on this world, for certain." Regge pursed his lips, still studying the readouts. Something wasn't right, and he hadn't decided what it was. He knew—as did all children brought up in the city's educational system—that raiders had visited Trasdrom'man before, just not in his and Carli's memory. It was the reason for the alarm system in the first place. Now, three times it had gone off, and just on their shift. Three times. They couldn't afford to ignore it, not with the possibility for raiders looking more and more likely. And, to top it off, it only showed up on the old and outdated systems, not the new, much-awaited and infinitely better interface that had only recently received the much-needed updates. That one was perfectly quiet, not a peep, one.

"Only the old system, it be on, and not the new. Make of that, what should we?" Regge rubbed his chin with one hand, undecided how to proceed.

"Worked very hard to find it on the new, I have, and only one

10

possible explanation there be." Carli had finished off a pre-wrapped snack, and he wadded the packaging before continuing, taking the time to toss it casually at a refuse bin.

"And?" Regge grumbled, thoroughly flustered by the jumbled and cantankerous warning system.

"Not finding it, because an out-of-date signal, it be." Carli chuckled and began unwrapping another snack.

"Noise." Regge snapped his fingers as an idea came to him. He knew he'd figure this out, if he let it ramble through his mind. "Too much radio noise, there be. Invisible only to *some* sensors, it be. See what's there, you will. Watch this."

"Watch what, my friend? You fail?" Carli, shorter than his friend by a hand, as well as rounder by many more, smiled. His red hair and freckles betrayed his teasing manner, even as his hazel eyes twinkled.

Regge reached to the old keyboarded system to tap a few more keystrokes. Glancing back at his partner, he shrugged off Carli's condescending glance. "The signal, very basic, it be, out of date, even, and hear it better, this old system can. To search for an old-fashioned signal, these old-fashioned sensors be the best. There be something there, you'll see. Getting a clear signal, I now be." He grinned as he twisted a few well-worn dials on his console, bringing a loud humming and squealing noise from an overhead speaker. Turning to Carli, he shouted, "That! The signal to run through your console, it be. Know this soon, we will."

Carli jumped from his seat, and with a violent shove, he pushed Regge aside. Tapping in his own instructions, the noise abated to a low series of chirps and buzzes. He cut his eyes to the man next to him, growling, "Deaf, I don't need to be. Enough it be just to hear the noise. Run your signal for you, I will. If this be anything, for you, find out, I will." Jamming a finger in one ear with a pained expression, he shook his head and returned to his seat.

11

A faint hum grew in strength, emanating from inside the machine. Soon, an image formed on the viewscreen above their heads. Carli looked up and saw his friend working with the old-fashioned keyboard at his station, and he threw a lightweight drinking vessel at him to get his attention. When he glanced up, Carli pointed to the image.

Regge muttered, his eyes taking in the displays, "Expected a cloud of gliderhawks, perhaps, or a ship lacking authorization. A cryo pod, this be? Flying free?" He looked down and tapped a few strokes. The image enlarged. He looked over at his friend. "Fly in space, they can? Never heard of this. Real, you think this be?" When Carli shrugged, Regge turned the sound back up a bit. At the other man's frown, he held up one finger to tell him to be patient. "Harmonics. A second signal, there be. Hear it?"

This time even Carli sat up and looked interested. Raising the volume even further, he pulled earpieces over his head and tapped on his console. After a few careful moments, he glanced up at Regge and pulled the listening devices from his ears. His mouth gaped, and he yelled over the noise of the signal, "MegaCorp, and real, it be."

"MegaCorp?" Regge yelled, also. "Sending a cryo pod to us, why would MegaCorp be?"

"Unknown," Carli yelled back. "Why be that important?"

"Cryo pods, MegaCorp doesn't have, not a one. Without spaceflight of any kind, they be." Regge flipped his controls to signal the spaceport remote guidance division. "A ruse, this must be. Send this to guidance, I will. Know what to do, they surely must."


THE ELECTRIC DISCHARGE spiderwebbed across one wall of the cabin on the great MegaCorp battleship, as the NeuroShok clattered to the floor. Electric fire shot between the eyes of CaptGen'l Willane Bofsky and UnderGen'l Ma'jene Holcum as their wills wrestled for control of the room. Shaking in fury, Holcum's acceptance of the military chain of command was wrenched from her hard rock of a soul and slammed at her captgen'l's feet with the dropping of her eyes.

"Damn you, Bofsky!" She spat her feelings at him. She knew he would do her one worse than anything she could do to him. She had seen it in practice too many times in the years they had served together. For her to exact retribution at this stage was to invite a rain of horrors upon her head.

"I've taught you well, Ma'jene." Bofsky grinned at her capitulation. He could afford to be magnanimous, now. He was in control of the situation, and she knew it. Looking at the blackened pattern the NeuroShok discharge left splayed across his wall, he laughed. "Even your anger has served me well."

Holcum jerked her eyes to his face, her flashing pupils narrowed to slits. "Just not in this. Is that what you think? For all the suns gone nova, I've worked these groundies over with a finetooth comb. Those that couldn't tell me what I desired to know paid with their lives." She turned her eyes away from the captgen'l. "None have been able to give us the answers we required. You're aware of my skill in this matter. I've let no one down. There are no answers."

Bofsky walked to the electricity-scarred wall and picked up the NeuroShok where it had fallen to the floor. "Perhaps. Even so, this is the final Rejuvie. If we don't get our answers from this one, there will be no answers." He said the words with a smirk that spoke of desire more than intent. He hefted the tool in his hand, remarking, "And to think, this wasn't even invented as a defensive weapon. Or one of coercion."

"You mock me."

"Mock you? Not in my dreams. I believe this was invented as a method of molecular bonding for metallic sheeting. It revolutionized shipbuilding in the airless restrictions of low planetary orbit. It became a well-known and useful tool throughout the inhabited systems. Industrial molecular bonding, only available for law enforcement once they added governors to control the power output."

"This is no civilian tool." Holcum's eyes were on the weapon, and she viewed it as such. "There's no governor on our NeuroShok wands. Spare me the lectures, Bofsky. You treat me as though I were a child."

"Ah, but it is." He laughed. "They are one and the same, as shown by a shipment of military and civilian NeuroShok wands that were once mislabeled." Although officially, the civilian NeuroShok was reduced in power to non-lethal standards, the unit was essentially the same as the military version. A simple power governor was used to contain the power output to maximize production capabilities. Reserves of completed tools could quickly be converted from military to civilian and back again as demand dictated.

"And I should care?" Holcum still had hopes of retrieving the wand. She must gain access to the final humanoid from the planet below. His death would be hers, and she would revel in it.

"Perhaps. A technician was, shall we say, distracted. On the input window where he should have checked *civilian,* he inadvertently left it blank, and because of that, the shipment defaulted to our fully powered military model. Many people died before the mistake was uncovered." Bofsky walked to his desk, opened a drawer, and dropped the weapon inside. He looked at Holcum and smiled. "We know that to inflict the maximum strength from a military model on the human body will fry the very nerves that allow the human body to operate. More than a few seconds, and it's possible to cook a person from the inside out. Hence, our wall." He motioned with one hand.

"Wrap this up, Bofsky. I wish to be away, if I'm not to be given access to the final suspect." *And I will gain access by other means, if you simply give me opportunity!*

"In good time. Let me finish. Financial fecundity is of paramount interest to MegaCorp. That technician was labeled as a sleeper terrorist, and he and his family were escorted to the newly set up prisonplanet, Rant. There his daughter died a painful death due to lack of medical treatment, and the corporation received the accolades deserved by their new status as the rescuers of vulnerable civilian populations. The terrorists responsible for inflicting the NeuroShok incident on an unsuspecting population were now incarcerated and unable to inflict further damage."

"And?" She bit off the word in her attempt to control her anger.

"What will MegaCorp do to those who fail to perform at this task, one that's so much more profitable? Do you wish to be the one to *fail?* I cannot protect you in this. I can only look out for myself." He straightened the bottom of his overjacket, and when he looked up, he gloated with his reasoning. He knew he had her.

"There are no answers. Why can't you admit that? You do in this final Rejuvie, and you'll have wiped this race from the face of the planet below us. Just that alone is enough satisfaction for me, but is that the real reason you're taking this opportunity from me? To protect me? Or just to have the pleasure of using the NeuroShok on this last one? You know it can't be because you expect to get results where I've found none."

Frustration made her heart pound. She couldn't let this last one escape from her. This was her final chance to enjoy her hand with the NeuroShok on one of these people, and with Mega-Corp's approval, too. She dreamed of this every night and could hardly wait each day for the next group of Rejuvies to be brought on board. Just to be able to press that electric tip against their skin and create rising screams of torment was better than anything she knew.

"It isn't always about the answers. You know that as well as

I, Holcum. The process used is the interesting thing. The answers, if they come, are welcome. If they don't, the process has still been well served." Bofsky opened his drawer and tossed Holcum the NeuroShok, watching her catch it efficiently, its power switch still in the on position. He raised his eyebrows, daring her to question his pinpoint accuracy on the matter. "Whether there were ever answers for you to find is now a moot point. This last Rejuvie is mine."

With a tightening of her lips, Holcum snapped to attention, tapped her heels together, and barked out, "Ser!" The door barely had time to open before she was gone, her angry storm taken with her.

A CLOUD OF black fury wrapped Holcum as she tore through the corridors; the faces she met were just flashes of annoyance in her path. Finally, reaching a corridor clear of intrusion, she stopped, her anger tearing her strength from her. Forcing her eyes shut, and her clenched jaw popping the tendons from her neck, she turned to the wall and pressed her forehead to its surface, one fist slamming into its hardness over and over.

No matter how furiously she beat the wall, she knew she could no more damage it than she could return to the captgen'l's quarters and claim this last Rejuvie prize. A memory of the final time she had been onworld flashed into her mind. Gods knew she'd tried to forget the horror that event dredged from her forgotten past. Forgotten? No, buried. Intentionally removed from her mind, boxed up, and buried in a hole dug by the dark deeds of nearly twenty years. That first uppercadet who had snubbed her. Rezalton, simpleton, had helped take care of that one. That'd been her most satisfying kill, better even than all the ones she'd blown back to their makers during those downside conflicts she hated. Well, she admitted to herself, she hated being downside, but blowing people away? That wasn't so bad. It had provided her *some* consolation while being onworld.

That last planetside conflict, though. She should have never volunteered for that one. They had been clearing the final rebels from MegaCorp's rightfully owned mining world, or at least that's what her team was told. Then, as her team battled the final group of rebels, she *remembered.* She'd been a little girl there. Her parents, her home, and all the things that were done to her in the intervening years until she was forced into the academy at fourteen. In her mind, on that day, those buried events had become yesterday. Gods, but nothing since had been able to wipe the pictures from her mind, the reeling, flashing images that now demanded her attention every moment of her day. Her little girl's shattered life. Her parents dead at her side. Her home torn to its foundations. Riding in the dark cage. The men. The men. Over and over.

She could feel freedom only when the stomach-rending surges of satisfaction from the Rejuvies' pain fed her raw nerves the sustenance they so craved. Bofsky was stealing that final opportunity from her. She could already feel the withdrawal. Her nerves burned, and she felt her *need* for the pain of others as they screamed in torment, their voices drowning out the horror in her head.

The last time she was on Earth, they had forced her to sit on that dais. She had sat there with *groundies,* her nerves still raw from that sudden remembering only a handful of sevendays before. They had seen bravery in her actions. She knew otherwise. Her actions had been fueled by blind rage and only blind rage. Even that had been a flyswatter against the black river of torment that had come flooding into her memories. Afterward, her terrors had refused to leave her alone, their blinding reminders here even today, even now in this corridor.

Her body leaning against the corridor wall triggered its built-in sensors. The molecules of its internal substrate realigned themselves, and the glassine, the strongest substance ever used to construct the giant behemoths that flew between the stars, let the light of the planet below, that beautiful world and its twin suns, flood the corridor of the ship.

Opening her eyes and looking around, Holcum could see her lonely corridor was no more. Now she stood on the edge of space. Before her was nothing but the floor on which she stood and the blackness of the universe stretching farther than her eyes could see. In this lonely stretch at the edge of the galaxy, there weren't even stars to break the inky velvetiness of its texture, only the twin suns, one hugging the beautifully jeweled planet as its own, and the other circling at a great distance.

Unmoved, only knowing how she hated groundies and anything associated with them, Holcum cursed the glassine window wall and slapped a palm to its surface, triggering it back to a featureless, opaque solidity. Turning, slamming her back to what she had seen and all it represented, she threw her head against it and let the tears flow as she sank to the floor.

"HERE IT BE," the control manager called to her overseer, "as Regge said, the signal, and coming this way."

The overseer stepped to the readout. "The signal, that of a civilian pod, it be. MegaCorp, you say?" He cleared his throat. "Remote, that possibility be."

"There it be, mas. From me, what do you wish? A warning, only, can I send. No weapons, we have; that, you know." She looked at him for confirmation.

He motioned to her. "A warning, then, send to them. Away, they must depart."

"Sending to them, already. Still, the signal, the same it be, mas. To do next, what be it you want?" She sat with her hands poised over her console.

Her overseer paused, and then he made a decision, snapping

his fingers in inspiration. "Regge and Carli. Them, we'll send. Then, take all the blame, they will, if this lands." He smiled. He had his scapegoats if something went wrong. Knowing Regge and Carli, things could go very wrong, indeed.

HOLCUM STOOD before the door leading into her quarters and drew in a deep breath. Back in control on the outside, she didn't want to lose her semblance of self-respect once she stepped out of the view of others onboard the ship. She needed to do that for herself. After a moment, she placed her palm on the lock and waited as the door opened. Casting her eyes over the sparse interior, the clean lines and lack of personal items were a comfort for her.

She stepped in and palmed the door closed. The jumble of emotions and pictures raging in her mind could sometimes be pushed into the background when she looked at the *nothing* surrounding her, as she stood alone in her quarters. Nothing to remind her of conflicts or people. No parents, nor the lack of friends, or even the cruelty she habitually visited on those she came into contact with daily. In this space, she could pretend her mind was this way, also. Clean. Uncluttered. She stripped her clothes off and flung them at the stor'lok, not caring for the moment if they were hung neatly or not. They could be in no more of a jumble than her thoughts. Stepping into the shower, she was glad her quarters were located at a great distance from the bridge and her workstations. The long walks and lift rides gave her transition time. At the start of each duty cycle, she had time to push the night's terrors away. Returning, she needed the distance to prepare her resolve. People who thought she was aloof and callus didn't see how hard it was to survive, to be strong, and to not let them know the terrors and horrors she lived with each day.

Stepping from the shower, she snapped a disposa-towel from

the dispenser, flinging it into the recycle slot when finished. Moving into her room, kicking her soiled clothing aside, she was disgusted at the disorder and disgusted at herself for not hanging the items properly. Snapping open the stor'lok, she pulled down a freshly pressed uniform and laid it out on her bunk. Clean clothes would provide a fresh start for the rest of the day.

Glancing at the crumpled clothes on the floor, she rifled through her overjacket and began removing the medals and awards she would wear as she exited the room to continue the day. Laying them out on her work surface, she stroked each one with care. These tangible tokens of her military success represented who she was. These were the sum of her life. Attaching each one carefully and lovingly to her fresh overjacket, she recognized the great strides she had taken in her career. Soon, she would be in a position to command her own starstrike cruiser. They had to build her cruiser first, and with a fifteen-year build cycle for the massive ships, that meant she had to be patient. She curled her nose at this outdated wreck she currently served on. Bofsky could have this one. She would be primed and in position just as the latest model came on line. Then, these medals and this uniform would serve her well. She stroked the letters emblazoned on the front of her overjacket. M. She traced the letter and smiled. C. Her smile grew larger. MegaCorp was her life. She would be the most successful captgen'l ever documented in the history of the corporation.

Of course, no one outside the highest echelons of the Mega-Corp Military Arm would ever know, as the best of the starstrike cruisers were top secret, but that was fine with her. She enjoyed running in an elite crowd. The fewer people she had to interact with, the better.

She pulled one medal apart from the rest. This one she would refuse to wear today. It was for *that* time, the time that had brought her buried memories alive for her. She wouldn't be reminded today of what she was trying so hard to forget. With her anger cleansed from her, perhaps she could reason with Bofsky. Perhaps this last Rejuvie could be hers, after all.

Opening a low and unused drawer, she set the medal inside. Perhaps, when she had enough medals, she would throw this atrocity out with all the other detritus of her life, just as she had that idiot, Rezalton.

She began to put on her clothing one item at a time, a ritual she knew well. Underclothing, clean and trim, and always in standard-issue white. Some people liked to wear special-order underclothing, but not her. It disturbed her carefully maintained MegaCorp image. Others might not see what was underneath her clothing, but she knew. She always knew.

Next, she pulled on her outer clothing, and finally, her overjacket with its many medals. The reassuring weight renewed her self-confidence. For the first time since stepping into her quarters, she felt her sense of pride begin to return.

Only now, with her fresh uniform and medals in place, did she dare to envision herself as her shipmates saw her, and she was pleased. This was what she wanted others to view, and this was the only way she allowed herself to be seen. This was the MegaCorp she represented. This was the Ma'jene Holcum that stood tall and brave before the world, no matter what she'd endured to get here.

CARLI HELD out a sheaf of paper to Regge. On most modern and prosperous worlds, paper was an unacceptable medium of keeping records or sharing information, but it was something very well known on their world. While other more advanced planets had superseded the use of hard copy with technology, Trasdrom'man wasn't one of them. It lagged far behind the rest of the inhabited systems.

Regge snatched the paper orders from Carli, the look on the

21

other man's face telling him he'd wish he hadn't. He glanced at the words and then back to his partner's face. Wadding the paper, he threw it at his console.

"Remote access? Achieve remote access, they think we can? How, when to us, the thing won't respond? Barely to get the signal to pick up, we can."

"Know this," Carli responded, "expect us to do anything, the 'seer doesn't. Just the ones who get to chase it down, we be, when it gets through and crashes. Out there, how hot be it?"

Carli had a valid reason for asking. Winters on Tras-drom'man were long and fierce, barely survivable, and never on the surface. Only in summer were the northern and southern portions of the planet tolerable for life, and then it was cruel, even at the poles. Near the equator was worse. The vastly elliptical orbit of the planet allowed it to freeze for half a year and roast for the remainder. Their world didn't have a word to adequately express the concepts of spring and fall as understood on Earth. This year there had been no transition at all. When the seasonal transitions were exceptionally sharp and vicious, people died, and that happened often. Now, it was summer, and to be outside without a water suit was to risk one's life.

Regge drummed his desk. "Just for a few days, summer has been here, and already dare go out without a water suit, I refuse. Want to be outside himself, the 'seer doesn't."

"Blame him, do you?" Carli gave a rueful grin. "Okay, give it a go, we might as well. An override, let's try. Remember that delivery, when here to work, we'd just come?" He grinned at the memory. "Intercepted it, we did."

Regge laughed at the mental images invoked. "Which one? That stimulant shipment, or the one for the year with all the women's personal hygiene supplies?"

Carli's eyes went wide. "Forgot all about that one. Fun after all, this just might be, Regge. That pod, let's the-what-for give it!" He leaped to his feet and headed towards the door. Regge rolled his eyes and called after him, "Or, give us the what for, it might." He exited behind his friend and closed the door, making sure the catch was firmly latched to keep the day's rising heat out of doors.

HOLCUM RESTED her hand on the topmost storage drawer alongside her stor'lok cabinet. She stood for a handful of breaths considering the contents: personal identification cards, information crystals, and other sundry goods suitable for blackmail or revenge. If Bofsky didn't give in, a little backup satisfaction might be in order. Making her decision, she snapped open the drawer and slid the pile of ID cards and information crystals into her hand. Thumbing through them, one in particular jumped out at her.

Rom'n Rezalton, ultimate pansy.

*Sentimental fool! Demoted to underpriv't, and at my hand!* Holcum laughed to herself. He'd been at her side from the first day she'd shown up at the academy, promoted along with her at each step of the way. His interest in her had been obvious, and she'd played him to the hilt.

Overcadet Timons was her first test for him. Rezalton capitulated without a murmur. After that, they crippled another cadet in the games competition, although Holcum had needed to plan it out for him. A little lubrication on the steps, then Rezalton setting off the ship's emergency drill alarm just as the cadet was starting down. Holcum even secured a copy of the security feed. The cadet made it to the bottom step in record time, and Holcum won the games that year.

Oh, she'd chewed on Rezalton when he'd complained about the girl being permanently crippled. Holcum had retorted that she wouldn't be if she hadn't tried to take away what belonged to her. For that, the cadet deserved what she got. Holcum had no sympathy, whatsoever, for losers like her.

She and Rezalton'd been a good team, too, until he got the idea to proclaim his everlasting love for her over the three days of their T404 Trainer downside mission. She might have kept him around even then, just for the occasional kick, but the final two days of the mission started to get cloying. It was when he used the word love that her stomach turned, and she'd written him off from then on. *Grow up, kid,* she'd thought. *Life isn't all about first love, candy canes, and fairy tales. Some of us happen to live in the real world, and true love doesn't happen out here.*

Hope wasn't welcome in Holcum's world.

Glancing up at the ceiling, she threw her head back and laughed a spiteful cackle, muttering, "The irony of it all is, he'll probably find a girl, and by the magic of the stars, he'll live happily long after I'm dead and in the grave." She reached and wiped her eyes, her frustrations bleeding themselves onto her face, as a second memory consumed her thoughts.

Years ago, just before she'd died for her insolence, an old gypsy woman had cursed her, warning her to be careful what she predicted, because what was set into motion by the prediction often outlived the very events that drove the prediction in the first place. Holcum had laughed then as she'd engaged her weapon. Just to spite that annoying sliver of a memory, Holcum laughed once again and spit her words in that old gypsy's face, "Some miracle might occur today, Rom'n Rezalton, and in three hundred star-sucking years, you'll get me just like you always wanted." Holcum turned her head and lashed her words to the four walls of her quarters. "How's that sound to you? You just have to wait three hundred years, but you can have whatever's left of my dry, dusty bones!"

Mollified, Holcum stuffed the IDs and the crystals into her overjacket pocket. Rezalton and all these others would have to wait. She had a final Rejuvie to practice on, but only if she could

24

get there before Bofsky. Striding purposefully down the corridor, she focused on how she would perform the interrogation. Many of the Rejuvies had refused to be captured alive. The early Vids brought back by the teams from downside revealed images of the welcoming inhabitants, so reasonable, knowing if they just *explained* to the soldiers, all the nice men and women in the black uniforms would go away and let them live their docile little lives in peace. Then, after a few rather delicious deaths, they had begun to run and hide. To get any up to the ship, they had to be tricked or captured. Those were the ones Holcum had enjoyed playing with.

Holcum had expected to get answers at first. She'd learned from Bofsky's use of the NeuroShok, his favorite techniques for inducing the most exquisite pain, the screams growing ever louder. Subjects regularly died at Bofsky's hand under the use of the NeuroShok, but until recently, she had assumed the deaths were due to the inferior physical specimens being interrogated. When she held that first Rejuvie under her NeuroShok, she knew Bofsky's kills had been no accident. Moreover, she was unsure how he'd ever let any subject on any world be carried from the ship alive, no matter what intersolar law stated.

With every press of that wand against quivering flesh, with every scream of pain, with every look of terror as she stepped closer, Holcum had felt crashing waves of pleasure course through her, stronger and stronger. Soon, she was hardly able to think as she pressed wand against tortured skin, the screams seeming to Holcum the cries of a lover's ecstasy. Trembling as she pressed the wand harder and harder into her victims, the final screams mirrored her own mounting waves of pleasure.

The room was finally cleared, and Holcum had known one thing for sure. Looking at the NeuroShok in her hand, she had been glad the Rejuvie hadn't had the answers she sought. No man had ever given her what this little stick just had. Whatever it took, it had to happen again. No one was keeping this from her.

Stepping into the detention block antechamber, Holcum opened the rack of NeuroShok wands, pulling one down and idly flicking it on. She had become very practiced with this during the past year, never allowing herself to think past the point when this particular thrill might no longer be available to her.

She rounded the corner, the opaque glassine wall ahead of her hiding its panoramic view of the various holding cells and interrogation theaters. Walking up to it, she tapped its surface, triggering it to clarity, uncaring how it worked, just that it *did* work. What she saw turned her rising anticipation into twisting hate as she caught a demonic vision of Bofsky, NeuroShok in hand, his actions already preempting her well-formed solicitous requests for this one last opportunity to experience that which no man had ever been able to bequeath her.

Turning, she slammed her still-powered wand back into the rack and erupted her anger into the corridor. He wouldn't change his mind now. She knew that look. She knew it because it was the same one she'd seen reflected at her during that fraction of a moment the glassine had thrown her image at her, as it was rearranging its substrate to let visible light pass through unheeded.

She couldn't stand and watch him take what was hers, to see his breath quicken, his nostrils flair, and the sheen on his skin that would tell of his rising pleasure. It was unfair for him to have this final thrill, when all she could do was watch, knowing that only a pale imitation of these pleasures waited for her from here on out.

Holcum glared at the ship's crew standing on either side of her as she waited for the lift, and was gratified to see them melt away from her even as the internal transport appeared. This was not a moment for the corridor, for sharing. Not her mood, not her life, and certainly not the reason a black cloud of frustration and anger darkened her face. She smirked to herself as the door closed on her view to the corridor.

"Maybe, Holcum, you're letting your true character shine, after all," she mused to the lift's sole occupant. "This does seem to *be* you lately." She laughed, the sound sour even to her.

Feeling the IDs against her breast, she pulled them out. Salving her wounds, she perused them. At Rezalton's, his image focused her anger, and she spat his name aloud in a string of vile curses. "May your tomorrow be three hundred years of nothing, Rezalton. May you never spend another waking moment in the world I inhabit. Once I'm finished with you, your life will never be the same. You'll be out of my world forever, you and your romantic little I-love-you's." She would take care of that before the day was done. Slipping the IDs away, she leaned her head against the wall of the lift.

She straightened as the lift drew to a halt. She had to look her part. She was MegaCorp, and she must portray that image to everyone around her. Weakness wasn't allowed. Glaring at the faces that looked in as the doors opened, her eyes dared them to enter the lift, to intrude into her space. Her presence melting them away once again, she stepped into the corridor and immediately felt the floor buckle underneath her.

*Blistering suns!* Holcum instantly crouched, falling into a battle stance. *The ship's been attacked,* she cursed, *and here I am without a weapon.* She ran, searching for something with which to fight, her eyes tracking to the ceiling as she heard klaxons screaming, and an announcement began repeating itself, following her as she moved.

"Emergency escape pods cycling online."

Dodging the other idiots that were getting in her way, she paid particular attention to the panels opening in the walls. *Gods, I don't want to be in one of those. Let these other bozos in. I want to fight.*

27

The ship jolted again, and the lights went dark, the immediate flickering on of the emergency lighting making Holcum pause to let her eyes adjust. She exulted in the realization that there would be no emergency pods escaping from this level. The wall access panels had frozen halfway open. These pansies would have to stand and fight. They had no choice, now.

She felt distant thudding explosions from deep within the ship, sensed in the floor as much as heard with her ears. Pressing against the wall at the massed sound of pounding feet coming her way, she saw soldiers running the opposite direction, a full array of weapons in their hands. That alone told her there were undamaged and viable armaments somewhere back along the direction from which they'd come. She waited until they passed, and her tensed muscles hurled her body toward the munitions cache she knew to be there.

Rounding the corridor that led to the nearest weapons bay, time slowed for her as she watched a slow-motion ripple begin twisting the corridor floor in front of her. The metal turned red, then, in a searing spray of sparks and molten metal, it flung itself at her, the hole her eyes dismissed as impossible reaching out to yank the very floor from under her feet.

Her eyes blinked, and in that instant, the shattering of power leads and metal bulkheads all around her became the staccato pop of primitive firearms, as old memories jerked violently into the forefront of her shock-shrouded brain. She peered through the darkness and saw them just there, over that low wall, her troops' invisi-suits discernible to her only when they moved.

Her armament could differentiate the suits, of course, and she had no concerns about her fire hitting her own men. If the armament sensed one of her own, it wouldn't engage. She knew the old-Earth horror tales told to every military cadet about soldiers dying from "friendly" fire. Thank the gods above and below that such events no longer happened, at least not during hand-to-hand combat.

She sensed the familiarity of this place. She blinked. She *knew*. Just there, down those steps was a room, and that was where the rebels would be hiding. As if led by an unseen hand, she moved forward, motioning for her troops to remain low. She shook her head in puzzlement. She couldn't know this place, and yet she did.

As a shell exploded just to her side, the reason was suddenly there. Another memory seared itself into her brain: the little girl she had once been. Twenty years of burying forgotten horrors were wasted as her demons rose up and slammed into her like an old-Earth freight train. In that moment, she was there again, buried in the revulsion of her stolen youth. All she had treasured and believed in had been taken from her by black-suited soldiers, who then repeatedly took her youth for their own.

Standing, uncaring whether she lived or died, Holcum let out a blood-curdling scream as she fired her weapon at the enemy. *Groundies* were her enemy, and she would wipe every one from the face of this planet.

As the floor dissolved from underneath her feet, Holcum's hands clutched empty air. She felt searing pain across her face as sparks and molten metal intersected her path. Her body floated in the space where her corridor had been. Sinking, she turned her head away from the throbbing, burning sensation on her face, fighting the pain, only to look deep within the inner workings of her dying home, revealed in the cavity of piping and wiring separating the level she had been on from the one she was falling toward, and then she was through and into the corridor below.

Her foot made contact with the floor, although not at the right angle; she didn't land properly, couldn't stand this way, and the snapping of bones and tearing of muscles and tendons yanked her memories back into the staccato beat of the present.

She felt her face, and the touch of her hand pulled away

seared skin, sending additional waves of pain coursing through her body. The explosion had taken everyone on this level with it, even if the escape pods had completed their cycle to escape-readiness. She laughed and with difficulty forced out the words, "All ready to go, and no one to use them." The final words were little more than a groan of agony.

Pulling herself up, using an opened escape pod as her hand-hold, with her crushed leg offering no support, Holcum considered her options. The ship buckled one more time, taking even that away from her, as she was thrown into the pod, its sensors automatically closing the hatch, filling the pod with cryo suspension gel to encapsulate the occupant, and accelerating away from the brutally stricken warship at upwards of twenty gees. Her last hissed beratement as the capsule closed over her was spat with vile anger.

"Coup de grâce, Rezalton! I'll outlive you, you pansy!"

EVEN IN THE HEAT of the early summer, the sudden roaring in the daytime sky brought curiosity seekers out into the glare of the sun, their hands held out to shield their eyes from the brightest of the sun's rays. Residents questioned each other, the unusual sounds pricking the wariness of those who had lived through long-ago raider attacks that had last come in a time young people only remembered as *before*.

Regge dodged those braving the sun's heat. He was grateful that with the intensity of the day, some of them were already giving up and heading back inside. He turned to his friend Carli, his words coming out in puffs as he ran, "Heard me . . . you did . . . Carli." Dodging yet another curiosity seeker, he continued, "Would not work . . . the remote tracking . . . told them, I did."

Carli agreed. "Stupid . . . all!" He grabbed Regge's arm and pulled him to a shaded bench. "Too hot in this heat, it be, like this to run." He drew deep, ragged breaths as he pulled a flask of water from his clothing and swigged a large draught. He held it to Regge, who also took this chance to replenish his body's moisture. "Not even a water suit, do I have on. Think you, raiders, this might be?" He cut his eyes from side to side as if he could see the dreaded and legendary raiders peering around the corners even as he spoke.

Regge laughed as he panted in the heat. "Nah! Fools, all those who think that. Raiders be insystem, only." He waved his arm wide to indicate the far heavens. "From out there this thing came. Tracked a long way, it was. Flying pods? Ever seen one, have you? Cargo holds, their place of transport be. Part of a wrecked ship, this may have been."

"Hurrying, then, why be we? Control its flight, we cannot. Dying with the heat, we be. Look around you. Giving up and going in a few at a time, the townspeople be."

"To *see*, Carli. Just to *see,* be why we hurry." Regge grinned with the look of a treasure hunter who knows this might be the mother lode of all the treasures ever found.

Carli smirked and nodded his head. "Think you more women's things aboard, there might be, like last time, maybe?" Regge laughed, his humor goading his friend on. "Or maybe this time a beautiful woman be aboard, one for you to marry?"

"Nah," Regge came back. "Be saving this one for you, my friend. Know, do I, old, she be, and crippled and crabby, being just the kind you like."

Carli jumped up and pushed his friend, sending him stumbling in the street. "Already have one like that, you do. Your sister, she be. Another one to want, why would I? Your misery to share?" He jumped back, crossing his arms, and daring his friend to come back with a response.

"Ah, friend, right, you be. Enough be the one we be stuck with, already. Send this one back to the skies, we will. That sister of mine, jealous, she'd be. All for her own, she'll want you. Tear

31

this one's eyes out, that sister of mine will." With that, he rammed Carli with his shoulder, sending the two of them into a scuffle, both of them trying to keep to the shady side of the way and out of the biting heat.

With their scuffles in the dust starting to attract attention, the boys soon had an attentive audience, with several of the onlookers venturing to cheer on one, then the other of the friends. A bruised elbow here, or a scraped knee there, and the two were having just that much more fun, the competition very real, the reason for the scuffle just another excuse to expend youthful energy. Then, both men were drenched, as a bucket of water cascaded over them, showering many of the onlookers, also. Carli and Regge stopped to find the cause of their drenching.

There stood old Mas. Tommeoseo, the local hair trimmer.

He yelled out, "Know your boss, I do, and like you here, he won't. Boys, on your way, you get, you hear?" He dropped his bucket to his side. "Early summer it be, and you boys, cooped up too long have been." He pointed to the sky. "That be your goal, and lost it already, you may have. A shame on you, it will be! Trust old Tommeoseo with that, you should." Having spoken his piece, the old barber turned and walked back through his door.

The onlookers finally dissipated in the heat, and Regge and Carli looked at each other hard; and with barely a pause, they were back off down the way with nothing to dodge, the heat having forced the people back into the coolness of the city's thick-walled buildings. They once again searched for their golden pot at the end of their much-too-hot rainbow. However, the next rainfall wouldn't be until summer reached its end, and even that would be only if the skies deigned to give up of their life-giving moisture. That was a long time away, and this dusty world would have to wait.

IN THE HIGHEST reaches of Trasdrom'man's sunbaked skies,

a gliderhawk skimmed the tops of thermal currents that extended from the shimmering deserts below to the tips of its bladder-filled wings. Its high-pitched screech reverberated throughout the thin air, warning other 'hawks to give it a wide berth. Very territorial, the scant food carried aloft and scattered in the vaporous winds was its to claim, and it wouldn't share what morsels it could find. Its feet never touched soil during the warm months, as its wind bladders slowly swelled each spring with the warming touch of the sun's rays, lifting it higher and higher, until it couldn't come down if it tried. Only the supercooling of the planetary atmosphere that signaled the start of the crushing winter ahead would bring the animal back to its underground nest. Then it would deposit the eggs that had been fertilized while on wing and die, its frozen body providing insulation and then food for its offspring for many months afterwards.

The gliderhawk first felt the trembling in its wings, as something bigger than it had ever known entered the atmosphere. With the first sensations of movement in the air, it turned its mandibles the direction of the incoming prey. Its primitive brain sending its signals faster and faster, its pumping heart driving its skin through the colors comprising the fiery side of the old-Earth rainbow, the normally tepid-hued creature now burned with the color of hunger in anticipation of its next meal.

As the object grew closer, the gliderhawk began to sense this was no ordinary meal. The pressure waves forced ahead of the incoming object began to shake the very core of the creature, even driving the sense of hunger from its primitive brain. Soon, even the heat the 'hawk thrived on had grown too great, and as it sought to find a rescuing thermal in hopes of escaping the monstrosity that was engulfing its world, the searing pressure wave came to meet the gliderhawk.

The gliderhawk's brain knew momentary pain as the overheated air in its wind bladders swelled and expanded, those membranes stretched past their breaking point. The animal's thermal lifting ability was ripped from it as it was shunted aside by the thundering cryo pod, and for the first time in many years, one of these creatures landed on the desert floor during the summer of its world. The gliderhawk didn't know that, though. By the time it hit the ground, it was already dead.

"LOOK! SOMETHING overhead." The worker shifted his water suit tubes as he stepped from the loading dock. Anyone who did more than venture into the heat and then back into the heavily insulated shading of Summer City's stolid, thick-walled masonry buildings found the fine net of tubing worn under his or her clothes a requirement in the heat of the planet's brutal summer. The suit's bladderpack would disperse a gradual amount of cooling moisture throughout the suit's net of tubing, easing the excessive warmth of the day, and beating back the heat-induced death that had plagued the earliest settlers of this formidable world.

His partner shifted her glare goggles and looked into the sky. "A retinal solar flash, it be. Your goggles be off, yes? Saw you pull them loose, I did." She turned to her coworker with a smile that showed she thought this might be another of her prankster partner's jokes. "In any event, why, skyward, be you looking at all?"

He poked her shoulder and pointed back to the sky. "There it still be. Laugh at me, you shouldn't." He reached and turned her head in the direction of the contrail high in the sky. "Just there, look, partner. See it, you will."

Satisfied, the worker pressed his palm against his bladderpack to infuse his water suit with an additional burst of moisture and turned to lift another package from the transport. He was pleased when incoming ships were unmanned and landed on remote. No people to deal with. No one to complain about the current season's heat or cold. Rare was it to have a day on this world

34

that was pleasant and comfortable, and discussing it didn't improve his disposition. It was when summer drew to a close that things would change. The roaring winter winds would hit one night, and the next morning, the driving snow would fill the skies. The runoff of the snowmelt on the still-superheated soils would fill the city's reservoirs until the ground finally cooled enough to allow the flakes to stick. That was the time to discuss the weather, to offer warnings, or to make plans for survival. Many a city dweller had been out for a time across town on a hot summer day, a water suit with a fully charged bladderpack keeping him or her cool, only to be found frozen the next spring, winter's blast having left him or her unprepared to simply walk across town. By then, most would have already begun the shift to Winter City in anticipation of the changing weather. There were always holdouts, though, people whose arrogance was no match for the extreme weather systems initiated by the vastly elliptical orbit of this planet around its life-giving sun.

The worker's partner paused to look, finally locating the brighter streak across the brilliance of the daytime sky. She stood watching until her partner shook her shoulder. As she returned to moving items off the transport, just one thought kept running through her head. *No good will this come to. No good at all. Whatever that thing be, gone from here, it should be.*

However, since she couldn't do anything about it, and these packages did have to be moved if she wanted to keep her job, she put the thing in the sky from her mind and grabbed the next box. *Moved already, one hundred thirty-seven be, and the day be just started. When be midmeal?* She looked at a time image on the wall and picked up another box, dreading the day ahead, as it already seemed to stretch on forever.

THE SMALL, furred creature froze. In its experience, unusual sounds usually meant something was going to die, and this small creature had survived a long time by paying attention. One ear twitched. Each small movement of its appendage helped it locate the direction of the sound. Its tiny muscles shifted their massed tension as the vibrations in the air seemed to draw closer, and the small animal stiffened, its ears pointed firmly in one direction.

With its dim eyesight, there was only the darker brightness of the land and the blinding brightness of the sky above. Any sound that came from farther than right in front of its face would come from something unseen, something to give the creature a reason to turn and run as fast as it could, zigging and zagging when possible, a hiding hole its goal, impending death its sure future if it couldn't find one.

The small heart inside the creature pounded in fury as the sound grew to pummel its sensitive hearing. It tried to break its muscles free, to run for safety, even as its weak eyes sensed the brighter brightness in the glare of the sky overhead. Its eyes hurt, but it couldn't tear them away. The animal always kept its focus on the dark places its eyes were made for, not the brightness up there where this new sound was from; but this new thing had it riveted. Only as its eyes were truly blinded by the brightness of the incoming assault did the creature's muscles finally break free of their hold.

With a flash of fur, the spot it had occupied was empty, the creature's attention to its surroundings serving it well once again.

BURIED DEEP in the soil, protected from the sun's penetrating heat, the small, burrowing insects that made up Trasdrom'man's most numerous creatures moved slowly through familiar territory: a grain of sand moved aside there, a small pebble slithered around, the morsel of food taken in for the energy to crawl yet another span of its body's length. Life moved at a very predictable pace for these creatures. Within their small world, they had no reason to fear, the top of their world's food chain belonging to them, with the gliderhawks far, far above, and most small, furred creatures preferring those widely-spaced patches of plant growth spread across the globe.

That's why they froze within their safe, cool, hard-earned shafts and miniature tunnels as the ground started to vibrate with the pressure wave that blasted the soil above them. At the same time, just over the safety of their buried homes, a pair of boots were planted on the vibrating soil. The person inhabiting them looked up from his troublesome transport, the power plant having failed him once again. The pilfered goods he'd managed to secure from an unlocked building in Summer City were at his feet, and he watched as the contrail moving through the sky toward him took on an orange hue. Then, in a gradual sharpening of intensity, he saw it become a fireball streaking through the atmosphere.

Jeanna'te Vapiro wiped the grime from his forehead, the dust of this world's desert swirling about him with each movement of his feet, the cruelty of summer already upon every part of the land. Resting his repair tool on the transport's opened power plant access panel, an absentminded movement of his hand pressed his bladderpack, sending moisture through his water suit's tubes to provide a cooling sensation across his entire body. The water suit was life-sustaining in the summer's extreme weather, and the man let out a curse as he remembered that his water suit's tubes around his left leg had a clog that he'd forgotten to clean out once again that morning.

Mesmerized by the incoming firestorm, his heart accelerated, driving blood through his veins, as his body released the adrenaline his brain knew it would need. His muscles tensed as his mind pieced together his location, the perceived trajectory of the fireball overhead, and its incoming velocity. His eyes looked in panic at his transport, the tool he'd been using still resting on the opened access panel, the power plant unable to be started. Then, his eyes took in the goods he had taken from the building's unsuspecting owners, and he cursed again as his brain and his age-old responses tensed and flung his body—without his conscious volition—into a desperate run for life. As he dived behind a rocky outcrop, the fireball impacted the broken-down transport, sending bits and pieces flying through the air. The rain of pulverized dirt, shattered machine, and pilfered goods showered the man and his hiding place.

Standing and brushing the dirt from his body, Jeanna'te reached to pick up several pieces of debris that lay around him. "Crikes!" he sputtered vehemently. "Last week, this new regulator, just installed, I did. There be the control stick off that transport that in the city I stole last year. Double crikes, loved that control stick, I did! To have it back, I want." Scrambling over the shattered pieces of his transport, he began to unscrew the control stick from the remains of the vehicle's shattered interior. As he did so, he glanced at the pit left in the ground where he'd just been standing.

Absently slipping the rescued control stick into a pocket, the man stepped away from the remains of his transport and peered into the crater left by the impact. Placing his feet carefully on the edges of the hole ripped from the desert floor, the pulverized soil gave way, and his boot sank deep into the ground. He scrambled backwards, muttering to himself as he did so.

"Something be down there, surely. Wow! What a story! *Taken Out by a Meteor, Unknown Man Nearly Be,* or whatever that thing be. How'd that look on the Vid service?"

As the man let his eyes take in the field of debris, he surveyed the damage, accepting that his pilfered goods and his transport were gone for good. Rolling his eyes, he slapped his hand to his head, calling out, "My frickin' comm unit! In the transport, it was. Of all the suns to go nova, why must my comm blow up? Now, the entire way back, I must walk. Thank the legendary twin suns that to put on my water suit, today, I at least took the time."

He slapped his bladderpack, then remembered the clog. "Crikes! Even if the leg on this suit works not at all. And a frickin' long way I have to walk!"

It *was* a long way, and the day was only going to get hotter. The thief ran his hand over the control stick in his pocket and began his journey. He paused and searched the horizon for a moment to orient himself, the explosion having thrown off his sense of direction. Finally, making a decision on the right way to go, he set off, shaking his head repeatedly, for this was turning out to be a very bad day.

Unseen to him, beneath his feet, numerous small burrowing insects were having a very good day. No more did every grain of packed sand have to be shunted aside in the hunt for food, and those creatures that didn't survive? Well, the insects that lived found them to be very tasty.

In the hole in the ground, the dirt continued to settle on top of the round device that, on its way down, had torn a hole in the roof of the world, stripped a gliderhawk from its home in the sky, pulverized a transport, and been the reason many small insects had paid with their lives that day. Despite all that, underneath the settling grains of sand, a green panel glowed, indicating life still lingered, waiting.

CARLI SAT at the unfamiliar control board, his hands slowly running over the sensors at first, then speeding up as the familiar movements returned to his fingers. He smiled at the opportunity to use these more advanced inputs. The old-fashioned ones in his department were certainly familiar and easy enough for him to use, but these were downright fun. He glanced at Regge, who was twirling some images on a glass.

"Regge, like to have one of those, I guess you would, huh?"

Regge shot him a half-grin. "Had one, I did, at my dad's house. Take it with me, I couldn't. Wanted it for his own, my dad did. Know how it works, that be why I do." He continued to push and pull information from the databases available to him until he found just the one he wanted. "Hey, Carli. Throw this one to you, I will." Regge flung the image from his glass and watched it appear on the display above his friend's console. "What you be looking for, that image will have. See, you will."

His fingers tapping several controls, the image sharpened, and one small icon grew to fill the screen. Carli grinned excitedly. "The one, friend, be it. This satellite feed, if follow it, I can, we might be able to track the landing position of that pod." As he brushed sensors and slid his fingers up and down the various controls, some images on the viewscreen rolled and tossed themselves off the display, while others grew larger, then shrank, as the console followed the information thrown to it from the glass, tracking it back to its source. He called to his friend, "To download this infodump, make sure the glass be properly set. A lot of information this will be, and interrupt the information dump, I cannot."

Satellite images began flashing across the display, stills grabbed from live feeds as well as short motion bursts. Carli's eyes remained glued to the images as he searched for one that showed anything that might lead him to the location of the cryo pod he and Regge had discovered.

"Regge, that first image we saw. How long has it been, and what was the time when the atmosphere, it hit? If I jump back these feeds that much time, a calculated track and a possible landing site I can extrapolate."

"Have to grab the image back. Bump it to me, will you?"

"Catch." Carli twirled his fingers on a sensor and watched as the image on the viewscreen overhead wrapped itself tightly into a ball and flung itself onto Regge's glass. Regge reached his hands into the image and pulled it inside out, pinched one side, twisted, then flung it back to the big display.

"This be when we were outside. The thing was just a contrail then, remember?" Regge walked up behind his friend to watch him do what he did best. He knew they were thought of as goof-ups in the city's port and satellite division, but this was why they still had their jobs. They had been whizzes in their final forms at school, and they were very good at manipulating the images. He grinned as he recognized one that flashed across the viewscreen. "Stop! There, Carli. Right there." He hopped around the console and pointed to the top of the image. "Contrails. Remember seeing that, I do."

"Ah, ha, Regge. There we be. Stymie us, the 'seer thought he'd do, but no such luck. Watch this!" His fingers, now fully refreshed on this more modern system, flew like the wind over the sensors. Then, with a flourish, Carli slammed his hand onto a palmpad, signaling the console to extrapolate the landing site of the foreign body detected in the image.

The two men watched with smug faces as the realimage changed to a very realistic graphic tracking the contrail's speed and direction, while factoring in the pull of gravity, the blistering summer heat, and the friction of the air as the object had knifed through the atmosphere. Overlaid on the moving shape were numbers, coordinates, and words telling what the console knew about the object at any particular instant, as the display ran forward. The picture finally showed the contrail ending on the surface of the planet with a giant X marking the spot, its coordinates overlaying the center of the X, indicating just where the men needed to look.

Reggeante slapped his friend on the back and laughed out loud. "Good at that, you be. These reminders, every now and then, I need, just to know why I put up with you the way I do."

Carli sprung from his chair and pushed the other man on the shoulders. "Say that, you just didn't! To put up with you, be what I do." He licked his lips in anticipation, expecting Reggeante wouldn't be able to resist his gibe, and he was right.

"What? You, you crude moron! Take that, I won't," and he shoved him back. When their overseer stepped into the room to see what the noise was all about, he rolled his eyes at the two young men wrestling on the floor, and then the display overhead caught his eye.

"Men!" He yelled the word, getting their attention. "The biggest two idiots I know, those you be, but impressive, that on the board be. Keep you around, that be why I do. Don't ever let me down, boys." He turned to look at them lying on the floor. "Now, out and get a cryo pod for me, go!" He turned and stormed out the door, slamming it as he exited.

Regge and Carli looked at each other, their clothes dirtied and their hair mussed. Regge reached up to flatten his friend's wild locks, and they both grinned. Leaping to their feet, Carli hit the download cue, and grabbing the glass, Regge followed him out the door.

CARLI LOOKED over the city transport he and Regge had been assigned. Not only did it have the most skin damage of any vehicle he'd ever driven, but even in the dryness of this world's atmosphere, it was covered with rust. He called to his friend standing in the cargo bay, "Rusted it be, but how? No water be anywhere in the city. Summer, now, it be out there."

"Winter, Carli. Winter be what puts it on. Runs good, though."

"Ah, Regge!" He kicked the side of the transport, his disgust apparent in his every motion. "A piece of junk, this be. Break down, it will, as soon as out of the city, we be. Thinking what, were you?"

Regge jumped down from shifting the load on the transport. He walked over and slapped his friend on the shoulder. "The adventure. All about the adventure, it be." He looked around at the loading hangar and motioned outside the open door toward the sun that blistered the buildings standing in mute defense of humans' attempt to live on this harsh world. He leaned in to Carli, "Better it be to sit inside, the glass display to stare at? Huh? Better than that be this day. This we do, and change, our lives may forever do. In me, you should trust, my friend."

"True, out of the office, we be." Carli didn't look pleased.

Regge vaulted back on the transport. "Your water suit, you have? Wear it enthusiastically, my friend. Cool, it will keep you, and fun, this day will be. Rejoice, Carli." At the continued look of disappointment on his friend's face, he grinned. "Cursed to you, be this day. Cursed with the joy of interesting times." Regge laughed out loud as he continued, "A curse for me to enjoy, that curse be!"

Carli pointed out another flaw in Regge's plans. "No windows be in the transport. So, in the heat for the day, we must ride?"

"Whiner. For adventure, today be! To have the adventure, live, you must! Come!"

Carli leaned against the bent and rusted transport. "My water suit I be wearing. Though hot it be, travel with you for the day, I will." His voice not sounding very glad at all, he continued, "An adventure, today will be, for sure. To me, though, a curse still a curse be. Thanks, Regge." He wiped his face and turned to his friend. "To do what, be it you need?" The best thing to do when his friend started on a roll was to give in and go along.

Both men made sure their bladderpacks were filled with life-saving moisture, and with Regge at the controls, and Carli holding the portable glass that would lead them toward the extrapolated and downloaded coordinates in its memory matrix, Regge paused the transport, giving Carli's glass time to orient itself to their current position.

After a moment, he looked at his friend. "Well, say anything, does it?"

"It does. Just hoping, I was, willing to turn around and not do this, you'd be." He reached up and pumped his bladderpack. "Turning into the hottest day of the summer so far."

"And not getting any cooler. Still with me?"

Carli sighed. "With you, I be. Straight, you must go, and direct you from there, I will."

With a grin, Regge stomped the power, and the machine crawled forward at the gradual pace it was designed for. Despite the driver's grin, that was very slowly, indeed.

Finally, Carli cracked a smile. "Look, friend." He slapped his companion on the arm and pointed. There were several examples of native fauna slowly moving through the sun-scorched desert. "Moving faster than we, the wildlife be. Be this all the power this transport's got?" Seeing the look of consternation on Regge's face, Carli laughed. "Get there before we do, the var'delk will. What a machine for us you've picked! The men we are, and with the big, bad machines; yet outrunning us the little four-legged furry things be. Leave this glass right here for you to see, maybe I will, and take a nap. Okay?"

Irritated, Regge mumbled, "Full, I hope your bladderpack be." He glanced at his partner, and smirked to see him sit up and take notice.

"Why that, do you say?" He glanced into the back of the transport, checking for additional water supplies. He'd ask his partner to stop before they got too far from the city, but he knew Regge wasn't about to do that, not with all the complaining he had done. "Why, about my bladderpack being full, should I have to worry?"

"Well," and Regge gave a very long pause, "pack any extra water, I didn't. Your responsibility, that was."

"What?" Carli twisted in his seat. He'd been giving his bladderpack extra slaps ever since they'd pulled the transport into the sun. It wasn't even close to full any longer. "Told me that, you never did."

Regge looked at him, an amused expression on his face. He tapped the glass with his knuckles, leaving it flickering through several images, unsure what he intended. "Pulled up your system's log today to check your information feeds, did you?"

"What? No." Carli's felt his panic on his face. "Straight to the transport, I came, just like you told me. To know, how was I?"

"Well," and Regge shrugged. "If the message you'd get, I wondered, so wearing a double bladderpack, I be. Okay for today, I think I'll be. How be you fixed?"

"Go back, can we, Regge? Want to get that water, I really do." He risked death without it. How could his friend do this to him? It was the making of an unparalleled disaster.

"Now, Carli. Get this job done and run back and forth at the same time, we cannot. Just fine, I feel sure you will be."

Carli sank into his seat, fighting the urge to tap his bladderpack. He wanted to, he really did. He didn't want to run out of water, either, and already the day was very hot.

Oh, Regge, pay for this, you will. Pay, you really will!

GUIDING THE TRANSPORT toward the magic X wasn't as easy as it had appeared from the city. It was way out, in the first case, and the roads indicated on the glass's terrain simulation were sometimes no more than dusty tracks between rough piles of stones.

In this region of extremely dry summer soils, the earth was usually hard-packed, and seeing the mounds of fine matter stirred up and disbursed by the movement of their transport was surely a signal of something unusual. They truly knew they were close when they started noticing debris scattered about, pulverized rock and dislodged dirt that were very out of place. It wasn't until they started to see bits of machinery that disappointment began to set in. They knew this was the remains of something. An object, most likely a machine, had blown up here, and whatever they were seeing, they weren't likely to find it in one piece.

At one point, Regge stopped the transport to get out and look around. They were nearly to the dead center of the coordinates, and things were getting worse, not better. Sighting a depression with impact ejecta piled around, they noticed the great amount of machinery debris mixed in with and even partially covered by the finely powered soil.

Carli finally broke the silence. "Too late, we be, Regge. Pulverized, it was, as soon as that thing hit." He stepped to the rim of the crater. "Hey, look. Here, footprints. Beat us here, someone else has, to scavenge the area. Even get to be first, we don't." He turned to glare at Regge petulantly. "Wasted the day for nothing, we have. Plus, hot out here, it be."

"Oh, not so bad, it be." Regge started to whistle. "Keeping me plenty cool, my water suit be. Having two bladders makes the use of water not a concern, and slapping my bladder be of no cause for worry. Great out here, this be." He grinned, as Carli shot him a look that could slice butter on the coldest day.

"Share, can you, Regge? Very low, I already be." He'd been very conservative with his water use, and he wasn't even close to emptying his bladderpack. That didn't mean he was cool, however. Just the opposite. Conserving wasn't practical when it came to keeping cool with a bladderpack.

"Nah. Okay, that be, Carli. Just fine, I be, with what I've got. Not that hot, the day be, yet. Long before your bladder runs out, back to the city, we'll be. Just be easy with it." Stepping closer to the depression, one of Regge's feet hit a soft spot on the ground, and down he tumbled all the way to the bottom, with his arms flailing, and sending sand and soil flying through the air.

"Regge! Be you all right?" Carli leaped to the edge of the

crater to peer over.

"Just fine. Not that far down, it be. However, Carli, all the debris? Not the thing from the sky, I think." Regge looked up at him with a grin on his face.

Carli shot him an astonished look. "Why that be? From just standing in that hole, to tell, how can you?"

Regge stooped and rubbed the dirt from a glowing green panel, and then he turned his grin back to his friend. "That be why, friend. Standing on it, I be. What we came to find, this be it," and he held out his hand for Carli to pull him from his discovery. "Need to dig it out, we will. That be for sure. Get on the comm, as need new hands, we will."

Carli was in agreement that more people were necessary, as he had no desire to use up his precious remaining water excavating in the dirt. "Right you be this day, my friend. There be no dissatisfaction in me at all, except getting very hot, it be."

Regge reached over and slapped his bladderpack for him.

"Hey, Regge. Too soon to slap the pack, it be. Make me run out, you will. Stop that!"

"Ha!" Regge laughed at him. "Be the fool, you always will. Plenty of water on the transport, there be. Loaded it myself. My silly joke, as always, you fell for. Because I like you, that be why I tease you, Carli. Smart, you make me look."

"With those looks, a lot of people you fool. Looking smart be far from the same as being smart."

"Ah, don't sulk. In fun, it all was. Some help, let's get, maybe even a remote digger, and this thing, out, we'll manage. To see what it really be, I want badly."

Carli looked thoughtful. "Safe for me, you think it be, to go down to look?"

Regge grinned and placed his hand on his friend's back. With his palm, he shoved Carli, sending him sliding into the hole. At his friend's look of disbelief, he smiled wider.

"Safe I be sure, see? Pull you out, I will, when you wish." With that, he walked to the transport to call for additional help digging out the cryo pod, ignoring the pleas that followed him.

"Regge, now would be good. Regge? Regge, be you leaving me? Don't leave me, Regge. Out, now, I want. Enough, I've seen. Regge? Regge?"

REGGE'S OVERSEER walked around the heavily damaged pod.

"At this, boys, look." He ran his hand over its surface. "Slagged, this whole side be. Even shapeless, the metal be, where the edges on the far side, crisp and sharp should be. What caused this, I wonder?" He scraped his fingers across the green panel still glowing under the grime. "A good thing, that be what green usually means, right, boys?"

Regge jumped up on the old transport he and Carli had driven out, landing next to the pod, now loaded and tied securely to the back. Hearing a shout of triumph, he looked at the workers who had helped pull the pod from its resting place in the dirt. They all turned toward a man wearing heavy glasses under his outdoor goggles as he stood up smiling and making an announcement.

"A transport, all these broken parts be. Sitting here, it must have been, when landed, the pod did. This be why the pod be slagged, I think." The engineer turned, looking at those around him, smug in his assessment.

Carli jumped on the transport next to Regge. Now feeling refreshed with plenty of water in his bladderpack, he quietly leaned in and quipped in his ear, "Not so smart, he be, if he thinks one transport, when hit, this damage would do to the pod. Much more than transport damage, this be."

"Aye, but what be the cause of so much damage, even to make the metal melt?" Regge idly traced the undamaged Mega-Corp logo on the one good side. "At least flash, the lights still do.

48

Maybe what be inside will come out, and the story of all this tell us."

As they jumped down, the overseer pulled them close, a cunning look of secrecy on his face. "For the pod, think you that someone will come? If not, what might be inside? Who knows?" He looked at the others helping to clean up the area. "Valuables inside, there could be. If so, maybe share it, we could. Keep quiet about that." He grinned at the two discoverers in anticipation of just what might be inside their find. "Track anything else, did you? For this pod to be here, somewhere out there, a ship must be."

"Nothing else on the feed was shown. All we found, this be." Carli and Regge both shrugged their shoulders at the 'seer.

The overseer jabbed them both in the chest. "If that be so, then ours, this be. What be inside belongs to no one but us." He turned, and with a self-satisfied strut, walked back to his transport and its artificially-cooled interior.

As the two true discoverers of this possibly abandoned object climbed into their summer-heated transport, they commiserated with each other. They knew if it was valuable, the 'seer would want to share. But if a deadly criminal were inside, the pod and all its responsibility would belong to them, alone.

Such was the life of the peons they were on this world, but still, they turned and grinned maniacally at each other. Today had been a grand adventure, and whatever the pod contained, they would do it all over again, if they had the chance, with no regrets.

# —Chapter 3—

*Hot . . . it is*
*so hot . . . these walls are closing in on*
*me . . . white . . . everyone wears white . . .*
*white is death . . . let me out . . . there are bars*
*on the windows . . . people on the other side*
*are laughing . . . I cannot laugh . . . I cannot*
*see them . . . I only hear them*
*laugh . . . it is*
*so hot . . .*

*—Found on the wall of an*
*abandoned mental ward*

EXPERIENCING repeated difficulty, Regge tried to start the old transport. Sitting in the intense sun had not been the most favorable of conditions for the old hulk. Just as Regge had said, it did run well, but getting it to run after it sat awhile was another matter. It didn't help that the rest of the team were already driving away when the two final members decided to fire up their ancient transport.

After tiring of the difficulty, Regge wearily got out and opened the access panel. Not really a skilled technician for these more advanced machines, he did have some minor talent at unplugging and replugging various connections. Doing so some-times worked when a machine wouldn't perform as asked. After much digging around in the interior, the problem defeating every attempt at a reasonable resolution, he noticed the darkness slowly eating the sky. The day's residual heat had sucked away their energy, and soon, even Carli gave up and crawled out of the transport.

"Hey, Regge? Do anything, will it? Ready to head back, I be." He stepped up and peered over the other man's shoulder.

"Know what be wrong, I don't. Comm in, we can, but," Regge fiddled with the connections for a time before finishing his thought, "fools, we would look. Fix it first, I would like to try."

Carli sat on the packed earth and leaned against the side of the old, beat-up vehicle. Regge fiddled with the inside of the transport's power plant access panel. Carli complained, "Filthy, I be, from digging out the pod. Found its way deep into the crevices of my body, all this dirt has. No hidden places be immune."

Regge pulled his head from the transport. "Then, lending a hand in loading the pod on the back of the transport mixed the dirt with sweat." He grinned and disappeared once again.

"Hot, tired, and very hungry, I also be. Crying out, my stom-ach be, telling me it be time to eat again." Carli stared balefully across the dissected soil that stretched as far as they could see. He slapped what was left in his bladderpack, and dust flew from his clothing. The team had brought out some food, but it had been consumed long ago.

He turned to Regge, talking to the half of him sticking out of the transport. "On the glass, a repair diagnostic, there may be. Look, should I?" He poked Regge's exposed backside.

Regge popped out of the compartment like an unplugged champagne cork, falling seat first onto the dirt. He clambered to his feet holding a long, colored cable with a large plug attached to the end. Satisfaction painted his face.

"Look!" He held up the cable. "Unplugged, it was."

"It goes to?" Carli leaned over to look in the opening, and he crouched on his knees to see inside. "Still attached, it be, at the other end?"

"Say so, I would." He yanked at it, and it didn't come free. "To what this end attaches, I don't know, but plug this in, and work, she may." He laughed, slapping Carli's shoulder. "Hot, it be in there. Whew!"

Carli grabbed the plug. "Do this, I can, plug something in." He poked his head in the opening and began searching.

"Find it, can you?" Regge teased.

"Dark in here, it be. Nice, light would be, but see a little, I can. Found it, I be certain. Plugging it in now, I be. Onto your shorts, hold, Regge."

"To trick the dog, that be the bone, my friend. Trusting you, I be." Regge climbed into the transport and palmed the ignition sequence. Hearing a satisfying vibratory hum, he leaned out and called for his partner to climb in. Long past ready to head back to the city, he stomped the power to full throttle.

With a stiff jerk and a loud popping sound from the back of the transport, it surged forward. Immediately, Regge released the power, letting the transport slow to a stop. Carli turned to him.

"That be what, Regge? That, it never did before." He glanced behind him, then back to his friend. "A problem, we have. Loose, the pod now be. Move easy, we must, or lose it for sure, we may."

Regge clambered out with an exhausted sigh to inspect the package they were to deliver safely back to the city. Sure enough, the sudden surge from the transport had snapped one of the ties holding the pod steady, nearly causing it to tumble off. He jumped on the back, calling to his friend, "Help, you must give, Carli." When his friend joined him, he reached a hand and pulled him onto the transport.

It was soon apparent that although the pod was not especially large, it was extremely heavy. The two of them could manipulate it, but only with difficulty. Three people moving it would have been better. That couldn't be helped, so they tugged and swore, cursed the heat, slapped their bladderpacks a few times, and finally got it repositioned. Loosening one end of the snapped tie gave them enough length to reattach it, stabilizing the prize they had almost lost.

Back in the transport, Regge looked at Carli with a sense of wonder in his eyes. "Whatever you did, more power it opened up." He grinned. "This transport, claiming it for my own, I be. Be thinking old and slow, everyone will. It, a sleeper be. Smoke others in the dirt, it will."

Carli gave him a thumbs-up. His grin was Regge's equal. They started off much more cautiously, though, with slight pressure to the power. They didn't want to snap a tie-down again. However, to have the power that the machine now had, who could have guessed?

"Good, we be, Regge. Fast, this may well be, and guess, no one will. A keeper, I, too, think this now be." Carli bobbed his head in an enthused beat as the hot wind blew over his skin. "Very satisfied, I be, to follow the glass's directions back to town. Into a day for surprises, this one has turned, and this one be ours, alone." He nodded his head confidently.

As they rode back, Carli, as usual, soon bored, wondered aloud, "How long out there in space has this thing been, do you think, Regge?" He looked at his friend. "MegaCorp on the side, we see, sure, but that means what? Across space, shipments in a pod to be thrown? Nah! Not that, would they do." He propped his feet up and looked at the passing view, although he wasn't sure just why. The light was growing dim with the evening, and it all looked pretty much the same.

"The answer to that?" Regge shrugged. "A military at one time, MegaCorp had. Sure of that, I be. Look it up, if you wish."

"Nah, too much trouble." Carli tapped the top of the door with the fingers on one hand.

"Too much trouble?" Regge laughed. "The glass, you have. Find what information it has, you can." He glanced over as he reached a hand and tapped the surface of the tool.

"Regge, watch out!" Carli sat up, horrified, seeing what Regge's glance away had hidden from him.

Flipping his eyes back to the front, Regge involuntarily yelled, "Freakin' blast torrents! A hole!" Both men braced themselves as well as they could, knowing there was nothing to be done about the load they were transporting. It would have to be entrusted to their tie-down skills, and anyway, it had survived a fall from space. How much more damage could be done by a fall from a transport?

Hitting the hole was as close to flying as they had ever come in a transport. Once they were over it, and their vehicle stopped swerving and bucking from side to side, they turned in their seats, relieved to see their tie-downs had, indeed, held. Looking at each other, they laughed and decided to let the discussion about Mega-Corp remain unanswered until they got back to the city. After all, it would be nice if the pod actually got there in one piece, and then they could look for their information at their leisure. No matter what they found, the news wouldn't do them any good if the pod were destroyed.

"Think we may get a reward?" Carli looked hopefully at his friend.

"That be all you want? Credits?"

"What if a criminal, this be, Regge? Give a big reward to us, they might."

Regge gently tweaked the drivestick around a rough spot in the path the glass directed them along. He didn't know a lot about cryo pods flying alone through space, but he did know enough to understand that a criminal flying in one of these was not someone being pursued with a reward on his or her head. Unless there was a cohort to catch the pod and release the occupant, it was as good as a death sentence. It was much more likely any criminal in a cryo pod had been ejected into space with the hopes he or she was never seen again.

No, if a reward was coming for anyone in this pod, they had escaped from a disintegrating ship, and somewhere, someone was still desperately looking for him or her. That was the most likely scenario, and it wasn't very likely.

He also considered that if someone was in the pod and still alive, responsibility would invariably come into play. Reward or no, whoever this was, he wouldn't be able to walk away. That was something he took very seriously, even if few people understood that about him.

"MUCH BETTER, this be, Regge. For us to lift the pod from the transport, this crane be perfect." Carli whispered his words to his friend. They stood off to the side, letting others do the work for a change. It was late, power in the city was spotty, and one lone spotlight illuminated the scene. "Hard work, that was, shifting this thing back into place, when broke, that tie did."

Regge put his finger to his lips. "About that, need to be aware, they don't. Shush."

They watched as an overhead crane moved over the pod, dropped a hook down, and winched the pod off the transport, holding it hovering in midair. The operator motioned for them to move the transport.

"Easy on the power, Regge. Remember at the crash site, how it took off?"

"The slow insect I will be," and he grinned. "Crawl away like an old granny, I will. Trust me." Regge fell into the battered heap, and with a wave to the operator, eased the rusty hulk out of the way. He spun the tires only once, laughing when his friend covered his eyes and turned away. The crane operator didn't seem to notice.

Once the beaten-up transport was out of the way, Carli strained forward, pushing a wheeled rack, and settling it just under the pod. The crane operator gently deposited it for him. Carli smiled in anticipation. The wheels were a bonus they'd be grateful for. No more tugging and pulling just to shift it a short distance.

As he walked around the old pod, he searched for power ports. It would need to be plugged in to reanimate whatever was inside, that was, if its internal mechanisms were still powered. He might not know much about these, but all school children with even a modicum of education understood that without power, the gel inside that sustained life almost indefinitely would liquefy. Once that happened, the occupant would expire within hours. He stopped, an idea coming to him as Regge walked up.

"A zoo specimen, Regge. Maybe that be what we found."

"Biting insects or NeuroShoks, or full of even solid gold, also, it could be. Exploding suns know, heavy enough it be to have gold inside. But, think, Carli. Think." The final word was thrown out very loudly and with a condescending tone.

Carli was hurt. "I thought I was. Animals, to ship, a zoo could, by putting them in cryo pods, and to the system they're destined for, just shoot them. Cheap transportation, it'd be."

"Good, Carli. The next time you and I on a trip need to go, get a cryo pod, I will, and you, ship that way. Hey, save this pod, I might even do, especially since found it, we did. Then, ship you in it, I will. That will prove that animals inside cryo pods can be shipped. Get it, Carli? The animal, you'll be. Now, rich that will be," and Regge laughed, poking Carli to get him to laugh, too.

"Come on. Serious, be. This thing to figure out, I be trying.

If a zoo, it be, someone there, they'd have, to reanimate the occupant. See? So, automatic, it couldn't be. To need to figure a way to open it, we must. Just to wait on it to open itself, we cannot. See what I mean?"

"Hey, you know, I think I do. Something would need to control this, when back to life, it was ready to come. Even have something to do that, they might, right here in the city. Offworld, nothing be ever shipped, so if on our world it once was, it be here, still."

Carlen'te grinned. "Yeah, remember that string of colonists several years ago that came? All on one ship, they couldn't afford to charter, so in cryo, they hitched on whatever ships were coming, especially on the drones. The first ship, the reviver machine had. I think a cryo-rejuv it was named. It was left so the other colonists, access to it, would have. Still in storage, I bet it be, right here in the city."

Regge slapped the pod. "Open, we'll get you, old girl. Just you be patient. Carli, where we've gone, you tell them, and the transport, I'll get." He winked at his friend. "To test out the power, this'll be our chance. We'll know how well you fixed us up, when plugged in that cable out there, you did. See, we will. Who knows, maybe, really fast, it'll be, or maybe the power plant will blow when up to speed we get it. Know, we never will, if push it hard to find out, we don't."

They pulled away from the warehouse very cautiously. Neither of them wanted the transport to be either claimed by another or reset to its original configuration. Once away from the building, they decided to have some fun. A quick stomp on the power, and the transport was sideways in the street. With a sharp intake of breath, Regge let the power off, and the machine came to a rest.

"Wow! Carli, tons of torque power, I always knew these transports had, but fast, they never went. I think from the torque converter you unplugged the power, moving it to the hurry-up-and-get-there port. Want to drive?"

Carli's eyes lit up. "Do I ever? Too greedy, I didn't want to seem. Out of the way, move, Regge." With a romp on the power, the transport was again sideways down the street. Leaving the paved surfaces of the city proper, Carli flew through the air as he put the machine through paces it had never been designed to perform. His heart pounding as he came to a stop among clouds of dust, he turned to the only other person who could hear him, his voice loud with the excitement. "Want this one back, will they, Regge? Keep it always, can we?"

Regge unwrapped his fright-stiffened fingers from the transport's handholds and took several deep breaths before answering. "Maybe. Just maybe, this be the one no one wants, so bad, it looks. Sort of suggested, they did, that keep it awhile, I should, before turning it back in. Bad, it makes the fleet look, they said." His eyes finally drawing back into his head, he turned to Carli with a gasp. "To do that, where did you learn?"

Carli laughed. "Prowling the databanks, I was, last year. There be this company, games for the glass, they build for kids. You know the kind we enjoyed as boys? Shoot 'em up, and all that stuff. Well, years ago, absorbed this old storehouse of files, they did, from centuries ago. To know what they had, the files, converted to glass technology, had to be. Racing games, some of them were, where transports used to slide race."

Regge barked a derisive laugh. "Slide racing? What the blazing suns be that?"

"*Make* the cars slide, they used to try. Called it *drifting*. Know, I do, to talk about it, silly, it seems, but back there, it, I just *did*. Slide racing. *Drifting!* At home, playing the games, I've been. Fun they be, but to get to do it in real life, I never thought a chance I'd really have."

Regge suggested, "Can I learn? Teach me, will you?"

Again, Carli laughed. "Sure! Over, if to drive, you want. Have a blast with this transport, we will. Great, this be!"

It was, too, until the blackness of the long night forced them to return to the city, and for many days as well after that.

CARLI AND REGGE rolled the cryo pod, still on its stand, into storage beside the cryo-rejuv they had rescued from the storage depot. They had found the rejuver, and it did seem to be in working condition. There was just one problem, and that was the information cables that ran from the rejuver to the pod.

"Disappointing, this be, Regge," Carli had whined when the cables didn't match the sockets on the pod. "All this work for nothing." It was hard for them to be this close, and for the pod to be abandoned in long-term storage.

Before the strange object had landed, they had been able to get a readout telling some very basic information about it. A beacon, a call for contact, for pickup, had steadily emanated across the airwaves. Being an emergency escape pod, they hoped there might be a person inside. The broadcast had proclaimed itself as MegaCorp, however that might be possible. MegaCorp had possessed a military arm years ago, but for this to be from that well-known but fractured corporation, it would mean it had been in space for upwards of a hundred standard years.

Regge had insisted Carli research that out. After a hundred years, who knew if it was still working? After some difficulty, although not excessively tiring, he uncovered numerous references to MegaCorp's military equipment, including digital operating manuals clearly stating that as long as the main display panel was glowing green, the pod was still functioning properly. If they could find the correct cables, they could reanimate the contents. Carli had joked with Regge about going to all this trouble just to find out there really were women's undergarments inside. In that case, they wouldn't have needed to let it reanimate.

They could have cracked it open at any moment they wanted. Carli had laughed, but Regge hadn't found it all that funny.

When they'd discovered the cables didn't fit, they'd sent out messages to all passing ships asking for those carrying cryo-rejuv cables to check their model numbers to see if there was a match. One distant colony transport had thought so, and had even diverted to Trasdrom'man to allow them to use the cables to reanimate the pod. However, when the ship arrived, Carli and Regge had gone to the port to check on the ship's rejuver. The connector on the cables had looked like it would work, but when they tried to unhook the cables from the ship's machine, they found they weren't detachable from the colony transport's rejuver unit.

The two men returned to the city's warehouse, loaded the cryo pod onto the transport, and brought the pod they'd found to the ship. Sure enough, the cables did align with the pod's external access ports just fine, but the cryo-rejuv kept giving them an error message, saying the files in the pod needed to be updated before the rejuv process could begin. Apparently, the cryo-rejuv carried newer programming than what was compatible with their pod.

Now, they were waiting on a passing ship's delivery schedule to be changed in order to drop a set of cables to them. If these new cables worked, and if they weren't attached to another incompatible cryo-rejuver, and if the ship didn't get an emergency reroute to another location, then, just maybe.

At first, they'd both been excited, and in the excitement, the only thing they'd seen was the possibility of what the pod contained. Knowing tomorrow or the day after hadn't been an option.

Instead, they'd found, because they were no more than lowly peons in their world's ranking of important people, tomorrow was an option they'd certainly better consider, because peons really didn't have a choice. So, the pod had to be put aside in favor of more practical concerns, such as those that would allow the men to keep their pay flowing and their bills paid in full.

They didn't like it, but that was real life, and real life was the world in which they lived.

"REGGE, THE POD, just modify it, could we? To make it fit, change the connectors, maybe? Perhaps, to adapt it, we could?" Carli sat at a table in a favorite eating establishment. Grabbing a paper napkin, unaware that on worlds across the known galaxy, the use of this substance was considered de facto "low class," he pulled a marking instrument from a pocket and began to illustrate his ideas.

This very thing had been one of his strengths when he was in his schooling days. It had also been one of his weaknesses. It wasn't that his ideas and the illustrations he had drawn from them had been poor. The opposite, in fact. They had always proven themselves to be very, very good. He had just drawn out his ideas whenever (and wherever) they came to him. Sometimes that was in his schoolbooks or on a locker door, and once, even on the metal of someone's personal transport.

He'd really gotten an earful for that one, even though that idea was eventually praised as a really good one. It was good enough, in fact, that the city planners had used his idea when they were rerouting the plumbing infrastructure for the underground Winter City. Fuel and heating resources were always at a premium on this world, and his idea had saved the city many credits over the next season.

For years, he'd been mulling over an economical way to cool Summer City, but the thick, heat resistant walls of the buildings were still all they had at this point. Power during Trasdrom'man's brutal summers was mostly allocated to water resourcing. Snowmelt from the winters was stored in massive Winter City reservoirs, but that went quickly in the heat of the summer. Someday,

Carli knew, he would have that idea, and it would be big enough that after he was paid, he would really have the freedom to do just what he wanted. Now, though, he had to find little ways to make his more immediate ideas come to life, and remembering his old attempts to bring cooling to Summer City sparked a fresh idea.

"See," Carli continued. "Studied that rejuver on that ship, I did, the one that with our pod wouldn't calibrate. How it was made, I understand, now. An old model cryo, we have. To work just fine with that rejuver we've got, it should. Just as old, our rejuver be. Connectors. That be what we need. Cable, I can rig, if your help, you'll give, Regge." He sat back, tapping his writing instrument on the paper.

"Push, why, on this, Carli? Not asking us to do anything with the cryo pod, the department be. Already written off as an interesting interlude in a string of uninteresting summer days, it be. Sure, someday, provide the necessary equipment to bring its contents back to life, maybe a passing ship will, but that happening be like an old-Earth story one of the department staffers once told about."

"Story?" Carli's sat up and leaned forward. "Tell, Regge."

"Ah, be it one you've heard, my friend."

"Be it one I've not. Now." He slapped his writing instrument down sharply, with a growl.

"Hey! Slowly, and I shall." Regge chuckled, popping his friend lightly on the side of the head. "Heard of Chrismast, you have, I be certain, the old gifting holiday?"

"Gifting? For free? Who gives, and to whom?"

"Not know of this, huh? Not surprised, I should be. Very old, the story be. A woman, there was, early on in Trasdrom'man's history. From the first planet, from the direct descendant of an original colonist, celebrated Chrismast on the first planet, her family did. Here, after they arrived, collected gifting items all year, they did, though they weren't to be gifted until the first green plants appeared. At the first shoots, to tie a ribbon on quickest gave the person the right to open the first gift wrapped for him or her."

"A joke, this is." Carli could barely keep a smile off his face.

"Nay. Wait, each subsequent member had to do, for another plant to sprout. Before long, covered with ribbons, the field would be. Only then, all the presents would be opened."

"Your point." Carli rolled his eyes once.

Regge explained very slowly, telling him how their department was content to wait for that first green plant, a passing ship that just might have that cable or attachment that would allow the "found" cryo pod to be opened. They were in no rush. They were waiting patiently for the Chrismast season, no matter how long it took.

Carli laughed and waved Regge's lesson away. He didn't believe in Chrismast. He didn't want to wait. He was determined to find a way to get in, and he also wanted to do it without bypassing the integrity of any of the pod's systems. They all seemed to be functioning perfectly, and he wanted whatever or whoever was inside to come out also functioning perfectly.

Regge turned the paper to look at it and rubbed his finger absently against his nose. "Custom, these be, Carli?" He glanced at his friend. Carli was good, but he was often the dreamer in the clouds when it came to his ideas.

"Well, admit, I must, not in the city's stores, these things be found. Custom, I guess, be the word." His eyes again lit with the possibility of actually getting into the pod. "Do it, though, we could. Care, the 'seer wouldn't. Thank us, he probably would."

"Pay us, though, Carli? Credits, this would mean. Credits to make, how much do you? Lots? Nah. Know that answer, I do. What you make, it be the same as me. To eat, I need, my friend. Smart in life, you need to be, not just smart in the head." He rapped his knuckles against his friend's skull. "Needed for this, credits be." He patted his pocket to emphasize what he said next. "Empty, mine be. Very empty, mine be."

"Oh," he mumbled, and his eyes drooped. "About credits, life always seems to be, and appear to have any, we never do." He wadded the paper and threw it in the trash bin at the table's side. Recycling never occurred to him. Not on Trasdrom'man. Here, life was still waiting to catch up with the rest of the galaxy, and without precious credits, that progress was proving to be very slow.

THE MESSAGE splashed across the display, as the cap't of the ship pulled it from his hand-held glass and flung it up for the others to see.

"This is what I'm talking about. Can someone check the requirements of the cryo-rejuv they need and run the cargo manifests for each of the different groups of colonists we have on board?"

With a nod, his first-in-command flipped the display on his personal glass off and stepped from the room. Pulling a manifest reader from a stor'lok near the cargo hold, he palmed the door open and stepped into the bay. He'd crewed on a private ship once, a small one that left the holds in zero gravity. It had been a real relief to sign on this large commercial vessel where everything was under artificial gravity. He'd also once crewed with a guy who'd been on a vessel so small that it didn't even have an environment in its holds. The crew had worn envirosuits just to check out the cargo being shipped. This was certainly better than either of those had been.

At each crate, he held his manifest reader up to the locking mechanism and idly watched it scroll through the contents inside. Occasionally, he stifled a yawn and tapped the reader, sending it back to repeat a series of items. Then, when the cryo-rejuver he was looking for wasn't seen, he would let it finish scrolling through the list of the stored goods the colonists had deemed important enough to pay to ship to their new home.

"Hey, First! What are you doing, taking the long way around the hold? You know you could just plug in a search from your glass, and it would tell you which crate to open."

First-in-command looked up and waved, one hand still holding the manifest reader to the crate. "Done that, before. Unloaded a few crates just to find the officially recorded manifests didn't match the crates' manifests. Had to reload a few crates, too. This way guarantees that if I unload a crate, what I want is really there."

Each item on the crate was affixed with a tag the crate automatically registered anytime the item was moved in or out of the crate's access wall. If the crate's manifest said it was in there, it was.

"I get ya', man. I've done that a few times, too. Good luck finding what you're looking for. What is it, by the way?"

"I'm looking for a cryo-rejuver, seventy to a hundred years retro compatible. Colonists carry a lot of old technology, so I'm hoping. At least the cap't is. A world we're passing needs one, and the cap't thinks they might pay if we've got one. Free credits, just for a quick stopover." When his reader made a series of sharp beeps, he turned to look at the item on the list glowing in red. "Got it! Hey, there's a palmcrypter there by the door, hanging right beside you. Bring it over, will you?" He took it from his crewmate, handed her the manifest reader, and then slipped it over the lock. Putting his palm over it, he twisted his hand a quarter circle, and the sound of the crate's locking mechanism let him know he was in. "Get with the cap't, and let him know I'm checking it out. I'll report in as soon as I get inside and see what we've got."

"Gotch'a. I'll report, and then, if you'd like, I'll come help you move all that junk around."

"My appreciation. This crate's filled with all their bulky stuff. In my experience, that means heavy, and heavy I don't do willingly, not by myself."

She laughed. "You and me, both, First."

REGGE HELD the hardcopy in his fist. He rubbed his lower lip with his thumb, and then he ran his fingers down and around his chin, taking a deep breath before glancing up at Carli.

"Want this much, just to layover, they do, for a few hours?" He worked his mouth, and then chewed on his lower lip for a moment. "For this, go, the 'seer won't, and this kind of credits, have, we don't. Know that, you surely must."

"Well, have hope, I did. This, inside the pod, would have gotten us. A three-week window they have. Something for us may come up in that time. Throw away hope, I won't, just yet." Carli grinned. "For now, more about MegaCorp, I want to know. Find out, I will, Regge, and the time when it comes for the pod to open, spectacular, it will be. Ready for that, you'll be, will you not?"

Regge grinned. "That, I will. Get the information, and bring my excitement for the opening of the pod, I will."

As his friend walked away, the grin on Regge's face faded as he murmured to himself, "Although, at this rate, an old, old man I may be by the time this pod, we get open, and out will, indeed, step a beautiful young girl. What a loss that will be!" Then, with a resolute sigh born of frustration, he shook his head and tossed the hardcopy on his desk. It would still be waiting for him when he arrived at work the next day. Whatever he left always was, one of the things that wore on his patience, sometimes. Ah, well, this was his life, and one more night wouldn't make a difference, no matter what he did, so he just shut off the lights and locked the door on his way out.

As he turned to start his walk home, Regge looked up to see Carli running toward him. He slid to a stop, barely missing Regge and breathing rapidly. His face was red, and he wiped perspiration from his forehead.

"Come with me, you must. A new idea, I have." He tugged on Regge's sleeve, excitement lighting up his face. "Know, do I, that MegaCorp be civilian retail, only. Just remembered, I did, though, my old great-uncle. Tell old stories, he used to. Just silly stories to me, they were." The two men stepped through the heat of the evening, the shade from the building protecting them from the intense rays of the late-day sun.

"Carli, talking about what, be you? Hot out here, it be, and much there be this night to do. Outside of work, a life I do have." Regge walked quickly. "Focus, you must. Three words for you: cool; inside; home." He paused and took in the excitement on his friend's face. "For you, my friend, with me, stop. A drink, we'll have. Be you okay with that?" He smiled, stopping at the door to an establishment they were passing. "Come in. Cool in here, it be. Little time, this delay will cost."

Carli acquiesced, and inside, where it was much cooler, the two of them took a table. "This great-uncle," Carli began, just as a server stepped up to them.

Regge held up a hand to slow his tablemate down as he requested two servings of a very strong beverage. Then he looked across the table, and covering his eyes with his hand for a moment, not entirely sure he wanted to hear the story about Carli's uncle, he massaged his temples with his fingers and thumb. Taking a deep breath, he put a bright look on his face and raised his head.

"Now, your great-uncle. About him, tell me, now. What be so interesting about him?"

Carli almost bounced. "That be it, Regge. Tell me stories, he used to." He paused for a moment and looked down at his hands, massaging the knuckles of one with the fingertips of the other. "Actually, to find the stories interesting, I didn't." He looked up to find Regge's bright look fading.

"Why do you tease, making me pull the information from you?" Regge slapped the top of the table sharply.

"Enjoyable, it be, this moment of fun, knowing what I know."

"So, Carli. Then, here, why be the two of us? Very tired, I be. Made me really disappointed, this pod has, and so many credit worries, I wish I didn't have." He paused, looking around. "Well, fine my personal credits be; anything extra, though, just not enough there be, like for getting the pod open."

"Patient with me, be, Regge. Let me play on his glass, Great-Uncle did. Embedded there, fun games he had, military-type scenarios that anytime I wished, I could run. Seemed real to me, they did. About MegaCorp, all his stories were. An old wishful thinker, I thought of him, maybe even slightly demented. Now, think otherwise, I do. But, Regge!" He slapped the table between them for emphasis, causing the server to almost drop the beverages he was setting down. "That glass! The real thing, maybe. Think about it. What if real, those games might have been? Mine now, that glass be, with the great-uncle's death, you know. At home, it be, somewhere. Awfully good games, they were, and seemed real, they did, like actual battle simulations. Maybe that be what they were. If that be true, and that was what was really on that glass, who knows what else there may be? Codes or directions to open this pod without a rejuver? Be possible, it might. After all, gravity drives or triangulation capabilities, civilian model cryo pods don't have. Seems to, this one does. This one we've got, other features it possibly has, like," and he grinned as he took a sip of his beverage, "built-in rejuv. Great, wouldn't that be?"

Regge sat back and looked askance at Carli, not feeling his

friend's enthusiasm at all. "A built-in rejuver right in the pod?" He balled his hand up, leaning forward, his knuckles ready to rap his friend's head for the second time in a very long day. "Heard of such a thing, whoever did?"

"Right! Just think, though. See, if top of the line this be, this being a military model, and from the end of the MegaCorp military era, them being the best around, then the pods, the very latest technological advances would have had. Says the same, does everybody I've spoken with."

"Yeah, but seventy or more years, and heard of this before, I never have."

"Two standard, old-Earth seconds flat. Know, did you, that to put a person into cryofreeze in two seconds flat, MegaCorp cryo pods could?" Carli grinned. He had saved this last piece of information to make his case.

Regge tilted his head back and barked out a laugh. "That made-up fact! For me, find it, where did you? Knows, everyone does, a minimum of three days to prep for cryo immersion, it takes. Without the proper prep, without exception, certain, death be."

Carli leaned back and ran his hand over his hair, his amused grin goading Regge. "Looked this up, I have. I know." Shifting his demeanor, he leaned forward, placed his elbows on the table, and his voice acquired a new level of intensity, as he pleaded for Regge to accept his proffered invitation. "On the shady side of the street, my home be. Already nice and cool this time of day. Come with me and look for the glass, we will. Tell us something, it might. Then, know for sure, we will."

Regge slugged down the final liquid in his drinking container, and slamming it down on the table, stood, glaring at the other man. "A sneak you be, Carli. A sneak, for sure. Twist my arm, you do, and be in so much trouble, I will. You, sometimes, a friend be not. This, though, find out, I would, to prove you wrong, or whether right, you may be." He threw several credits on the table and walked out the door without looking back, having visited Carli's multiple times, and certain that he wouldn't be alone when he got there.

REGGE STEPPED over the piles of stuff in Carli's place, calling out in frustration, "Carli, if crawl from that pod, a beautiful girl did, run back in and close the door she would, should she see this mess you keep." His foot caught on something heavy, and he stumbled and nearly fell. "Vow a hundred more years to sleep, she would, just from this to keep."

Carli grinned at him, not caring about the insults. "Good stuff, this be, all of it. When Great-Uncle died, wanted the collected possessions from the storage place, no one else did. Lived with my family for many years, Great-Uncle did, ever since I was very small. Too small, in fact, for me to remember otherwise. Nearly all he owned, he kept in a nearby storage facility."

He reached in and pulled a container from underneath several others, and he read a label on the end. He grinned and stood, tossing it at Regge.

"This container, Regge. Found inside be that glass we be looking for. Er, maybe. Look, will you?"

"So much, Carli." Regge pushed a place clear and set the box down.

"No so much. Nah! Just a little." Chattering, he went on to tell that perhaps to some people, there was a lot to look through, but when everyone else had threatened to send the stuff away, Carli had pulled every single item from his great-uncle's carefully organized storage niches, and he had kept anything that seemed of value. Most of it had seemed very valuable at the time. Still more of it had been gifted away.

"Only part of what your uncle collected, this is? Get into his house, how did he manage?" Regge dug through the container, still, and didn't look up.

"Nah, from when my parents died, most of this is."

Regge didn't know that, but he knew the story of Carli's parents and how they died. There had been a sudden transition from summer to winter the year when Carli was just getting out on his own. His parents had been moving things down to their place in Winter City over the span of several days. Tired, they fell asleep after packing up things in their Summer City house one evening, not really planning to spend the night, just exhausted from the heat. There was an expectation of several more days before the weather changed. The cold had hit suddenly and early. They had been found several days later, frozen, the snow whipping through the window openings and dusting their bodies.

That had been hard for Carli, but he'd not been there, and they were taken down to the city before he was told. There was no other family, and their house was his, now—half of each year, anyway, the half he spent in Summer City. Their things had been harder to prowl through. It was the accumulation of both their lives and his own, and it was much more difficult than sorting out his great-uncle's effects had been.

He imagined uses for much of it, however, and he had turned their old room into a storage area. For security, he'd filled in the existing window openings. No fresh air was needed just for the stored items, and with the original window openings being just that, openings, he'd wanted to be able to seal them up against the weather and intruders. Things in Summer City did get stolen from time to time, especially from those who chose to vacate early. That was one reason so many people stayed right up to the weather change, that and the residual heat below ground.

Carli finally pulled out a container that somehow looked and felt right to him. Cracking the lid, he called out, "To quit looking,

71

you can, Regge. The magic one, found, I think I have." He dumped the contents on the floor. Shifting through the mess, he snatched up a familiar item just as Regge's shadow dusted his activities. Holding up the glass to catch the light that filtered in around his friend, he smiled. "Answers we now can see, if be found in the glass, they are."

"Well, Carli, no power." Regge waved his hand over the glass several times. "Turned on, your house power be? If so, power access nodes? Near a power source, we need to be."

Carli pointed to the other room. "In here, off, all power be. In the front room, access nodes, you'll find. Soon, join you, I will. These things for many years I haven't seen." He squatted and began to sort through the rest of the items in the container. "This, to do, just a moment will take. Go." He waved his friend away. "Pull up the glass, you can. Enjoy, my friend."

Regge stepped through the doorway, moving forward until a power indicator came to life across one edge of the glass. Finally, he smiled, and with a practiced motion from his youth, he tapped its surface. There, as bold as day, was the well-known rolling image of the realtime old-Earth spinning across its screen with the letters M and C emblazoned across its surface.

What really caught his attention, though, was the image that flashed up afterwards. There, in black and gold, were the words the young Carli either had never seen or never paid any attention to. MegaCorp Military-Issue Glass. The only problem was the blinking window at the bottom ghosted with the words, INSERT PASSKEY HERE.

"Carli!" When he got no response, Regge called again louder, "Carli, in here you must get, quickly!" Seeing the other man appear in the doorway, he held out the glass to him so he could see. "Old military, for sure. Just, to get in, we can't, unless the passkey, you have."

Carli paused in thought, then his face brightened. "Easy,

Regge. Just a boy, I was. Easy for me, Great-Uncle had to make it. Just my hand." He placed his palm over the glass and pressed it flat.

Regge gave him a surprised look. "Never have I known a glass to have a palmkey." He watched as the image changed, now showing the new words, PASSKEY ACCEPTED.

"Forgotten that, I had, until, saw that image, I did. For the passkey, sometimes other things could work, too, I think. A ring they wore, or a tag on a uniform." He snapped his fingers. "Remember, now, I do. Used to carry a button from an old uniform on a chain, my great-uncle did. Called it a key. Knew why, as a boy, I never did. Nothing for it to fit, I thought. Buried with him, that key was.

"Hey, but find what's inside, that we must; so to see, let's have a look. Search for cryo pods. From long ago, the information be, but old the pod be, too." Carli looked up and grinned. "The same age they both be. Bet, I do, that something in there, will be."

In the much-practiced way of glass users for hundreds of standard years, the two pulled, pushed, and threw away information as the glass accessed its data files. Although it had been old when Carli had played with it those many years ago, it was old-MegaCorp military grade, and that had been very good, indeed.

IN THE storage facility where the pod was being pulled from its parked position next to the cryo-rejuv machine, Regge and Carli almost couldn't contain themselves. They had found what they needed in the old military glass from the long-deceased great-uncle. Deep in the bowels of its passkey protected files was the clue.

The military-issue escape pods like the one that had landed on Trasdrom'man were built to an equal or even a better quality than the MegaCorp military-issue glass in which Regge and Carli had found the information about them. Now they knew that not only could these pods gel someone into cryo suspension in two seconds or less, they could triangulate their position relative to the known locations of over 40,000 recorded heavenly bodies, and when in the proximity of a star with a habitable world, use their simple magnetic gravity drives to adjust their trajectories to eventually land there.

More importantly, though, the two men had found out the pods were indeed equipped with a rudimentary reanimation feature. While not as rapid as tying in to a cryo-rejuv machine, it could, however, successfully pull a fully suspended person from the chilling cold of the pod's life-sustaining depths. After all, even the military personnel who designed them had shown enough sense to understand that of the ever-increasing numbers of habitable worlds out there, most were not going to come stocked with the convenience of a military-issue cryo-rejuv machine just in case an emergency escape cryo pod should happen to land there someday.

They also snagged the crucial piece to the reanimation puzzle, the codes. Without access to a cryo-rejuv machine, the digital codes the military-issue glass could transmit to the pod were the only method of initializing the pod's internal reanimation feature. Without those, the military-issue machine's built-in algorithms to bring the contents back to life were nonfunctional. What would happen if the pod landed on an enemy's world? It was a built-in protection feature.

Carli held the glass, its information swirling across its surface in its security protection mode, while Regge grinned a nervous smile, rubbing his hand across the tortured metal of the pod's surface. He tapped his nails on the glowing green panel that indicated life might still be possible within the powered mechanism. Its scarring also told of years battling microscopic space dust and perhaps even of the disaster that had sent it this way so many years ago.

Regge found the two depressions the glass had told them would be along the top edge of the green plate. Placing his fingers against them, he pressed and grinned at Carli, whispering to him to do it, to hit the first code. As Carli palmed the surface of the portable glass in his hands, the image stabilized. He tapped his fingers above the surface of the glass as he triggered its internal mechanism to send the first code to release the pod's outside access panel.

With a subtle click, a large slice of the pod's skin turned loose and lifted from the spherical surface of the battered machine. Regge reached his hands to either side, and following the directions found in the glass, gave it a sharp yank, staggering at its weight as it came off in his grasp. Dropping the bottom edge to the floor, and then shifting it to stand against the unused cryo-rejuver stored next to the pod, he took a deep breath and rubbed his hands together. This was very exciting. They could see the translucent inner shell of the pod with its glowing, yellow light suffused just beneath their faces. This was just what he and Carli had been waiting for. The old glass was working its magic, all those stories from the great-uncle, the life's collection that had been nearly disposed of, with only the great-nephew to want all the things. They were actually inside the shell of the old cryo pod. Of course, they were only halfway to the true contents, but this was certainly the first step to eventual reanimation of whatever was inside.

In reality, removing the heavy section of skin had only exposed the more sensitive controls within. Regge ran his fingers around the inside surface they had accessed, finding the internal rejuv socket for the thankfully unneeded cryo-rejuv as well as a panel he knew must be there. Pressing on a notch, he motioned to Carli, and with the chattering of Carli's fingers once again across the surface of the glass, the second military code was sent. A string of lights flashed along the cryo-rejuv's panel, the indicators turning green one at a time. The men cheered and backslapped each other as the yellow glow from the pod brightened. They still had half the evening to wait, plenty of time to go get refreshed at a nearby establishment, but it was certain, now. Whatever was inside was going to come out, and it wouldn't be months away, either.

FOR THE FIRST TIME, each man felt two conflicting emotions, both at the same time. They felt the exultation of success after having found the pod and chased down opportunity after opportunity for attempted reanimation, and they also felt the fear that came from opening a door into the unknown. What would they be releasing when that inner panel disgorged its contents? Would they be glad to have turned it loose, or would regret dog them for the rest of their days?

They couldn't know for certain, but this they did know. If they didn't open the pod, regret would be theirs, for sure, the regret of not knowing what new path might have been opened on the roadbed of their travels through life, the most exciting opportunity they had ever come across trampled into the nothingness of yet another set of tedious days at a job neither one of them particularly enjoyed. That might have been the better choice, but to two young men in the hot flush of success, nothing could have seemed further from the truth.

*Only time will tell.*

The prosaic phrase had been said many centuries before. There was one way to look at its meaning. If the end result were known ahead of time, the future might not be allowed to happen.

For these two, Regge and Carli, only time would indeed tell, and that would be in about the amount of time it took to consume one of the strongest beverages of their choice, and maybe even repeat that consumption in more than one establishment. The pod would surely wait. After all, it had already done so for many years. What was the importance of several enjoyable hours in the pursuit of few extra celebratory nightcaps?

Only time would tell.

# —Chapter 4—

*"What happened when the clock struck twelve?" The little girl was breathless with excitement as she stared into her daddy's eyes.*

*"We don't know that yet. We'll find out when the clock begins to chime. Now, listen quietly as I continue the story." Her father reached to tweak her nose, and then he turned the page. "The beautiful girl and the prince danced far into the night, the glimmer of her glass slippers sparkling in the candlelight . . ."*

*—A little girl's favorite memory*

CARLI AND REGGE sang to each other very loudly as they walked down the darkened street toward the storage facility. This night had been very good to them, or rather, they had been very good to themselves. Not often did they make this merry. Their finances didn't allow it, and certainly, their heads, the next day, often complained strongly. This night, though, had not been one for restraint.

They glanced at a timepiece in a still-open shop and noted the numbers in their drink-fogged heads. The pod was due to open, and they wanted to be there when it did. If there was a person inside, they accepted that they *needed* to be there. After all, what if the person was disoriented, or even more importantly, injured? Pods were always attended; everyone who knew anything at all about them knew that; and they knew about cryo pods now, because since finding theirs, the two friends had studied up. They now understood quite a bit more than they had before all this started.

One thing Regge had already done was to purchase a brand-new, top-of-the-line glass, one with all the bells and whistles. It could draw its energy from any source, including the power plant of a transport, the brilliance of the sun's rays, or even the beating of his own heart. He'd had it custom loaded with all the latest software, so it would operate flawlessly for as long as he owned it.

Of course, Regge had done none of that, not in reality. In his dreams, though, the reality was there, and it would be if this pod came through. He just had to wait until he could see what was inside the soon-to-be-opened machine. Only the confirmation or denial of the possible riches inside would allow him to keep or release his purchase, the release so much easier if it became necessary.

Crashing through the warehouse door, Carli nearly tripping and falling, Regge reached to grab him, then let him collapse into a noisy heap on the floor as he reached for the light. He turned and laughed at the scrambling Carli, as he pawed at loose items for support, taking them down with him. With a hiccup, Regge stepped to help his friend and tripped on the debris Carli had strewn across the floor. Now on his back, he laughed with the indignity of it.

"Carli," he called out. "Now, need help from you, I do. Fail me now, please do not," and he slapped the floor in mirth at his perceived humor. He searched with bleary eyes to find his friend, as a sudden beeping wail pierced his ears. Shaking his head to clear his thoughts, he blinked his eyes widely and shook his head again. "That was what, Carli?"

His friend pointed, directing Regge's eyes to the pod. "Think that, I do, Regge." Turning his eyes back to his friend still lying on the floor, he spoke solemnly, "Opening, it may be, do you think?"

Carli pulled himself to his feet, shaking his head to clear his thoughts, murmuring that they might finally know what was inside. He turned at the sound of movement behind him to see Regge also stumbling to his feet and motioned with his hand for him to catch up. "Come, my friend. Alone, I do not want to be." He laughed, holding his stomach, barely able to keep from falling once again.

While it had been easy to imagine the thrill of looking inside the pod, now, as the top released its hold on whatever had been sealed inside for so many years, the reality was very different. The two men had spent too many hours discussing the possibilities, and not all of them had been pleasant. Sure, precious metals, valuable documents, or a beautiful young woman would be a welcome sight. What about a raging beast, a rampaging criminal, or an explosive device that had been contained and jettisoned just in time to save the people stationed on a space platform? Cryo pods weren't used just for people, although that had been their original purpose. They did work well with flesh and blood, but just as the the people inside were "stopped" in time, so were inanimate objects.

However, both men had laughed over the idea of a beautiful young woman stepping from the pod, her clothes having rotted to the point of disintegration, and her only way out being with the help of their hands. Those chances were very slim, indeed.

"Glowing brighter, be it not?" Regge put his hand on Carli's shoulder, as they drew close to the lighted pod. He placed his hand on the yellow panel they had uncovered earlier. "Warm, now. Feel." He grabbed his friend's arm, placing his hand on the glowing surface.

"See movement, I can, Regge." Carli whispered as if there was a person inside already listening to them. "That, should it be correct to see?" He wiped beaded sweat from his eyebrows. "Stars!" He looked at Regge and quickly back to the pod, blinking his bloodshot eyes rapidly. "Coming out, steam be. Normal, that be?"

Regge shrugged his shoulders. "As new to me as to you, all this be."

With a click, the panel made a whooshing noise and released itself to open a hand's breadth. Regge and Carli stared as a very real, flesh and blood human hand reached out and grasped the rim of the opening. Startled, they stepped back, their faces blanching nervously. It wasn't so much the hand that filled the two with such sudden anxiety. It was the blood that covered and dripped from the fingers that were attached to gods-knew-what that was still hidden inside that machine.

As they backed up, their feet caught Carli's earlier mess, and in a wild tumble of flailing hands and arms, the men went noisily down. Once the clattering pipes had settled back into silence, Regge heard Carli whisper rather loudly, "Maybe, opened it after all, we shouldn't have."

"Correct, you may be," was all Regge had time to reply, before a final pipe rolled against an upright stack of poorly stacked materials, sending them crashing around them. The racket they made would have awakened the dead.

MOST OF THE voices sharing the tale of the pod's unexpected and rather forbidding opening moments wouldn't start up until the next morning. In the heat of the night, the utter shock of seeing a torturously disfigured human emerge from the golden egg was shared only by the two men.

As the hand retreated into the cryo pod's interior, the groan of a severely injured person drew the men forward, the bloody handprint that had been left on the outside of the pod suggesting injuries they didn't even want to contemplate. After all, these two men weren't soldiers, experienced in the personal devastation that war can do to the human body. This was a peaceful planet. Perhaps that peace was sustained by the world's very lack of desirability, but peace was peace, and the occasional weather-related casualty was about as extreme a death as Regge or Carli had experienced. What they saw here, though, was much more.

After the hand released the pod's access panel, the bloodied section of the pod slowly rose to its full height. Hesitant to move in too quickly, the two men looked at each other with wide eyes. As the access panel opened more fully, the glow from the pod faded away, leaving the interior shadowed and dark. Unable to see clearly inside, Carli looked up at the row of darkened bulbs running along the side of the warehouse.

*More lights, should I turn on?* Carli mouthed to Regge, giving his shoulder a nudge. His friend shook his head and motioned for the other man to move forward with him. When Carli bumped a metal item on the floor, causing it to ring out, a harsh voice from inside the pod accosted them.

"Who's there?" The rasping words carried the razor-edged sharpness of someone accustomed to unquestioned obedience, yet it was filled with the pain represented by the bloody hand and its accompanying handprint, the one that had driven the men back from the pod in the first place.

"A woman?" Regge leaned in and whispered to Carli. His friend shrugged.

"Answer, Regge." Carli nudged him. "Quickly, before she climbs out."

"Here be two of us. I be Regge, and my friend, here, be Carli. Cycled the pod to open, we did."

82

The pod barked at them. "Get over here, fools! I need to see you. Are you pansies? I require help."

They jumped forward at the demand. What they saw when they looked into the pod was much worse than they had imagined. It was impossible that the disfigured shape inside could still be alive. Carli froze with a gasp; Regge grabbed his friend's arm to break his concentration, quieting the man's involuntary sound. He leaned in, unsure whether the one good eye left in the poor woman's ragged face would be able to see him at all.

"Help you, how can we? Tell us, if you can, and try, we will." He swallowed the rising bile in his throat at the sight of her face, one side raw and bloodied.

The woman took several ragged breaths, clearly building her energy to speak. Then she rasped, "This place. Where is it?"

Regge glanced up and around the inside of the building, and then back into the pod, phrasing his answer carefully. "The warehouse. The city's warehouse be where you're at."

The woman closed her eye and rolled her head, sending a series of curses aimed at the pain as well as at the man's stupidity. Her voice punched her words at him, "Planet. What world am I on?"

"Trasdrom'man." Regge gave a nervous laugh. He hadn't imagined she wouldn't know that. "Summer City, this be."

"Gods, it's hot in here. I guess the city's name should tell me why—" Her voice crumbled in a gasp of pain, and she paused, the failure of her words complete, her rapid breathing the tell-tell, letting the men know just how weak she really was.

Regge turned to Carli and whispered, "Medpac. In the locker, over by the door. The white emergency kit."

"What are you whispering? Tell me, fool." The woman inhaled an audible breath, and her words were sharp and cutting in their intensity.

"A medpac. Have painkillers inside, it will. All right, that be?"

"Gods, yes. It's about time you said something sensible." She held up one arm, the one still in good shape. "Quickly. Apply it here."

Regge reached to take the medpac from Carli and pulled the painpack from inside. Reaching into the pod, he grasped the woman's arm, placed the painpack in the crook of her elbow, and pressed her wrist to her shoulder to burst the nodule inside. He held it for a moment to let the painkiller absorb into the woman's skin. As it did, he watched the good side of her face, where he could see it, anyway, relax in response to the drug. Taking a moment to look around, he was shocked to see one leg twisted up under her in a way no human could possibly bend a leg.

*That leg, a goner be. Even to be saved, surely not. Be battle wounds, these must. Helped this woman inside, some good friend or faithful subordinate must have, when how severely injured they saw she was. For them to do this for her, as harsh as she sounds, a friend to someone, she was.*

"Feeling any better, be you?" Regge released her arm, removing the painpack and laying her arm to rest on her good leg.

"The date. How many days have I been in this pod?"

Carli reached to touch Regge's shoulder. When he turned, Carli shook his head rapidly, mouthing, *Tell her, do not!*

Regge turned to look at the creature still curled in the escape pod. Although he and Carli guessed it had been as much as a hundred standard years, they really had no idea. He phrased it as gently as possible, "A very long time."

"Good!" She spat the words. "That pansy, Rezalton, is dead by now." She struggled to rise, grabbing Regge's arm, and in an unexpected tirade thrown out into the room, her voice surprisingly loud, she expended the last of her energy. "Damn you, Rezalton! I outlived you after all. You'll never have any part of

84

me, not even my dry, dusty bones. Telling me you loved me . . . showing the fool you were!" With those words, she collapsed against Regge, her breath coming in great torrents of air, her hot blood becoming one with his shirt.

When he gazed at the pitiful mess in his arms and at the blood now soaking through his clothing and smearing his skin, his resolve deepened. This poor creature was now his responsibility for as long as she needed him. He knew he would stand by her, no matter what. It was obvious she would need someone to.

Regge looked over the woman's head at his friend and grimaced in pity, his eyes cutting to the wreck in his arms. He motioned with his chin for Carli to come closer and help. Even with the painpack, he knew it would be agony for the woman to exit the pod. The injured leg wouldn't support her weight, and to manipulate it as she came over the lip of the opening would be torturous. Yet, there was no other choice. She could not be left inside.

"Move you from the pod, we be doing. Help, can you, at all?" Regge spoke softly to the top of her head. He watched her head nod against his chest. "Cause pain, this will. Sorry for that, I be, but know no way to help it. Make it somewhat better, the painpack should." He turned to Carli and spoke urgently. "Step inside to the offices, you must. For laying her down, find a bench. Do this, we should. Hurry." Turning back to the wreck of a woman he held in his embrace, pressing his arms around her, he murmured, "Holding you for a moment, I be. Have help from us, you will. Do all we can, that we will."

At the sound of Carli dragging the bench through the door and onto the warehouse floor, Regge called to him, "Carli?"

"The bench. Have it here. Something else to have me do, what would you, friend Regge? For me to know, just say."

"Hold her, you must." Regge leaned around her to reach deep into the pod. "Her weight, hold tightly. Up over the edge, lift her legs, I must. Ready?" At his friend's nod, he counted, "One, two, three, *lift*." With a wail of agony from the exhausted, pain-laced person in their arms, Carli pulled her tightly to him and lifted her torso. At the same time, Regge lifted the good leg that hadn't been damaged in whatever melee had caused these injuries, as well as the leg that was twisted beyond belief, the ankle showing at the bottom of the trousers already blackened with bruising and distended with the pressure of the swelling.

"Down! I will walk," the tortured face growled.

Regge looked up to catch his friend's eye, then did as she requested. As he set her good foot on the floor, the injured one dangling beside it, yet another groan welled up inside her, the obvious fight to keep the sound under control seen in the tensing of her body and the sharply drawn breath. "Give me your shoulders," she ground out, hanging onto Carli and grabbing at Regge's unseen support, grasping his clothing as he moved to step under her arm.

Hopping along on her one good foot, her jaws clenching as they absorbed the pain, she spat at them, "Holcum. UnderGen'l Holcum. Help me lie down." As they did so, she lashed out as a new wave of agony blazed throughout her frame. "Gods above and below, I'm being torn apart! More painkiller, if you have it." Raising her head to view what she could see of her twisted leg hanging from the bench, she laid her head back and commanded, "Pull the leg straight. Pull it hard and fast."

Regge and Carli looked at each other in dismay. They weren't med technicians. They might do more damage than good. Trying to postpone that requested duty, Regge offered, "The painkillers. Look first for them, please let me." As he stood, she grabbed his arm and yanked him back to her.

"The leg," she hissed. "Now, before I pass out." With the finality of an order she expected him to follow without question, she released him, pain crossing in waves across her face.

Regge glanced at Carli and shrugged with a look of, *Her pain, it be.* He glanced down and calculated, then spoke quickly, "Take her foot. Under her shoulders, I'll pull." He looked at his friend intensely to make his point clear. "Carli, pull firm and quick, you must. To do this again, we cannot." He glanced down at the woman lying beneath his face. "Ready?"

"Gods, no!" She spat her words at him. "Do it now, and make it hard and fast." She took a deep breath, and Regge watched her face tighten in preparation for the agony she knew was to come.

Regge knelt, bracing himself against the end of the bench, as he slipped his hands under the woman's shoulders. "Brace your own feet, you must, Carli. Ready? Now!"

As Carli took the damaged leg's foot and threw himself backwards, his feet firmly planted against the end of the bench, the sounds of shattered bone moving against shattered bone startled the men. Even louder was the woman's scream, at least until she passed out. When Carli finally released the straightened leg, the woman was very still. Life could be seen in the rise and fall of her chest, but her biting words were now deep within her, unable to be released on the two men, her pain trapped inside of her.

Regge stood, and Carli joined him. Side by side, they looked almost as badly injured as the woman. They were smeared with her blood, their clothes were ruined, and their faces were distraught. Even in their most ominous discussions, this hadn't entered the equation. An injury, yes, but this woman was mangled. They looked at each other, locking eyes for a moment, their unspoken questions riveting their gaze back to the vision of horror lying before them. What could have done this much damage to her? The answers, if they were ever known, would come from inside her head, that they knew. They also knew, no matter how bad the scenario they could possibly imagine, the truth she might tell was bound to be much worse.

Carli turned to his friend, his eyes reddened with the horror of what the woman must have gone through before being placed into the cryo pod. "In the pod to have gone, all these years, these injuries to carry. To do this, how could anyone?" He rubbed his opened hand over his mouth, and then down his chin and neck. "This, to travel in a pod, I couldn't." He turned his eyes back to the woman on the bench.

"No choice, she might have had. Forced in, she may have been. Know, we don't, only that find help for her, we must." He reached out to grasp his friend's forearm, his eyes widening with the realization of where they might do just that. "Old Tommeoseo. Help, he would. Know him from long ago, and also know his heart, I do. Gruff, it be, but soft as the warm butter inside."

With the woman in front of them breathing her painfully taken breaths, and with blood congealing on her blast-scarred face, he grinned with the prospect of parceling out some of the responsibility of what he and Carli had released from the cryo pod. Someone older would know what to do. Someone wiser would make better choices. Mas. Tommeoseo would know the correct decisions to make, and the two who were the ones carrying the real burden of responsibility were ready to give that up to another, even if just for a time. In the sudden shock of the pod's opening, Regge wanted it to be so. He even hoped it would be so. In this instant, he *needed* it to be so. It would have been nice for him if it could have been so.

Old Tommeoseo was a good man who watched out for others and often took the responsibility on his shoulders when others wouldn't. He would help here, once again, but for the moment, there were more immediate concerns for Regge and Carli to deal with. That first adrenalin rush of immediacy, that rush of urgency that had been thrown upon them with that first bloody hand that had escaped all those years of imprisonment in the cryo pod was beginning to ebb, and that left room for other feelings to rush in and take over.

The bile rising in his throat, his stomach suddenly churning, Regge turned a bilious shade of green. Clamping a hand over his mouth, holding the other on his stomach, and without explanation, he exited to the outside of the building just as fast as he could go. Carli heard the results of Regge's sudden rush burbling just outside the door. Soon, turning his own shade of green, Carli was alongside him, his own contribution to the pile of residue left by Regge warmly fresh and not smelling very nice at all.

A FACE PEERED through the door, not happy at being awakened at this early hour. This was not the proper way to start any day, and when he saw it was that pair of fools, Regge and Carli, Mas. Tommeoseo cursed.

"Ehh! What be it that you boys, at this time of the night, want? Not for many long moments of treasured sleep will, in our sky, the sun burn. How be it that here I must stand with my eyes open, with you facing me in my doorway?"

He refused to open the door farther, no matter how urgent the looks on their faces. He'd watched these boys grow from children, and he knew their reputations. There was more than once they'd been brought to his shop for a hair clip, and he, old Tommeoseo, had found his clippers trimming carefully around a new head wound or peering at the boys in the face, overlooking one more black eye. Goof-ups, these were, and the whole of Summer City knew it.

Right then, the two young men looked every bit the part of old Tommeoseo's goof-ups. Both Regge and Carli were breathless at having run all the distance to old Mas. Tommeoseo's home, and although the sun was banished to the far side of the globe, it wasn't all that cool, even in the darkness of the night. Not only were they breathless, sweat pooled in their hair and ran down their faces.

With quick, run-together pleadings, they reminded the old mas of what had fallen from the sky not so long before. They ran through the efforts they had undergone to open the heat-slagged pod, ending with Carli's final solution, the old military-issue glass. Almost dancing in their desperation for him to come with them, to relieve them of some of the responsibility for what they'd done, the need to have someone to bear this burden along with them, they described to him the horrible pain the woman had been in, and how they'd had to pull her leg straight, how she'd insisted they do it, even though it brought even more pain. She'd passed out right before their eyes, they told him. Mostly, they told of her face and the skin that was peeled from one side, the raw muscle that was visible underneath. When Mas. Tommeoseo finally relented and opened the door more than just a crack, he became aware of the boys' clothing, and how it was blood-soaked. That was when he began to wake to their urgency, taking it on as his own.

"Boys, come inside, you must. Be it as bad as you say, see, I can." He laughed a rueful bark. "Would have locked my door on you, if during the day, like this, you'd come to me. Wait here, you must, and get dressed, I will. My help, that I can give."

Using one hand to rub the rest of the sleep from his eyes, the old mas exited to the back room to ready himself for a terrible situation. If this was half as bad as those boys had described, then it was twice as bad as he wanted to deal with. But Tommeoseo wasn't a man to shirk duty or responsibility, and this he would take on. After all, he had been asked, hadn't he? Regge and Carli had made a good decision in choosing to go for help where they did. Yes, Tommeoseo mused, they had finally made a good decision, probably for the first time ever in their goof-up lives.

OLD TOMMEOSEO followed the smooth-faced young men, although they would always be boys to him, their small bodies

90

sitting underneath his cutting tools, as they led him back to the warehouse, even taking some rudimentary medicinal supplies with him. Seeing the disfigured woman lying on the bench, her wounds untreated, and what could be seen of her leg grossly blackened and distended, he let the boys have another of his tirades. He couldn't imagine they'd left her unattended. Old Tommeoseo didn't know what he'd imagined in his fogged brain as he dressed, his old body just dragged from a solid night's sleep, but somehow, he hadn't expected to find the woman abandoned in such serious condition.

Kneeling at the injured creature's side, he demanded the boys bring him a container of water. Pulling a clean cloth from his supplies, he gently began rinsing the blood from her face, arms, and neck. Looking her over as best as he could, he could see her heavy, military-issue type clothing was torn and shredded in multiple places, but there was no obvious damage underneath most of the uniform she wore. Taking in stride the massive Mega-Corp logo on the breast of her jacket, remembering the boys' jumbled rantings about the little they knew of her, Tommeoseo didn't bother to look past what she needed at the moment as he helped her.

Once most of the blood was gone, and Tommeoseo could begin to sort out just what he might need to do to really help the woman, he turned to Regge and Carli. "A splint, boys. This leg, walk on it, she won't. Wrap it, we must, with a splint inside." He looked around the warehouse, its contents unfamiliar to him, but warehouses themselves very much the same no matter where he had traveled in his long life. "Something flat and stiff, boys. Go. Find it. A cutting instrument, also. To remove much of this clothing, something that will cut and cut cleanly, I must have."

"Mas. Tommeoseo," Carli hesitated, unsure of just how to approach what the old man had asked, "her clothing, to cut away? Um, mas, here to watch, should Regge and I be?"

Mas. Tommeoseo felt the heat rise under his collar at the young man's callous response.

CARLI GLANCED at his friend, their nervous gazes matching in kind. They had hoped and even counted on the old barber relieving them of their direct involvement in all of this. Perhaps tomorrow, they'd hoped, they could address the situation from a more remote attachment. Maybe they could even be the under-stated saviors of this ragged remnant of humanity. No, it didn't seem Tommeoseo was seeing it that way. In any case, they had no desire to see this woman, badly mangled as she was, with any of her clothing cut away.

Tommeoseo, his neck now flushed with anger, and only now starting to truly wake, turned and spat in irritation, "Carli! Know you, I do, boy, and surprise me, what you say, it shouldn't. To be in this condition, do you think she asked? Huh? Die, she yet could. Cause this, you didn't, but die, she still could, and on your heads, it would be. Regge? See you there also, I do. Feel the same way, you do? Yes? Do this alone, I cannot." He glared at them, his irritation at their youthfulness and their irresponsibility goad-ing him to continue. "There be a healer in the city, newly arrived. Learned her craft on Rondeo World and just returned. There for many years, she was. Perhaps, to her, this one we might take. To do that, be it what you want?" At the sudden relief washing across the young men's faces, Tommeoseo turned back to the woman in front of him.

Almost to himself, but as much to the injured soldier and the two standing behind him, he continued in a quieter voice. "Needed, surgery be. Alas, many systems away the nearest medic resides. My lady, sorry, I be, that no more help than this can I give. Found us, you have, and a sorry thing that be for you. To move you, I hate to do, but do this, we must. Assemble a gurney, we will, makeshift though it be. Also, provide a crutch for you, my shoulder will."

Carli felt hope in the final thing the old barber said. His shoulder, not Regge's, and certainly not Carli's. It was the highlight of the night in his youthful eyes.

THE OLD MAS had known his share of pain. That was where he had derived his strength and his compassion. That was also where he had learned his brusque manner, his defense against the cruelties that life had served him. He could see this woman was a mess, and observing the military uniform, he wouldn't be surprised to find she had brought much of it on herself. Yet, no matter what she had done to precipitate this, pain was pain, and no one deserved to suffer in this manner.

She would be disfigured, for there was no surgeon available to correct this level of damage on this world. Crippled, she would probably also be, what with the injuries he could see to her leg. He reached down and rubbed a remembered soreness from an old leg injury. He knew what severe pain could do to a person, and the scars it could leave behind. He knew what damage, left untreated, could do to a person's psyche. One side of her face showed the remains of a beauty slowly going hard. She would wrestle with the loss of that. Perhaps she would triumph, or perhaps she would allow it to defeat her. That, old Tommeoseo couldn't help her with. However, her injuries, for those, he would do his best. He turned back to the two *fools* standing behind him.

"Clear it be what you want, boys." He growled his instructions as they prepared to move someone who clearly needed immobilization. However, that was not what she was going to get, no matter how much worse it made her situation. Tommeoseo stood and put the necessary gears into motion, the moving of the woman to the healer their most important priority. "Something for a gurney? Found it, have you?"

"The bench?" Regge offered the solution hesitantly. "Carry

her, we could."

"And make it worse. Think, man!" Tommeoseo was out of patience.

Looking around for anything else, Regge finally cried out in frustration, "Nothing here there be, Mas. Tommeoseo." Then his face brightened, and he slapped his head. "Gods, the transport. Outside, it be. Work, will that?"

Old Tommeoseo jerked his eyes to the frustrated boy. "Have a transport, you do? Using this, we could have been, all along? Start to think, you must, boy!" He turned to the woman who was beginning to moan on the bench. Using the moist towel to sponge the good side of her face, he called to Carli to bring him fresh water.

Glancing up to take it, he saw Regge still in the room. "Think, Regge, please! Watched you grow from a boy, I did. Now, found your time to be a man, you have. Be that man. Need that transport, we do. Here it be, already? Or, invisible, it be?"

REGGE KNEW he'd messed up yet again in the old man's eyes, and that made him feel very low. Mas. Tommeoseo was well liked among the inhabitants of the city, and Regge and Carli had worshipped him as children. They had run from him in fear a time or two, also, but the worship had been there, still, even as they had run.

Mas. Tommeoseo stood, the look of distress on Regge's face revealing the small boy he still remembered so very well, and he took pity on him, speaking more softly. "Help her, we must, Regge. Die, she might, without our intervention. Leave now, the transport to bring around. Use the last medpack for the painkiller, Carli and I will. With the moving, feel pain, she will." Tommeoseo stepped to Regge and touched his shoulder. "Helping, you thought you were, when opened this pod, you did. Not what you expected, this be, my boy. Understand how you feel, I do.

Get through it, you will, and to help you, I be here." He turned to Carli as he pushed Regge out the door. "Come, son. Show the medpack to me. Get this done together, we will."

Carli turned to help Tommeoseo. Together, they broke the last painpack onto the woman, Carli telling old Tommeoseo the name she'd given them. As they finally lifted her to the back of the transport, not even the medications could alleviate all the pain. Rousing, her voice lashed out at their efforts, commanding them with the barbed tongue of long-established authority. Despite the harshness of Holcum's threats, Tommeoseo, with his own bristled insulation, showed the tenacity and determination that were needed to spite her cruelty, her words washing from him like the rains at the end of the hottest summer day.

All three of them stayed the night at the healer's. The woman was finally awakened after much knocking, but her pay had to be guaranteed by the three men. This time Holcum's clothes did get cut away, and just as old Tommeoseo had hoped, the worst damages were in the areas he had been able to see. The healer listened to their story, nodding at various parts, filling in with her knowledge of the pod assimilated through word-of-mouth, and finding a measure of humor in the situation as she recounted others' tales of the escapades of the two fools who had chased an old cryo pod falling from the sky, only to be unable to open it, no matter how hard they tried. Regge and Carli squirmed at the stories, even as Tommeoseo gripped their shoulders to keep them at the healer's side.

Peeling the uniform from the swollen and discolored foot, the healer's first suggestion was to remove the damaged limb. There might and probably would be an infection of the worst sort. The woman could die even with the best medication she had to offer. Would a missing foot, or perhaps even a missing leg not be the better choice? Regge and Carli were horrified at the suggestion, but they did concede the seriousness of the damage, hoping that the instructions they had been given by the woman hadn't made matters worse with their pulling on it. It was Tommeoseo who decided the situation, though, taking the responsibility for his own, knowing the ways of women. He'd been with a few in his life, he shared, several for very extended periods of time. Vanity was the rule, and women wanted to be whole. Even death might be preferable to the loss of a part of the body.

The healer, after some argument, finally surrendered. The leg would stay, and the woman, Holcum, would remain whole. The face was another matter. The skin was gone, and there was no way to replace that. Of course, the healer surmised with some vexation, on a more developed planet, with a first class med-center, this repair would be quick, and the damage would be virtually unnoticeable. However, this world didn't have a first class medcenter, or any medcenter at all. The medpacks and the occasional requested drop of specific medical supplies were all that the people who were forced to live on this isolated globe were given. This night, this incident totally unexpected, this healer was caught unprepared, and the three men had to watch as her hands took what measures she could with Holcum's face and leg.

Just in from her healer's training on Aretne's Colony out on Rondeo World, she did have a supply of local remedies. None of these remedies could be found on Trasdrom'man, all being local to Rondeo World, hence the sharply escalating price quoted to the three men by the healer.

During much discussion among the three, Carli's face flushed with the thought of spending credits he didn't have on someone who might die anyway, someone whom, just that morning, had been safely sealed inside a cryo pod free from mak-ing demands on a workingman's meager wages; and with his vivid memories of so recently being unencumbered by her needs and injuries, he admitted he didn't want to commit to the extra charges.

Even Regge had some misgivings about the numbers the healer quoted. It was old Tommeoseo who swayed their opinion. It was true they still held enormous respect for him, and no, they didn't want to spend the rest of their lives watching the woman suffer, knowing a few credits might have made the difference, a few credits Regge and Carli weren't willing to share. What really convinced them, though, was Tommeoseo's readiness to foot half the expense.

Watching the healer pull out her remedies bag, taking the pouches and jars from inside, the pungent unguents and crushed plants creating a medicinal aroma in the air, Regge sat between his old barber and his friend, guiltily remembering his earlier conviction that he was responsible for whatever came out of the pod, and how he had already tried to shirk that duty. As the healer pounded one plant, added a piece of another, and then dug a fingertip of unguent from a jar, crushing them all into a paste, he knew he would pay the others back, no matter how much he had to give up. He didn't know how, because he'd heard the healer tell the cost; but his earlier unwillingness to pay weighed heavily on his heart. The price he would pay in credits would be much preferable to the price he might pay in self-respect.

He was already feeling better as he watched the healer smear her concoction across the skin-stripped face, wrapping its healing substance in long swaths of a lightweight cloth. He was less secure in his feelings when the healer started on the leg. Perhaps it was just his stomach turning rather than his new inner resolve, but he certainly knew it didn't feel very good as he watched a sharp cutting tool dipped in a sterilizing compound slice through the discolored skin, releasing a strong-smelling mixture of blood and bodily juices.

Holding his stomach with his hands and his determination, he watched the healer pull the skin back, cutting through to the bone, and working the shattered pieces back together. Though the new damage was done to repair even worse injuries, the long thread the healer used to repair the skin seemed to be one more way to torture an already overburdened human body. How could any person withstand so much pain and still live? That, Regge didn't know.

Before his stomach finally overpowered his determination for the second time in one night, he watched the healer smear more of the compound she had prepared over the cuts she had made, wrapping the entire leg with more of the lightweight cloth used on the woman's face. Then, as a stiffening paste was brushed across the cloth-wrapped leg, the fabric almost immediately hardened, the time for healing now counting itself down. Finally, his stomach took control, and Regge bolted into the safety of the darkness outside.

Returning from the night's second sudden sojourn to the outdoors, his deposit faithfully made, Regge passed Carli, the man's color as green as his own had been. As they stepped by each other, Regge was able to grin and wink about his friend's discomfiture, something that hadn't been so very funny to him just a few moments back. He arrived back inside to find old Tommeoseo with a smirk on his face, and Regge hung his head. He knew Tommeoseo found his and Carli's weak stomachs to be as good an entertainment as the most fast-paced Vid ever made.

They were all surprised when the healer looked up and told them Holcum needed to be awakened. When questioned, she told them the health of the ill one couldn't be assured without a more comprehensive exam. She needed to assess the woman's coordination, hear her speak, and look into her eyes to judge the response times of her pupils. Only with this could the healer assure the men their money was well-spent. When Regge protested, she quietly shared that if this woman died, her own unsecured reputation as a healer of the best caliber would be greatly damaged. Her standing as a successful healer greatly affected the prices she could charge. This one must be saved, and that meant waking her. Tommeoseo grudgingly agreed, and with reluctance, Regge fell dutifully in line.

A strong-smelling plant was placed under her nose, and the woman wrestled herself away from its stink. Sitting up, supported by hands at first, and then by a cushion, her one disoriented eye struggled to take in her surroundings. Glancing down, she saw the cast on her leg, and her eye grew wide.

Realizing that her face was partially covered, she reached a hand to gently feel. At that, the unbandaged side of her face fell in disbelief. Finally, she spoke, her gravelly voice forced into the room, a harsh and heinous vapor, her eye leaping from person to person, as she made her demand.

"A mirror."

Carli, jumping to retrieve one visible on a nearby counter, was quickly stopped by the healer's next words.

"A good idea, the mirror be not. Heal, my dear. Let yourself heal, first." She nodded reassuringly, placing one hand on Holcum's good arm.

"No!" Holcum's vicious reply was insistent. "I will not be coddled. The mirror!"

So, it was retrieved and handed to her. As she held it up, she turned it to reflect her bandage-covered face, her expression reflecting the memory of the pain that had inflicted the damage just a few short breaths ago in her memory; and she reached a hand to press on the cloth wrapped on her face, with even that gentle motion shooting a look of pain across her exposed features. The healer put her hands out to stop the wrappings from being touched again, warning Holcum that the damage was deep. A whirlwind of a reply thrust the healer away from her.

"I was there. I felt the blast, and I pulled the skin from my face with my own hand. Don't tell me how bad it is! How badly will it scar?"

"For me to work with, no skin, there be." She shrugged. "A bigger world? Find a medcenter there, you might. Here, there be none. Scar badly, it will. How badly, I do not know, but badly." She paused for a moment, glancing at the additional injuries the woman bore. "The leg. Even worse, it be. Walk, perhaps, with a stick or crutch, you might, then, perhaps not."

The healer turned to put away her things. What caught the men's eyes after the healer's final comment were the tears rolling down Holcum's face. Her lone, uncovered eye was reddened and wet. They watched as she closed her eye, leaned her head back, and let silent sobs wrack her body.

She didn't stop for a very long time.

"SEE IT, did you, what came from that pod? Found it, those two boys did."

Old Maggents, her face lined and leathery, stepped to the side of the street, the shadows giving her the coolest part of the morning, before the air truly started to lick its fiery breath up and down the buildings that protected Trasdrom'man's human occupants from the worst of the sun's assault.

Her companion, an old woman by the name of Rodricks, who made a point to walk with Maggents daily for their morning trip to the foodsellers, laughed. "Too old to remember things in the present, Maggents? Two boys, you say." She wiped several rising beads of sweat from the crevices around her eyes. "My baby gran, no longer a child, be as old as those two." When Maggents looked at her in disbelief, the old woman nodded her head repeatedly, emphasizing how quickly children seem to grow when someone wasn't there with them every day. "Out on her own, she be, and seeing fit to give even one kind visit that her old gran would enjoy, she can't."

Maggents leaned in to whisper in a conspiratorial, sotto

voice, "At least, all in one piece, your gran be. Not so, it be, that atrocity that emerged from that pod, from what I hear. One leg, *sewn back on,* had to be." She shivered even in the early morning heat, and then reached to touch her companion's arm, the news she was telling making them the very best of friends, at least until the telling was done. Glancing up and down the street to make sure no one was watching or listening, she slipped the juiciest of her tidbits to her friend. "No face, it be said. A pulpy mess, all of it be. Not even enough for an eyelid to sew back on. Imagine that, friend." Maggents giggled at the atrocity of the idea, not seeing just how that could be true, but glorying in the macabre details, anyway.

Her companion put a hand to her lined mouth, its creases drawing down her face, as she contemplated the fantastical story. "Help, does she need? Perhaps some of us, together could get, and using our skills, some money make. To help out, we could." She reached into a fold of her dress, pulling out a cloth with which to dab her eyes. "Sorry for her, be you not, my dear?"

A cackle rose from the old lips. "Sorry? To bring trouble to those such as us, be she not the one? Old military, I be told." Maggents shook her hand in the face of the old woman, one finger rising to make her point crystal clear. "Old enough I be to remember. Was a part of old MegaCorp, he was, my old Chariel. Loved him, I did, damn his mean old soul to the underworld. Took me and Chariel with it, when went down, MegaCorp's military did. Rough times, it were, and remember them well, I do. No good from this effigy of a woman will there be. My words, mark them, you should."

Maggents nodded her head sagely, the stern and unsympathetic expression on her face telling more of what she thought that her words alone. She remembered how much she had loved her Chariel as a boy, and then adored him as they grew into adulthood together. He was the handsome one, and she was quite

101

a beauty herself, though no one would guess it in this old body she wore now. They'd loved each other from early on, never once regretting the sacrifices they made for each other. Never, that is, until his involvement with that corporation from hell.

Never really a military man, Chariel had worked as the liaison between the two, both MegaCorp's commercial enterprise as well as the military arm that ensured its success. Slowly he had been turned. Maggents had lived with it, had watched him lose his humanity to the compromises and deceit he had been forced to accept just to keep his position. If there had been more warning, she felt her Chariel could have mitigated the disaster. As it was, he was in direct negotiations between the two MegaCorp arms when the catastrophe hit, and fallen, he had. Fallen and taken Maggents with him.

She felt no compunction in harboring an inbred anger with which to lash out at MegaCorp. Unable to wrestle with his sudden loss of identity, Chariel had taken the easy way out, ending his own miserable life. Damn him! Look what he'd left her with on this sad little world. She'd been here so long, no one would ever guess the properous life she'd lived at one point. No one even asked her anymore if she was from offworld. Even her speech had degraded to the locals' butchered syntax.

Maggents no longer cared about that.

MegaCorp, though? That, and that alone, she cared a great deal about. Hate it, she did, with a vengeance. Fight it, she would, and fight this woman, if she supported that damned-to-hell corporation.

She looked up at the sky and raised a fist, holding her hand in an age-old arrangement of fingers that spoke of the most vulgar of epitaphs. *Came to our world, woman from the pod, you did! Ran to this wasteland long ago, I did, to escape ever running into the likes of you, and now at the end of my too-long life, chase me down through time, anyway, you do.* The fury in her face was

102

unmistakable.

The old woman walking with her laughed at Maggents' fist shaking towards the sky, although she certainly didn't understand the way the old woman held her hand. Perhaps, even Maggents didn't really understand what her hand was doing. Someone from old-Earth's past would have, though, as she stood thrusting her arm at the sky, her middle finger extended heavenward. She was sending MegaCorp's long dead military arm the most offensive insult she could muster, even as in her heart she was aiming it at the poor creature the old woman next to her so wanted to help.

Glancing beside her, Maggents knew this would be the last time she would converse with Rodricks. Anyone who would help MegaCorp was no friend to her, even if they didn't know why.

RODRICKS KNEW more than Maggents thought.

She also felt emotionally moved in response to the injured person from the pod, no matter whether the battered woman was from MegaCorp or not. That didn't matter to her. It was the escape pod bringing the injured woman to Trasdrom'man that captured her sympathy. The old woman could identify closely with the thought of being cooped up inside one of those, captured without hope of escape, knowing that no matter how long the journey was, no matter how many years passed, the damage that had been taken inside with you was the exact damage you would still claim as your own when you once again climbed out. She'd seen this before, had lived through it herself, and pitied anyone who had to do the same.

Unknown to Maggents, Rodricks knew Maggents' story, and she also knew Maggents thought it was a secret she kept inside as her private pain. The old woman knew, because Maggents' husband had been instrumental in sending the old woman's sister to a distant prisonplanet *locked in a cryo pod* after the old wo-man's sister was severely injured in a MegaCorp takeover of the world her sister had helped colonize. For that reason, Maggents had better be careful. If she went too far, her day would come, because the old woman was keeping an eye on her.

Later, Rodricks did attend Holcum, sitting at her side as she awoke in her excruciating pain, the painkiller from the medpacks now worn off. She watched the injured soldier rail at her agony, the damaged woman's body fighting with itself, attempting to heal those areas that were injured, yet the healing process itself ripping all peace from her devastated body; through Holcum's railing tirades, the old woman quickly understood the volatile levels of anger she carried, and that Holcum's fury could be frightening.

One afternoon not long after, in a part of the city not too far from the healer's place, visiting the room rented for Holcum by the credits the old woman had helped gather for her, Rodricks was surprised to see a glimpse of a smile on the good side of the injured soldier's face. She soon found that the healer had given Holcum hopes that the leg had healed enough to allow her to attempt to walk across the room. This seemed to buoy Holcum's mood, and the Rodricks was glad to be the one to have this opportunity to help her in her attempts. Surely, she thought, if Holcum could begin to see progress, she would learn to come to grips with her situation, eventually fitting in with the world that was now her home.

She soon found she didn't know Holcum at all.

Helping the devastated soldier twist sideways on the narrow, rented sleeping ledge in the cramped, unfamiliar room, the mutilated leg was placed gently on the floor as a companion to her undamaged one. A carefully made crutch the old woman had paid for of her own money was placed under her arm, and she gently supported Holcum's weight until she was standing fully upright. Then, at Holcum's insistence, she released the woman to stand by her own devices.

As soon as her weight shifted to her damaged leg, with a scream of agony, Holcum collapsed to the ground, the leg skewing out from under her. Once Rodricks had helped Holcum back onto her narrow sleeping ledge, making her as comfortable as possible, she quickly ran and brought the healer for her evaluation of just why Holcum's leg had caused such excruciating torment when she had at last tried to stand on it.

Feeling the leg, sensing its bone structure was healing well, the healer told them it was as she had suspected. The fall and the crushing of the leg had damaged a nerve. Without a trip offworld to a major medcenter, there was nothing to be done. Perhaps a crutch or a rolling chair would be a reasonable adjustment for Holcum to be able to forge a livable existence.

With the violence of the truly angered, Holcum called the healer and all the people of this world she was stranded on names that even the healer and the old woman had never heard. With tears in her eyes, seeing the two women simply standing there and taking her abuses, Holcum screamed at them to get out of her sight, throwing whatever small items she could get her hands on, the small breakable things shattering against the walls and doors, and the things that wouldn't break, chipping and breaking whatever they crashed into.

When the old woman and the healer finally escaped to safety, Rodricks touched the healer's arm to show gratitude for all she had done. She apologized for the ill behavior and callus disregard Holcum had heaped upon her, asking if there was anything else to do for her. Telling the old woman she had just changed the bandages the previous day, the healer allowed that all that was needed was to remove the bandages from the face within a week. Dismissing the healer with her thanks and a packet of credits, the old woman listened until the sounds from the room quieted. Then she knocked.

"Mos? Be you okay? Come back in, I would like to do." The

old woman waited several long moments before her patience was rewarded with a reply.

"If you must. Come in and observe the crippled and disfigured invalid. Certainly, come on in."

Rodricks opened the door to the sight of an anger that had decimated the room, only to leave a broken and crushed woman behind. The anger would be back, she had no doubt. This one had trouble inside that went much deeper than just the injuries the healer had tried to repair. But, during this small interlude, Holcum needed all the nourishing she could receive, and nourishment was something the old woman was very adept at giving.

"Why did you not let me die? To live like this on a backward world—" Holcum's voice broke, and she turned her bandaged face to the wall. "On any other world, my injuries could be repaired without a moment's hesitation. Not here, though. Here, I have only that pathetic creature who calls herself a healer." She twisted her head, able to see from both eyes, now, and riveted them upon the old woman, flinging her insult at her as if to sully her along with the healer. "Witch doctor! Grinding those weeds and only calling things 'expected' after she sees what they've become!"

"Whatever she be, saved your leg, she did, Mos. Holcum. Thankful, you may someday be." The old woman paused, very aware that what she'd said was not what Holcum wanted to hear. Shifting her tactics, she spoke to the woman of other people who'd been instrumental in helping. "Wanting to visit be the two who found you." She prattled on as if this were a social visit, and seeing Holcum's eyes soften, knew she had followed the correct path to provide just what the woman's injured psyche needed. If she could find a way to create a social bond for this woman, there might be redemption for her, after all.

HOLCUM TOOK a deep breath. She wasn't really interested in

106

what the woman was talking to her about, but she did know who buttered her bread. For now, that was an important consideration, although she struggled to hold to it through her anger.

"The names of the two, remind me, please. I've had trouble with keeping track."

"Ah!" Rodricks smiled at Holcum's apparent interest. "These two and the old barber, Mas. Tommeoseo. Helped you, they did, from the start." She leaned in closer, as if wanting to make her own healing bond with Holcum, and hoping this was the start of that connection. "Carli and Regge. Resist your command, they couldn't. Pulled your twisted leg for you, the healer said. Believe her, if you will, but saved that leg, they did."

Holcum, in a brief moment of magnanimity, laughed as she leaned her head back on a cushioning mound of bedding. "That, I remember. Gods, they were the fools!"

The old woman laughed also. "About that, right, you be. Fools, they be thought of, by all."

Reaching a hand to gently touch the leg that she suspected would never support her weight ever again, Holcum recalled the events aloud to the old woman, momentarily empowered by the small vestige of her authority she had displayed that night. "You should have seen them. Pain! I had never known such pain, and the heat of this place! I was dying, and not from any of my injuries. I could almost feel sorry for those Rejuvies in all those interrogations." She cut her eyes to the old woman, and seeing no sign of recognition of those events played out just a short time ago in her mind, relaxed and continued. "Those two boys didn't know their armpits from their backsides, and to watch them jump! It was almost worth what I was going through." She smiled, her story winding down, the memory turning melancholy in the retelling. "Not quite, but almost."

"Feel responsible for you, they do. The old barber, too. When you need help, be there for you, they will. Just to ask, be all you need to do."

"Get offworld? Can they help me do that? That's the only thing I need from anyone." In an unexpected and virulent blast, she snorted her contemptuous hatred for Trasdrom'man, the world Regge and Carli called home, and then spoke, almost in a whisper, to herself, "That and a new leg, and just perhaps, a new face. Yes, if I could get all that, I might be able to start again." Holcum paused, her anger only smoothed over for the moment. It wasn't gone, even if it occasionally exhausted itself, and she wan't impressed by her visitor's offer. Holcum sat up and quizzed her. "My things. When I arrived, I wore a uniform. In one pocket, I had a number of things. Were they saved?"

The old woman walked to the sleeping ledge and knelt, pulling open a drawer. Looking up at Holcum, she indicated the contents. "Saved, everything be. Here." She smiled. "Not to wear again, but clean, your uniform be, just in several pieces. The other things you speak of, here they be, also."

"Hand them to me." Seeing the old woman's fleeting expression of hurt at the harshness of the request, Holcum relented. She was a pragmatist. She knew she still needed her for a time, and she softened her voice. "Please." The woman's expression relaxed into a smile as she placed the items in Holcum's outstretched hand.

Unlikely though it was, and it was very improbable it could ever be called a friendship, but a bond of sorts had been formed. That had been the old woman's goal, for she knew Holcum wouldn't survive without one. Exist, yes, even without a personal bond with another human, but survive, no. That wouldn't have been survival to Rodricks. That would have been the barest level of existence. She knew that for certain, as she, herself, had faced the same dilemma herself many years ago. Even Holcum deserved better than that.

# —Chapter 5—

Book of Gollium, vs. 1,459-1,462

*Give a man riches; he will spend until he is poor.*
*Give a man health; his abuse will leave his body sore.*
*Give a man a woman; he will want to mount a whore.*
*Give a man peace; from you, he will ask no more.*

*—From ancient text found on Getsl IV*

*MA'JENE HOLCUM. One ex-military officer, Ma'jene Holcum.*
She looked at her fingers, seeing the dirt ground into the cracks
of her knuckles. *UnderGen'l Ma'jene Holcum. That's where I
was, and I don't even know how I got here, what caused my life
to fall apart, what took my ship from the sky.*

She turned her hands to study the ends of her fingers, this
world's dirt packed under and around the nails she had once kept
so fastidiously perfect. She looked up at the sky, the brilliance of
the day just creeping in to devour any pleasantness that the night
might have begun to give, the morning unwilling to even pretend
it planned to gift the people of this world with temperatures close
to tolerable.

For an instant, the old feelings wrenched her heart, and her
breath closed up, captured in her throat, leaving the air in her

lungs unable to scream for escape. She felt her heart freeze in her chest. She closed her eyes, hoping beyond hope this time, wanting that hard rock she had carried in her chest for so many years to not resume its thumping cadence of life, that driving beat that drove her to endure each day of her life here as a *groundie*. Just to feel the cleanness, the *spareness* of metal walls and metal floors. Just to know she was surrounded by the black purity of unfettered space. That was all she asked from life. Without it, death was preferable.

Then, in an explosion of reality, her body exhaled the now-rotten air from her lungs, her chest heaving as she gasped for breath; and the heaviness of the world around her came crashing back onto her shoulders. This was her world, now. She knew that, even if she didn't like it.

She shook the dirt from her hands and reached for the crutch standing against the wall at her side. Even these growing things she had planted to supplement the meager handouts she received from others knew life on this world was too horrible an existence to endure. She laughed to herself as she looked at yet another of her foodplants that had given up on life and just accepted suicide as a better option. She gazed with envy on the plant that had died.

*There should be a lesson in this for me. There are other options besides continued misery.*

Back in the dimness of her rooms, Holcum reached for the package someone had left on her doorstep the evening before. She had refused to answer the knock, and had, in fact, refused to bring in the package until the morning. She hated the feelings of gratitude she was expected to show. She took these things because she had no other choice.

Except to die.

*Thank you, anyway, small plant in my garden. For this one day, I'll resist your sweet exhortations to join you in your proffered avenue of escape, even if that means I must accept this despised charity.*

From the package, she pulled out small containers of dried legumes, sun-hardened green plants that could be boiled to return them to an edible consistency, and, worst of all, a loaf of the flat, hard bread this world considered a staple of continued existence. Her stomach turning sour at the sight of the same foods for yet another day, she allowed herself to fall into a rough and ill-fitting chair, and she covered her eyes and let the tears flow. This, she could do no longer. No longer. These foods, these endless days of heat with being unable to go outside except at the earliest dawn.

*Water suit!* She barked the word to herself. That one, Regge, had even offered to provide her one so she could go out during the daytime. She had known him for a fool the first time she saw him, and the very idea she might be able to wear a water suit proved his incompetence. Her leg was *crippled.* How was she to put a water suit on; and with her crutch as her constant companion, how would she manipulate the water bladder? *Besides,* she let the tears again start down her face, *torn up, it would be, by the crutch.*

She took in a deep, ragged breath of realization and jerked herself to her feet, her hands gripping the edge of the table next to her to keep the pressure off her leg. *No! I'm even speaking like them. I will not copy this world's reversed syntax patterns. I will hold to who I was, be the starcruiser cap't I was destined to be. I'll keep that pride with me, even if no one around me knows.*

She reached to pick up one of the bags of legumes, and breaking it open, she spilled it across the food preparation surface. She would have to eat, and these would take a long time to cook. *Thank the gods I don't have to haul combustibles to build my fire, too. At least fuel is piped directly into this hovel of mine.*

She would eat again today. Her body required that of her. No matter how hated, no matter how sick she was of these culinary basics, her body would convert their substances into useable fuel for its continued existence. Why she bothered, she couldn't have said. Just one more day, that's all she allowed herself. All she had for the rest of her existence was just one more day. That's all she knew she could stomach at a time, and that was only marginally better than the legumes she was sorting on her table. Sometimes, however, she thought it wasn't better after all.

Pulling out a large pot, she filled it with water and carried the food she'd sorted to the counter. Dumping it in, she ignited a flame underneath the pot. Holcum grasped the side of the work surface and stood, her crutch keeping the pressure from her foot, the nerve inside bearable as long as she was careful with her movements. At first, she would forget from time to time, putting pressure on the foot in the old way. After a few trips to the floor, the fire shooting through her leg, sending its flaming spears deep into the very core of her body, she learned to keep her crutch at her side, it serving as her most treasured friend.

She had also learned to keep a cloth with her to force back the heat from her skin. Her leg, while an insult to the military woman she had been, would slowly become a part of her background. That, she accepted, but the heat. The heat, she would never get used to. Without thinking, she paused, her free hand sweeping her cloth across her face, its dampness sliding smoothly across the good side, the roughness of the other reminding her of what she would forget if she could. She leaned against the room's rough wall, its coolness through her thin clothing and against her shoulder refreshing to her overheated flesh. At times, during the hottest part of the day, she would simply stand and press her face against an interior wall, letting the manmade stone that the city was built of draw the heat from her skin as the sweat ran from her scalp, soaking the collar around her neck.

She knew the day was warming, but it wasn't yet overbearingly hot, and she hobbled to the door, just needing to see something beyond her walls. This wasn't an ancient world, as compared to other inhabited planets. It had been here long enough, however, for its isolation to allow the local speech to bastardize into the idiocy that grated on Holcum's hearing.

The walls of this place told a similar story, too. Stained from the darkness of hands that had rubbed along the edges of doorways, and furniture formed up against too-close walls, the lives of many people could be seen within this dwelling. It was just that Holcum wasn't interested in any of them. She'd been told of the winters this place would afford. With a clever look, the knowing local telling the unlearned the secrets that would make the difference between Holcum's life and death, she had been told how she would long for the heat of the summer afternoons once the winter set in.

Holcum reached for the latch, releasing the mechanism that would allow the world access to this small slice of privacy that kept her trapped and safe. Trapped, because she couldn't be outside in the brilliance without the young man's proffered water suit. Safe, because only here could she pretend her injuries were a temporary setback that would one day be resolved, and her military honors-filled life could resume. A dream, only, it might be, but sometimes, a dream was what she needed.

The door swung open, the brilliance assaulting her eyes, her pupils still adjusted for the dimness of the hovel's interior. As she turned her head to shield her eyes, she felt the now-familiar tightness on the side of her neck, the stiffness that told of scarring that ran deep. She snorted as she reached to massage the skin, although it wasn't skin as most people knew it. It was rough cording mixed with sandpaper, the feeling of sensation mostly coming from her hand. Her face felt almost like someone else's. Her flesh knew almost none of the sensation of being touched, just the pressure that one often easily dismisses when wearing a snug piece of new clothing. Her face's corded skin was that new piece of clothing, but one she could never remove.

Her eyes were now adjusted as well as they would, although the summer sun's brightness even at this early hour was more brilliant than human eyes were designed to block. Holcum peered out. This group of rooms was located on a slight rise, and if she looked at just the right angle between two of the buildings across from hers, she could see far into the distance; and when she lifted her eyes to the distant horizon, a shimmering rise that might even be a mountain range graced the distant break between land and sky.

A breath of longing kept her immobilized for a moment. She had heard of an unnamed sea trapped by a group of mountains, and while she didn't know if it was those she could see from her hovel, she hoped it might be. That was where she'd be if she could travel, the idea of the cooling water drawing her. In her mind, having never seen more of this world than the few city streets she'd walked, or more precisely, hobbled, on her very seldom and very brief forays, she somehow pictured the sea buried in the mountains as a retreat for the revitalization of her over-baked and worn-too-thin life.

She sighed as she pushed the door to, retreating into the relative coolness of the room's interior. For these many months, this had been the course of her days. Wake. Prepare food, wallow in a moment of self-pity, and prepare for sleeping. Then, tomorrow it would be time to tackle that pattern once more. There was no one to take her away from here, and there wasn't a thing she could do about that.

Finally, the water in her pot boiling, Holcum turned the heat down. Covering the container, the food preparing itself all on its own, she dared to really look around the room. She had little out. She knew where the medals were that had been taken from her uniform. The remnants of the uniform itself had been stripped of its buttons and snaps, the gold cords pulled off and wound up, and the fabric disposed of long ago. Even with no mirrors in this place, she couldn't keep too many things around her that might make her look back. She didn't need reminders that this was now her home, as permanent a residence as her home aboard Mega-Corp's mighty ships had ever been.

Throwing a few of the dried green plants into her pot, careful not to overcook them, Holcum lifted the flat bread. Rapping it sharply against the edge of the work surface, she broke off a tough end piece. Live here, or there, or anywhere else. She knew it didn't really matter if she liked this place. It was hers, and that's all that counted. Right now, she did have to eat, and all the trials of this world would have to wait.

CARLI WHISTLED as he dodged the sun, keeping to the shady spots along the street. He and Regge still had the transport, although they had tried to return it. He laughed aloud, startling those around him, as he remembered the looks on the faces of the city workers when they had driven up in the old, dented, and rusted transport. The transportation workers hadn't wanted it back. The ownership papers still said it belonged to the city, but he and Regge had been made to promise they would keep it somewhere else, never, ever returning it to the storage facility.

Now, Regge wanted to go for a ride, and Carli was feeling good. Regge had told him they were heading someplace they'd never been before, someplace a friend of his wanted to visit. It usually wasn't like him to be so vague about what they were planning together, but Carli didn't care, not as long as Regge let him slide the transport on the desert. They had a whole series of tracks, worked out by trial, error, and excitement since they'd discovered the cryo pod.

That was still a spot in Carli's craw. Regge actually felt responsible for that pitiful creature that had crawled forth. Why, Carli didn't know. They had helped her get to the healer that first night, and the old woman, Rodricks, had helped her after that. Plus, old Tommeoseo had even tossed his hat in the ring, and Tommeoseo wasn't the tiniest bit responsible. Even after all that, Regge still took her food and had helped arrange her a place to stay.

At least, today was reserved for Carli. And Regge, of course. Of course. Regge had the transport. He would have to be there, although, if Regge would let him, occasionally Carli would be glad to take the transport out from time to time, just to keep the power plant from seizing up from disuse. If he had the transport for his own, though, the power plant might just seize up from *over*use. He laughed out loud again, his humor at the prospect known to everyone that might be listening, and maybe even to a few who weren't.

Seeing Regge in the distance, the transport waiting for them in the shade, it wasn't until he was closer that Carli noticed the third person already seated inside. When he got near enough to clearly see the shape of the person inside, the glimmer of the day's excitements began to wane, as he suspected who it might be. He was almost fooled, though. As he waved to Regge and glanced at the person in the transport, he thought for a moment that Regge had invited along a new girlfriend, someone dark-haired and very attractive, if too mature for Carli's taste.

Yet, when she noticed his arrival and turned to watch him, he could see two people there. On one side was the woman who still retained much of the beauty of the attractive girl she had been at one time. Turning, though, it was clear the other side was deci-mated, the skin corded and red, something for hiding away in dark rooms where no one goes. It was the first time Carli had seen her since delivering her to the healer. Regge had shared stories with him, ones revealing little of the anger from that first night. Other people seemed more willing to tell blacker shards of the woman's story.

Now, it seemed Regge wasn't content just to tell him about her. He expected him to spend the day with her. Would she be able to endure the sliding he hoped they would do? Finding out Regge's plans was the next thing on Carli's agenda. In fact, it was the first thing he intended to do now that he was here.

With a nod to the woman, Carli motioned Reggante to the far side of the street, as he pretended to show him an item in a just-opening shop. Pulling him inside, he whispered in a disgruntled tone, "This be what, Regge? A cripple, she be, and invited her, you have?"

Regge laughed. "Whisper, you need not do, friend. Inside, we be, and hear you, she cannot. To you, in a word, an answer to give, yes. A cripple. A lonely cripple who needs help."

"Regge," Carli peered at him with squinted eyes, looking closely for signs in his friend's face that might show what he truly hoped he did not see, "in love, be you not, I hope most sincerely. Please, the truth, tell me, otherwise."

REGGE GRABBED Carli's shoulder, and he smiled indulgently. "No, my friend. Not so. Needs a friend, she does, and allow me to be one of those, not even that will she do. Someday, an older man for her to need, one to find, perhaps she will. But for this day, a ride to the inland sea be all that willing to accept from me, she be. Invited you, that be why I have." Regge unexpectedly laughed. "That, and in the transport for us to take a ride, this day be. Taken it a long distance, we never have. Thought you might like to go."

"Told me, you could have, Regge." Carli's mouth showed signs of a pout his friend was very familiar with and instantly tried to ward off.

"Not until today was I sure she would go." He glanced at Holcum waiting in the transport. "If not, go anyway, we would, and a great time have. Okay, be you with this, friend?"

Carli's face relaxed. "Drive, I can, Regge?"

Regge let himself return the pleased expression, smiling and indulging his friend. The woman hadn't *promised* she would go, had in fact *begged* him to take her. She would have gone today if she'd needed to walk, she'd ranted, as he'd dropped off his regular food delivery the night before. But, Carli was pleased again, and that would make for a far better day.

Together, they returned to the heat of the morning, having purchased nothing in the shop. As they stepped into the direct rays of the sun as they crossed the street, Carli hissed from the side of his mouth, "Wearing a watersuit, she be?"

Regge slapped Carli's arm. "Stupid, I be not, no matter what some say. Helped her put it on, I did. Ready, she be, Carli. Remember her name?"

Carli ducked his head for a moment, then looked up brightly. "Um, be it Hol . . . um, Holcum? Correct?"

Regge grabbed him by the back of the neck and squeezed until Carli twisted his shoulders to get him off. "That, for you, be a yes."

"Fool!" Carli slapped him away. "Just say, next time."

Regge jumped onto the back of the transport, sitting on the makeshift seat he had assembled there. He leaned forward to speak through the missing back window to the two who would ride in the front.

"Holcum, my friend, this be. Remember Carli, you might. Drive us, today, he will." Turning to Carli, he spoke in a much firmer voice. "Remember, friend, in the back my seat be, and firmly fixed, it be not. Into the dirt, please don't throw me with the driving of the slide race you so love. To remain aboard be what I wish."

That brought a grin to Carli's face, and when his eyes glanced at Holcum, seeing her looking straight ahead, trying to mind her own business, a grin also played at her mouth.

118

ALTHOUGH Holcum knew these men to be fools, she was amused for the first time in a very long time.

*Groundie.*

She pictured dirt flying, and for the first time in her life, she saw the term in a humorous light. It hardly dampened her underlying anger, but it was a welcome respite from the mundane repetitiveness of her endlessly routine days. Unable to stop herself, she began to smile broadly as she looked away from the two men.

Riding in the old, windowless transport towards the inland sea was too far for the weathered vehicle, had the plugs inside not been rearranged by Carli's bumbling hand. The speed he'd opened up made this day possible. Upon arriving, a sense of disappointment washed over Holcum.

Both Regge and Carli had always known the desolateness of the inland sea, and had Holcum told them what she was looking for, they could have saved her a day traveling across the desert. She had hoped for something soothing, something cool, and the shores of the sea were anything but. Instead, there were sheer rock walls plunging preciptiously into the water around much of the shoreline, some vertical, others gracefully curving, the water lapping at their bases, the discoloration showing the sea's seasonal rise and fall with the changing environment.

Only in a few areas were there actual beaches, and many of those had to be reached by water, either that or by falling down the cliff faces directly into the churning waves. The men knew a few places where the waves could be accessed through a series of caves. Carli carried a bag with foodstuffs for their lunch as the three attempted their way through the honeycombed rock. Regge helped Holcum when she would allow it, or leading the way when she wouldn't. An easy trip for the two men, the passage was much more difficult for a woman needing to navigate the entire distance with one hand attached to a crutch. At many points, the outer walls opened to stunning views of the sea broiling under the midday sun. From the relative coolness of the caves, the sight was stunning. Even so, the heat emanating from the openings assured them the reality of the beauty was otherwise.

Long before reaching the bottom, worn out, Holcum stopped by one of these openings, telling the others she could go no farther. Exhausted, bonded for the day by a shared activity, by help given and new surroundings, she began to tell something of her fears of others laughing at her, the public side of life in the city not allowing her the emotional freedom to roam freely while others were out and about. The men listened, pulling out midmeal items, sharing the food, as she talked to them about how angry she'd been upon first arriving on this world, and how hard it had been to accept that she would never leave. For a time, the three appeared almost as friends out for a day in an exotic locale, enjoying a good meal in the coolness of a cave far above the thundering of an inland sea. Of course, appearances can be deceiving, and what might appear to one person as a bonding experience may, to another, simply be a release of exhausted emotion, clearing the channels for the anger that still boils underneath the calm surface.

Whatever the reasons the three had for being there that hot, hot day, no matter whether it was from a desire to help, a longing for escape, or just because a friend had been slightly dishonest with a misleading invitation, these three people were good for each other, if just for this one time-out from life. Before heading back to the city, as the men were gathering the food supplies, Holcum sat for a bit staring out to the sea. To herself, she whispered softly, "I would stay here some day, away from everyone and everything that hurts me. I would run away to this, if I could. I would find my peace here."

She didn't know if that might ever be possible, but this had been one day away from her hated life in the city, and that was the good that had come from the day. She now knew there was an existence possible that could be more than just an endless string of days spent in that hovel in the city. She had to find a way to live it, and she didn't have any idea how it could be done.

The tears in her eyes were dried before she stood, and Regge once again helped her to maneuver through the system of caves. She again had tears in her eyes during her return to the city, tears of dread. For her, it was a return to her prison. She was glad that by the time they had returned to the city, the heat of the dwindling day and the wind from the movement of the transport had dried them all.

HOLCUM SLAMMED the door against the flames chasing her through the ship. She looked for her crutch, then remembered she'd left it in the hallway. Realizing she'd felt no pain in her leg as she'd darted through the open door, she smiled in relief. Her injuries were getting better after all, in spite of what that crank healer had said. All her *"as I expected"* mumbo was just that, mumbo.

Stomping her foot to the floor to prove to herself the injured limb no longer hurt, she laughed in exultation, and she turned to the door to check to see if the flames had died down. Catching a glimpse of her reflection in the polished metal in front of her, she paused, running her fingers over her face. Her skin! It was whole, again. Her face was once again beautiful.

"MegaCorp! Rezalton! Bofsky! I'm back, and you'd all better watch out!" She would save this ship, and it would be given to her to command as a reward. Throwing the door wide, she flung herself with abandon into the adjoining smoke-filled corridor. "Soldiers! Follow me! We must fight this enemy!" When she saw no one rising to her challenge, she shook her head in disgust, understanding she would have to do this herself.

Tearing down the corridor, adrenalin pulsing through her blood, her muscles flowing with the power of the gods, she ran to meet her fate, to *control* her fate. Life wouldn't beat her down again, not now that she was back in control. Seeing a wall of flames in front of her, she dived through the middle, certain she could reach the other side, and then she'd be able to keep running, never giving up her ship. The flames brightened around her, their touch burning her skin, her clothing turning into flaming torches, and when she was finally through, there was nothing but empty space. Floating, she was flooded with pain. She moaned with the torment, searching for a cool spot in all the burning. *Find it,* her mind cried, and she searched; and in reaching out, she located it.

Reaching her hand to her forehead, she felt a cooling cloth pressed there, and along with it, heard a voice. An angel? She knew there were no angels, but out in deepest space, what else could it be? She tried to open her eyes and look around, but they wouldn't respond for her. She moaned, knowing the burning must stop, and only the coolness was able to do that. Again, she heard the voice, and this time she understood its words of comfort.

"Holcum, dear. Wear heavier clothes over your skin, you must. Shot, those boys should be, allowing this to happen. Sitting out, overlooking the water. Told me, they did, when I pressed them, where you were yesterday. The worst place you could be, it was. Made the sun worse, the water did."

"Needed to see," Holcum mumbled. "Hot. I'm so hot. Thirsty, too."

"Badly burned, you be. The face, worst burned be its scars. Shush, be quiet. Watch over you, I will. Sleep, lady. Sleep."

"Who are you?" Holcum began to drift back into her state of slumber, the medicine the healer had given her beginning to take effect once more.

"No concern to you, that be. To get better, now be the time. Just sleep, and look after you, I will. Shush, now. Just sleep."

In spite of Holcum's earlier abuses and accusations, the healer was good. She was very good. She knew that injured people often threw their worst insults at the first person to help them. That was part of the training she'd received. She would take care of her patient no matter how long it took. Of course, she would charge, too, and she would expect to be paid. That was also part of the job, and when she did the first, she could always claim the second.

HOLCUM LAY in bed and shivered under her thin coverings. The summer heat at night was bearable only with these thin pieces of cloth draped over her. When the wind was still, this was sometimes too much.

She wondered if she was ill. It wouldn't surprise her: the heat; trying to take care of that poor sod of a garden that barely produced enough for her to think of its "bounty" as supplementing her basic dietary staples; then, her daily legumes, those green reconstituted leaves, and that hard bread. They were hardly adequate to keep the human body fed.

Also, a high-pitched keening noise kept slicing through her sleep, her *attempted* sleep, about to make her explode with frustration. She pulled her coverings closely under her chin, any air on this night unwelcome against her chilled flesh, and she closed her eyes, hoping to find sleep.

Eventually, her breathing deepened, and she felt herself starting to drift off. She could tell, had always been able to tell when she was drifting into a sound slumber. Just as she began to slip into the welcome respite of sleep, repeated rapping at her door jarred the darkness. Her eyes sprang open, the noise jarring her back to the chilly reality of the night. In the past, the noise would have angered her. Now, her heart pounded with fear. She was no longer the strong and agile military woman, able to quickly respond to emergencies while commanding others to do the same. At one point in her life, she would have leaped from her sleeping pad at an intrusion like this, her weapon in hand, leaving the intruder dead before a second knock was even considered. However, not now.

She slipped a hand down her near-naked body, touching the leg with the errant nerve, the damage repaired what seemed like an eternity ago, and sighed. She massaged the skin, the muscle underneath revealing the knotting of the bones where the medic had worked her shattered leg back into place. Running her fingers down her thigh as far as she could reach, she knew the scar she could touch stretched to her foot. Although it had healed over, even the itching that she had endured for months finally ending, its presence on her leg told her she would never be "fixed." She felt her belly, its flatness just as she had always known it. When her hand caressed her breasts, her fingertips tracing the ends where a baby would never suckle, but men had, her hand cupping the fullness that was there even with all she had gone through, she let her thoughts wander.

*A man's hands might touch these and never know that other parts of my body are damaged beyond repair. These a man might still desire, if only the face above them was not so hideous. In the dark, if only someone would come to me . . .*

She closed her eyes, and the insistent rapping at her door became, to her, the knock of a stranger seeking companionship for the night. He was someone who didn't know her, had just heard that someone lived here who might be willing to share her warmth for the night. He slipped his specially made key into the lock, opening that door that kept the world at bay, and he stood by her, his clothes falling from him in anticipation. In the darkness, he stood out sharp and clear, his pale skin the color of a moon on some distant world, his hair a ghostly cap. Tall and trim, she could see that he wanted her. She moved the thin bedcovering to invite him in. She smiled, offering him the unseen gesture in the darkness. As he knelt on the sleeping pad, he placed his hands on either side of her, reaching his lips to gently kiss the rough side of her face.

"What's hidden in the darkness is not there at all." His whisper caressed her ears. "You'll be beautiful to me tonight."

He lay beside her, his warmth becoming hers. Holcum drew in a sharp breath as she felt his lips and the roughness of his tongue take over where his hands had rested.

She reached to kiss the side of his face as he leaned into her. She was jerked back to reality by the rapping once again, repeated with greater urgency. Gasping with the dream that was suddenly undone, she looked for the man who had come to her, hoping against hope he might still be there, not wanting to turn loose of him. And yet, he was nowhere to be found.

Throwing the covers back, she sat up and realized it was *cold* in the room. Pulling her crutch to her to stand, she draped a cloth over herself to hide her nakedness and hobbled to the door, releasing the latch. She snorted with disgust at the intrusion, uncaring who was there, and unwilling to wait for the door to open. She turned and fell into a chair.

The door burst wide, a frigid gust of air making Holcum's skin crackle, as a voice cried out, "Good. Still alive, you be." It was Regge and his friend, Carli, both bundled in more clothes than Holcum possessed, carrying a portable light in their hands. "Too late, afraid we might be."

They crowded in and pushed the door firmly shut behind them. Holcum laughed at the audacity of these fools who were making no sense at all. "Raiders are out tonight, is that it? An asteroid is falling from the sky. Or, and I think this must be it, I'm dying of my lack of male company, soon to be dead because no man will have me." She sat in the shadows, irritated at the intrusion, and she snorted her acrid derision at them.

Carli spoke with urgency. "The winter. Here early, it be. Hear the wind, you can, the wailing. Soon, from the vast salt oceans, the snow will come, covering the land. To Winter City, take you, let us, you must." His desperation hummed.

"I have no home in Winter City, and why would I want to be trapped underground? It's bad enough knowing my life will be spent walking the dirt of this world. Underground, pah!" It *was* cold, though. She would admit that.

Regge stepped forward and knelt at her side. "Died, Carli's parents did, on a night such as this. Days early, came the cold, and ready, they weren't. Found days later, they were, frozen on their sleeping pads. Come with us. Go, you must." He grasped her hand, holding it in his own as he continued. "Came to me, Carli did. Searched all over Winter City for you. Knew, we finally did, come with the rest, you hadn't. Insisted, Carli did. Another death on his shoulders, he didn't want."

Holcum sat for a moment, holding the fool's hand, the hand of the idiot who had come with a friend to rescue her. She would have stayed where she was, even if she'd known just how cold it would get. She'd assumed the upcoming winter weather would be an inconvenience. Maybe not, she was starting to realize.

Not having intended to go below, the very thought abhorrent to her, she was, however, holding the warmth of a man's hand in hers, and she could still feel the ghost man's warmth next to her, his touch on her breasts, and his lips on her face. Her eyes misted as she remembered his words: *You'll be beautiful to me tonight.* She didn't need those words, and had, in fact, refused to listen to them once before. But, for this one, lonely night, with the still-vivid memory of his body warding off the chill in the room, they had been the only words he could have said that she would have believed.

For some reason, she needed a man tonight. She didn't expect these two men wrapped in their many layers of clothing to come to her as she lay to sleep, but to be with them, to hear their voices, and to perhaps touch them in passing, that would do for the moment. It was also more than she could expect from any man, anymore. Only in her dreams would a man see past her face and want the rest of her. That or someone very desperate, someone who wanted to take every woman he could find, no matter how old or dissected she looked.

She smiled to herself as she pointed out the location of her things, the water suit left behind for use on another hot day, many months into an unclear future. Bracing herself, an extra coat her rescuers had brought helping her fight the cold, Holcum stepped outside, gasping as it took her breath away. *Gods,* she thought, *I never could have imagined this level of coldness. No wonder the man's parents froze to death. It's a wonder all the inhabitants of this world don't freeze to death.*

On the way to the underground city in the windowless transport, she kept tucking the coat in wherever she felt the cold, and that was everywhere. As the vehicle reached the lower city, Regge maneuvered it through what would eventually become a vast ice hanger for offworld transports arriving to service Trasdrom'man's sparse economy, once the cold weather was in place long enough to build it. The hanger would offer some protection from the brutality of the harsh winter. Building it would have to wait for a time, though. The ground was still cooling, and, in fact, the blanketing snows hadn't even arrived. They would, though. They always did.

Now, the trio would get to face the worst drawback about Winter City. Its internal heating system, though not enough to keep the city really warm during the worst of the cold, operated all year. During summer, Winter City was an underground furnace and couldn't be accessed for any reasonable length of time, due to the planet's naturally occuring geothermal activity. This world had no other readily available fuel source, and using the geothermals was what made the city passibly tolerable in the severity of winters so brutal that a person could freeze to death in the amount of time it took to cross the city on foot.

Stepping from her rooms in Summer City, Holcum had felt the cold all over, but most strongly in her leg. As never before, she'd been able to feel every break in the bones up and down that mangled limb. During the ride, she'd bitten her tongue to keep from groaning aloud. Worse, though, was the heat below. Winter City *would* cool, Regge and Carli assured her. It would cool, they said, far too much, becoming a place where the very warmest of clothes were worn at all times. Only the well-funded or those directly over the geothermal piping could count on any really comfortable heat throughout the bitterness of the upcoming season.

Holcum was relieved to be ushered in under the cover of night. However, the walkways and interior passages were not free of people. Many people had waited until the last possible opportunity to move below, because of wanting to keep safe those items in Summer City they wouldn't be moving. Until the actual winter hit, the city above would be subject to looters, no matter how much policing the city leaders tried to do.

Then, there was the second reason: the heat below the surface of the planet. It was, perhaps, a stronger motivating force than the first.

As they traveled through the passageways, Holcum tried to avert her face when possible, but she saw the looks, and they weren't pleasant or welcoming. She hadn't tried to be the charming newcomer, but she also hadn't been intentionally abusive to anyone unless they had come into direct contact with her. Even for one such as she, the looks cut deeply, compounding misery upon grievous misery.

After much waiting and checking, a place was found for her.

It seemed that Rodricks, the old woman who had been so helpful to Holcum at the start of the summer, wouldn't be coming below this year. As her own life had drawn to a close, her years great, and her relief at no longer having to live them palpable to her, she had looked out for her new ward in one last way. She had ensured that her quarters would be allotted to the woman from the cryo pod.

Soon, deposited in her new surroundings, the quarters utilitarian and basic, Holcum stood her crutch by the sleeping platform and lay down. It was very warm in the room, something Regge and Carli told her indicated nearby geothermals in the walls. She wasn't grateful for her small blessing. Quite the opposite. To her, this was the start of the summer all over again on this sanity-forsaken world. For many years, she'd thought the nightly abuse she'd suffered from the soldiers who had wiped out her family, eventually sending her to the MegaCorp academy training ship, was the worst thing her life had dealt her. Here, this night, she knew that wasn't true. On those long ago nights, the child she had been had learned to close her eyes until the men were finished, and if they'd been gentle and hadn't torn anything, the next day, she could look in a mirror and pretend her life was all right. She'd heard screaming the first few times the soldiers had taken her. It was hers; she knew that, now. Back then, however, it had been a sound that went with the pain ripping her apart. Finally, one of the men had slapped her repeatedly until the screams stopped, and she'd never heard the screams again. She'd soon learned to treasure her days without the men. Only when the nights came did she have to close her eyes to forget what they were doing to her.

She closed her eyes once again and tried to forget. This heat was no better than the first day she'd climbed from that pod, curse those two who had stupidly allowed her to wake to this hell of a life. This was worse. Much worse. She wouldn't turn fourteen and be rescued, sent to the academy for a fresh start where no one knew what had been done to her. This was forever, and everyone could see, could laugh at her, and she would never be able to hide.

With tears running down her face, she lay on the heat of the sleeping pad, and with the anger inside of her, reached out and stuck the stone wall by her side repeatedly until her fist painted the surface red. As the cold rushing across the face of the city above began to seep downwards into the underground world the city's inhabitants would call home for the next half a year, Holcum's quarters slowly began to cool. With that cooling, her tired eyes began to close, and the sleep she had nearly grasped hours before finally became hers.

LIFE TOOK Holcum for a ride that night, her first experience of the underground municipality the local inhabitants called Winter City. Not only was she exhausted with her move, but for the first time since arriving so many months ago, the air had licked her skin with the sweetness of release from summer's grasp. As she slept, she began to dream.

The light was bright in her dream, and the air was warm. Flowers surrounded the grass where she played. She looked up to find her daddy at an outdoor cooking center. He smiled at her through the smoke that rose from under the cooking surface's cover. As he raised the cover, smoke billowed out, causing him to wave his free hand to try to clear the air.

When he began to cough, she laughed. He said something to her and laughed back. She didn't know what he said, but she knew it was funny, causing her to laugh even more.

Just then, her mommy walked up with a tall glass filled with ice and a cool, brown liquid. As she handed it to her daddy, her mommy kissed him on the cheek. He grabbed her around the waist, kissing her neck over and over until she pushed him away, laughing at him. Her mommy came over to Holcum and gave her

130

a big hug and a kiss.

Everyone jumped when a loud noise startled them. Up in the sky, a big explosion happened, causing a giant red flower to appear against the blue of the sky, and black smoke started pouring from it. They all looked to see what was going on when a pop, pop, pop sound started. That was when her daddy grabbed her around the waist, then he grabbed her mommy's arm, and they all ran into the house to be safe, but they weren't safe at all.

In another dream, she watched the boy on the bunk over hers. He was asleep. All he had on was his priv'tshorts. They'd told her about him, how his bunkmate had been killed in a hazing. Well, she'd had worse, so he could just grow up. She used to wish she'd been killed when her parents were. Now, she was glad she hadn't. All that had made her tougher.

She was fourteen that year. The boy in the bunk was, too. Just like her, he'd already changed, was no longer a kid. She also knew that boys who had just gotten their manhood always thought about it, wanted it, and all the time, too. What they wanted was what she had to offer, and she didn't mind using it. She needed him, but he wasn't going to get her, because she also knew that boys would do whatever she wanted as long as they wanted her. Once they got what they wanted, they didn't care, anymore. She couldn't control them, then.

She laughed as she called out to him. He acted like he couldn't understand why she was a girl and not another boy. That was funny.

Her dream shifted, and she stood on the elevated bridge of a massive starstrike destroyer. She was the one with the officer's bars on her uniform, not the others standing below. They had to do what she said, and they knew it. She wasn't the captgen'l, yet, but she would be, just as soon as she could get Bofsky out of the way. He was good, though. Good at keeping control of his power.

She imagined his life, sometimes, how lucky he must have

been. Even as a baby, he probably had his parents jumping to do anything he asked. She smiled at that, causing some of the bridge crew to look away, not wanting to be the focus of her attention. They were right about that, too. She had no compunction about corrections for any member of the crew, no matter how harsh she needed to be to make her point.

When Bofsky was a boy, all his instructors had probably been afraid of *him*. His life had been a charmed one, straight to starship captgen'l; she was certain of that. She should have been so lucky as to have had a life like Bofsky's.

She did remember the cryo pod cycling her back to life. Some people say you enter the pod, and the next thing you know, you're climbing out again. You don't know the difference, except the calendars have changed. Well, she'd known what was happening. She'd felt cold and stiff. She'd known the cryogel was still around her, and she'd felt it sucking back into the hidden bladders in the pod where it could be reused again and again. She had *felt* that happening to her. She'd known when it left her face and emptied from her nose, and she'd felt it when her leg started to hurt again.

That and her face. Her face had certainly hurt, the blood all over, still running from her wounds. She remembered the pod's hatch springing open, seeing the light coming in from around the edges, and reaching with her hand, grabbing it to open it, then realizing she couldn't. She had so needed to get *out*.

She hadn't really intended to fall in, only the ship's floor had buckled, knocking her inside, and the pod was so small, too small to stay inside. She also remembered the smell of herself inside that pod before the hatch popped open: the blood, the sweat, the smell of her ship's burned, scorched, and melted parts. It had all entered the pod with her, and it was all there as she was brought back to life.

If only it had malfunctioned. She could have flown on in

space for another three hundred or a thousand years, never waking up. That would have been better. That certainly would have been much, much better.

THE NEXT MORNING, Holcum's fury at the previous evening's debacle had her out of bed when Regge arrived. Hobbling to the door, she opened it, returned to her bed, and leaned her cane to the side. The young man perched nervously on a built-in seating niche in the wall. For a time she glared at him, the tension thick between them, and then her pent-up anger boiled out.

"Did you know about her? Her death? The old woman helped me, tried to be a friend to me, only I wouldn't let her, wasn't ready to let her or anyone close to me. She even gave me this room."

Her body vibrated with her rage, and her shaking finally knocked her crutch clatteringly to the floor. When she leaned to pick it up, her foot brushed against the stone and began to fire pain throughout her body. She crashed to the floor, flinging furious curses at the man who had invaded her morning.

Her memory of the dream man who had come to her the night before was still strong in her mind. Her need of him was still physically powerful in her senses, her body tingling at the slightest memory of his pale, strong shape and the firm touch she had felt when he'd lain with her. From her position on the floor, she screamed at Regge, "He loved me, do you know that? For all those years, he loved me!"

Regge watched as she started sobbing, her hand drawn up to her mouth. He leaned in to listen as she continued, whispering as if to herself.

"I didn't love him back. I couldn't. I never could show that. I would have seemed weak. Instead, I used him, and meanly, too. I wished him sent away to prison or worse. For battle after battle, I wished him dead, always cursing the gods that he still lived.

Even when I was thrown unwillingly into that cryo pod, I still carried his ID card, meaning to ruin him even as my ship was attacked and that pod carried me to this hellish world. All because he loved me."

She glowered darkly at the man sitting on the edge of his seat, just waiting for her to ask for his help. He'd learned her lessons that well, at least. She only took help that she requested.

"I've made no friends here, Regge. None. Not even you. You've helped me, for which I'm grateful, and I admit I've not acted as your friend. Still, why did you not let know about old Rodricks? Surely you knew she was dying, that she was finally dead. You didn't tell me. Is that so?"

He nodded. "As she wished, that was what I did. Thought enough troubles you had, she did. This, done for you, I knew she had." He smiled in apology, motioning around him to the room they were in. "Knew its location, I didn't, and the reason for the wait last night, that be."

"I would have told her thank you, if only I'd known." Holcum reached to wipe her eyes with the back of one hand.

"Now, Holcum," Regge prodded, with some of the wisdom he had been finding in his encounters with her and the people who were helping her even without her knowledge. "Done that, would you have, really? Think not, I do. Seriously, now, to feel better, do not, about this, lie."

Holcum looked up, surprised at Regge's response. This sounded more like the old barber, the old mas, whatever his name was. She felt a moment of respect for the man sitting in the room with her. This was what she needed, not the pansy-pity most people wanted to give her.

"Help me up, will you? I never thought I'd say this on this world that now seems to be my home. It feels to be getting cold, even here."

He smiled. "Get much colder, it will. Get additional clothes for you, we must, and warm ones, too. These things, not warm enough, they be." He reached to rub a few of her fabrics between his fingers. "For summer only, these be."

Holcum took a deep breath, considering just how much to tell this man. He didn't seem vengeful that she had lashed out at him, and living here certainly made her feel very weak. Even so, just speaking to anyone was sometimes a relief. She didn't always like herself, and without the ability to command respect from others, her own self-image had suffered immensely.

"I want to thank you again for helping me. I know I'm an angry woman, and these injuries have made me worse. I even hate the gods, wherever they may reside." She barked out a laugh. "I'll not be a friend to you, Regge. I don't have that in me. I won't be nice much of the time. My anger boils inside of me, always. But, I can be grateful, and I am. I really am."

Regge laughed out loud, inciting a sharp look from Holcum. She softened as she heard his reply.

"Honest, you be, and for that, grateful, I be. Take brutally honest from you, I can. Deception, I cannot. For that, thank you, I do."

At that, she smiled at him as he helped her to her feet, her needed crutch once again in her hands.

# —Chapter 6—

*Beware of the man in red,*
*Dressed in his stocking cap.*
*He forces all the small children*
*To climb up and sit in his lap.*
*He comes to them in their dreams*
*And strokes their sleeping heads,*
*Then he leaves his special gifts*
*Hidden underneath their beds.*

*—Trasdrom'man Chrismast verse*

THE WEATHER had turned, and for once, there was promise in the air. It seemed that during this change of the seasons, the people of Trasdrom'man might even be blessed with that rare specialty given only on those few days a year when one major weather pattern changes to another: a spring.

Of course, this was Trasdrom'man, and any spring here would be necessarily brief. By any old-Earth standards, it might not be very spring-like, either. However, these people knew old-Earth only as a distant legend, a Vid-world, a place of children's dreams and stories.

If they had been able to visit that distant world, they might have looked and possibly would have found many similarities in the great planet they thought of as so different than their own. They would have seen the massive oceans and the beautiful polar regions frozen year-round. They would have recognized snatches of their Trasdrom'man in those.

However, the massive rainforests of Earth covering huge swatches of land were still in place, and the pollution of old-Earth had long since been dealt with, its scars mostly hidden. In those, old-Earth would have seemed very different from rugged and brutal Trasdrom'man.

For a time, the beauty of that distant world might transfix them, but despite that initial charm, reality would soon set in, for living from day to day would become just as tedious, the finding of those "special" moments just as difficult. The stress and pull of person against person would be no different. The cities would be crowded, and the weather patterns would drive their days just as they did on Trasdrom'man.

This spring was one of those special times on Trasdrom'man, a time that would be spoken of for many of this planet's seasons for its beauty, its sweetness, and for one more dark, dark event.

The raiders.

The first advent of spring, that initial suggestion that the long winters days might be at an end, was first felt as a warming of the rooms inside Winter City. Piled coverings were kicked from too-warm bodies at night. Instead of three of the warmest shirts that day, only two were chosen, then one. The great ice windows to the sky that blocked the gusting assaults of the world above them began to drip their rain of promise to the humans sequestered below. Life outside of Winter City was returning.

As the first brave humans ventured forth, they noticed one thing that was especially odd. It wasn't bitterly cold, yet it wasn't torturously hot, either. The great movements of air across the surface of this world, driven by the vastly elliptic path of the planet around its sun, normally shifted without warning, forcing themselves across its surface, bringing changes swift and sure. At the end of the frozen hell of winter, a blisteringly hot wind would sweep in from the equatorial regions and into Summer City, wrap itself around the spaceport and its ice structures, and within days, these great winter behemoths would be gone, the flash of summer's heat boiling away any moisture that couldn't be quickly gathered and stored for the city's use during the dry months ahead. As bad as it was in the city, no outposts had ever survived at the poles or the equator, and the planet's inhabitants didn't have the luxury of chasing the quickly changing temperate regions that flittered across the globe.

This year was indeed different. Even the plants seemed to know it. Rather than the usual frantic, scrambling burst of life given by the melting snow and ice, the heat's tongue licking the moisture from the ground before the growth could mature, the plants fading in the sun's brilliance, the rains came. Cleansing water ran down the streets of Summer City, drenching people as they moved their things from their Winter City quarters, some cursing, many more laughing with the joy of the seldom-seen water flooding from the skies at this critical junction of the seasons.

This year, the plants grew more slowly, those citizens practicing the Chrismast gifting holiday having to contain their impatience as the rains teased their green children from the ground. For nearly three local weeks, the world these people knew seemed to stop, the days pleasant, the nights sliding into the languor of outdoor activities that had been stored away for years, waiting for a spring just like this one. Even the water suits were left packed in storage or simply stagnated on shopseller's shelves, the pleasing sun on too-cold skin bringing a forgotten joy to the city's populace.

Then, the rain ending but the languid temperatures still hovering over their world, a few began to talk of the distant columns of dust seen high in the sky. *Duststorms,* some whispered. Others claimed to have been told of weather events from their long-distant past on a world so far away that it was now more legend than history. *Tornados.* Even so, it was yet another word that struck fear into their hearts, one that at first, only the fewest of the few dared to whisper. It had been scores of years since anyone had experienced its touch, but those who had, remembered. The very murmurs made them shiver, and the word's meaning crawled up and down their spines.

The whispers grew as the sound of the voices began to permeate the city, pricking the joyous bubble of the extended spring until its very substance threatened to collapse, washing the people back into Winter City.

*Raiders,* the whispers said. *Raiders have come again.*

WHEN THE RAIDERS finally arrived, the people had already emptied Winter City, the blazing beauty of green plants and glorious weather pulling them to the surface, the city below the ground beginning to warm to uncomfortable levels with the planet's geothermal heat coursing through its walls and floors. It was a difficult transition for Holcum. With her crutch, she had been able to navigate the interior passageways of the city below, albeit mostly at the times of day when others weren't out, but in reality, almost never. The clothing required, even in the confines of the city, was too tedious for her crippled body to endure, so she stayed in her rooms, the geothermal heating at first keeping her as warm as most, and later, only warmer than some. In the deepest of the winter, she had lain still in the dark, covered, shivering through the nights as the insidious cold reached ever bolder fingers in to torment her. Yes, she had to admit, she did long for the heat of the summer days, even though she'd never thought she would.

She finally made it back to the surface and to her hovel,

abandoned when the cold winter winds had attacked the city a half-year before. The climbing of the stairs alone, the long trek to the city, her refusing to ask for a repeat of her ride from many months earlier, these were Holcum's statement that she was determined to state her independence, to make the journey on her own terms. She had basked in that first brush of the sun, not knowing she even needed its brilliance, not having lived under a sky for most of her years. The preceeding summer, the sun had been a punishment, and she was being told it would be so again, but for this short time, she let it fall on her skin as a treasured companion.

At Regge's insistence and reminder of their time at the caves, she allowed herself to enjoy the treasured heat only when the sun was low in the sky or by covering her face from the sun's direct touch. When her one and only friend found Holcum in her Summer City rooms, he was unhappy with her for not asking his help moving back to the upper city. However, instead of showing the anger she had expected, he had talked with her, cautioning her about the summer sun, but letting Holcum reach the decisions she needed to make to forge ahead on her own. He took the time to warn her, telling her of the talk around the city, the fear of the raiders he only dimly remembered from his time as a very small boy.

"Your door, you must lock. Be safe," he'd cautioned. "If come, they do, safe, no one be."

Even so, after a winter of frozen bones, she exulted in the time she could be outside to touch its warmth, refusing to sequester herself in her rooms like a quivering and fearful animal. It was one of those times, the evening pleasant, her doors open to catch the breeze, when she saw the sudden scurrying, the people rushing by her rooms' entrance, their arms carrying things that must have seemed valuable to them. As Holcum rose to her feet, her crutch taking her to her door, she heard the voices, the words that made her heart quicken. *Raiders!* At first she laughed, thinking, *Fools!* before considering the warning cautions from Regge.

His stories, those of others, mostly, were ones that wouldn't have fazed the woman Holcum had once been on her ship. But she was a practical woman, and as Regge told her the stories of the Raiders' atrocities that had long ago been visited on the inhabitants of the city, she saw herself as she was. This new Holcum, weaker and unable to fight back her fears so easily, this *changed* Holcum, knew her fear, and she felt it as a deep flaw in her strength, a crevice of terror that hailed from her childhood. This was the fear she'd kept locked away, boxed up and pushed into a dark corner, a fear from her childhood and the atrocities she had endured from the black-suited soldiers. She had lived the nightmares Regge told her of.

Calling out to those passing, Holcum tried to find out what she should do. Stepping to the street, she finally grabbed one woman's sleeve, forcing her to stop.

"Tell me what to do," Holcum pleaded. When the woman tried to pull away, the fear apparent in her eyes, Holcum shook her as well as she could with just one arm, her frustration growing inside of her. "Tell me, or you will stay here until whatever happens, also happens to you."

The woman's voice finally broke through her fear's hold, and it wasn't comforting to Holcum. "To Winter City. Go there, we must. Defend ourselves there, we can. Here be the raiders, and take all, they will. Please, to go, let me, you must. Take everything, they do, even from us, their pleasure. Hide, I must."

Holcum looked her in the eyes hard. "Do you know Regge or Carli? I must find them." The woman frantically shook her head no, and with that, she ripped free to run toward protection and safety.

Holcum grabbed at another city dweller, this time a man who looked vaguely familiar to her. "Regge and Carli, do you know them?" When he tried to pull away, she repeated her question more harshly, adding, "I must know."

The man glanced up and down the street, and then at the sky. He took a deep breath and looked at Holcum, his eyes flicking to the side of her face. "Her, you be, from the pod. Know them, I do, commandeered by the city, help to give. Not here, they will be. Run, mos, run." Then he, too, was gone.

Holcum stood, her crutch at her side, and watched the city swirl around her. Her eyes glanced to the rising dust clouds in the distance. Under her breath, she prayed, "Oh, gods that be, I need your help now."

Suddenly, she was hit by a too-large box carried by a man who couldn't see around it. Her crutch was flung from her as the sudden fire in her leg slammed her to the ground. The man, realizing he had hit someone, turned, saw Holcum, and called out, "So sorry, mos. So sorry, I be. Forgive me, you must." He turned, and like lightning, was off down the street.

Holcum watched in horror as her crutch was kicked by the throngs and finally stepped on, crushed and broken. She lay there as the crowds eventually thinned, the city's inhabitants slowly finding their way to safety in the underground city that had so recently been their home. As she had been so much of her life, she was once again alone.

She could already see a vast transport lander making its way toward the city. The reaction of the city's inhabitants told her the seriousness of the situation. She had a fair idea of just how the events would play themselves out. The lander she could see off in the distance would approach the city, observing its defenses, or lack of them, from the air. It would watch the people running for safety, and that was where it would plan to head once it had finished doing whatever damage it wanted to the vacated dwellings and shops.

The noise of its landing would be atrocious. The small native animals, and there were a few even on this extreme world, would run from the great machine in fear. Those flying creatures that might be in the vicinity wouldn't try to compete with such a behemoth, instead riding their thermals and currents to safer surrounds. Holcum pictured the vibrations from the lander's descent that she would feel even here on this street, no matter where the craft chose to land.

The unloading of the troops would be a sight to see. Even though she was to be on the receiving end of this violation of the city's environs, she could still wish to see that. The great wall of the transport lander would release with the resounding thunder of seals giving way against the push of massive metal actuator arms. The groan of the metal gears lowering the ramps would vibrate the very doors and walls of the closest buildings. The mighty *whump* of the ramps on the ground would send clouds of dust flying through the air.

Then—and Holcum could envy those aboard as she imagined their entry into this world's atmosphere—striding strong and tall, their steps thundering down the ramp, they would stir cloud after cloud of dust, hiding the thievery and destruction she knew they wouldn't be able to resist showering all around them. She knew, because not so very long ago, she had felt the same, done the same. Not on a world such as this one, of course, but on the inhabitants of a world far way under twin suns, a yellowed-roofed world she and Botsky had finally left emptied and dead. There, the inhabitants had been brought to her aboard her ship as it flew far overhead. This time, Holcum was the one on the face of the planet. They would be coming for her. She considered that as a fellow soldier, she could perhaps reason with them, pandering to their pity at her grevious injuries.

With a better glimpse of the arriving transport, its sides rusted and battered, she saw with a sinking heart that this was no MegaCorp military vessel, meticulously maintained and filled with well-trained troops. What she had so enviously imagined was very different from what would exit the great ship. This would not be a organized troupe of armed forces, qualified to canvass an enemy territory, strike where it would do the most damage, then systematically move about, taking what they would from the world they had conquered, including their pleasures from the subdued inhabitants. These were raiders in the worst meaning of the word, rough and ragged, and they would do damage just for the sake of damage, taking what they could, anyway.

She could drag herself. She wouldn't allow herself to lie here in the open, to be the target she knew these raiders would make of her. Already, she could hear the sounds of the transport, the deep-throated rumble of its engines vibrating the dust at her side. She could feel the wind stirring from its passing, catching that dust and whipping it into the air. This airship was huge, at least by the standards of the transports on this world. In spite of the desperateness of her situation, she could still smirk at that, the backwardness of this credit-poor world where just having any transport at all was to be envied, where energy was so scarce, hovels such as hers were often unpowered, and cooling a building in the heat of summer was unheard of, even for the wealthy.

Finally, reaching the doorway to her rooms, she paused, her arms exhausted, her leg ragged from being dragged across the ground. Partially hidden, she listened, the sounds of the men on the ground now coming to her, running, unconcerned about who knew they were here. She heard yelling and occasional projectile weapons' fire. Just that told Holcum something about those whom she would be dealing with. There would be no rules of engagement. This would be kill or be killed. This would be every raider for whatever he or she could take, and most of that would be whatever hadn't been carried down to Winter City. Goods didn't matter to Holcum. What made her heart beat fast and her blood run cold were the people who remained in Summer City. She was one of them.

Even Holcum cringed when she heard the first screams. Some of the city's dwellers had obviously chosen not to run. The initial cries she heard were those of a woman, but she could also hear the voice of a man trying to protect her. She knew they couldn't be far away, so there wasn't much time for her to prepare. As she tried to push through her doorway, forcing herself with her good leg, she was jolted to hear several sharp reports of a projectile weapon. Freezing, she listened. She could hear the woman from earlier still screaming, but now, the man's voice was silent. She heard other sounds, those of a raider long without a woman, taking that which he considered his due right of conquest, even if the woman's protector had to be eliminated first.

Holcum's eyes turned at sensing motion across the way. Dark-suited men, rough and filthy, were kicking open doors, disappearing inside, and throwing out items they could easily lay their hands on. They didn't seem to care what happened to the items, whether they broke or scattered. She watched other men and a few dark-suited women run along, digging through the household debris that piled up in the street. Holcum closed her eyes at what she saw next. Even with all the cruelties she had heaped on hapless victims throughout her military career, this she had never done, had never even imagined being done.

One of the raiders reappeared at a door, yelling for one of the others to look up, and with both hands, threw something to him, laughing as the item, a child, its face still showing the smoothness of youth, flew flailing through the air. Not seeing if it was a boy or a girl, Holcum knew what was coming as the raider threw the child down on a cushion right in the middle of the street, ripping its clothes to gain access to it. Even with Holcum's eyes closed, she could envision what the raider was doing to the child. Finally, the raider moving on, Holcum searched, not sure she wanted to know, and saw the shape that had been left there, unmoving and quiet. Alive? She didn't know, but she did know she needed to hide herself quickly, or that fate might also be hers.

She flattened her head against the wall, her door just behind her, as she heard a voice from the street yell out, "Hey! You, Rat-hole! Have you checked this side of the street? Barf said he saw someone moving over here." She heard the sound of a door being kicked, one very close to hers. She slid through her doorway, pulling herself up, using the door latch as her crutch.

"Barf is horny." Another voice, different from the first, so Holcum now knew there were at least two of them outside. If she had a weapon, she could enjoin them in a fair fight. Or, and this would be her way, in a not-so-fair fight. She heard the second voice call out, "Besides, Barf's already taken one. It's someone else's turn. Like, mine."

"Rat-hole, you're too picky. Barf's had two, by the way. The difference between him and you is that he's not picky. If you'd take whatever we find, you'd get your share, too."

Holcum heard the sound of things being smashed, as if the goal here was to have fun, not steal anything of value. Then, angry, the second voice flung its response back.

"Hey! Bristle! You want some of this fist? Maybe up yours? Maybe you'd like me to knock you out, give you to Barf. He'd never know. That screwball'd probably take a boy, if we found one."

The other voice barked a laugh. "That last one was, Rat-hole! I watched the kid scream, or at least until Barf hit him in the head with his gun. He was quiet after that."

"Freakin' suns, Bristle! I didn't need to know that. I, at least, got some principles. Barf'd probably even take that one we heard about, that really ugly one with only half a face." He laughed. "I want one presentable enough that at least I don't have to close my eyes when I put this baby between her legs." There was a pause and the sound of footsteps on hard stone, then a rough laugh chortled. "See? My tool's primed for the first opportunity I come across. It wants out. Check it out, Bristle. Ever seen one bigger?"

"Yeah, maybe that's why you don't take the ugly ones, Rathole. You've always got your hand on your crotch." The voice blasted out a rough laugh. "Instead of waiting on the women, you take care of your own needs. At any rate, you're not a beggar, not for your personal satisfaction. I'll give you that . . . or at least, I'll give your hand that."

"You wuss! I'm just pointing out how big it is."

"Sorry, Rattie, I couldn't see what you were talking about. Try again when you hit puberty. Then maybe you'll have something big enough I can see."

"Shush! That door! It wasn't like that when I came by before."

"What do you mean, it wasn't like that? It wasn't like what?"

"Shaddup! Listen and look, Bristle. I think we might've found someone."

Holcum cringed as she heard footsteps just outside. *Gods, she wished, If only I had my leg back. I'd take out those two pansies without a second thought. They're just ruffians with weapons, no match for someone with military training . . . at least if that person with military training has the use of her legs. However, maybe I can still put my military brain to use and come up with something.*

Quietly, she released the door, holding her hands to the wall as she hopped on her one good foot into the adjoining room. Moving, holding onto the door as she passed into the second room, she pulled herself behind it, trying to position it as if it had been casually opened and left that way. If luck was with her—and that would be much more likely than the help of any gods out there—if the raiders came in, they would glance in here, not see her, and move on. She had nothing of value for them to take, and little for them to destroy. She breathed slowly and listened, and as she did so, she realized the absurdity of her hiding spot. Cursing herself for not making a better choice than this for a redoubt, she knew she should have chosen a defensible position where her leg wouldn't prevent her from acting aggressively. This was surely not it.

She heard the man she had identified as Rat-hole yell once more to the one called Bristle. *Stupid names,* Holcum thought. *The names of stupid men who cannot think further than their crotches. Give me half a chance, and I'll see that their crotches never take another woman, or,* and she shuddered, *another boy.* She listened carefully as Rat-hole told Bristle to check the next dump of a building. He'd check this one, and that Barf might've been wrong about what he thought he'd seen. Holcum watched through the space between the door and the wall as the dark-suited man peered into her room and backed out again. Hearing him in the street, calling to his buddy, she saw her chance to do something besides hide behind a door, and she hopped back into the main room, grasping the food preparation surface for support.

Her eyes locked on the shelf above the cooking surface. She kept a knife there. If she could find a way to protect herself with it, a way to be safe from their primitive projectile weapons, then if they returned, she could at least take a few of these pansies with her. Sliding her hand down the edge of the cooking surface for support, very careful of her one leg, she reached up and grasped the knife, holding it by the handle as she looked around the room, her search finally finding the garden space out back. *That might do. No way out, and only one way in. They'll have to go through that door to get at me, and I can take them out as they do so. Not perfect, but in times of desperation, things rarely are.* Balancing on her one good foot, Holcum let go of the table and pivoted to grab the doorframe leading to the garden space. She moved outside, and her back was soon against the wall, the knife firmly held in her hands.

Reaching a hand to push a strand of hair from her face, her fingers ran along the scarred skin. The feel of the scars caught her off guard. With the danger of the raiders, she'd been distracted, forgetting her disfigurement, and just for a quick moment, she had to think to remember what the scars were all about. The worries about her safety had forced her to concentrate only on her long-unused skills as a soldier. For the briefest of moments, she had been that soldier again, not the scarred cripple that frightened small children. She breathed easier, *At least they won't want this.* She ran her fingers over the corded, rough skin. *If I'm discovered, maybe they'll just kill me, and all my troubles will be over.*

"Yeah, Bristle, I was just in there. That dump is empty."

"You sure? Or just lazy?" Rough laughter accompanied the questions.

The voices were in the outdoor space of the rooms next to hers, and only a tall wall separated the two areas. At least Holcum now knew where they were. They argued about which set of rooms Barf'd seen the movement in, at times their voices rising, until their argument grew heated, and Rat-hole finally yelled at Bristle to go ahead and double-check that last building if he wanted, but there had been no one there. He'd looked in every room, and he was sure. Just to prove Bristle wrong, he'd go back with him. Then he'd laugh in his pus-ridden face when he was proven right.

Holcum smiled. That was his first mistake, because this set of rooms wasn't empty, and Rat-hole hadn't checked carefully. He'd soon find out. She would make sure of that, and with a glint in her eye, she tightened her grip on the knife she held in her hand, as she prepared it for use.

As her hand hefted the killing instrument she held at her side, her balance shifted. She gasped as her bad foot touched the ground. Then she froze as the knife clattered from her fingers. When it did so, the voices on the other side of the wall became deathly quiet.

Kneeling to pick it up, cursing herself and her leg for identifying her position to the men, she held the knife at the ready, mentally preparing herself for what she knew was to come. She could take one, she was sure, but the other, she didn't know. Perhaps. Just perhaps. If the nerve in her leg didn't incapacitate her so completely, she could and would fight in spite of it, but that was chasing an empty dream. She couldn't fight past the pain of the nerve, and that's all there was to that.

Her eyes watched the shadows flickering across the doorway. That's how she would know when to strike. Her mind remembered the heat of the previous summer, and also how quickly it had turned to the bitter cold. She hadn't been comfortable even once during the previous year. Now, here in her garden space, she had enjoyed, yes, actually enjoyed the past few weeks. Even today, with the sun shining, with the sky above clear, and the temperature satisfyingly pleasant, it didn't seem right to die. Not here, not this way. However, war was like that, and like it or not, this was a day for war, as witnessed by that child in the street and that couple she had heard just before the poor child had been dealt that vile brutality by the raiders.

Holcum's eyes saw the flickering as the shadows in her doorway moved, bringing one of the men within her grasp, and her military training served her well. With a downsweep of the knife held high in her hands, the long blade pierced cleanly into the side of the man's neck and into his chest cavity, his collapse pulling Holcum off balance just as his partner stepped through to point his primitive weapon at her as she fell to the floor. The man with the gun on her turned his eyes to look at his partner, the knife handle protruding from his neck, the muscles in his body jerking their final dance of death.

"Ha!" He laughed, as he turned his eyes back to Holcum. "He was a fool, anyway, always playing with his crotch, as if I cared what was down there." He looked more closely at Holcum, his face crumpling in disgust. "So, the stories are true. There is one in this city so ugly as to be a freak. I've found her." He threw his head back and threw a guffaw to the sky. "So, this is the one I'm given to satisfy my needs." He raised his fist and called hoarsely to the open sky, as if his words might be picked up by someone unseen. "I won't hide my taking of her as if I'm ashamed. I'll take her in the street where all can see that I can take pleasure in any woman's body, no matter how disgusting a face she wears."

Leaning over Holcum, he reached a muscled arm and touched the scarred side of her face, licking his lips as he whispered to her. "This might be an interesting treat, after all. How many men could possibly have wanted the likes of you? That will make my pleasure so much sweeter, to know that no other man has been there before me. I'll enjoy running my tongue over this *beauty mark* as I lay on you, your body rising to meet mine. You'll not be able to control yourself with the pleasure I'll give you. I know how to make your body work, even as your thoughts curse me, and I'll enjoy knowing that you hate what I'm doing, even as your body gives itself to me." With that, he placed his weapon against Holcum's throat and knelt over her to run his tongue over the scarred side of her face.

"I'll kill you, first," Holcum hissed. "I'll kill you as you take me, even as my body responds to your invasions. Do not underestimate me. You're not safe when you're within my grasp."

He jerked away, glaring at the woman on the ground. "That will make my conquest all the sweeter, to have fought for it, and to have the danger at my throat every moment. This day I will have something worth taking, even if its face does look like it should be hidden under a mask."

As he let another round of raucous laughter roll, he didn't pay attention to what Holcum's unseen hand had been doing. She now had the partner's small knife from his belt firmly in her fingers, and as the man pulled his booted foot back and kicked her over and over, she vowed he would die this day, whether he took her or not. She would run on that foot, no matter how much fire it burned through her leg. Today, this man would meet his maker.

Finally, tired of his brutality, he squatted by Holcum. "Come, now. It's time to plead with me to spare you." He grabbed her chin and twisted her face to him, reaching down and pulling one eyelid open. "Beg me not to do this, woman. You never know. You might even be successful."

His grin told her otherwise; besides, now she only wanted to kill him. Let him take her, let him think his advances were being successful. Her greatest revenge would be to have him die just as he was in the final throes of his conquest. He would least expect it then, for his body would be overcome with sensations no man could ignore. To have him die just then, his surrender to his body's conquest of her own interrupted by a knife through the heart would be her revenge. He thought she would be his conquest, but Holcum knew something this man didn't. He had already signed his death warrant, and the poor pansy didn't even know.

HOLCUM DID scream as the man dragged her into the street. He dragged her by her leg, the one she had nearly lost just one year before. In her torment, her hands drawn up into fists of pain, the knife was secure, even as the man ripped her clothes from her, the brilliance of the sun washing across her body, the man seeing something much more desirable than he'd hoped for.

Standing over her, yelling for his unseen comrades to watch his taking of this woman, proof to them of his superior masculinity, he pulled his clothing loose, his pants dropping to his knees, and his shirt pulled up to his chest. He stood over Holcum to gloat. His body had been ready from the moment he had seen Rat-hole jerking his last dance on the ground, his life bleeding from his neck. Death did that to Bristle, and he wanted her to see. His was no imaginary manhood, one he had to brag about. It was something for her to be afraid of, and he wanted her to be terrified as he took her.

Dropping to his knees, he put his hands on her shoulders as he fulfilled his promise. His tongue traced the tough cords of damaged flesh on Holcum's face even as she gripped the knife in her hand. He was everything he claimed, and he did to her body everything he said he would do.

However, even as her body responded to him, she prepared the weapon in her hand. She knew how far the human heart was below the surface of the back, and she knew just where to strike to avoid any bones or other obstructions. She also knew that the blade in her hand, the blade that had cut into her flesh cruelly as the man had dragged her into the street, would reach that organ, and she would twist it once it was inside, causing the man's heart to spasm, its electric beating shorting out its life-giving flow. The man would have but a few moments before his body registered that it was already dead. He would have enough time to realize, even as his passions finished their ecstasies, that his heart was no longer beating, and that his body's release into her would be the last one he would ever know.

It was his eyes she watched. When his tongue stopped licking her face, and his grip tightened on her shoulders, she remained fixed on his eyes. When they rolled up into his head, and he was no longer looking back into hers, the time had come. She readied the knife over his back, and as his body pressed tightly against hers, and his voice gasped with his stolen pleasure, she drove the knife deep, her hand grasping it and twisting it in a clockwise fashion, tearing the organ inside. She smiled in satisfaction as she watched his eyes spring open, the *knowledge* of what she'd done sure in those orbs, and knowing with it the damage she'd done, and that he was already dead. As Holcum's attacker slumped against her, jerking spasmodically, she closed her eyes and remembered three nights on a warm, humid world too many lives ago to even count. As she did, tears began to run down the sides of her face.

She had lain with a man then, a man who had loved her. She hadn't loved him back. She still knew his name, but the name wasn't important to her any longer. This man on top of her hadn't loved her, and he had paid for that with his life. What was the difference? That man all those lives ago had loved her, and he had also paid with his life.

There would be no loves for her, she knew. There would only be men who died over and over in her arms. She was a curse to this world and to all the people around her. How she wished she could board a ship and leave behind all that her life had become!

The inland sea, perhaps. If only she could run there. The caves had been cool on that summer day with Regge and Carli. There had been no one else. She would be all alone, and that was what she needed, to be all alone.

When the man was through with his dying, Holcum didn't have the energy to push his dead body off hers. She let her tears flow, the sobs of her self-pity making him seem almost alive to those who found her hours later.

As the dead raider was rolled from atop her, and she was covered for respectability, she looked up to a familiar face. It was the only friend she had on this world, Regge, who had been concerned and had come to look for her as soon as he could. To Holcum, however, it was another face that rescued her, a man who had spent three nights with her too long ago. This time she allowed him a name, one that was written somewhere on an old shipboard ID card that she had stored in her meager things. As she was carried back into her home, Holcum smiled in gratitude at the face she saw above her, even if the man she saw wasn't the one who was there.

# —Chapter 7—

*Chos'n, chos'n bebe,*
*Who ya' momma be?*
*Take ya' finga' an' reach it ou';*
*Pick one fa' me.*

—*Old spiritual song*
*remembered during an*
*ancestral dreamtime trance*

THE ROOM swam around Holcum. For many weeks after the vicious attack by the raiders, she'd been unexpectedly exhilarated by the *vigor* of her fight with her two attackers. The assault itself, of no more consequence than an inconvenience and deprivation of the battlefield, was pushed aside. The important thing, it gave her back a bit of her old life, the one she'd lost when she'd come to this dusty rock of a planet. She'd been one of the best at ground fighting, leading her troops to victory after victory. The raider attack had been a boost to her self-image to know she *could* still fight and take out the opposition.

She had done that, too, fought two armed men in hand-to-hand combat and beaten them both, taking out a superior force with her bare hands. Today was awful, though. If she tried to stand, her stomach attempted to dump itself all over the floor.

Only sitting down again would stem the flow of nausea, and as now, at times, only the prone position was good enough.

She remembered the twinge of this the past few mornings, but each day she'd recovered by the time she'd started boiling her water to cook her daily ration of legumes. This day, though, she didn't know if she would survive. Perhaps she was suffering some lingering space sickness or radiation poisoning from her injuries in the cryo pod. After the length of time she'd been inside, floating through space, who knew what seals had broken, allowing gods-knew-what poisons to leak into her body.

One thing she'd become keenly aware of over the past year was the return of her monthly cycle. While she'd thought it unusual to have such a flow as her body was giving out each month, especially when she'd barely done anything her entire life, she'd attributed it to her body's injuries and the healing process speed-ing up her bloodflow. She'd refused to call that quack healer. That witch would make up something after Holcum was better, telling her she had known it was whatever it turned out to be. Then she would expect to collect a sizable fee for her services. No thanks.

Holcum had been able to put up with the inconvenience, and she'd been very glad to have the blood flow stop after the raider attack. She'd confidently marked this up to the vitality she had grasped that day and her exhilaration at her conquests that had make her feel she was back aboard her ship again. At least, it made her feel a little bit as if she were once again the person she'd been in her previous life, even though her surroundings contin-ually whispered the lie she was telling herself. To tell the truth, she hadn't even paid attention to the stopping of her flow. That was as it should have been—in fact, as it always had been when she had lived aboard ship.

This, though, and the cramping. Oh, she should have let that raider just kill her. As she lay still for a time, the cramping released its hold on her, her head started to clear, and her stomach no longer swam with each passing moment. She swung her legs off the sleeping pad, and reaching to her new crutch, she finally accepted that the pain was gone. Surely, it had been no more than a virus or food poisoning, she reasoned, although it would do no damage to her ego to search out what these symptoms might mean.

As she used her crutches to find her way to her food preparation area, her one free hand now easily reaching to do things she had struggled with only months ago, she pulled out a pot and filled it with water. Starting it to heat, she took the now all-too-familiar sack of dried legumes—beans, she had been told by Regge on one brief visit—and began to look through them in preparation for their immersion in their watery grave.

IF HOLCUM had known what to look for, she might have noticed a small stirring in her belly, one that wasn't really all that similar to an attack of a virus or the overwhelming discomfort of food poisoning, but one that was something else, entirely. It was still there, and it wasn't going to go away. One day it would make itself known in a way that not even Holcum could ignore.

That day was coming, and it was coming soon, but for now, the small stirring just shifted its position and waited. While it did, Holcum mindlessly prepared her food for her meal, not even aware that another life had already begun, consuming the energy her body produced, taking from her what Holcum wouldn't wish to provide to it freely. She'd known a contraceptive world onboard the MegaCorp military ships, although she'd never been told about the medicines she was given in every meal she ate. None of the troops were. It was de rigueur that copulation had no consequences except emotional ones. As soldiers, they had been expected to be able to deal with such superficial issues as conflicts they brought upon themselves.

Now, it never occurred to her that this might be something other than an ordinary illness. Well, an illness it might be, but this illness would someday, not too far in the future, be a screaming, crying illness, one that would drop unbidden into Holcum's world, whether she wished it to or not.

HOLCUM WALKED the streets of her adopted world, her vile step-parent of a city. It wasn't her world, she would have decried, but then, what other world did she have? No world was hers, and none had ever been. She'd been ripped as a child from the face of the only world she'd really known, and then she'd returned, unknowingly, many years later to finish the destruction for those who had managed to hang on against the huge corporation that had claimed the planet as an industrial resource to be mined and consumed at their leisure. She'd become the hand of MegaCorp, and they had stolen her, owned her, used her to destroy others, and destroyed her, although not necessarily in that specific order.

This world was the one she'd been left with when MegaCorp no longer cared. The powerful corporation could have chased down her errant escape pod. She knew what her military over-lords were capable of, the unparalleled power in MegaCorp's outstretched claws. From Regge, on his visits to her, and even from Carli and old Tommeoseo, when she happened to meet them in the street, she now knew that MegaCorp's military arm had long ago been dissolved. But it hadn't been gone when her star-strike battle cruiser was attacked. The whole ship had gone from conquering victor to dead in the water in only a handful of moments, and Holcum didn't know why. She struggled to accept that she probably never would.

Now she explored the streets, Regge's water suit keeping her cool. When Regge first brought it to her, she'd only worn the suit because he wouldn't take her to see the inland sea unless she agreed to put it on. Then, when she had gotten there, the sea had been nothing like she'd imagined, and she'd wished she hadn't gone. The caves had been peaceful, though, and in the end, she hadn't regretted her day. It was many months before she donned the hated suit once more. She'd been trapped in her hovel, and in desperation, she found that she could manage the suit alone, and with careful adjustments of the tubes, she could wear the contraption and manipulate her crutch at the same time. Lately, however, the suit had slowly become more and more difficult to put on each day, the waist growing ever snugger. Holcum scoffed at the notion she could be building body fat with the stringent diet she subsisted on. Her garden did provide a few extras, and she'd taught herself to find her way to the shopsellers, learning she could trade a few of her things from her garden for things she couldn't grow: ground leaves to boil for a hot drink; a sweet cake, occasionally. But those things were rare, and she'd already reduced her intake to offset the tightness of the suit. A measure less of Regge's beans in her pot of water, a smaller portion of the hard bread broken off to soften in the plate of legumes. Yet, just this day, she'd needed to hold her stomach in tightly in order to slide the water suit on. Perhaps she'd forgotten some specific adjustment. She would need to ask Regge to check on it.

At least her stomach had stopped giving her troubles. She didn't know what that had been about. However, she did know one thing that was't the same as the time before the raiders, and she hadn't decided whether it was a good thing or not. The people of this city now treated her differently. Thank the gods of this hellish world, they weren't friendly to her, but, and she had to search for the word, having rarely acted this way towards anyone, but she was finding them to be *deferential* to her. Was it due to fear? Probably not, she thought. In her crippled body, what could she do that would inspire fear? Respect? For the woman found naked under a dead man, because she had no strength to push him off? Ha! As she hobbled down the path, that made her laugh, startling the others walking near her.

She looked around as they did so and considered how crazy she must seem, crippled, disfigured, and laughing aloud to herself over nothing they could see. She patted her bladderpack, amazed at the cooling spreading from the tubes that encapsulated her body. Maybe this *was* her home. She was adapting here, growing to feel like she could survive in this extreme weather, and perhaps even feel comfortable with it.

She laughed out loud again, startling a woman just in front of her, and Holcum noticed the small child by her side. For some reason, her vision blurred just for a moment as an image flashed in front of her, the street scene before her replaced with that spring day not so long ago, the child left lying there after the raider had taken what he wanted. Holcum closed her eyes tightly and shook her head, forcing the image away, sending the present once again crashing back around her. *The children. There have been children around me all along, and I've been so full of my own misery, I've never noticed. I wonder if that child survived. Perhaps Regge would know.* She tightened her face, determined not to think of it again, knowing she would never voice that question to her lone benefactor. It might make her seem as if she *cared.*

She pumped the bladderpack once again as she stepped into the sun, and the day's heat assaulted her. Her bag of surplus foodstuffs over one shoulder, Holcum made her way to the town shops, considering what to trade for today. Pausing at one stall, the smell of unfamiliar spices pulling her forward, she set her bag on the stall's counter, questioning the stall keeper.

"I have these small, green melons to trade." She reached inside and pulled one out, then she added a small fruit to it. "Also, I have a handful of these. What can I get for them?" Holcum tugged her bag closed, her fingers resting around the top, and the remaining foodstuffs trapped inside.

"Grew these yourself, you did?" The keeper picked up the fruit. "Very nice, they be. Take all of them, I will. The melons, too." Smiling, she added, "From my supply, what do you wish?"

Holcum loosened her bag and began removing the remaining foodstuffs, placing them on the counter. Then, reaching to point, occasionally picking up something to smell, she selected a number of spices, letting the keeper wrap them for her.

"For the little one's health?" The keeper smiled knowingly, nodding at Holcum's waist. Holcum frowned, puzzled, causing the keeper to laugh, "See now, I do. Wish to keep this a secret, you intend. However, soon to show, you will, my dear. Lucky you." She handed the spices to Holcum, pushing her gently away. "Go. Have a little one to care for, you soon will," and she stepped back to her spices.

Turning away, Holcum pressed on her stomach, remembering the discomfort of the many mornings she had felt so ill. She wondered if the woman could possibly be correct. A child certainly would not do. Besides, she had been with men her entire adult life, and she had never worried about conception. She could only think of one possibility, the raider. He was the only man she had been with in her year here on this world, and she had ended his life as he had taken her.

Holcum staggered, her thoughts carrying her back to that day. She knew the facts of conception and pregnancy. She silently tallied the time since the attack, the remembered monthly cycles ended, and the days of her illness. It had to be him. She had ended his life, but she remembered, too, waiting until he had consummated his rape of her body, her knife stopping his heart just as he was in the final throes of his lust. She had never actually considered he might *impregnate* her.

She looked for a bench or a rock to sit on, her legs suddenly too weak to stand. Sitting, holding the crutch at her side, she groaned, knowing she must get this *aberration* taken from her. A child? She could not raise a child. No, it would be even worse. It would be a baby. That would be even smaller than a child.

Her thoughts swirled, a black fog, and she couldn't lift herself to make her way home. She also knew she couldn't stay here on this street for the time she would need to see this thing out of her body. That might take days, just the finding of someone to remove this from her belly. What an inconvenience this would be, and to pay for it? How many melons and fruits would she have to trade? The added complexities so carelessly heaped upon her disaster-of-a-life here on this world threatened to swamp her reserves of strength.

Her newly acquired spices left on the bench, she stood, holding her crutch as her support, and began to make her way to the healer. Quack though Holcum knew her to be, it was the only solution she knew. If the healer couldn't do this, perhaps she could suggest someone who would, but Holcum knew this for a certainty. This thing she was now certain was inside of her must be gone from her belly, and yesterday would not be soon enough.

"NO, MOS, for this, find no one, you will." The healer searched the woman's eyes, remembering the day she had been brought to her over one planetary year ago. There had been other visits with her since then, but that first success with this one had jumpstarted the healer's reputation across this city. The healer knew she must be careful here.

"No? How can that be? This thing inside of me is the result of a rape, the taking of my body by a man who had killed the others he had taken. He would have killed me, too. How can this not be done?" The very thought of the healer's refusal enraged Holcum, and her voice lashed the woman she'd come to for help.

"The facilities, the law. For people, a need we have, and a life to take, an atrocity be. When numbers matter, be wasted, none can." The healer offered a comforting hand, just brushing

Holcum's arm. Holcum's instantaneous rebuff as she jerked her hand away was an electric shock filled with hurt, one that nearly brought the healer to tears.

Pulling back and standing, the healer stepped to her medicines, refusing to turn to face Holcum. "To take this child once it is born, someone, glad will be. A worry to you, it need not become. Need to have schooling, the child will. Barren, some families be, and grateful for any child. Consider all this, Holcum. Call you that, may I?" She turned to face the pregnant woman, her concern for the unborn child overriding the hurt Holcum had dealt her. "Provide schooling, can you? A world poor in resources, Trasdrom'man be, and much money, this place hasn't. Yet, much prized the education of the children be. To think hard on this, you should be prepared."

HOLCUM SAT with the healer's eyes on her, disbelief coursing through her veins. It was now well into the hottest part of the year, and here she was being told she would have to carry a child through the heat of this world's summer. Gods, no! Then, with winter upon them, possibly even while buried under that mound of a habitation they called Winter City, she would have to give birth. To have a child in that gods-forsaken place when the world above was covered with its frigid blanket of white, keeping the ground frozen and dead for months, seemed too heinous to be true. The schooling? She knew nothing, absolutely nothing about that.

She screamed inwardly that life could not do this to her, force her to endure this, yet in her twisted heart, she knew it could. She had barely begun to accept that she might be able to forge an existence here, to survive at some level, and now this knife thrust of fate had been driven deep and twisted with vicious irony. She had no choice in this matter, except whether to keep the child or give it away, and it seemed she might have little choice even there. This burgeoning atrocity in her belly soured her stomach, and she wondered just how hard it would be to take the life of this thing herself. Would that be possible? She would have some days to think on it, and then she remembered. The spices. All her fruits and melons wasted, the packet of spices left on the bench. Her face twisted in torment.

"Mos, be you all right?" the healer inquired.

Holcum stood wearily, wordlessly forcing her crutch to push her decimated body through the door. As soon as she was out of the healer's sight, she leaned heavily against a wall. She sank to the rough paving, and she let her tears flow as she spat her frustration on the roughness of the manmade stone at her side.

"I will have this thing around me forever. My life is now the stuff of others' nightmares, and it simply goes on and on. There's no point to my life. I should end it now."

Yet, before it became completely dark, Holcum's military nature forcing her into the familiar footprints of rigid patterns and decisive action, she rose, making her way back to her rooms where she might hope for a semblance of peace in the night, the tears pushed from her face for a time. The walls of her rooms heard her words as she lay down to sleep, but they didn't care. No one did, no one except the one who spoke them.

"I don't even have the man who did this to me to be angry at. I have only myself to blame," she cursed to herself. "I have only myself to blame."

HOLCUM PANTED with the exertion of walking across her room. Winter was late this year. Trasdrom'man was still in summer's full swing, and it was predicted to be weeks yet before the cooling blast of winter would break the back of this monster oppressing her, this tearing, mind-numbing heat. She looked at the ceiling above her, the dust and oil-stained rock telling of the many years these rooms had been in use.

165

Closing her eyes, sweat running across her scalp, she could see the coolness of her ship's quarters, the metal walls and ceiling, the grilled inlets for the cooling air. She'd never thought of these while on the ship, not unless she was chilled and needed to adjust one. Those precious air inlets were a part of the background, just another item forming the parameters of her life, something to be considered or ignored—and mostly ignored—at her leisure.

On this day, she'd give almost anything to have one of those air inlets at her side. To stand in front of one of them, her hand reaching to adjust the airflow, increasing it until the coolness washed over her in a torrent, her hair blown from her neck, the air reaching around her face, its fingers dipping their touch between her breasts, drying the sweat there.

Laying her crutch against her side, she felt her arm brush the *thing* she carried in front of her. She also felt the bile rise in her throat at the remembrance of how it had come to haunt her, and how easy it would have been to prevent this. *All I had to do was drive the knife just moments earlier, and he wouldn't have consummated his passions inside of me. Then, this* horror *wouldn't have grown to fill my clothing until I must wear this sack of a tent and walk panting in this heat just to cross the room to sit in a chair.*

As bad as it was, she could still be grateful. She'd learned what the city's inhabitants saw in her, now. In spite of the heat and her discomfort, she chuckled, a sour bark of a sound that ending in a fitful laugh. She had become a symbol to them, the warrior from the distant past who was the survivor of a great military campaign, and who had vanquished two of the enemy on their own world, even as she had risked her life, a hero even now bearing the burden of that attack as this child grew inside of her.

That didn't mean they liked her, but they did respect and defer to her. And they brought her food. That was especially appreciated, particularly since she could no longer get her water suit around her belly, even with the most generous adjustments Regge had been able to make to the tubes.

Holcum knew she should have already made arrangements for the child once it was born, but she hadn't been able to force herself to deal with it. Instead, she had treated the child growing inside of her as if it didn't exist at all, and was, instead, simply something in her way, something too large attached to her body that would go away after nine standard months. The child had never seemed quite real to her, not one coming from her own loins, no matter that she could daily see and feel the evidence. It was on its way today, too. She'd been having pains where it would be exiting her body. Labor pains, she understood they were called, and she knew why. They were pains she couldn't ignore, although she labored hard to do so.

With a ripping surge of torment, she gasped. She was having one at that moment, the intensity nearly too much to bear. Her body squeezed her insides until she thought she could no longer take it, and then the driving pain suddenly released its hold on her, and she sank into her chair, her exhaustion total, compounded by the heat that was wrenching her life from her.

*Oh, that the medic would come and take this hated thing out of me,* Holcum moaned. *I don't want this thing. Why did I not make arrangements for someone to take this aberration from me when my body tired of it? Gods, I've done it to myself, again. I do* not *want to be stuck with this mewling little brat. It couldn't even wait until the heat of summer has broken.*

A second spasm of pain gathered between her legs and began to spread throughout her abdomen. Finally, the intensity too great to contain, Holcum let her pain fly from her, her voice calling it out to whoever would listen.

Then, surprising her, fluid soaked her legs. Knowing this must be the start of it all, she fell to the floor, accepting this as her own private hell, knowing that there was no one to contact that crock of a healer to look out for her, and anyway, just a little bit of her hoped that maybe this thing would die as it was torn from her womb. She corrected herself, her words ripped from her and slashed across the room with razor sharp intensity, "All of me hopes this misshapen creature chokes on its cord, so that I can watch it die before my eyes. I wouldn't share that satisfaction with another. I want its death all for my own."

Then, as a scream of anguish tore itself from Holcum's throat, the life inside of her erupted, its own scream upon hitting the floor letting Holcum know she was not alone and would never again know the peace she so desired.

HOLCUM OPENED her eyes, groaning at the realization the day was already in full swing. People in the rooms around the one assigned to her and Girl were already in motion, and in the process, making noise to wake the dead. Thankfully, most had vacated Winter City, already. She'd worked out one especially good reason to postpone hauling her and her daughter to Summer City as long as possible. If they waited long enough, they wouldn't notice the heat, because being up there wouldn't be any hotter than it was growing down in this underground warren of a rabbit hole. She placed her hand against the rock wall, its heat noticeable even in the overly warm space. She'd been assigned these overheated rooms only because of the child, those in power seeing a small human as something to be protected, as if it couldn't survive on its own just fine. If it couldn't, it deserved to die, but Holcum had shown the good sense not to express that thought.

She became aware of the sharpening realization of something not quite right. The door, open. The light from the ice-free sky openings flooded brightly into the room. *Gods! That child is gone again! Damn the city for not taking that creature when they*

168

*threatened to do so last summer. I didn't make plans to have someone take her when she dropped from me like an unwanted bowel movement, and now, no one will.*

Groaning, she shifted, her leg's nerve warning her to be careful, and slowly, she sat on the edge of the sleeping mat, swinging her legs to let them hang near the floor. Without looking, she reached for her crutch, its wooden handle having become a second part of her, there within her reach always, and never forgotten. When it wasn't where she thought it should be, she took an exasperated breath and glanced over, knowing it must have shifted from its place against the foot of the platform with her movements during the night. Cursing, she saw it on the floor *across the room!*

"Girl!" Holcum didn't care who thought she was harsh with the child. "Girl! Where are you?" The child would bring the crutch to her, if she were close enough to hear her name called. However, and Holcum knew this was more likely, the child was nowhere near, and the crutch would have to be retrieved by her.

Rising to stand on her one working leg, the other held carefully from the floor, she worked her way across the room with one hand on the wall for balance. A memory from long ago flashed across her mind, and her eyes misted with self-pity at the difference between then and now. She'd been on her great MegaCorp ship, young, just having received a promotion. Rezalton was with her for the celebration. She growled his name, *Rom'n.*

Why she was thinking of him now, she wasn't sure. This wall her hand was running down, perhaps, her feeling of unsteadiness. Then, they'd both had far too much to drink, and the fool had wanted her, had tried to kiss her. She'd teased him, then walked down the hall, her hand sliding along its smooth metal surface, its solid rigidity giving her inebriated self a false sense of balance. It had been sweet when he'd run up to steady her, to keep her safe.

She laughed, thinking to herself, *And he did it just to get his arms around me. He never did get that kiss. Maybe I should have . . . No!* She caught herself, feeling the foul slime of self-pity crawling up her spine. She would never regret what she'd done. She'd been strong, independent. No one had taken advantage of her. She'd risen in the ranks, and she was only one step from captaining her own star cruiser. Standing in the bowels of Winter City, with her arm against the hot rock wall, she straightened her back with resolve. *I was being strong, and I will be, still.* Reaching the crutch, she bent to it, standing again to slip it under her arm. She needed that child back. Holcum stepped to the door.

"Girl Child! Get yourself back here. We're moving, today." *Gods, I hate having that creature around me and in my way every moment.* Holcum turned back to the room, her eyes evaluating just what she needed to pack today, then making a decision.

"Nothing," she said aloud to no one other than herself. That resolved, she headed out the door. Girl Child could find her own way home. After all, she'd lived in the city above for two summers. She should remember. If not, then Holcum's responsibility was done, and she'd be glad for that.

As Holcum hobbled slowly down the underground passage, she spat in a harsh whisper, "Abomination! Come and find me, if you can."

She didn't look back. She really didn't care.

HOLCUM BLINKED in the glare from the sun, and she realized she'd made a mistake. She should have moved from Winter City days before. This year was no gradual shift from the bone-chilling cold of Trasdrom'man's winter to the blast furnace of summer, those sweet few days given as a peace offering of transition from one to another. Under the blaze of the relentless sun, she staggered under the pulse of a raging thirst, and sweat poured down her back.

"Gods," she cried in frustration. Sweat burned her eyes, and she could barely see.

For months, the cruel fist of winter had twisted the above-ground world with a blizzard of snow, with even the ice windows to Winter City below too obscured to let in any appreciable light. Then, during the blackness of an extremely miserable night, the weather had unexpectedly changed, and by the morning, the water from the massive slabs of ice that had been cut from the inland sea were running down the walls of the vast passageways they had kept lighted all winter, the people below dodging the frigid rivers that were soon cascading from the ceiling overhead. The heat of summer had slammed its fist into Trasdrom'man this year, and Holcum's water suit was in her Summer City rooms.

"My hovel," she cursed to no one in particular.

Finally reaching the shade of her doorway, Holcum pushed the partially opened door with her shoulder, turning to look back at the brightly lit street scene, knowing it had been blasted clean with the winter's winds, and yet still seeing the awful deed that had forced this child upon her. She hadn't seen Girl Child on her way to her Summer City abode, and that didn't particularly concern her. Holcum couldn't lose her if she wanted. These people in this city, these groundies, these *losers* who deferred to her so, her mystique something beyond understanding to their groundie minds, would corral the child, returning her to Holcum's care, if what she gave her could be called that.

Stepping into the relative coolness of the rooms, she made her way to the door leading into her protected garden space. She was glad she had at least taken the time the previous fall, those two relatively tolerable days when the weather had shifted half a year ago, to plant some of her seeds. She'd been told they would come up earlier if she left the seeds in the ground over the winter season. She'd cursed as she'd pressed them into the soil, not sure

171

of the sense of it, but now she could see she'd been given good advice. She'd have something to trade, these plants already on the way to giving her that which was her only income, the barter that helped her have those things she could not grow or make herself.

She no longer had even Regge's help, not really, what with his newly bonded one. At one point, Holcum had even imagined he might take care of her in a more intimate fashion than just leaving food for her. He still brought the food each day that Holcum gratefully took, along with the occasional items left by others. She accepted that his sense of responsibility was strong, and that he would continue to provide that for her no matter if she snubbed him or not. However, she hadn't dared snub Regge and wouldn't do so now. Did she attempt to be likeable? She could never be that, but she and he had formed an understanding.

He simply had no time to give to her now.

A chattering of voices distracted Holcum's musings. As they slowly filtered into her awareness more and more loudly, she began to recognize one. *Girl Child. I have tried and cannot get her to speak her be verbs correctly. Gods, that grates on my nerves.*

Holcum raised her eyes as the door banged against the wall, and there the child was, together with those other two children Girl seemed to find so interesting. Two adults followed the three small creatures inside, smiles of indulgence for Holcum's child on their lips, their eyes revealing their deference to a person who was a mysterious savior to them.

Holcum waved them in from where she stood at the back of the space, their unctuous voices endured until they shared what Holcum didn't care to hear. Once they were gone, Holcum made her way in and fell on the musty sleeping pad, calling out, "Girl, stay inside. I need to sleep."

She did, too, uncaring and unaware of the child, and leaving her daughter to play in the garden, the funny plants hers to do with as she pleased.

"MOS," THE VOICES started.

Holcum pushed Girl Child away from her as she turned from her cleaning of the dried beans to the group of city citizens entering her door. She knew why they were here, and she was both relieved and angry at the same time. Girl Child might actually be taken from her, and that would be a relief. For nearly three years, she had endured the crushing oppression of the creature depending on her constantly for her needs, the changing and the cleaning, the watching after. Always, especially in the heat of summertime, Holcum was exhausted with her care, and the child never slowed down. To have it gone would be an easing of everything that was wrong with her life.

She dumped the beans into the pot of boiling water as she stood to answer the voices. "This is my home, although I'm not proud to claim it as such. You're intruding. What do you want?"

She reached for her crutch, releasing the back of the chair she'd been holding to walk toward them. As she aggressively bore down on her intruders, she dared them to stop their asinine deference, and to do what she really needed them to do, just take the child.

"Your pardon, we beg, mos—"

"Just gather what you want and leave. I have no need of anything in this hovel." She looked down to see Girl reaching out, grabbing onto her good leg.

"Mos," they started again, "to take from you, here, we be not. Only to help. To aid the girl be the only thing we want. Not even a name, she has. Comes and goes, she does, with no supervision."

Now Holcum saw how things would progress today. They weren't here to take the child from her as she wished. They wanted her to *parent* the abomination the raider had forced her to bring into this world. Why could they not do this simple thing? Her anger boiled over at them.

"If you will take nothing, then leave my home. You were not asked to enter, and you are not welcome here. Out!"

She moved toward them on her crutch, and her sudden change in position knocked Girl Child to the floor. A wail of protest let the others in the room know of her discomfiture. Holcum's anger and domineering presence forced the intruders from the comparatively cool darkness of the room into the brilliance of the day. As she listened to her child wail her frustration, Holcum slammed the door on the last unwelcome guest, sealing the group into the heat already withering the moisture from the skin of anyone who dared its embrace.

Turning to the child, she remembered she hadn't fed her today. Dipping a spoon into the boiling soup of beans, Holcum drained a handful against the side of the pot and ladled them onto a shallow eating dish. Setting the dish on the floor in front of the child, Holcum was relieved to hear the wail stop.

As she stepped through the door to the garden outside, needing her own space for a short time, she gasped at the heat that already hung in the air. She moved her crutch in the dirt, knowing the plants also felt the scorching of the sun's rays. She'd become a gardener of sorts. At least she knew that plants died if they didn't get enough water to their roots, so she reached to the barrel of water she had filled that morning and began to dip the water a pitcher at a time, watching it soak into the soil as the heat shriveled her brow.

*Even here I need a water suit, and I don't have the energy to put it on.* As she covered the barrel, Holcum heard the wail of the child start back up inside. *That creature probably needs watered, too. One more chore,* she thought.

She had no idea how long this life would last, but it was far too long. It had been far too long three years ago, and she suspected there would be many more years before she would be released from its torment.

*Maybe this is payback from the gods of this universe. That'd be like them to torment me to teach me a lesson.* She paused to blink away sudden tears. *I'm finding it hard to care, anymore.*

Her tears belied her protest, even if her care was more for her present situation than it was true regret for wrongs she had fostered upon others. Before she walked inside, she reached a hand to wipe the moisture that had started to flow, only to find the heat had already done that for her. She laughed to herself as she turned. *I can't even cry on this world. It's too hot,* and she stepped back inside to the child that once again demanded her care.

NOT ALLOWED to be anything more than a distraction in Holcum's day, Girl Child wandered as she would that summer, often climbing to drink from the water barrel in the garden, her days in the streets whelping blisters from her repeated sunburns. Many more times the officials came to offer their help to Holcum, the visits always ending in them being ushered to the door, at times with yelling or the sounds of things breaking against the door frame, or at those times when Holcum had no energy to respond, with the tsk, tsk of knowing that no improvement had been attempted.

It was the broken leg that finally drove them to give Holcum what she claimed to want. Girl Child had wandered all the way to the Winter City entrance. Trying to explore down steps that were too tall for her to navigate, she tripped, and a passerby heard her wailing from the lowest level.

Holcum didn't look up as the officials arrived to collect Girl Child's things, what little she had. She waved her hand at them in response to their directives on what she needed to do to regain possession of her daughter. Just to think was too much for her to do at that point. Her life had dragged her through the lowest dregs of what could possibly happen to her, and she'd found no relief. She had to leave this city, these people. She could no longer be a part of what her life could become. In the darkness of her thoughts, she could see only one bright spot in all her time here on this world.

She had felt at peace in the caves overlooking the sea. There she had known her one day of escape from the misery of what this world had smeared across her life. That was where she'd go to die. Surely Regge would take her. Maybe, just this one last time, her only friend on this world would do that for her.

*That is*, she laughed dryly, *if I haven't driven him away, too.*

This time the heat didn't dry the tears from her eyes. They came too hard and fast for the day to beat them back, and she didn't even try to wipe them away.

"REGGE, TELL THEM no, did you?" Carli expertly tromped the power to the transport, and as he pressed the steering hard to one side, the old machine slid sideways, showering dust and grains of sand across the small, hardy plants growing nearby. Shooting a grin to Regge, he shifted the steering the opposite direction, narrowly avoiding letting his slide take them directly into a rock.

Regge held a handgrip on the roof with one hand and his seat with the other as he laughed at Carli's maneuver. "Yes, told them, I did, my friend. Brand new, it be, too. To dig in the power leads, let you, I will, if you want. Then, as fast as this, it might be. Shiny red, it be, and very pretty. See, you will, my friend."

"This one. Do with it, what will they?" Carli bounced in his seat as the vehicle skittered over a series of ripples in the hard ground. He knew what he wanted, and that was to have the old transport given to him. Now that his friend had a bonded mate, the two old buddies couldn't always manage time together like they used to. They were out today only because Regge's woman wouldn't let him honor Holcum's request without Carli along.

Carli didn't understand what possessed the mutilated woman from the pod to want to make her home by the sea. How anyone could live there was beyond him, but he was glad to have dropped her off, even if Regge had insisted they help carry her things deep into one of the darkened spaces buried within the rock. Carli couldn't believe the things Regge had loaded on the transport for her: foodstuffs for many months, cooking supplies, and even bedding. When Carli had teased him, Regge had reddened around the neck, saying he felt a sense of responsibility for her. He was the one that had insisted on opening the cryo pod. He'd shrugged and tried to laugh it off. Then Carli had begun tallying up the cost, and Regge had told him old Tommeoseo had given him the credits for most of the items on the transport, so it wasn't like he was taking funds out of his family's pocket to purchase all the things they'd left out there. Best, Carli hadn't had to share in the expense.

Carli asked about the girl that had been taken from her. Was the woman being banished, he'd inquired with a knowing grin. He'd never seen the woman's child, but he'd heard. Everyone'd heard. Most people thought of the crippled survivor as being *military,* and many considered her baby as an unfair penalty on her life after driving those two raiders to their deaths, killing one even as he was taking her for his pleasure. Perhaps they were correct.

Regge had cautioned him to be generous.

Carli didn't know what to think, but he did know children needed some sort of parenting. Perhaps the city officials should have given the baby another home just as soon as it was born. Then, he'd shrugged, telling Regge that it wasn't his responsibility. He couldn't worry about things he had no control over, well, not unless he was interested, of course.

This transport? This was something that interested him.

He grinned as he once again gave the transport full power.

177

Surely the city didn't want it back, not to *scrap* it. His mind was already hard at work coming up with a plan, any idea that would allow him to keep this transport for his very own.

At Regge's yell for him to pay attention, he laughed with the thrill of the adrenalin rush, as the transport narrowly missed yet another huge obstruction in the course the two men had worked out many years before. The thrill of the near miss was one more thing to convince Carli he couldn't let this transport go, even if he had to buy it from the city with his own funds. He thought, perhaps, he could work around that. After all, it was old, and what if they walked back to town and reported it as broken down or wrecked?

With a flash of insight, he remembered the cryo pod. What was said about all the debris they'd found? Part of a transport— was that it? One that had been impacted by the pod as it had hit?

Carli began, "Hey, Regge. Try this idea on for a fit. What if . . ."

After he heard Carli out, Regge laughed, even as he admitted the idea was a good one, and ideas given are solutions in the making. Carli would have his transport. He didn't think it would be at the hands of a cryo pod, but he was convinced Carli wouldn't let go until this racing machine was his.

As Carlant'e rounded yet another curve, the transport again sideways, Regge laughed at his friend's joy in the machine, telling him he thought he had a way he could help him out. Carli deserved that from him.

Carli enjoyed the machine even more now that he knew Regge was on his side, and the transport would soon be his.

HOLCUM HAD known the day would be hot, and it was, blisteringly. After all, why should this day be any different from all the other dreary, exhausting days she had lived through this summer? For that reason, she'd worn her water suit on the way to the caves, lethargically patting her bladderpack when she felt she could no longer tolerate her life's energy being wrung from her by the drying, cracking heat.

It was, as she'd remembered, comparatively cool in the caves. Even that made her laugh, or it would have if she'd had the strength. It wasn't remotely cool, but it was certainly better than being outside. It *was* cooler than it had been in her rooms back in the city, and she had been able to, at last, remove her water suit.

What she hadn't been able to understand was why Regge and his friend, that other man, Carl . . . Carli . . . Carli-something, had brought all these items out with them. She wouldn't be using any of it. She only wanted to lie in the shadowed silence, letting the quiet of the caves comfort her, as the distant sounds of the sea at the base of the cliff lulled her to sleep. As the light waned, she grew groggy. She made her bed from the pile of textiles they'd unloaded, leaving them tied in the bundles they had been in on the transport.

Awakening to the gentle sounds of the surf whispering through the cave openings and caressing the interior of her new home, she felt the gnawing of her stomach prodding her to find food. She groaned. To give up and die was one thing. To lie here in pain when she knew there were foodpacks somewhere in these piles of goods was another thing, entirely. Slowly, she drew herself together, and turning to the things Regge had brought for her, she began to paw through them, the drawing of her hunger driving her lethargy away.

There was more to this sudden restlessness than just the food. She had become used to the constant sound of noise from the child. It had been in her waking moments, and her last sound before sleeping. All she'd wanted for the last three years was for the sounds to be gone. Now, they were, and the silence was louder than the sounds had ever been. That, Holcum had not expected.

With food finally in her stomach, the pit that had deepened there now sated, she stepped to an opening in the cave wall and looked down at the sea below. In the deepening twilight, she pictured herself as she'd been when she was here once before. In in the city that first year, she'd started to come to grips with her life, or at least that was the way she pictured it. She knew she really had, though. Her bounty from her garden, though small, had provided her with a few luxuries she enjoyed. She'd learned to speak with people and not drive them away. She had been *adjusting.*

Then came that child. Holcum hadn't been exposed to children in MegaCorp's military environment. For her, people sprang into being as full-fledged adults, or at least at the age of thirteen, the age at which they could begin life at the academy.

She let her thoughts fade as she stood looking disinterestedly over the sea, standing there until the darkness washed the last of the light from the sky. Finally, her eyes unable to see more, she turned, and feeling her way back to her things, she tugged on them to make them comfortable enough for sleep. As she dropped to them, she let the night pull the heat from her body.

She hadn't forgotten how to be grateful, as she noted the coolness of the air that night. Never had her rooms in the city cooled this much during the summer months. For this, the cooling of the night by the waters of the sea, she was exceedingly grateful, and in the darkness, even the quiet of being alone couldn't keep her awake. For the first time in many months, she slept her exhausted sleep the entire night through.

# —Chapter 8—

*Lucy: That's just it, Ricky. How did I know Ethel would barge in without being invited?*

*Fred: She's got a point there, Ricky. (snort of mirthless humor) You have to admit, that's Ethel, always barging in on everything.*

*Lucy: Besides, if she'd simply rung me on the phone, I would've taken down all those nasty comments I had my mother needlepoint about her. She wouldn't have had to see them.*

*Ricky (angry look on face): Lucy! Ethel is your friend. You go down there and apologize to her.*

*Lucy (smiling brightly): I already have. She's keeping Little Ricky this Saturday while we're at the club. And, as you can see, all the needlepoints are down. (motions around the apartment with her hand)*

*Fred (grinning): I wish you'd kept them. I saw a few I'd like to put around the building.*

*Lucy (stepping to closet and opening door to show a huge stack of framed needlepoints): Take any you like, Fred. Just return them afterwards. After Saturday, I may need them again.*

*Ricky: Lu-cy!*

*—From a lost episode of* I Love Lucy

IT HAD BARELY warmed in the underground Winter City, although summer would arrive before long. The beautiful Arianna pulled wrappings away from a small face held within their warm embrace, and she turned to the man beside her.

"She does have a grandmother." She smiled as the baby quivered in anticipation at the sound of her mother's voice. "Yes, you do," she whispered, reaching to rub her finger against the side of the child's face. "What shall we name her, Frenki? Let's make it a good name."

Her bonded man and best friend reached for the bundle in Arianna's arms. "Hmm. Hold her a bit, I will, and come to me, her name might." He wrapped the small bundle into his strong embrace. "Perfect, our life be, with this little one." He rubbed his nose against the child's. "Perfect, she be, Ari, and glad, I be, that this one, birthed together, we have."

Arianna pushed his shoulder in mock exasperation. "So, Perfect be her name. That be what you want?" She laughed at the very idea of a child named Perfect. What a legacy to live up to! "A real name be what I want to hear. Now, tell me, Frenki. What real name has come to you?"

She reached to the man she loved and ran her hand across his strong back, his muscles through his warm, winter clothing providing familiar memories to her hands. He was good to her, and he loved her daughter. His daughter, too.

In that moment of closeness, she pictured Frenki in labor—having *his* baby—and she laughed out loud, the thought of a man physically having a baby too funny to ignore. He looked at her with a mystified look on his face.

She reached to touch his cheek. "I was thinking of what a great father you'll be. Even at times when I be not around, you'll take this child and make her the happiest and luckiest of children, caring for her well. I love you, my precious Frenki." She reached to kiss his cheek, letting her fingers run through his hair.

"The one she'll need, you be, my dear woman. Without a father, live, a daughter can, but without a mother? Never. Now, a grandmother she has, you say. For real? Never for you to speak of her, have I heard a word. Tell to me abut this, you must, Ari." The baby hiccupped, and he put the child against his shoulder, patting her back to settle her stomach. "Find a strong name from the grandmother, perhaps we might."

"I never knew her. They tell me I lived with her until I was three. She was some sort of war hero, but she'd been severely injured. She was scarred and crippled, from what I've been told." Arianna absently reached and stroked the wisps of hair breaking free of her daughter's wrappings. "My two old uncles, just family friends, really, told me of the time she drove an entire band of raiders back from the city with her bare hands."

"Old uncles? Be they Carli and Regge?" When she nodded, her eyes glued to the precious one in her husband's arms, he laughed with gusto, startling the child. When the baby let out a wail, Frenki shrugged and offered her to Arianna. As soon as she traded arms, and her mother touched her face, the child let out a long sigh and reached to suck on the finger she felt there.

Frenki grasped his daughter's hand as he whispered, "Not so old, they be, even now, Ari."

"I was but a child, and they were very old to me. One day— when I was a bit older—I made them tell me the rest of the story. You see, it had always seemed too convenient to me. The raiders, they came to my mother's city, my mother unbonded, mind you, and then I was born. As I grew older, I knew something was amiss with the details of the story. When I pressed them as a teen-ager, old Carli—one night after a few too many, you under-stand—let the cat out of the bag." She let out a deep sigh, her eyes moist with her pending revelation. It was old news to her, but at times, it still struck close to home. "The raiders were why I was born."

Frenki sat up, leaned back, and looked at his beautiful, bonded mate. "Heard of this, I never have. You say a raider, your father be? How interesting, and still turned out to be so beautiful, you did! However," and he laughed quietly, "explains your temper, this does."

Arianna rolled her eyes as she stood with her daughter, not angry, and turned away from him. "I've always wondered when I would see my father in me, see the raider that he was." She turned back, her eyes red with threatening tears. "I was taken from her, Frenki. I didn't just live with her and then go to live with someone else. The city officials came and took me from her. You know that almost never happens, not even with the worst of parents."

Frenki stood to put his arms around both his partner and child, as Arianna's tears followed through with their earlier threat, the tracks down her face making her even more beautiful. "Turned out well, you did. You, the one that I hold in my arms at this very moment, love with all my heart, I do."

"How bad could she have been for me to be taken from her? I don't remember any of it. Uncle Regge let it slip one time that she still lives out at the inland sea."

"To know that, how would he, Ari?"

She laughed as she raised one hand and wiped the remains of her tears away. "This be where the story gets crazy. My mother, a woman I can't remember, came from space."

"From space? To Trasdrom'man? Comes here, no one does, my love."

She laughed at his raised eyebrows. "A very long time ago, a cryo pod crashed to our world from the sky, and Uncle Regge and Uncle Carli devised a way to open it. When they did, there she was, a survivor of who-knows-what military campaign from some place far across the galaxy. Uncle Regge's always felt responsible. Uncle Carli, not so much." She smiled when she thought of her Uncle Carli's opinion of her mother. Arianna knew, because she'd asked him one time, throwing a youthful tantrum until he shared what she needed to hear.

Her mood buoyed once again, her eyes still twinkling with the remnants of her earlier tears, she continued, "Uncle Carli feels the responsibility not at all. All Uncle Carli cares about be that old transport he's had since before I was born. Uncle Regge, though, told me he brought my mother and me food during the years we lived in the city, and he still takes her food and other items out to the caves where she lives on the sea. How horrible it must be out there, Frenki!"

"With Regge, send her word, you can. To help you out, I'm sure your Uncle Regge would be glad. About your mother's grandchild, I'm certain he would agree. Want to know, your mother would."

"I suppose so," she murmured, her attention now taken up with preparing to feed her baby. She smiled as Frenki leaned over to kiss her. She knew by his smile that as soon as the baby was asleep, he had hopes of some private time with her. With three people in the house, he didn't get as much of that as he'd like, and perhaps tonight she would enjoy his company equally.

REGGE RAN his fingers through his grey beard, this winter having taken the remaining dark streaks from him. He liked it, though. He felt it looked distinguished, and as he looked at Arianna, his heart warmed. It was Frenki's words that make him glance away.

"Tell her, Regge. Go to visit, she must." Frenki put his hands on the table, clasping them together as he did so. He nodded at Arianna with an intent expression. "Know her grandmother, the baby must. To do otherwise, be fair, it wouldn't."

185

Regge treasured Arianna. She was, to him, the daughter he had never had. His bonding had lasted a number of years, but when no children had come, his mate had decided another man would be a better choice for her. Now, it was back to old Carli and him. Sometimes he thought Carli, always skirting marriage, had been the smarter of the two. Now, to take Arianna to visit Holcum? He didn't know about that. That ragged old woman living out on the sea was not his idea of a loving grandmother. He paused and laughed, studying the ceiling and tracing old cracks that were darkened with age. He was nearly as old as she. Still, she barely tolerated his presence during his quarterly supply runs, much less asked anything about her daughter. He wasn't sure Holcum even remembered she'd once had a daughter, she had lived in those caves so long.

How she survived the winters, he didn't know. He always made sure she had the warmest of clothes, and one winter, he'd even taken a heating machine out to her, an extravagance he'd spent far too much to purchase. When he had gone back mid-winter, it hadn't even been turned on, and at Holcum's insistence, he'd reloaded it, taking it back to the seller's shop to trade for something more practical for his own use.

He responded carefully. "Likes living alone, your mother does, Arianna. Argues with even me whenever I visit." He paused, not wanting to venture too closely to feelings that might be barely submerged. "Happy here, you be. Mess that up, please don't, as what you and Frenki have, very special, that be." He truly did not want to see her get involved with that hollow shell of a woman that still existed out there in those caves.

"Uncle." Arianna's smile always melted his heart. "My dearest Uncle Regge, Frenki has talked me into this, and I agree. This thing I need to carry out. For me, yes. Especially for the baby. A grandmother would give a good name to her. Will you take me for a visit?"

"Fair, you be not, Arianna." Regge took a deep breath, knowing his good sense was lost when this young woman smiled at him. "To tell you no, certain you can be that I cannot. Know that, and you ask me, still."

He stood, catching Frenki's grin, recognizing the look of success on his strong face, understanding that the young man had helped make these plans, and that he was very pleased they were going through. The smile on Arianna's face spoke to him of the pleasure of anticipation, but Regge knew neither of them had the slightest idea just what they were getting into.

"When breaks, the cold does, then go to the inland sea, we will." Regge pursed his lips in thought. "Perhaps have a few good days, we will, and be at her best, your mother will. Know this one thing though, Arianna, like this, I don't."

Before leaving, Regge did spend some time with his godchild. Finally, with a hug from the daughter he'd never had, and a shake from her adoring husband, Regge was on his way.

He couldn't get over his feeling of dread. Nothing good would come of this. Nothing that touched Holcum ever turned out the way it was intended. He'd long ago admitted the truth to himself about his marriage to his ex-bonded. It wasn't the lack of children that had driven her away. It was his devotion, however platonic, to Holcum that had tipped the straw, and the camel's back had come crashing down hard.

Regge didn't know just how this trip would go bad, but certain of it, he was. If it touched anything to do with Holcum, it would go very badly, indeed.

"FRENKI, all our things be not moved yet, and already the heat be here." Arianna sat on a box next to the baby and ran her fingers through her hair. Winter City had grown entirely too warm for continued habitation. She looked at her husband pleadingly. "So many things to move for this little one, and Uncle Regge will be here any moment. I cannot go and simply leave you here. What will you do?"

Frenki moved to her and put his hand on her hair, caressing it between his fingers. He knelt to look her in the eyes. "For this day, 'can' and 'will,' for you, both be words of importance. All this moving, I can do. Enjoyed the pleasant temperatures of spring for two days, we have, and ask for more than that, we cannot. Lucky to get that, we were. Just go, my Ari, and meet her grandmother, our child will. To come back with a name be what I wish from you."

"I will miss you." She placed her hand on his, fighting tears.

Frenki leaned in to kiss her on the cheek, then he cupped his hand around his sleeping baby's head as he continued, "Good for her, the ride will be. What a child needs, fresh air, also, be." Standing, he took Arianna's hand and pulled her to her feet, giving her a push to the next room. "Mine, all this be, and done, it will be, also, when return, you do." With a wink, he waved her away; and she smiled, turning to the adjoining room.

She pulled out her water suit and began checking the seals. The suit needed to work properly, for this was the first real day of summer, and she couldn't afford to be outside and about without the suit working as it should. Next, she pulled out the tiny water suit she'd purchased for her daughter. It was more a jumpsuit with the tubing running between layers of moisture-wicking cloth, but it did have a water bladder that Arianna would need to keep an eye on. She felt an uneasy disquiet overwhelm her. Without Frenki, how could she do this for an entire day?

Then, with resolve, she took a deep breath. Steeling herself, she knew she could manage this. Frenki had coached her under Uncle Regge's watchful eye. Every time Arianna pumped her own bladder, she must reach to give the half-sized bladder next to her a gentle pump for the baby.

She carried the water suit to the other room, and Frenki

turned from his daughter to smile at his wife. Arianna ran her hand down the front of the small suit as she whispered, almost as if to convince herself, "I can do this, Frenki. This will be fun, both for the baby and me. Even to put this water suit on her will be a new experience to treasure."

Just then the door opened, and gray-headed Regge burst in, with a wide smile on his face. "Ready, we be?"

"Where be the man taking me to the sea today?" Arianna laughed when she looked at him, running over and putting a hand to his freshly shaven cheek. She turned to Frenki. "This be not my Uncle Regge, not with this smooth, beardless face." She laughed as Regge hugged her, pulling her to him and swinging her around, her toes curling as they swung in the air.

"Down," she laughed. "I must get dressed." As soon as her feet touched the floor, she ran to the other room, returning after a few minutes, her water suit on and her water bladder full. She let the baby's "uncle" help with the tiny water suit, and finally ready, with Frenki gently carrying the smallest member of the troupe, the four of them climbed Winter City's steps into the morning's already too-hot sunshine.

"Old Red, I see. I've always loved this transport, Uncle. It be so clean, today. Be you sure you wish to drive it to the desert? Rather, perhaps we should pick up Uncle Carli's." The vehicle's wheels gleamed, and the glassine side windows were in their door recesses, stored away securely. Arianna laughed mischievously as she walked up to the door he had already opened for her.

Regge laughed with her. "Always clean, it be, my girl. To-day, just for you, it be especially so. And to you, my thanks. Love it, also, I do."

Kissing his daughter's head, Frenki stood next to Arianna. He whispered as he looked at the small face, "Keep her covered, you must, and her water bladder, push often." He smiled, handing Arianna their little girl.

Regge chuckled at Frenki's concerns. "How responsible my goddaughter be, I be well aware, and no fear for the baby do I feel." He finished loading the few things Arianna felt she needed for the day, most of the items already on the transport being those he was taking to Holcum, anyway. Then he helped his god-daughter inside.

Arianna snuggled the baby next to her and leaned through the open window to kiss her husband. "I'll do all you be asking and more, besides. I love her, too, Frenki." With a wave of her hand as her uncle eased the transport away, she turned to watch her bonded man disappear as the transport rounded a corner.

She turned to Regge, cautioning him in spite of the trust she professed in him. "Be careful today, Uncle. You may have let Uncle Carli toy with this transport's workings, but that doesn't mean you have to use all that power. A baby be here with us, today." She smiled at his *Who, me?* look, and she reached to pat his arm. "Another day, and you must take me out and slide race. I remember you and Uncle Carli doing so when I was a child, and it was always a treat. I'd come in laughing and would want to tell everyone. You and Uncle Carli would panic, advising me strongly to never tell anyone of the sliding, the *drifting*, as he likes to say, and I'd laugh at the both of you, not understanding why anyone would care."

Regge peered at her thoughtfully, a question he wanted to ask clearly brooding in his mind. At her amused glance, he let it burst from him. "Fast, though. To drive fast, will you let me?"

"I was waiting for that question. The wind would feel good in my hair for a bit, and the little one be wrapped up and out of the worst of it. Go fast, Uncle. Go as fast as you dare."

He laughed with pleasure. "Then, when builds, the heat does, close the windows, we will, and run the cooling unit."

"I never doubted you would." She smiled and caressed her baby's cheek.

With a nod and a grin, the transport began to rapidly pick up speed. In a nearby stand of scrubby shrubs, the scattered woody plants freshly leafed out in a violent burst of spring as they prepared themselves for the onslaught of summer shook their verdant limbs at the transport's passing. Several var'delk held their heads to the ground, nibbling the crusts of the leaf pods that had begun to fall away, as the shrubs' greenery unfurled with life. The shortsighted creatures with their furred heads and small, recessed eyes, raised their noses as they felt the rumble in the ground as the transport passed. However, these delicacies fell only this one time each year, and besides, a flash of red was all they saw. When the ground settled under their feet, their hearts also returned to their normal, slow-pulsing rhythms, leaving the grazing var'delk undisturbed, the exquisite taste of the pods the only coherent thoughts running through their furry little heads.

In the transport, the heat having finally become too much, the machine's glassine walls soon enclosed the trio, keeping the heat at bay while they were en route. Regge turned to Arianna with a hint of a grin. "Have a bit of news for you, I do. Remember, do you, the old woman from the city Carli and I told you about? The one, the cause of all the trouble when you were small?"

Arianna thought for a moment. "Old Maggents? She be one who hates the cold and always insists on the warmest rooms in Winter City. Council fought her over that this past year." She laughed with the memory. "She lives for the first day of summer and always beats everyone else to Summer City. As a girl, I had to dodge out of her way a few times when I tried to claim the prize of first outside."

Regge patted her arm. "Worry no more about that, you will." What went unsaid was that it was Maggents who had repeatedly reported Arianna's lack of care by Holcum, finally getting the three-year-old removed and sent to adoptive parents. Regge had never figured out what had driven old Maggents, but even after

Arianna had been adopted by her new family, the old woman had kept petitioning to have her sent offplanet.

"Why be that, Uncle?"

"Tripped and broke something, she did, the last day of this winter just ended. Had to sit and watch Winter City begin to empty, and broken by it, she was. She be dead as of last night, never seeing outside of Winter City this year."

Arianna, unsure of just why her uncle was telling her all this, ventured, "Be you sad, Uncle Regge?"

He laughed, and seeing the baby between them stir, lowered his voice to a whisper. "Sad? Know all the trouble that woman caused, you don't. Just as an interesting conversation tidbit, I say this to you, telling you of the death of someone known in common, the news shared with a beautiful girl I love."

Arianna had long thought there must be much more to the Maggents story than she'd been told, but she also accepted some things were better not asked. She thanked him for the news and reached to place her hand on her little girl's cheek. This was all that mattered to her at the moment, her love for her daughter. Some old woman who had caused Arianna trouble many years ago couldn't compete with this treasure she held now, right this moment, her sweet skin warm against her hand. Love, *this* love, was the more important thing, and Arianna was sure her Uncle Regge understood that, too.

ARIANNA STOOD, holding her daughter in the cool darkness of the caves, watching Regge carrying in the supplies from the transport. He made repeated trips, disappearing as he ferried supplies deep within the mountain. Everyone in the city knew of this place, but she'd never visited or seen the inland sea in its crashing fury as it attacked the rocks below. Travel over these distances was difficult in the best of times, and impossible at others; and she'd never had a reason for coming out this far.

When Regge had taken her to look out through one of the openings in the cave's wall, the stark beauty of the sea stretching to the far cliffs in the distance took her breath away. She was very surprised to find just how cool, almost cold, really, it was sequestered from the biting teeth of the summer sun. With the cooled air in the transport and now here in these caves, she was beginning to wish she'd left her water suit back in the city.

Regge had assured her the caves did warm each summer. This was the first hot day, though, and the rock walls still carried the winter's cold inside of their slow-to-warm cores.

"Brr! What will it be like in these caves when winter hits again?" Said to herself, Regge off again, and no one around to respond, anyway, Arianna was surprised to hear a gravelly voice reply.

"Colder than hell, that's how bad it gets. Cold enough to make you hide in the deepest cave just to stay out of the wind."

Arianna was appalled at what stepped from a connecting rock-walled room directly across from her, the shadows covering part of the figure, the harsh voice not one she associated with the reason she had come to this place. Surely this was an intruder, or perhaps another person living out here that Regge hadn't thought to tell her about. Arianna pulled the baby closer as the first brush of uneasiness tickled her skin.

"Who be you? My friend, Regge, be here helping an old woman who resides in these caves." Arianna's eyes searched to see if she could find a sign of him. She hadn't expected to run into this old, decrepit hermit out here, and with the baby in her arms, this unkempt person made her distinctly uncomfortable.

Wearing nothing but rags, her clothes grown tattered, with new layers constantly adding themselves to the old, Holcum did look the decrepit recluse. She laughed with her seldom-used voice, and her words cracked and shattered as she spoke.

"An old woman? Well, now, that's a story. Did old Regge

tell you that? Now, you tell me this, *girl*. Who are *you*?" The words were harsh, and even in their brokenness, they slashed cruelly at the young woman standing with her baby in her arms.

With that one familiar word, Arianna knew. She remembered. *Girl.* People had called her that. She'd answered to it for a very long time, and then she'd forgotten it. Hearing that word again in that voice, though, there could be no mistaking who this was. This ragged creature was the woman with whom she had lived for the first three years of her life.

Other memories also started to fill Arianna's thoughts. A garden and playing with the plants. Getting hit afterwards. The painful blisters from the sun. Hunger. Her mother not waking when she needed her. Crying . . . a lot.

She whispered, the acoustics of the cave making her voice louder than she intended, "You let them take me, and you didn't care."

"What, girl? Speak up if you want me to hear you. Otherwise, leave now. If you came with Regge, I don't know what he was thinking. Go back to the city where you belong." Holcum squinted at Arianna and saw she was holding something. "Leave my things alone. They don't belong to you. Whatever you have, put it back."

"This? This be not yours."

Holcum started her way, and stepping out of the shadows, Arianna caught the light across her face. Startled, she took a step back. She could see the crutch as Holcum shifted her weight from her good leg to the crutch's support, the rocking walk looking a bit like the waves on the surface of the sea she had recently admired to her Uncle Regge. With Arianna's sudden movement, the baby in her arms started to cry.

"A baby?" Holcum snorted and turned. Without looking back, she paused and spat harshly one more time before disappearing back into her shadows. "Take that thing from here. Next time, tell Regge his lady friends are not welcome in my presence."

Arianna stood frozen for a moment, her breath taken from her, and as her daughter began to softly cry, so did she. This wasn't what she'd expected, not what she'd wanted. Frenki would be horrified when she told him. She looked at the baby she held and treasured. All the preparations and the trip out here, and her daughter still didn't have a name. As the child grew quiet, Arianna noticed her daughter grabbing at the tears from her mother's face as they fell, her puffy fingers slapping at the droplets as they slipped from Arianna's chin. Laughing softly at her, Arianna reached to wipe the tears away, her fingers then gently stroking the little one in her arms.

*How could she not have wanted the bond I have with my baby? How could she not have wished for that with me?*

Her tears starting up again, Arianna walked out the way she'd been led in, finding Regge unloading the last of his delivery from the back of his transport. Turning to her, seeing her face, he pushed the package back onto the transport and ran to wrap his arms around the precious young woman he'd brought to this devilish place.

Pulling her head to his shoulder, he spoke into her hair as his shirt dried her tears. "See that you've met your mother, I can. So sorry I be for you, my little Ari. Know, now, you do." Stepping back, he touched her chin and lifted her face to look into her eyes. "Know one thing, you must. Loved, you be, even if not by that old woman. Hard, her life was, long before she came to this world. Her hurt, with her, she brought, and let go of it, she never could. A hero she be to many, but seen the real woman, you have. Not even there with you when you met her, was I, and saw the real Holcum, you must have, these tears tell me. To our home and those who love us, let's go."

He grabbed the final package, set it just inside the cave

entrance, and helped the heartsick little girl that Arianna wrestled with inside her grown-up self, that little girl she'd forgotten she had once been, back into the transport. On the way to the city, Regge let her be silent. In sympathy, he held her hand all the way.

HOLCUM TURNED from the room where her supplies were stored, and her disgust boiled inside.

Regge had been a godsend to her when she'd escaped to these caves. That didn't mean she had to like taking his help. That would never be easy for her to do. Every time she walked across this cave or tried to climb to those on different levels towards the sea, she cursed this leg and the ubiquitous crutch her life had dealt her.

One day, not too long after she'd come here to stay, she'd struggled and finally made it to the water. She'd been too exhausted to enjoy it, and after a short rest, had begun to hobble her way back to her refuge from the world. She almost hadn't made it, and indeed, for one night, hadn't. Stranded without food or water, the strange darkness of an unfamiliar cave had claimed her company for those black hours, offering her only the stone floor for her comfort, releasing her only the following morning for the remainder of her journey back to the caves where she made her home.

Her face, though. When she was alone, she was able to forget for a time. What she felt each time she brushed the dissected skin didn't seem so disfiguring with no one here to share what she'd become. Then, Regge brought that girl to remind Holcum of what her life had been, and just what she'd lost when her escape pod had carried her to this barren world with its wildly erratic seasons and backward people. She paused and listened to the sounds of sobbing softly echoing throughout the caves, telling her the girl was still outside with Regge, her crying satisfying Holcum very much.

196

*She should know that cave acoustics carry sound exceptionally well. Stupid girl,* Holcum sputtered.

She reached her hand to touch the skin on the ragged side of her face. She had truly almost forgotten this was here. Her breathing sharpened, and her heart began to race as her fingers traced the cording that comprised half her hideous features. She could see it in her mind as if it were the first time she'd looked in a mirror after the accident: the redness, and the edge of her eye down turned and misshapen; her ear twisted as if torn away and hastily reglued; the way her lips blurred into the corded skin as if it were all one piece. She'd forgotten, and now she was forced to endure the memory all over again.

She cut her eyes to a darkened shape in the corner. She was glad the girl hadn't found that. It would have to be removed soon, what with the warm weather of summer here at last. It would soon begin to stink. That was one man who wouldn't steal her things any longer. That's what she'd thought the girl had been doing, taking some of the things she needed to survive, the things Regge brought her.

In the depths of winter's cold, she'd known she was running short of supplies for some time, and she'd been cutting back, conserving, not daring to question Regge about it. What if he brought nothing at all? Even if she ran a little short before he returned each trip, at least she could be grateful that he *did* continue to return.

Then, one day at the start of winter, the supplies stored just where Regge had left them, Holcum had ventured from one of the deepest caves she had found within the caverns. It was the one grotto she had stumbled across in her wanderings where it was warmer than elsewhere. Even in the deepest part of the cold that gripped her as winter settled in, the back part of the floor and one wall radiated unexpected but welcomed and continual heat.

As soon as she had seen the movement in the shadows, she

197

had known. A *thief* was taking her supplies. She had been doing without, and for no reason except to make it easier for a *thief* to survive.

She hadn't been able to stop him that time, and not even the next. It had been too bitterly cold for her to remain by her supplies and wait for him. Then, over time, she had discovered a pattern in his thievery; she had determined he would pay for being so careless. There he lay, his price the one she had taken from him: his life for a few items he had thought so necessary.

He had tried to tell her his name before she twisted the knife in his gut. He'd desperately blathered a crazy story about how bad the last twenty years had been. A meteor had fallen from the sky, blowing his transport and all his worldly goods to the heavens. He swore he'd pay back everything he'd stolen from her, but he'd stolen her full belly and her security. Those could not be repaid. Worse, he'd looked at her face, and he'd cringed when he'd done so. That mistake had to be redeemed at the greatest possible price.

He'd given her his name. Jean, Jeanne . . . Jeanna'te! She was often frustrated by her lack of recall of the most trivial facts, although she chalked it up to her insufficient mental stimulation. Gods knew, she didn't get much of that, anymore. Even so, the man's death had awakened a pleasure in her she had long thought dead.

The knife had driven deep, and when she'd twisted it, he'd fought her grip on the hilt as she held it pushed inside his body. She hadn't needed him to die quickly, so she had only twisted the knife to tear him inside. That would poison him from his own bodily toxins as they leaked into his internal cavities. She had smiled her crooked, grotesque smile, making sure he took in that side of her face as his own twisted with the pain and the knowledge of just what she'd done. It had been remarkably easy. No matter how degrading the life that she was forced to live on this world, her innermost being was still full of all things military, and killing was one of them.

She had left him, and over the next few days, she'd returned periodically to kick him to see if he'd finally decided to give up and die. On the third day, she could see he'd tried to crawl across the floor, but he did lie still when she kicked him. That satisfied her. He was scum to her, and scum needed to die.

She would have to take care of him soon, though, or he would start to stink. She hobbled to the opening overlooking the sea below and sighed. She could not throw him from this cave, with its rocky beach just below, but the opening she could see just to one side might do. It opened out over the water, and the waves would carry the man's body far from her. She smiled with the plan forming in her mind. A few rocks wrapped up with him, and the sea floor could claim him.

*Yes,* she thought as she turned back to gather some of her fresh supplies, *That could certainly work. A few rocks would take care of the problem just fine.*

"YOUR YOUNGER brother be telling me stories, Innocetta. What be your dreams of?" Arianna placed her hand over her daughter's, the warmth of their two skins helping keep the cold in the room at bay. "I trust them, you know. Never have I known one to have such strong dreams, and such true ones, too."

"Mother." Innocetta looked away. "Please."

At the embarrassed look on her daughter's face, Arianna squeezed her hand. "Not everyone believes in them, I know, but I think there be something in those dreams. Yours, my dear, have always seemed to steer you in the right directions. Your strength. Part of it comes from your dreams, I think."

"They be just dreams." Sometimes, though, Innocetta felt as her mother suggested. Her dreams unnerved her at times. She preferred to be in control, to be strong, and she felt confused when the events she imagined during her nights couldn't be explained.

Arianna caught Innocetta's downcast eyes, and she softly encouraged her. "No, I don't believe dreams be mystical. They be a summation of all you've seen, what you've experienced, and the things your brain recognizes as important. The dreamer, he or she simply be the one who can assemble all these things into a dream that explains what the person already knows, and does it in a way that makes sense. You have that ability. Not your brothers or your father, the gods watch over Frenki's spirit, poor man to die so early in his good life. Not even your father had the dreamsense." Here, Innocetta's mother laughed. "You won't find that word in a list of meanings anywhere. It be my own, but I like it. Dreamsense. Sometimes, I think it means to have the sense to pay attention to your dreams."

Innocetta smiled and withdrew her hand from under her mother's. "How much longer until the warmth returns? I be so tired of the cold this winter. You be assigned the coldest of rooms in the city this year."

Arianna pulled her collar more snugly around her neck. "No children at home anymore, dear. That be the price I pay for letting all of you grow up and move away. Would you become my small child again, just to let me have the warmer rooms during these cold months?" She laughed to let her daughter know she wasn't offended to live here, whatever the reason. She prodded, "The dreams? Can I know of them?"

Innocetta laughed timidly. "They seem so silly to me. I know nothing of what I've dreamed, and in fact, be still dreaming almost every night. It be all so similar, too, that which I see in each one." She stood and walked around the small room, none of the walls emanating much warmth from the underground geo-thermal heating. Arianna's rooms were on the very edge of Winter City, and there was little heat that reached this far.

"I dream of a old woman in a cave." She looked at her mother, seeing a face that had lost none of its youthful beauty, and was surprised to see a flash of recognition before Arianna could mask it with a smile. Innocetta stepped toward her, her heart telling her this dream could make sense to her today. "You know what this be, Mother. Tell me."

Her mother worked her lip beneath her teeth before answering. "More of the dream, daughter. Tell me more of the dream, first."

Innocetta sat to look her mother in the eyes, knowing she could read her responses well if she could catch all the cues. "It be hot outside and very cold inside. The old woman be not very nice, and that part of the dream always makes me cry." She watched closely, taking in the tears pooling in the corners of her mother's eyes. This was striking home with her. "I also remember the color red and the smell of water. Now, Mother. Tell me what I've dreamed."

Arianna breathed carefully, each breath long and measured. "Do you know anything else about what you've dreamed?"

"Only that some people tell of a crippled woman who lives in the caves by the inland sea. But I don't think that be true. No one could survive the winter in a distant cave." She motioned around her mother's frozen room and at the sweaters and coats they both wore constantly. "Even here in the city, some of us barely stay warm enough to survive." Then she turned and riveted her mother's eyes with her own, holding her to the truth. There would be no dissembling allowed on this day. Innocetta needed answers to these dreams. "Tell me, Mother. I can see this means something to you."

HER MOTHER looked at her beautiful daughter, remembering that awful day, her hopes for a renewed relationship dashed as cruelly as anyone had ever endured. She didn't want to tell her

201

about the grandmother who had thought Innocetta was a package of goods, was, in fact, only interested in her as something to protect from being stolen. When she'd found out Arianna was holding a baby, both Arianna and her baby were dismissed summarily, and in the unkindest way possible. Yet, Arianna could see that her daughter needed an answer, and she knew she must give it to her. Her decision made, she lowered her eyes to her hands and began to share.

"Your grandmother be whom you've dreamed about. You met her once." She looked up at Innocetta, wondering if recognition could be there. After all, she'd only been weeks old, and they hadn't really met, not like Arianna had hoped. Seeing none, she went on. "Your Uncle Regge. You've not seen him in years, but you may remember him from your Uncle Carli's services, may he drift the skies in peace."

Innocetta interrupted, "Drift the skies in peace? Mother? You be starting to worry me." She laughed.

"Just a joke. Ask me about it some other time. Uncle Regge, you rode in his red transport on the way to the services. It was many years old, and you commented on how quickly it took off."

"I do remember that. Go on, Mother."

"That transport be the red from your dream. You were a baby, and he took us to the caves, the transport as old as me, even then." Arianna paused, wishing she didn't have to tell it all. At the insistent look on her daughter's face, she went on. "The old woman, my mother, had lived there for twenty of our world's years, even then. Uncle Regge kept her supplied with what she needed. He still does, though not for much longer, I think. He be several decades older than me, and I be no longer young." She smiled and ran her hand through her still-dark hair.

"Mother, don't start," Innocetta reproved. "You be very young, and the men all say you be very beautiful, still. They would love you, if you'd let my father go."

"I loved him too much. He be still in my heart and thoughts every day." She took a deep breath and turned back to the dream. "The tears you cry from your dream be the tears of rejection. I took you to meet her, wanting to perhaps even love her, and she didn't care, throwing us out amid harsh words."

Innocetta took a breath and held it, a smile of anticipation growing on her face. She exhaled and turned to her mother. "I feel so sorry for her. I have a grandmother, and I never knew. I feel drawn to her, already."

Arianna was very sharp with her reply, surprising herself as well as her daughter, although later she would consider that perhaps an even sharper reply might have been better. "No! Do not say that! My Uncle Regge told me before I took you there that it was a very bad idea, and no good would come of it. I didn't believe him, and I took you, anyway. She hurt me cruelly. Don't develop an interest in this idea of a grandmother. She be a grandmother to no one. Especially not to you. Remember that!" Slapping the table for emphasis, Arianna stood and turned away, her daughter looking at her in astonishment.

Innocetta went to her, and in her hug, she whispered to her mother, "My strange dream has hit a nerve, and it clearly be a tender one. Don't be angry, Mother. You be the most loved of all the people in Winter City. Your daughter and your sons' daughters love you so much that you must feel you be drowning in that love every day. If you don't feel that, then we don't tell you enough."

When she drew back, tears were flowing down her mother's face, and she grabbed her again, the hug meaning even more this time. Love was being shared, and in that, they knew things would be all right, no matter what transpired in the grandmother's caves.

UNCLE REGGE was familiar to Innocetta, but only indistinctly. She remembered this old transport more vividly.

She smiled as he lectured her, his words intended to protect, she could tell. She knew there was certainly something between this old man she knew only vaguely and the old woman he was taking her to see. Innocetta peered out the glassine windows and was relieved the transport seemed well maintained. Old machines were treasured on this world, because credits were very short to replace them, but old did require care. If the heat went out on this trip, they could certainly freeze to death. The winter flying past the transport's cold glassine sidewalls was beautiful, though, Innocetta admitted without reservations. Great mounds of wind-whipped snow were battered into fanciful shapes. Overhangs like frozen waves towered in the air. Occasionally, the stiff arms of exposed trees made striking shadows on the ground. The sun, although weak in its winter straightjacket, caught ice crystals on the slickened surface, and they were diamonds, things of beauty in the desolation. Not many people in the city had ever, not even once in their lives, come outside to see the winter snows. They knew how easily they could die of exposure with just a short visit. But, to see everything white, this was amazing.

Innocetta was bundled up, even in the warmth of the old transport. She had been shocked when she had stepped into the ice hangar to enter Regge's vehicle, although she'd known beforehand the cold would be much worse here in the open. The wind buffeting them across the open desert was certainly easy to dismiss with the heated warmth inside the transport, but she dreaded opening the door when they got to the inland sea.

How did that old woman in her dreams survive this? Even her Uncle Regge, who was taking her there, was unsure of that, but she was still alive. He'd told her in his faltering voice about caves opening into more caves, forming caverns that stretched deep into the mountains around the sea. Perhaps she'd found warmth there, he'd suggested. Although he'd told her he sometimes hired others now, drivers younger than himself, to ferry the supplies out, he thought he'd like to go out this time and check on the old woman, since he'd have company for the trip. Regge didn't know it, yet, but he would be returning to the city alone.

Right now he was telling her about the old woman she would soon meet. Innocetta saw the irony in the fact that she had pressed everyone for answers and information, and the one person she hadn't thought to ask was telling her everything she'd wanted to know without her posing even one question. It seemed as though the old woman wasn't very welcoming to strangers. It also seemed the old man didn't want Innocetta to get hurt. The facts she learned were jumbled, but they were very informative. According to this ancient "uncle," the old woman had come from offworld in a cryo pod, crashing far from the city. Innocetta knew cryo pods, and she didn't see how that could be possible, but she humored the old man. Raiders had been driven from the city by the old woman's solitary actions, and they had never returned. The old woman never left the caves, not in summer or winter. Crippled and disfigured, she didn't like to be seen by others. The old woman's name was Holcum.

Innocetta now knew more than she'd been able to find out in all her searching, and it was enough. All these things were the old woman, and they had made her fearsome to others; but the old woman hadn't yet met Innocetta. Innocetta was stronger than all these things, and the old woman that was her grandmother, this Holcum, would soon know how strong a granddaughter she had helped bring forth.

Regge turned to look at her when he heard her laugh out loud. "So, what be funny, my dear?"

"She will know me, Regge, and then she'll know how strong she used to be."

"Strong, she be, still. Misled, you should not be." He gave her a reproving look for not taking his words to heart.

She just smiled, but inside she thought to herself, *She doesn't yet know strong. She just thinks she does.* And she turned to the window to watch the snow fade into the distance, farther than her eyes could see.

# —Chapter 9—

*. . . although it is one of the most beautiful of fishes, it must live in isolation. When penned with another of its kind, it becomes vicious and will fight to the death . . .*

—*Excerpt from* The Diversity of Biology, *Jamis T. Bowen*

THE NIGHTS had been too cold to endure. They had bored to the core of Holcum's bones, even in her warm retreat deep in the mountain. For years she'd felt the bitterness of the winter more severely each time it attacked her mountain fortress. Her leg and its errant nerve complained to her constantly as of late, often screaming out to her even as she lay down on her pallet against the warmth of her rock-walled retreat, with only the surging of the planet's internal fires to keep death at bay.

Then, there was the other thing. It worried Holcum even more. Worried? No, that was the wrong word, she knew. Dreaded was perhaps more accurate. She *dreaded* this other thing, because she knew it might bring pain that would make her leg feel as nothing.

It was her skin. When she pressed on it, it no longer retained the pink hue of life, the color of healthy blood flowing back into anticipating tissues. Yellow was her skin's color, now. She tried to remember from her days aboard the ship just what that meant, and she couldn't recall it anymore.

She had been here too many decades. She'd lost count, even as she tried to tally them in her head. Was it four or five tens of this planet's years? At one time, the years would have ticked themselves off in her head, dividing their contents into neat little compartments, and she would have known the date without thinking. The events themselves would have been the stepstones guiding her measured walk through her life. Now, she only knew that she was very old. She had no events in her life to be her stepstones, and her skin was yellow, slowly shading itself to brown, even here in this blasted winter, with not even her warmest cave able to provide her the heat she so craved.

She had begun to see half-real shadows of the past gather at the mouth of her cave. At first she'd ignored them, shaking her head as if to drive them away. They were nothing more than the encroaching memories of what could have been. Sometimes now, those memories were more real to her than the present. They didn't stay with her, so she knew they weren't alive. At least she didn't think so. She refused to live in the shadowy world of past events, but they flashed without warning into her mind as if she had turned a corner, and with a single step of her foot, entered into this hellish life she now lived, those events of long ago left only a few steps behind her, just around the corner. They felt so strong, sometimes, that Holcum was tempted to turn around and see if the people and the places in her head were really just the other side of the rock wall she had a moment ago rounded. They never were, though. For that reason, she knew the half-real shadows at the mouth of her cave weren't real, either. When they refused to fade from her sight, she drew in a deep breath, realizing these were physical people. The staying of a dream or a memory frightened her, but the presence of people angered her, and in the heat of her emotions, that anger overrode the sensations of pain in her leg, as well as the bitterness of the cold. Clutching her crutch with one hand and grabbing at containers of foodstuffs piled next to her with the other, she drew herself to her feet as quickly as her stiffened joints would allow.

"Get away," she yelled in her disused voice, and then she stumbled against the wall as a fit of coughing wracked her frame. This, too, she now had reason to remember. This was a third thing that she knew was wrong with her body. Her breathing had been tight, and while it had rumbled in her body for most of this cold winter, the yelling of those two words shot knives through her chest. An old, familiar voice called to her as she raised her eyes. She shook her head back and forth to clear her vision. Although indeed familiar, the voice *was* very old, and that was *not* as she remembered it. Regge had come to harrass her once again.

"Holcum, Regge, it be. To check on you, I wish."

He stepped forward to steady her, his helpful hands freezing in place as she jerked away from him. She quivered at the hated touch, and she braced heself on a tall container of supplies.

His voice quavering, he continued, "Very sick, you be." He stepped back, his feet catching on tumbled bundles of clothing. "Brought someone, I have. Someone you've met before. Many years ago, she came, and very small she was, too." He turned to motion for Innocetta to step up beside him. "Your granddaughter, Innocetta."

As Innocetta stepped up, Holcum raised her head, her yellow-tinted skin catching in the dim light trailing in from behind her two unwelcome visitors. She squinted, and she laughed a harsh, rough rumble of sound, again ending in another fit of coughing. After a pause to regain her breath, she spoke, spitting her harsh words.

"I have no granddaughter. I've never met you and don't wish to do so now. As far as you, Regge, I continue to be grateful for the supplies you've provided me over the years, but I detest these uninvited guests you insist on traipsing through my life. I call down curses on them all and damn you for bringing them. I would be left alone, and if I'm sick, then there's that much less time you have to be responsible for me."

She pulled herself up straighter, her anger focusing her, and with determination, she continued, "I know you, Regge. You've no love for me. You know only responsibility, and I've always been a thorn in your side. I'll be gone soon enough, you can trust in that. Now, go, and take this girl with you. I have no need to be reminded of what my life was and of what I've become. Leave me in peace." She turned and began to walk towards another chamber, unable even to lift her crutch from the floor, dragging it behind her with each step, to awkwardly fall back onto the rude stick, barely regaining her teetering balance as each struggling lurch threatened to twist her to the floor.

REGGE STEPPED forward to offer assistance, his own balance not that much more stable, only to have Innocetta stop him to let her pass. Grasping her grandmother's arm, thin through the layer of filthy clothing she wore, Holcom jerked away to throw off her granddaughter's help. However, true to her word, Innocetta did possess the determination she'd claimed to Regge in the transport. This grandmother would not deny this copy of herself the satisfaction of helping an ancestor, even if that ancestor intended to curse her to whatever hell might reside far underneath the soils of this world. How much worse could that hell be than the one that pirouetted its death dance across the soil of Trasdrom'man each year?

Though her grandmother growled and spat, Innocetta didn't release her. She was concerned with how thin her arm was. Regge had told her of the kinds of food he supplied and how it had to be of the most durable kind, able to be easily opened and consumed. What he'd described, though, had appalled Innocetta. She'd made sure there were fresh foods in what she'd brought. It was still sitting in warmth of the transport.

Healthwise, her grandmother's condition was about what she expected, considering the woman's isolation and lack of access to the simplest of care. But the clothing . . . Innocetta was determined Regge would return with more decent items. The filth of the fabrics her grandmother boasted was atrocious. Innocetta suspected bathing had been an unnecessary luxury to the old woman for years, and with winter abusing the world's surface just outside the cave's walls, the last time she'd worn a fresh change of clothing must have been during the long-ago warmth of summer.

Innocetta did take in the scarred face, the one side showing the remains of a sort of beauty, the same striking looks Innocetta saw peering back at her from her own mirror. The damage didn't bother her. This woman was her *grandmother,* and for Innocetta, a bond had already been forged. She knelt by the withered husk, her strength holding the bundle of rags firmly, the woman inside fighting her still, yet surely realizing her battle would be a lost cause with this one.

Whatever the reason, whether the illness that cried impassioned pleas of sympathy to a strength of character that never relented to her bodily weaknesses, or the years that had simply worn the old soldier's resolve to the thinness of a breaking point, something was triggered in that old, obstinate brain by the events of the day. In that moment in that cave, Holcum relented, her twisting away from the granddaughter less violent, her endurance not that which she had known in her youth. She might not understand the reason her resolve broke, nor would she have wanted to contemplate why she suddenly let this young woman take control of her the way she did, but relinquish control, she did.

Regge, never able to predict or sense a pattern to the whims of Holcum's violence, even after their long association, watched the events unfurl in front of his eyes. Who knew what might cause Holcum to lash out in anger or frustration? Yet, this young woman, the very likeness of what he'd always imagined Holcum might have been in the freshness of her youth, had tamed the old-Earth lioness with only a grip of her hand upon the old woman's arm.

He finally cleared his throat, calling gently, "Innocetta?" She turned to look from her comforting of the old woman to question him with a look. "Some meds there be in the transport. For me to get them, would you like?" He made a move as if to step that way.

"Please. I be afraid to move her or to leave her alone. How could she be so ill and not ask for help?" She paused to adjust one of the woman's arms in an attempt to make her more comfortable. "You must bring me more clothes. Warm ones, of course, but more importantly, clean ones. Soap. Yes, I will need much of that." She did allow herself a smile at the image in her mind of just how much of the winter's grime might have to be removed.

"Clothes, Innocetta? Sent clothes, I have. The wearing of them, the problem be."

"Help me, then. How can I find them?" She looked to discover that her grandmother had fallen asleep, and she stood to look around. "Also, it be remarkably warm in here. Can you tell me why?"

Regge shrugged and readied his heaviest of clothing to retrieve the meds he had promised. "Why survived so long, she has, it must be. Perhaps, as in the city, there be underground heat. Used to know the name for such warmth, I did, but starting to forget things, I am." He furrowed his forehead, then opened his eyes wide. "Ah!" He knocked his knuckle against his temple. "Geothermals, they be." He smiled at remembering the hard-to-recall word. "Tap these, and rich, someone could be. Sell the heat in winter to make a profit."

"Someone would have to live out here to want to pay, though, wouldn't they? It be a very long way from the city. My old grandmother certainly be not rich to invite guests, so I guess that idea be one for the back burner." Innocetta already searched through the many unopened containers scattered around the cave. It seemed Holcum took what looked easy to get to, and she suffered without the rest. It was a shame that no one had done the simplest thing, to come out here and be willing to help make all this more usable for a cripple. She could, though, and she would. For anyone to live like this would be unacceptable in the city, and it was unacceptable here.

"The meds, Uncle. Bring them to me, please. I must see what they be, so I can put them to use. I may need others that you can bring back to me in a few days."

"Bring back to you? Innocetta, be with me, you will. To stay here, you certainly cannot. If thinking that, you be, reconsider, you do, I hope."

Innocetta smiled grimly, her plan finally revealed. "Certainly I be planning to stay. Not much longer will winter last, and this be what I must do. She be much worse than I expected, and I would have stayed in any case. I come prepared."

"I know that look, it being the positive side of your grandmother's mean determination. Strength, you have, that I cannot fight." He smiled indulgently at her. "Give in, I do. See the look on your face, I clearly can, and one, it be, that I have seen before."

"You have? Where be that?" She didn't expect his answer, but when it came, it didn't surprise her. He pointed at the woman asleep on the floor, and she followed the line of his finger and laughed, knowing what he was saying with his silence was all she needed to hear. His proffered connection filled her with satisfaction that she had journeyed to this place to help this unknown woman. Unknown was certainly right, but not unlike. They were the opposite poles of the same magnet. Holcum's life had ground her into the person she'd turned out to be, and her granddaughter had been allowed to grow into the person she had become. Yet, both of them were the same, just as both of them were also the opposite ends of all the possibilities that their lives had afforded them. Holcum would never admit such a thing, even if she ever allowed the thought to enter her mind. Holcum didn't know another thing, yet, either. She would, though. Her granddaughter didn't plan to ever let her go.

INNOCETTA STOOD at the mouth of the cave letting the strength of the wind blow the winter chill from her skin. She didn't for one moment regret having stayed to care for the old grandmother she'd left lying on her pallet back in the deepest of the interior caves. However, she'd learned what true cold was after surviving the past few tens of days. It had been a bone-numbing in her body that told of old age before its time and had torn the enthusiasm from her waking moments.

Today, though, was the best of the time she'd spent so far out on the inland sea. She'd never before experienced what was happening to her, this that she was seeing as she looked out over the frozen water. The change of the seasons. She'd known it would come while she was here. To be prepared for her stay with her grandmother, she'd gone to the city atmospheric conditions center. From them, she'd carried with her the latest guesses for the arrival of this year's blistering summer heat. For the past three sunrises, she'd come and stood at this opening overlooking the sea, waiting in hopes that each day would be the day; now, it was here, and this hour was her time. The water was still ice covered, but the air was what was amazing. The snow had only moments before been whipping from its drifts across the frozen expanses, sparkling in the intensity of the early morning sun, the coldness of the winter's winds unabated, and then the air had grown quiet.

With the expectation of a long-anticipated event, Innocetta had felt the stillness build, the air charging itself with built-up energy, the very molecules of its smallest particles beginning to vibrate with the gradient changes that were already tearing through the atmosphere, preparing to sweep the cold from the surface of the sea.

Then, it happened. She watched it, this event that she'd so needed to experience in order to burn the cold from her bones. She'd stared out as the smallest of the sea's snowdrifts had begun to stir, and her heart raced as those same drifts churned when the suddenly rising winds grabbed them up and flung them across the ice. Then the drifts were gone, the steaming vapors of their transformation showing the life they'd led, the fingers of the summer's sudden warmth reaching to them and snuffing them out. Innocetta had stood watching this, her air in the cave still cold and motionless, and then the changing winds had reached their tendrils of summer warmth towards her. The coolness of the air around her as it had just started to move belied what was rushing upwards from the surface of the sea. As her hair began to lift with the currents, she had felt the shift, and suddenly the wind was warm. Then, the heat was upon her.

She had breathed in the freshness of the coming summer's new life, standing there looking out over the frozen sea. Holcum had told her over the last few weeks that the caves would warm but slowly, and she had even warned her the innermost recesses would never really warm at all, some of winter's coolness remaining even in the brilliance of the summer heat. Right now, however, Innocetta didn't need what remained of winter's coolness; she needed the heat proffered by arriving summer, and it was here.

She luxuriated, knowing she would come to dread this heat that would soon be too much to bear without a water suit, but for this morning, just to feel the warmth of the wind against her skin was enough. To wash winter's chill from her, she'd gladly trade all the days of wearing her water suit during the coming summer, for just this one hour of heat. When the sun finally reached into her recess and brushed across her face, she lifted her hand to protect her eyes from its fingers of brilliance, and turning, she sensed movement at the far side of the cave.

"Grandmother!" Innocetta stepped away from the sun's warmth, the sudden coldness of winter's chill still very much alive in the solidness of the old woman's mountain retreat. She rubbed her arms for comfort. "You've been so weak, Grandmother. You should have let me help you. It be warm only by the cave mouth where the sun be beating away the snow." She smiled at the memory of the quickness of the transformation she'd just witnessed. "The sun's first kiss burned off much of winter's residue, it being gone even now. The water runs down the cliff face already, a cascade of sound. Listen. Can you hear it?"

HOLCUM FELT a hint of a smile crack her face. That's why she was here, how she had known the weather had turned. In a handful of tenyears, did the granddaughter think she'd learned nothing about the change of the seasons in these caves? Although she was aware of how thin she was under her layers of clothing, and it distressed her to have another's hand touch her, she let Innocetta take her arm. Even with her crutch at her side, she no longer possessed the steady stride of her youth.

At least she didn't stink anymore. Holcum hadn't liked the intruding eyes being there when her filthy rags were taken from her and replaced, but once she was dressed in the fresh cloth of unworn clothing, she was mortified at how badly she must have smelled. She'd cringed when her granddaughter had pulled crates of hygiene supplies from the containers stored for years along the walls. She hadn't known they were there. With no interest in living, she hadn't bothered to look.

This granddaughter that Holcum didn't remember from that visit so long ago told her the illness of her skin was probably the cause of her exteme weight loss, but she hadn't been able to tell her the source of the illness that caused the wasting. Yes, it was a wasting; Holcum knew that. It would have been gratifying had it been something so simple as the decrease of a few pounds, a seasonal loss that would replenish itself when better weather returned. Yet, even with the better, fresh foods from Innocetta that she had been eating these past days, there had been no improvement.

Worse, yet, sometimes Holcum's food would come back up unbidden, and when it didn't, her stomach churned with a burning sensation. The granddaughter had finally convinced her to look at her face and neck in a small mirror she'd brought with her, and Holcum could see the yellowing in her skin most especially where the flesh was thin around her eyes and her neckline. She hadn't wanted to visit the mirror again.

"Help me to the sun, Granddaughter. I will have some warmth today, even if for the rest of this vile summer, I curse the crushing heat." Finally, standing in her precious sun, Holcum struggled to remove the many layers of insulating clothing that had ensured her survival during the cold of the passing season, needing the sun to burn the frost of winter away.

"May I help, Grandmother?" Innocetta took one step her direction, only to be stopped by a twist of the old woman's hand.

"I'm not a child, whatever you may think of me. I can remove my own clothing." Her words bristled with a brittle edge, but after only a few minutes of exhausting effort tugging at the layers of fabric, she gave in, panting with the fatigue of just standing, and she motioned for Innocetta to help her sit and remove her outermost coverings. Once that chore was completed, she waved the granddaughter away, barking roughly, "If I should die today, summer's warmth would be far from my bones. Leave me, girl, and let the sun bake my skin. I'll call for you when I need your help."

INNOCETTA TURNED to face the warmth of the opening, accepting that the old woman would tolerate no further assistance at this time, and it was best to leave the grandmother to her own designs. Learning her ways was what the grandmother had needed done for her, and the granddaughter that was so much like her knew just how to do that. She stayed close, but she stayed busy, and when Holcum was finally tired of sitting on the hard stone, Innocetta was there to wrap her for her return to the caves' winter coldness.

Tomorrow would provide another day of warmth for them to delight in, but the exhaustion from this first day of worshipping the long-neglected sun had taken all their energies. Holcum must rest and rebuild her scant reserves to attack her tomorrow, fresh and new. Innocetta looked forward to the emotional reprieve of the darkness. The heat that had come to them in small amounts this day wouldn't be lost with the passing of the night. It would cool, certainly, assisted by the ice of the lake stridently fighting for its life against this new assault of the sun and the wind. But for the heat to be gone, lost after only one day? It wouldn't be lost for the passing of many of Trasdrom'man's months, and by then, everyone would wish just as fervently for the returning touch of winter's icy fingers.

Not today, though. The coughing that Holcum had battled despite the medicines Innocetta brought had weakened her, and the old frail body, nourished by her granddaughter's willing hand, had barely survived winter's final days. During those times when Holcum had found no strength to fight back, she'd been forced to listen to Innocetta's favorite tales of her own life. There were many of them, and Innocetta had enjoyed regaling her captive audience of one, knowing this was a time when they could learn of each other's lives. Occasionally, the granddaughter was relieved to find Holcum smiling during her tales.

She told one story of her father. It had been the start of a winter when the coldest of the winds had taken many days to arrive. Summer's iron grip was broken, but the cold blast of winter had yet to set in, the season's arrival more hesitant that year. Before the inland sea could freeze and the thick ice blocks cut for the expansive sky windows of Winter City, the condensation of building moisture in the sky had poured torrential rains through the massive gaps that opened to the heavens, flooding the lowest of the streets. The bitterly freezing winds arrived days later to reach their long, chilled fingers to attack the city's inhabitants. Until the ice windows were sealed a week later with the slabs of frozen water carved from the inland sea, cruel fists of cold had slammed into Winter City's open maw, crushing the city's dwellers into their homes, and freezing the water that had poured down the unprotected walls of the city. That year, the water already pooled on the lower floors had turned to sheets of ice.

Innocetta and her brothers had learned to skate that winter. Her father had smoothed strips of a hard, wedge-shaped material and strapped them to their feet. She and her brothers had flown down the corridors, terrorizing unsuspecting inhabitants who were simply trying to navigate the ice on foot without falling down. Innocetta told of one poor woman who had tumbled on the ice, and seeing one of her brothers coming at her down the corridor at full speed, unable to stop, the woman had fainted dead away. The brother had known he couldn't go around the woman sprawled across the width of the corridor, so he'd skated faster, leaping into the air over the woman, his arms flung high over his head to pull him aloft. Innocetta had been skating ahead of him, and had turned, watching, her heart pounding as she prepared for the woman to be sliced in half, only to see her brother land on the other side, his knees bending his body into a graceful crouch as his legs absorbed the impact of the landing in a perfectly executed move, flinging his body laughing down the icy path past her.

With Innocetta's vivid descriptions and wild gesticulations, she occasionally observed Holcum's eyes darting to follow her hand movements, her interest at least aroused. With two brothers and a wonderful family, it was easy to come up with an unending array of stories to decorate the ramparts of the stone-walled rooms that had been so lonely for Holcum for so many years. Innocetta's words danced to the song of companionship and bonds being formed between two women who had no common ground in their lives except that of biology.

They were both of the grandmother, though, and that biology made them very much the same, even if their lives had taken them down roads so very different as to form them into opposite ends of a very powerful and determined lodestone. Just like that magnetized rock, spinning to locate its true path in a storm, no matter how hard life twisted the granddaughter and her grandmother, Innocetta was determined they would endure it together, their dance forming a level of harmony that others might struggle to understand.

"GIRL!" THE OLD woman's voice, at times weak and faltering in its presentation, wasn't weak today. "It's hot in here, and I need you to fan some air over me. Girl, where are you?"

Innocetta stepped from sorting through the myriad disorganized deliveries, much of which had remained in disarray for decades, and some of which was ruined beyond use. There would be days enough for this, she knew, and these things would not go away, no matter how intensely she attacked them. The grandmother was a different matter.

Hearing the strength in the old woman's voice, she smiled. Today was a good day for her grandmother. Some days she was delirious, her body unable to even stand, her mind obviously living back on her great starcruiser, her life as a military woman of importance and power filling her thoughts and clearly there for her, even in the touch of her fingertips on the substance of that imaginary world around her. Innocetta had found many of the things she learned from the rantings of the grandmother's deliriums so outlandish as to hardy be possible, yet the grandmother bore the scars of a great battle. Innocetta especially enjoyed the stories of the black-clothed warriors who could melt away in the darkness, their warriors' suits shifting them to invisibility in others' eyes, with Holcum's weapons alone able to pinpoint their location in the melee of battle. Believe it? Innocetta didn't know that she did. It seemed more like the imaginations of a deteriorating mind taking a remembered fact, and having that fact twist itself as it was pulled across broken synapses in her aging brain. Yet, the stories themselves were fascinating.

Some had been very touching, the stories of a boy's youthful attraction for a girl who played hard to get. The story of the first time the grandmother had met this boy, this *Rom'n,* on the first day of her time at the military academy had made Innocetta smile as she held the old withered hand attached to that faltering body, its palsied shaking telling of advancing nerve damage underneath the yellowing skin.

He must have been some boy, to hear the grandmother describe him in her quavering voice. The surging emotions of the fourteen-year-old she had been came through in her stories as if the events had happened yesterday. She'd been scared, her grandmother had confided, not really wanting to be there. The others had been at the academy for a full standard year, that first important year of getting to know one another, building friendships, and forging bonds that would last throughout a military career that might easily span a century or more.

The girl the grandmother had been had painted a mask of

bravado on her face as she'd brashly strode through the academy dorms, daring others to question her competence or her right to be there, knowing she had no choice where her classes would be or with whom she'd bunk. She'd pretended strength, but she'd indeed been frightened that year, masking it with brittle aggression. She'd found power in the way the other cadets had stepped aside, their whispers coming to her as she walked by, their voices telling her what she needed to hear, that they were impressed by her, envied her, and more importantly, were afraid of her.

When she'd seen the boy, he'd been lying on his bunk, obviously just come from the showers, his hair shiningly damp, and droplets of water still dotting his skin. Everything but the boy had faded from her vision, his pale coloring and white hair an angelic perfection to her. Her own life had been anything but heavenly, and to find such innocence and perfection in that fresh and new boy lying over *her* bunk . . . he was all the good things life had to offer. His was the life she should have had, not the hell foisted upon her when her world had been dashed to pieces as a child. She had blinked away the surprise of moisture in the corners of her eyes. He was a fresh beginning, *could be* a fresh beginning, the start of something better than she'd known; better than the men, the laughing, brutal soldiers who'd come to her at night, her screams only arousing them more; better than the cesspools she'd cowered in, hoping they wouldn't find her; better than her parents killed within her reach, casualties in an unfair and impossible war that had shattered her world many years before.

In that moment, to fourteen-year-old Holcum, the real world had crashed back around her. It hit her hard that his world was a place she could never go, and her past was something she could never undo. Standing there, she took a deep breath, crushed her internal weakness, and she moved forward, her bravado a shield once again. With roughness in her voice, her disguise to cover

222

the attraction and envy she felt roiling inside her, she brusquely awakened him, tauting him and setting him in his place.

When the old woman finished the story, she had lain quietly for a long time, her eyes misty, and her lips mumbling faded and incoherent thoughts to herself, her words not for her granddaughter's ears to hear, the memories leaking from someplace only Holcum's thoughts could travel any longer. Finally, feeling her grandmother would be fine for a while immersed in her past, Innocetta had stepped away.

As time moved into summer, the stories built a new, unknown framework around Holcum, one of intrigue, a life lived among the stars, and a woman who had excelled in a position of power and command, expecting others to bow to her will. Soon Innocetta began taking notes to keep track of what the grandmother had to say. As the old woman began taking more of each day to rest, sleeping on a pallet in the coolest of the summer chambers, Innocetta reread her notes, noticing similarities between the tales. Regge regularly returned with supplies, riding along with those he'd hired to help him, and Innocetta's queries about what she was learning led him to remind her there was an old pod he had taken her mother to visit as a child. It was still stored in the city's warehouse. He even remembered the uniform Holcum had been wearing when she'd been pulled from the scarred machine. Holcum had kept the metal artifacts from the uniform, some memory crystals, as well as all of the buttons and trim that had been removed from the uniform before it was disposed of. He suggested that Innocetta look for the items. It might be a link to the past Holcum told about in her stories, something for the old woman to touch, to trigger even more of her memories.

Innocetta hoped it would be so, and she kept an eye out for the things her uncle had described.

REGGE ENJOYED the beginning of that summer, making numerous trips out to the caves. He no longer dreaded his interactions with Holcum, the fending off of her outbursts, or having to search her out in the caves to make sure she was still alive. Innocetta was his buffer, and the trips once again gave drive and purpose to his life.

On one visit, when Innocetta expressed dismay that the buttons and memory crystals couldn't be found, Regge offered to check in Summer City. It might be possible they'd been left when Holcum came to live in the caves. If so, someone would surely have collected them and stored them with the pod. Holcum was still revered in the city as the stuff of legend, both for her role as a vigilante who had rid the city of the raiders, and as one who had chosen to live out her life as a recluse, alone, surviving even the severity of this world's extreme seasons. They wouldn't have thrown the things away, not on this world where things were rarely disposed of. He also told her of Carli's old military glass that had been able to access the pod to release Holcum. He had reservations about whether it would be any good without Carli to unlock it, but possibly it was still with all the things stored from his friend's life. Perhaps it would interact with the pod one more time. If it could be found, it was worth a try.

On one trip of his trips, he brought exciting news. The glass had turned on and worked for him. He didn't know why. He'd stopped by to search for it among Carli's things. Then he'd visited the warehouse to see if Holcum's artifacts might be stored with the pod. With the glass at his side as he rummaged through the items inside, he must have pressed on something, because when he picked up a small bag he thought might hold the items he was looking for, he discovered the glass up and running, a highspeed download in progress.

He had taken the glass to the city spaceport, aware from long association that the bulk of the city's funds for technology went into keeping those facilities updated with the best of equipment. They would be the ones to tell him what the information on the glass was all about if anyone could. Going back to pick up the glass several days later, he'd been surprised at the excitement among the spaceport's engineers over the contents. Apparently, the pod had overridden the glass's security locks and downloaded all its information into its data files. However, as soon as the engineers had opened the glass, and the pod's information had been downloaded from the glass to the city's database, the glass had locked itself again, and it had stayed that way despite their efforts to reengage it, including taking it back to the pod and placing it inside.

What they'd found amazed them. It seemed the pod they'd been unable to communicate with a half century ago had decided to communicate with them. They were unsure just what had been done to trigger the communication, but they had everything. The information dump off the glass contained even the most confidential information from the pod. One of the city's port engineers suggested that the trigger might have been a combination of the military pod, the military-issue glass, and some other possible trigger device, that it wasn't unusual to have emergency equipment set up to release all important data under a specific series of circumstances. It was only conjecture, he said, but it made sense since after they'd downloaded the pod's information, the glass's security protocols resumed control, sealing it against additional access.

The information they'd received told them the pod was a MegaCorp military escape pod from a hyper-secret starstrike cruiser whose construction had been so closely guarded that the ship was never officially named. The download revealed all the ship's recorded battle information up until the actual destruction of the ship. Apparently, the survivor of this pod had been very high up in the old MegaCorp military echelon. If that could be proven, the woman who'd ridden it might be able to command help from the remnants of the economic arm that had spun off the original MegaCorp corporate structure.

Regge questioned Innocetta, asking her if she wanted him to try to get help for Holcum. Obviously, she was very close to the end of her life, but to live so miserably was not what either of them would wish for her.

She pulled him aside, finding the coolest of the caves to try to offset the heat forcing its way inside. "Regge, she be getting so bad, and nothing seems to help. I keep her cool in the heat of the day, and I watch her carefully when her mind seems to wander. However, her weight falls more and more. That and her skin. It be not as it should be. The yellow tint and the brown color just keep getting worse." She looked him in the eyes, her own moist with tears. "I fear she may die any day. When she coughs, it seems it will tear her apart, and her mind be so often not clear."

"Many doctors on this world we don't have; but know that, you already do. A healer in the city, there be. Send her this way, I could, if that be what you wish." Regge shook his head in doubt. "Like this healer, though, Holcum never did. If she'll see her, I cannot say."

"There be no one else, then? I must stay here and watch her die?" She turned her face away, and Regge could see the emotion bleeding from her in the heaving of her shoulders.

He stepped to her, her attachment to the old woman he and a one-time friend had released from that cryo pod so many years ago stirring his desire to help. "Lived a long time, I have, and claim to know many people, I can. Have friends, I do, Innocetta. Ask around, I will. To offer me help, they'll be quick. A little time you must give me, though. To do that, can you?" He touched her chin to get her to look at him. "Be that acceptable?"

WITH HIS OFFER of help, Innocetta felt the bulk of her load lift from her shoulders, and she looked at him with tearfully grateful eyes, nodding her head. She'd grown to care for the old woman, that was true. She'd learned to wrestle her for control, also, but they now wrestled in a dance they both understood. The old woman had learned she needed help to survive, and Innocetta had learned what help to give and when to let well enough alone. Together, they had formed a partnership of sorts, and together, they'd survive.

At least, they would if Innocetta could get someone there to help with her grandmother's failing health. However, she'd done all she could, and now it was up to Regge. She hoped he didn't let her down.

"NO! DON'T ASK more of me, girl. You've asked too much, already, and I've given too much as it is. I'll die before this summer is done. I have no more life left in me."

Holcum's ever-more palsied nerves were giving her a break today, and she drew herself up from the floor, pushing away the granddaughter's offered hand, her crutch the only support she would accept. This had turned out to be a day of strength for the grandmother, except this time, she and the granddaughter were tightly entwined in their dance, the will of the grandmother matching steps with one equally as good as she.

"Grandmother!" Innocetta spoke with the full force of her will, brooking no resistance on this. "We've finally read the information from your pod, the one you arrived in many years ago—"

Holcum's hand flew up to stop that which she didn't want to hear, nearly overbalancing her tenuous act of standing, as she interrupted, refusing to turn to face her granddaughter. Her crutch wobbled as she spoke, taking direction from her inflamed muscles, and revealing the rising levels of her anger. She attempted to steady it as she  barked her next words.

"It wasn't mine. It never was, and don't remind me I ever spent time in that monstrosity." A stab of fear at her granddaughter's revelation coursed through her limbs. What would the old pod tell? What *could* it tell? She tried to think, to remember. That life had been lived so long ago. Why did it have to return to haunt her now?

"We know the years now since the accident that caused your injuries. Somehow, Regge got an old glass that had belonged to someone you both knew, his friend Carli, to read a signal from the pod. All your old shipboard information was there, even about the other pods that also escaped the destruction. We know information about you now that no one knew all those years ago." Innocetta's face shone with excitement. "You were an important person. We might be able to get medical help for your illnesses."

Important person? Like a flower just opened, the events and memories of a lifetime ago were, for Holcum, as fresh as yesterday. Her eyes narrowed with the jolt of memories her granddaughter's revelation flashed through her mind. Holcum's abused authority. Her direct superior, CaptGen'l Bofsky, and their fight over the last Rejuvie. The deaths they'd caused in the name of MegaCorp. Her youth and undamaged body. Gods! She'd been beautiful, with a perfect body! It was as if, for that one moment, the intervening years had never punished Holcum's poor body and soul with the life she had endured on this, her unwanted home.

Only one of the memories was a good one. The rest were as distasteful as bile, the things no one on this world knew, things Holcum had long accepted as part of herself, but things she thought had disappeared into the shadows of the past. She didn't know which of these might surface with the information the granddaughter had uncovered.

One memory was stronger than the others. Her youth.

Holcum collapsed in on herself at the unwelcome reminder,

and her eyes misted over. She brushed them past Innocetta as she turned towards the opening in the cave wall. Out there, somewhere, gazing out to the sea, deep in thought about what she had been told, she saw her reflection in time's mirror, her dark hair, and the smooth skin she had used as a tool for her own advantage. She'd never dreamed they would be taken from her. Death as a possibility she had always accepted, knowing that living a military life meant living the edge of existence, its end at times sudden and quick. But to *live* death, to endure the massive disfigurement she now bore was never contemplated by that long-ago military officer whose one career goal had been to captain her own starstrike battle cruiser. That was what she saw in the distance, as the white-capped waves tossed their spray over the surface of the inland sea.

Holcum's mind was jarred, and she felt the fragile control she had managed to maintain over her abused remnant of a life slipping away with the loss of the pod's silence. She shook a fist at her granddaughter, lashing out in her raw, cracked voice.

"You'll take everything from me! My life was stolen on this cursed-awful world, and I've only managed to claim the right to live here alone. Now, I no longer have that. Do you also plan to take from me the right to die a death of my own choosing?"

She struck at the granddaughter using her crutch as her weapon, the very action creating a maelstrom of cloth, limbs, and wood as Holcum tried to stabilize herself, before collapsing with her compromised dignity against the roughness of the stone floor.

INNOCETTA STEPPED forward and knelt to rescue the brittle old woman puddled in front of her. Reaching a hand to touch her face, her fingers came away wet with Holcum's tears.

"Grandmother," she whispered. "I be not trying to take anything from you. I be only trying to give life to you. You deserve better than this lingering death you be living. Please let me do this for you. You were important on that long-ago ship you helped command. Regge feels those with power on distant worlds will respond with requests to aid you. Please, Grandmother. Let me do this for you."

As she lifted the husk of the military officer that Holcum once was, the old woman let herself lean against her grand-daughter's strength, unable to stop the tears of regret for the loss of her youth and her body's perfection that flowed down her cheeks. They were losses too much for anyone bear.

"Grandmother? May I help?"

Holcum's eyes remained on the floor. "Do what you must, girl. You'll do it anyway, and I don't have the strength to fight you over this."

Innocetta looked up at the ceiling and smiled. Her grand-mother would get the help she needed. She was confident of that. All she needed to do now was get word to Regge, and that would happen when he made his next trip out to the sea. She could wait. She had no choice, but she could still wait. Having no choice just made it easier to bear.


"I DON'T like this, leaving her alone." Innocetta turned to Regge, studying his lined face in the coolness of the red trans-port's interior. At her side, she fingered the glare goggles he'd offered. Even in the comparative dimness of this protected space, the sun was still bright through the deeply tinted windows, mak-ing the man's furrowed visage tell the true length of his years. She knew he must be nearly as old as the grandmother he had provided for all these years.

His summer trips had aged him. She could see the difference, one she'd noted with each visit he'd made to see her. The many trips to the inland sea were tiring. An old man like Regge ought to be able to rest at home, enjoying grandchildren and good food. Instead, he was here once again, this time transporting her back to the city, and hopefully returning her to the sea before nightfall. In his age-roughened voice, he reassured her, "Fine, she was, for many years before you came. Do her in, one day will not. What you be taking this day to do just might make her well." He smiled at her, his look reassuring and honest. "Pick up the things from the pod, we will, and off to make a request, we will be. Bring quick results, your grandmother's name did, those officials my friends contacted knowing of her well. Quite important in the military, she was, and the heavens and planets, they said, move for her, they would." He smiled as he continued. "Quite impressed, my friends were. A little more prestige, I now have, after all these years."

Innocetta smiled at his small pleasures, as she slipped her goggles on her face and sat in the coolness of the old, much-loved transport, watching the scenery fly by at the breakneck speeds that were possible on this very flat, empty part of the desert. Occasionally, she caught glimpses of green, the plants in the low areas able to reach long roots to draw moisture from the submerged water table. Those were the places that looked cool and welcoming to her, but she knew as a fact they would be roastingly hot, just like those areas that were hard-packed dirt. Watching her reflection in the surface of the shaded glassine, she idly queried Regge, "The information from the pod's download will convince them to send the message for a medic to come?"

"Aye, be surprised, I would, not to see on the next transport a medic of the very best caliber. But the only proof we need, the download be not. Stop to get the ID crystals and uniform trim, we will. All together, convince them, it will. Send the request, they must. For us to have this information, know, they will, that researched, our facts be, and from the military, the old woman be." Regge laughed aloud in the comfort of the transport, causing Innocetta to look his direction and smile. "Called her the old woman, I did. I be as old. To call me, use what names, other

231

people do?" He looked over at his traveling companion and winked. "Old, do not get, Innocetta. Not on this world. To keep us young, no means, here, there be."

She rested her hand for a moment on his arm, returning his smile. "Just to keep the grandmother alive be all I could wish for now, my friend. Youth I cannot keep, nor can I collect it for the grandmother. A medic would be a nice second option, though. Do you think your friends can get me that?"

"Try, they have, and continue to try, they will. If be done, it can, then have your medic, you will. Trust my friends, I do."

Innocetta rested both of her hands in her lap, leaning her head back on the seat, her eyes finally heavy with the steady rhythm of the ride and the coolness of the transport's well-maintained, luxurious interior. "Then, so do I, Regge." She pulled the goggles from her face, and then she was still. Within a minute, there were the soft sounds of snoring from her side of the transport.

REGGE TRAVELED the rest of the way in silence. From time to time, he glanced over at the young woman sleeping in the transport next to him, her profile outlined against the desert scene visible through the far window. His mind raced with thoughts that many would think should only come from a much younger man.

*Gods, what a beautiful profile! All those years ago, if come out of that pod, this had, how different my life might have been. How different Holcum's life might have been.*

Then, with a shake of his head, he turned back to the terrain in front of him and whispered his reproach to himself, "On you, shame, old man. A girl, she be, and lived four of her lives, you have. For still looking and being attracted, on your old body, shame."

However, that didn't stop him from turning to glance again at the beautiful creature next to him. And again. And then one more time before the transport pulled into the city proper. She was that beautiful.

Regge finally reached to wake her, knowing he might chastise his body time and time again, but Holcum's granddaughter would be just as alluring every time, and he could not stop himself from enjoying that.

IN THE SMALL CLUB, of which he was a respected member, Regge ran his hand across the swirled wooden surface of a table, moving his fingers in a semicircle as he neared the base of his drinking container on each pass, the dim light in the room making it seem somewhat cooler than it really was. Much of the perceived coolness came from the ice in his container, the brown liquid caressing its frozen surface carrying a bite when it touched his throat. He looked up to see an old friend pause and then sit in the chair opposite the low table, placing his own drink there, also. Nodding, Regge raised his glass to take a sip as his mind prepared his words. The friend spoke first.

"Want to come, the medic does not."

Regge frowned. "Under contract, he still be? Told, I was, required to come, he'd be." He swirled his drink, the ice inside making a tinkling sound as it contacted the container's clear, brittle surface. "What be there to do about this medic, that to come, doesn't want?"

Smiling from under a heavy helmet of naturally gray hair, the old friend chuckled. "Doesn't want to come, I said. Not, *won't* come." He took his own drink, allowing himself the time to sip the liquid and run it around inside his mouth, its sharpness assaulting his tongue and traveling all the way into his nostrils. "Just married, it seems he be, and at a very young age, at that, all on a world several systems over."

"Come, then, he will?" Regge, unsure of the friend's response, worried. Always, he worried. Innocetta had wanted to return to her grandmother before nightfall, but then they'd seen

233

her mother, Uncle Regge's sweet girl, Arianna, as she was out walking to the shops. Not to miss this time with family, it had been easy to get Innocetta to stay the night. That had given Regge plenty of time to dandy up for this evening with his friends and associates. He tapped the wood under his drink with his fingertips after he set it down. "Realwood. To flaunt the wealth."

"Here it be for no other reason than to impress the locals," and his friend coughed softly. "Doing the same, it be, for me. Very impressed, anytime with realwood, I be. More impressed, though, I be with the ice. Cut from the slabs in the winter and sold in the summer. Thought of it, I should have, then as rich as these around us, I'd be. More money than you or I have together there be in this room in these deep pockets." His friend rubbed his leathery old hands together in anticipation. "Deft be my hand, and rich these pockets be. Start a weight loss program, shall we? To take the few credits I propose will be as nothing to these deep-pocketed corporation officials."

"Come," Regge softly redirected, "the medic will, you say?"

"Rest easy, old friend. Enjoy the night. Your good friends, these be, whom you've asked for help, and fail you, they will not. Another drink, and to tonight's special guest, you, I will introduce. A good one to know, he be, with connections to the people we wish to enjoy as friends and associates." The friend stood, downing the last of his drink. "A night for pleasure, this be, the finest of our world's things to enjoy. Some from other worlds, not impressed, would they be. Ah, for us to be content, we must." He turned, heading to the next room, the furniture set up for dining, with the entire gathering able to sit at the one enormous table.

*Yes*, Regge thought with relief. Innocetta would have her medic, and old Holcum would have her renewed chance at life. Too bad they hadn't known this information from the pod all those decades ago. If they'd had this new knowledge about

Holcum's position in the military, they might have been able to command help from offworld for her, and Holcum's injuries might have been corrected. If that had been possible, she might have lived a very different life. Better? Regge had no way to know that, but he was certain it wouldn't have been as bad as the nightmare she'd survived for the past half-century.

When Innocetta and he were again with Holcum, he'd ensure that her final few things from her previous life were hers again, the ID cards and memory crystals that had been left behind in the city so long ago. Poor Holcum had so little in her life. Perhaps those things would be the source of better memories than the ones she'd built for herself. He could only hope. That, and he could trust in Innocetta's determination to cushion her grandmother's life as much as possible for the rest of her days. In his own, final moments, he should be so lucky as to have a grandchild to care so much about him.

*Luck be tough there*, he thought to himself. *Have to have children first, I would, and that be one thing to go back and redo that I cannot.* The others looked at him as he laughed to himself in that old man's way that makes others see the elderly as peculiar. Regge didn't care, though. He didn't even notice. Suddenly, all he could think of was the food he could smell and how he hadn't eaten all day. That's one of the reasons he was here, after all, and he did enjoy himself as his friend had suggested.

# —Chapter 10—

*indentured servant (en den' chərd sər' vənt) n. a person who signs a contract guaranteeing a pledge of service in exchange for a certain benefit*

*—Wang's Cross-Cultural Dictionary, c. 2079 AD*

THE MEDIC closed his eyes in exhaustion. The trip had ground into his bones, and he couldn't believe this place, this *world* could possibly be so primitive. He rested his hand on his medic's bag at his side, his fingers toying with the latches as if already reaching inside for the medications he would find there, the rocking of the transport not restful to his stomach in any form or fashion. He groaned as the transport shifted violently over a rough place in the roadway—if this track through the heat and desolation could be called that—and his stomach hurled bile into his throat. Soon the day would be over, and he could contemplate his return to his new bride.

He cursed the contract. He'd signed it. It had paid for his medical training and for his relocation to that world he loved, and that his new bride loved even more. He'd been so pleased with himself, and now he was paying the price. He let his eyes rove the passing landscape. Dirt, with dust swirling with the slightest breeze. The sun, washing death upon everything. Occasional small trees—the medic didn't pretend to understand how they survived. He pictured the woman he'd left behind on a distant world. A year or more he'd be gone. Maybe less, if his patient healed quickly. He hoped his bride would be waiting when he returned. He quickly brushed that thought from his mind. She would be waiting. She would be. She must be.

He focused on his more immediate mission. He didn't know what he'd find when he reached this "inland sea" where his patient resided. Without a comprehensive system of communication across the surface of this world, there'd been no way to find out anything without actually going to meet her.

*Her.* At least he knew that much, so he'd brought supplies appropriate for female applications. He'd been instructed to take a DNA scan, also. He had no reader, so he wouldn't be able to do anything with the information, other than send it back to Mega-Corp for evaluation. What the point was in that, he was unsure. What could MegaCorp have to do with this? In his time aboard the ship, he'd pondered that day in and day out. His patient had to be either a political or military person of some importance to have this trip forced upon him by the very highest authorities. Yet, MegaCorp had no political or military presence in the galaxy, at least not that the medic was aware of.

He cleared his throat, asking, "Much farther?"

"Aye, mas, patient, you must be. Arrive, we will, in time." His driver nodded with a smile, his eyes hidden by his gold-tinted goggles, but his hand giving the medic a thumbs up.

It was proving to be quite far to this inland sea. He assumed this personage of importance chose to live this far out because of the beauty of this isolated location. He readied himself for greenery, real greenery, perhaps even stretching down to a beach fronting a gloriously wet, cooling beach. Trees must grow in such a location, their leafy heights providing glorious shade from this *awful* heat. That would be something to make this trip worth while, an adventure to share with his bride when he returned to her arms.

A hand on his shoulder startled him, and the medic jerked erect, his eyes open, as he realized he'd actually fallen asleep. Outside the transport's windows, he could tell no difference in the terrain, other than a rise of mountains that seemed to be their destination. He breathed deeply, the extra oxygen taken in to wash the grogginess from his system, and he smiled, antici- pating what must be on the other side of the rise. At last he would know something other than dirt and sun on this world. His own was hot, but at least it was green. This one was miserable, and if his contract had assigned him here, he'd have torn it up and found some other way to repay all the expenses he'd incurred in his training.

As the transport slowed to a stop, a voice spoke softly to him, "Ready, your water suit be, and need it, you will, mas, outside of the transport. Pump your bladderpack. Remember, you must." With those words, a wall of heat slammed into the cooled com- partment that had protected them from the sun, as the sides of the transport swung wide to reveal the fury of the day's torment.

The medic gasped, as he stood from his seat and pulled his bag of supplies into the sunshine with him. He held one hand to shade his eyes as he stepped after the men leading him to the darkness of a cave opening just ahead, the light painful to his off- world eyes even through the protective goggles.

He groused to himself, *Cursed medical degree that brought me to this! I should have been a politician. At least then I'd have been able to stay home with my beautiful wife, eat the foods I so enjoy, and not be here on this cursed world. At least these caves should provide some relief, as I traverse them to the other side.*

Moving into the dim relief of the cave's interior, the medic pulled the goggles from his face and was taken aback to see what looked like rough living quarters just inside.

"Where's the estate?" he asked.

From the shadows, invisible to the medic, with his eyes not yet adjusted, a pleasant, well-modulated woman's voice called out, "Estate? What do you mean?"

"The woman who requires my services. I was summoned from offworld. I'm headed to her home on the sea. Has the driver brought me to the wrong location? If so, surely you can tell me where it is. "

The woman in the darkness let out a ripple of laughter, laced with only the barest of humor in its undertones. "I understand. I be so sorry for the misunderstanding. It be not what you expected. Come, I will show you the sea."

Into the light stepped something else the tired medic found quite unexpected. The voice was attached to a beautiful woman, and that surprised him. Still unsure whether he'd come to the correct location, he followed her, the path meandering through a series of several caves, each partially filled with boxes, crates, and containers. Finally approaching a bright opening in the rock wall of one of the caves, the woman paused, cautioning the medic to shield his eyes.

"The sea is through here?" He motioned to the light.

"Not here, but the next cave opens to the sea. The sun be bright this time of day, and hot, it will be, also. The sun off the sea will burn skin quickly. Guard yourself. You have a fresh bladder on?" When she saw his perplexed look, she smiled. "Your water suit. You understand what that be? I can see you wear one, and smart, that be. The bag of water. Press it against your chest to cool your limbs. You'll be glad you did once the sun hugs your skin." She smiled. "Also, your goggles." She pointed to them with a finger, then nodded to the next chamber. "Ready to brave the light?"

The medic nodded. He was puzzled when the woman touched his arm and motioned for him to join her at the doorway. He froze and his heart beat faster as she stepped to him, a smile forming on her lips. She reached one hand to his chest and pushed. He laughed as he felt the cooling moisture from the forgotten water suit caress his body, and at the same time, he was both relieved and disappointed. She was beautiful, and for a moment, he'd misread her attentions. He'd wanted her for that instant, thinking his wife was far away; and then he'd been overwhelmed with relief to know she hadn't been interested in him.

She stepped back and nodded her head at him. "Being from offworld, you don't realize the truth of the heat. Now, you be ready." Innocetta stepped forward towards the final cave, then turned to the medic to encourage him to follow her. "Let's go inside to see the outside."

She chuckled as she walked into the brightness, the medic once again unable to see until his eyes adjusted to the change; in spite of their golden tint, the goggles gave only a partial relief from the strength of the sun.

"I MUST give a dose of painkiller first." The medic looked up from his position on the rocky floor of the cave, as he knelt at his patient's side. He pulled a pad from his bag and tore the wrapper open. With a stroke, he moistened the strip of skin just over Holcum's bared backbone. "I'll need it to rest for a few moments, and then I can apply the strip to draw the DNA." He watched the old shoulders shift as the woman under his care twisted her head to question him.

"How much pain will there be? I must prepare for whatever you do." Tiredness of life filtered through each word.

He smiled in reassurance. "None, my dear. There'll be no pain at all. You'll feel the pressure of my hand and nothing else.

I don't have a reader to tell me the results of the DNA scan, but that's the responsibility of MegaCorp, in any case. They are funding this trip for your care, and that's where I'll send my readings."

He was horrified at her condition, in spite of his easy words. He was a medic, and although he was still young, he'd seen his share of damaged and abused bodies. However, he'd never observed battle damage this severe left unrepaired. When he'd first rested eyes on his patient, he'd known another thing, too. The test for the skin condition would require him to cut; and once he was gone, the damage he did would provide all the pain it wanted. Only time would take that away. He would make the cuts, because that was what MegaCorp required, but just to look at the old woman was all he needed to know exactly what was wrong with her, and that it was something that couldn't be fixed here in this place. On another world, the mend would be as minor as a repair to a long-ignored tooth. Here, the old woman would suffer and die. The medic couldn't prevent that. Her liver was gone. It wouldn't repair itself, and all the medications he had in his bag couldn't replace the function of that precious organ.

It broke his heart to think about telling her beautiful grand-daughter. He'd thought for a moment she'd be his. He chuckled at how he could have imagined that. All she cared about was what was best for her grandmother, and all the grandmother cared about was herself. Even the medic could see that. Alone with him one day, the old woman had pleaded with him to do something to let her die. As soon as the granddaughter had stepped in, the grandmother had changed her words, mumbling as if she hadn't said anything.

The medic later told on the old woman, and the grand-daughter laughed, trusting in the medic's goodness and trust-worthiness. Still, he'd actually considered the old woman's request for a moment; but just for a moment, as there are some roads that are best not traveled, even if the way tempts the traveler to take them every now and then. Sometimes, safe is the way to go, because safe will lead the traveler home, even if safe and tedious are sometimes two words for the very same thing.

THE PAPER, folded and refolded many times before it was finally handed to Innocetta, had all traces of wording erased from the creases. She was surprised to find the report had been returned so quickly. After Regge picked it up in the city, she hadn't been disturbed to find he'd looked at it, but she couldn't understand what it was really about. For some reason, the report contained a request for her grandmother to travel to the city. Someone thought it vital Holcum meet with a person of some importance who couldn't take the time to come to her.

Innocetta had argued with Regge about that. Walking back and forth as he'd tried to explain to her just how important this was, she'd felt the frustrating pressures of her grandmother's needs combined with the *must* this paper had thrown at her, and the walls had started to close in. She had taken the report and followed the caves' circuitous paths down to the small beach at the bottom of the cliffs. She needed to think, and while the cool of the interior caves where Regge waited on her was wonderful during the heat of the summer, it was also dim in the shadowed spaces, and sometimes, only the sun could brighten her dark thoughts of confusion.

She unfolded the report. Tracing its words with her fingers, she came to a much-folded spot, and holding it up to the sun's light, she searched for fragments of lettering in the near transparency of the fold's softness. This information would need to be pondered, in spite of Regge's argument that Holcum should just get in the transport and ride away. This was the grandmother's haven of safety, and she wouldn't give up that security without good cause. Her grandmother must understand all this paper asked, and how could Innocetta convince her if she herself was unsure of its importance? Vast sums, perhaps, Regge had encouraged. For that, he was certain Holcum would travel to the city. Innocetta knew funds would be appreciated, but just how they might be involved with her grandmother was another matter. She'd have to quiz him again, drawing out the answers she desired from him one at a time.

Satisfied to finally have a plan of approach, she rose from her beach and made her way into the coolness of the caves. If her mother's old "uncle" couldn't accommodate her in this, there would be no trip to the city for the old woman. This understanding was important, because the grandmother would ask. When she did, her granddaughter must feel secure in her knowledge of the matters. Innocetta knew this about herself: she had no skill in supporting a side she didn't believe in, and to encourage this trip to town for her grandmother with no understanding in her own mind would be impossible.

Laying out the paper before the man who had been the grandmother's longest and most faithful ally, Innocetta tried to make her questions very clear. One line at a time, the impart of the words did make their meanings apparent to the granddaughter, a woman who was doing her very best to be the buffer and supporting mettle for the old soldier resting nearby. This letter told of a great corporation that had incurred the wrath of a generation. The rising tide of incensed anger at the abuses of public trust exposed behind the corporation's benevolent facade as it was being torn asunder had polarized the civilized worlds into stripping the corporation of its military arm, leaving the only substantial military organization in the galaxy to splinter off to be sold to the highest bidders, enabling world governments to gain control of what should have rightfully been theirs in the first place.

Along with this shattering of long-held military might, a umbrella of protection was put firmly into place so no military personnel would ever have to worry about being shunted aside, their service record discounted, and their pay accounts unreimbursed for time served and duty honored. Every MegaCorp military conscript or adjutant, from the lowest underprv't to the most highly decorated stargen'l, must remain on the payroll in perpetuity until DNA evidence firmly and unequivocally determined that person's demise. Should evidence be discovered that an employee of the now-extinct MegaCorp military arm was still alive, no matter how distant in time that discovery might be, all accrued funds and accumulated interest must be immediately disbursed to that person, no matter where he or she currently resided.

REGGE'S FINGER traced the words on the paper. He lifted his eyes to catch Innocetta watching him, and he let a broad smile cross his face. He ran a tongue over his lips as he chuckled.

"See, you do, now. Care for the old woman, I have. Responsibility for her life, I've felt, but to care for her, I also feel. For you, too, my dear Innocetta." He turned his head as his eyes misted, and with a sniffle of emotion, he continued, "When small, a daughter to me, your mother was, and consider her dear to me, even now, I do."

He turned his eyes to look back at the beauty he'd seen twice in his lifetime, once in the mother, and now in the daughter. He knew Innocetta would never be his, and at times damned his body for wishing in that small way men's bodies do in the presence of great beauty; but just to be in her company from time to time had been his life made over these several months.

"For you, now, the same I feel. Brought joy to this old man, you have, and do anything for you, I would." Regge dropped his eyes in embarrassment at his confession.

Innocetta placed her hand on his old man's arm, the brittle skin underneath tortured by the many years it had fought with this world's extremes, and she whispered with a smile, "Your concern for my grandmother when no one cared or would have faulted you for letting her go has won my heart, dear Regge. In the city, I didn't grow up with you at my side. Even here, in my heart, I've never called you Uncle, but you've come to be that to me. May I call you by my mother's cherished name for you?"

A new bond had formed between the two, a bond of family, one they would need in order to convince the old woman in the next chamber. They would go in as one, and their combined strength would be required to sway Holcum's decision to go where she didn't want to go, no matter how much assistance it might bring. Holcum didn't care about benefits that MegaCorp might provide, but Regge did, and with Innocetta now on his side, Holcum wouldn't be the victor in this upcoming war of the wills.

BLOOD RAN down the walls of Holcum's memories.

This *going,* this *MegaCorp!* They wouldn't let even this long-ago memory slip from her into the darkest recesses of her furthest nightmares. They wanted to bring her past back to haunt her, again and again. She wasn't that person, anymore, and to go, to make that portion of her life part of her existence again, was to be accessory to her soul's torment as it was bared to this world's scrutiny once again.

Holcum turned on her pallet, her ravaged face brushing the smooth cloth pillowing her head. Her breath tore from her old body as a choking sob rose from her chest. She brushed one knobby-fingered hand across the roughness of her face, letting her thoughts escape into the night's darkness, her lips mouthing the words.

"Once, this was beautiful. A boy desired this from me, and I only saw it as a way to control him, to make him do my bidding. Now, I'm to parade the parody I have become in front of the people of this world, and they'll laugh at how low my life has taken me."

She wrapped her fingers around the hem of her coverings and flung them back. Struggling to stand alone in the darkness, her breath wheezed as she grabbed the top of her crutch, pulling herself painfully to her feet. In the darkness of the cave's interior, she hobbled across well-remembered steps, slowly finding her way to an opening to the sea. The sounds of the water, night-still, its *swish-swish* as it rounded the boulders bordering the cliff's base, told of the waves' touch as they amorously encouraged the rocks, sharing the promise of the lovers they could become, their nights given back to them in ecstasy, if only they would just fall to join the waves in the watery depths. If not, the waves sang as their promises floated forth, they would never leave their adored ones alone in their pursuit, promising each night to faithfully return, the sensual caressing of the stones always giving their assurance that they would honor their lovers' suggestion of joy and ecstasy at the bottom of the sea. The whispered sounds brushed Holcum's ears in a familiar melody, one she had learned by heart over the decades of her isolation.

There were times Holcum had known the stones to accept the waves' offers, the storms crashing through, the stones rearranged and occasionally gone when the sun's brilliance returned. She could join them, be gathered in the arms of the waters, carried to the ecstasies of joy the waves offered at the bottom of their sea. One step was all she needed to take, just to stand with her crutch and lean out a bit too far. She would gasp as her balance was shorn from her, the scrambling of her hands perhaps leaving marks on the rock's surface, her involuntary cries waking no one. She would, perhaps, be dead as she hit the water, and if she weren't, she would slip under the waves, the sea covering her leg that no longer worked, the torn and decimated skin of her face, and the age that had taken what her cryo pod couldn't. This could happen now, and it would be seen as the disoriented night wanderings of a senile old woman, the death regrettable but not unexpected. How easy it would be!

She sighed. That way wasn't hers. In the morning, old Regge and that damned granddaughter of hers would give her their reasons, and they would plead with her to give in. Holcum would fight them. To do so wouldn't satisfy her and wouldn't make her happy. Only the return of her youth would make her happy, and being honest with herself for this one night, she admitted she hadn't been happy even then. Too much had already been stripped from her, had been done to her, and had been scarred across her soul before she'd left her childhood behind. Happiness was someone who had parents, a home, safety, and whose child-body hadn't been ravaged as the spoils of a war that should have never happened to her world.

She wouldn't let her past rule her now. She'd do what the granddaughter and the old man asked of her. She didn't want it, and wouldn't submit peacefully, but she would submit. Those choices had been taken away from her, and this choice at which she now stood, this opening on the cliff face above the sea, this precipice she could retreat from or step over, was not a choice she would ever make, but the pretense sometimes made it easier to accept the choices others made for her. After all, even a wild animal prefers to run, that being its first option. It will attempt to do so when being hounded by its pursuers. Only when it knows it has tried to escape and failed will it give up and fight, to do that which is necessary for the wildness in the animal to finally accept defeat, letting the stronger attacking force take its throat in its jaws, its lifeblood drained in the doing.

Holcum still had some fight left, even if she knew the final outcome; and the fight *would* give her some pleasure. No, she wouldn't make it easy for them. She smiled at the thought as she turned and made her way back to her pallet, sleep finally slipping its warm arms into her bedding to snuggle with her for the rest of the night.

HOLCUM BARKED her laugh to all in the transport. She was seeing this city for the first time since she'd left it all those decades ago. She'd seen Regge's old red transport repeatedly over the years, and was riding in it even now, but it had always been the same. She'd imagined the city remaining as she'd known it, but she knew better. Nothing remains the same for half a century. Not caring, she'd left it behind without regrets, and she'd found no reason to show an interest in it for all these years.

Now, she knew she'd been wise. In spite of the changes she knew to expect, it was the same city. Not just the same name, but the same city. She looked as the transport moved through streets vacated by the heat, the daytime sun keeping people indoors, the look as empty as it must appear during the deepest of the winter's cold.

"Pitiful," Holcum's cracked voice spat out.

"Grandmother?" Innocetta turned to the old woman at her side. "What be pitiful, Grandmother?"

The old woman turned to look at her granddaughter, her eyes narrowing as she saw her against the backdrop of the city. As she had at first those final months of winter, she saw again in Innocetta's face her own, looking back from time's mirror. What pained her most cuttingly was knowing the face next to her, the one that had been hers so many lifetimes ago, another world ago, in fact, could exit this transport and exact nothing but praise and admiration from anyone who might pass by. Meanwhile, she, Holcum, who had been given that face as a child, only to have it taken away with no explanation of what had caused the destruct-tion of her world, wore only a monster's face. The reflection of her image in the glassine window openings told the truth. Sitting beside the young woman, Holcum looked old and beaten, one side of her face revealing the remains of the beauty she'd once touted, and the other boasting the monster her scars had made of her. She blinked back tears. The information from the pod, once she'd relented to hearing some of it, had told only of the damage, not the cause. There was no one for her to rail at, to curse for what had happened to her, no one to absorb the misery she'd endured all these years.

She spat her answer, "All these years, nothing has been done to improve this place. It's exactly the same, only older and more worn." She blew out a disgusted breath of air. With hearing her remark, Regge, driving the old transport for this trip, laughed loudly. Holcum jerked her head at him. "Why do you laugh, old man? You live here, and this place reflects on you."

"In fixing up this old place, a point, there be? Hmm. If to waste your efforts, you want." He laughed again at the thought. "Built for sturdiness, this place be. Not for beauty. Rule this world, cold and heat do. Holcum, change that, none of its people can. Focus on what be important, we must, and living, that be. If live, we cannot, then important, the city be not."

"You old fool," Holcum barked. "The fight hasn't even begun, and you've given up, already. Why don't you just pack up and leave this hellish world?"

He laughed at the absurdity of it, this time loudly and long.

Holcum hissed, "What's funny about my question, old man? Tell me that before I take my crutch and knock you in the back of your head."

"No real answer, I have for you. That, for me to answer, I've never been asked." He chuckled. "To gather all the things of my life and just leave? Impossible, it be."

Innocetta diverted Holcum from her tirade with a simple response. "Grandmother, this be home. Why would we want to leave our home?"

Holcum spat, "Home? Thank the stars this isn't my home."

Innocetta laughed softly at Holcum's remark. "Why, it *be* your home, Grandmother. I've grown up here, and my mother before me. You were here before that. If this be not your home, then where?"

Holcum worked her jaw, her eyes narrowing at the very idea she should consider this her home. "Up there," was all her anger allowed her to manage.

Innocetta leaned in to hear her more clearly. "Where, Grandmother? I don't understand."

Holcum pointed with her hand, indicating the sky she could see through the transport's glassine sides. "Up there is my home."

That triggered Innocetta's funny bone, and she laughed until tears came to her eyes. As her laughter worked itself out, she turned to her grandmother. "That be so funny, Grandmother. Uncle Regge, my grandmother has a sense of humor. I never knew that, did you?" She turned back to Holcum. "Thank you, Grandmother. I needed that laugh."

Holcum didn't laugh with the granddaughter, nor would she, ever, for any reason. Behind slitted eyes, she looked at her and back away again. *You'll never understand, and that's why you're a groundie, and groundies are not worth the air they breathe.* She huddled into as small a ball as possible in her seat and was moodily silent the rest of the way to their destination.

INNOCETTA RETURNED to the transport where Regge and Holcum waited in the coolness of its interior, and she climbed inside. "Grandmother, all this way, and you need only walk inside those doors. Please, Grandmother. I've spoken to them as you've asked, and they won't budge. They do have confirmation about the DNA the medic took, and they have all their approvals lined up and ready. There be one more thing they need, though. Grandmother, they need you." Innocetta looked to Regge, hoping for help, but he just shrugged his old shoulders, and she knew this part would be up to her.

"Let them come to me," Holcum growled. "I've walked the

streets of this city, and I've dusted this vile place from my feet. I'm here under duress, and I don't want to give in on this." She wedged herself into the seat and pulled her wrap tightly around her, her hands twisted inside the cloth in spite of the blistering heat just outside the transport's door.

Innocetta, frustrated, sat for a short time and then turned to the woman next to her, seeing her as she really was, a mean and spiteful woman. She also saw the smugness on her face, and she knew she'd have to work to get this from her.

"Grandmother." She paused, making sure she was saying what she wanted. Out in the caves, it didn't matter how intractable the old woman was. She'd lived there alone for many years, so Innocetta could let her be and attack any problems that arose at a later time. It was not so, here. This problem had to be attacked now. If they left without a resolution, there was a half-day trip back to the inland sea, a full night, and a half-day back, if they could even get the grandmother back into the city. Her wording needed to be sure.

"Grandmother, there be no people out on the street. Besides, the streets be very clean today." She turned her foot so Holcum could see the soles of her footwear, hoping the humor would win the old woman's concession. "See? No dust on my feet." She smiled at the grandmother and was taken aback to see a glimmer of a smile on the old face next to her increase in size.

"Oh, well, girl. That's fine, I suppose. No dust in this dirty city. I'll go up there with you, if I must, as you've now removed all my reasons for staying behind."

AFTER HER granddaughter's face was turned, Holcum did smile in truth, a cruel, mirthless smile, and she glanced up to see the old man's face looking back at her, his expression reflecting his awareness. She'd been caught, but the granddaughter didn't know that. She pointed a finger at the old man's reflection, its strong message one that would keep his mouth shut, and if not, then there was nothing she could do about that. It had been satisfying making her granddaughter work for what she'd wanted from her.

When Holcum stepped through the money house door, she was surprised to find the people inside most deferential, and then she remembered how they'd acted all those years ago after the raider attack, when she'd killed those two fools who had come after her. She was glad they remembered, although it didn't make her dislike them any less. It just meant they kept back from her, giving her plenty of space to act out her charade of being disgruntled about being out of the transport. To admit the truth, it did feel good to be out of the transport's cramped passenger compartment, even if she had to brave the heat to do so.

Just as the granddaughter had said, there was no waiting. They scanned her palm and then ran the DNA report once again. After that, an account in her name was opened, and she was given a credit crystal. Immediately, they were on their way back to the transport, lucky old Regge still inside and waiting, cooled by the ancient machine's efficient and well-maintained systems.

"Worth the trip, do you think?" Regge quizzed the two women. "Much they owed you, Holcum, and paid up, they did, I hope."

She slapped the credit crystal onto the seat beside her, taking her hand from it as rapidly as her shaking muscles would allow. "Blood money," she growled. "The amount is unimportant. Is it worth this?" She pulled at the scarred side of her face. "Do you think credits can replace this face I wear, the leg I can no longer use?" No one responded for a time as the three sat in the quietness broken only by the low hum of the transport's powerful power plant. The tension churned thickly.

Innocetta broke the silence in a soft voice, "Grandmother, nothing can replace those things. No one expects anything to do

252

that for you. These credits, though. They be yours by right, because you were trapped in that cryo pod all those years. Think of all the time you've lived on this world since then, handfuls of decades out there on the sea. You deserve this."

Holcum grabbed the crystal and thrust it at the woman next to her. "Take it, then, if it means that much to you. Me? Now that I've taken from that corporation that which they owe me, I would seal the account and destroy this crystal. That would teach them. They would have given up their credits, and they would still be lost forever."

"Grandmother! No! These funds could be what makes your life better than what it has been."

"Granddaughter!" Holcum twisted the words out of her mouth and spewed them at Innocetta. "There is no *better* for my life. In your time with me, have you not seen that? My skin is yellow and brown. My face is destroyed, and I walk on a leg that would be better if it were taken off. What do you know of making a life better? You sit there with the face I used to have, and you don't even know what you've got. I sit here and can never regain one moment of my youth or beauty. How can you make that better with the money that god-forsaken corporation has given me? I'm offering it to you. Take it, or I'll drop it now and crush it with the foot of my crutch. Now, girl, or it's gone forever."

The crystal shook, wavering in the old woman's hand, waiting, waiting.

INNOCETTA DID TAKE the crystal from the old woman as tears began to run down her face. She'd thought she'd been building a bond with her grandmother. She'd really thought Holcum was coming to appreciate what she was doing to help her. She didn't require her grandmother's appreciation, but she'd thought it was there, at least in a small way; and today proved to be a very rude awakening for her. She glanced up to see a small cloth held out to her, an offering from Regge to dry her tears.

"To see your mother, let's stop by, Innocetta. Wait in the transport with your grandmother, I will, for as long as you wish." He began to guide the transport towards her mother's house. Reaching to Innocetta, he offered a hand for the offending credit crystal. "Have that, I will, if you wish. See that a portion in an account be opened for you, I will."

"Thank you, Uncle Regge. I will enjoy that." She turned from her grandmother and refused to look her way. She couldn't, not for a time, anyway. If she did, she might cry, and then her grandmother had won.

HAVING NO IDEA of the actual compensation Holcum had been receiving during her years as a MegaCorp military officer, Regge had picked a possible pay rate at random, figuring as closely as he could what the accumulated amount that Holcum would receive might be. However, Innocetta explained she'd been much further up the ladder than either of them had suspected, and the pay that had accumulated was commensurate with her much higher level of advancement under MegaCorp's generous military pay scale.

When Innocetta revealed the amount, he was floored. It was an amount that could put him above the league of the people with whom he had eaten all those months ago. It was all here on this credit crystal, even if the funds weren't actually there. He hadn't been worried about Holcum's threat to smash the crystal. This carried only the authorization to access and transfer a portion of the funds. She could certainly seal the account as she'd threatened, but she'd barely gotten herself here to get the funds, and he didn't think she would be so interested in sealing the account as to consider the deed worth traveling back to the money house to do so.

He also knew none of it was his. He didn't consider any of it his due for the many years he'd spent from his own funds to ferry supplies out to Holcum. That had been his duty, and he wouldn't consider scaling back that responsibility now, no matter how much money the old woman might have on this crystal.

HOLCUM WAS impressed by the number Innocetta quoted. Her interest, however, was because of the financial bruise she hoped it gave to MegaCorp's ledger books; for her own benefit, she didn't care. Her pay had never been a concern to her when she was on her great military ships. She'd rarely spent much of it. The occasional drink with a ranking officer. Someone to clean her quarters. She'd never kept track of it.

Then, on this world, she'd never provided for herself, other than her meager crops grown for trade. She recognized the amount on the credit crystal as a very, very large number, but in truth, she had no way to equate it with the goods or services it would provide. She just knew she had done what they wanted, and she had made them pay for asking. That had been the most she could expect in satisfaction, but it was better than giving in willingly. That made her smile as she sat in the coolness of the transport's interior watching the woman with her face walk up to Girl Child's house.

REGGE SAW the smile cross Holcum's face, and he immediately regretted offering to sit in the transport with her while Innocetta spent time with her mother. He faced the front and made himself as small as possible. It might be a long time before Innocetta returned to keep the old woman's sharp tongue at bay, and he hoped to become so small she'd forget he was there.

In fact, it *was* a long time before Innocetta returned to the transport. She didn't notice that her Uncle Regge was ducked so far down in his seat that he was hard to find, or that he seemed especially relieved to see her. For him, her visit with her mother had been a very long one, indeed, and his stay with Holcum had been even longer.

INNOCETTA DIDN'T give up on Holcum's health. In her years in the city, she'd seen the local healer at work. She was the same one who had been there for Holcum those many years ago, and her success in helping Holcum with her injuries had been noted by the local populace. In reality, she had been very good then, and she had gained substantially in her skills over the years. For that reason, the healer never felt guilty in charging whatever she wished for her skills. She knew, as did the people of this world, that people get what they pay for, and to get her, her prices were fair. If a few people groused every now and then, so be it. No one could make all the people happy all the time.

She did come when the granddaughter called on her services, bringing others with her as her assistants, even agreeing to travel with Regge all the way to the inland sea. It wasn't a service of charity. She would be paid, and if the rumors of the old woman's gifting from MegaCorp were true, she would be paid well for her efforts.

The healer had copies of the medic's determinations, but she'd known local remedies to work where other methods failed. From those many years ago during her training offworld, she still had contacts for roots and herbs that could work miracles, if one was trained to use them.

Pulling a well-aged pouch of foul-smelling seeds from the backmost corner of her bag, the healer ground them into a paste mixed with the most potent of fermented grains. Wiping it around the most discolored areas of Holcum's skin, the old woman seemed to respond, saying she felt better, but that, the healer knew, would only be temporary. A true healing would take months, and she turned to share this knowledge with the grand-daughter. The poultice could pull the sickness from the old woman's liver, but the healer was starting this cure much too late. Months were needed, and the healer needed to be honest. The old woman didn't have months. However, the illness she suffered would offer less discomfort if the granddaughter kept the poultice smeared around the worst of her places and then periodically let the old woman soak in a hot solution infused with the herb.

The healer bound a small package of seeds, separating the contents by kind and use, before sealing it up.

INNOCETTA SMILED inwardly at the healer's suggestion. Could the woman not see there was no place to soak in these caves so far from the running water of the city? Still, she did take the seeds and the liquid, and she paid the healer generously.

After the healer was gone, for a very long time Innocetta held the container of fermented grains the woman left behind. She had heard about the customs of some worlds to take grain distillations internally, that it deadened the senses. Perhaps the healer had offered a workable solution without knowing it. It looked like water, but it had smelled very sharp when the healer had poured it out. Innocetta opened the cap, pouring a bit on the palm of her hand and touching it to her tongue. With disgust, she spat the taste from her mouth onto the floor and looked at the liquid anew. It was a disgusting brew, and even for her grandmother's health, not even at the point of death would this touch her lips. This would be the cure that was worse than the disease, and that was not what Innocetta wanted for her grandmother.

She set the container aside. If the healer should ever come this way again, she could have the liquid back, unused even, and Innocetta wouldn't ask for her credits to be returned. She knew her grandmother would refuse to use this on the outside, and Innocetta would not force her to use it on the inside. There were many things she could not do for her grandmother, but protecting the old woman from this was one thing she could, even if the grandmother would have no knowledge of what the grand-daughter had rescued her from.

She turned to her grandmother, and seeing her resting fitfully at last, spoke softly so as not to disturb her. "Be grateful to me, my grandmother, even if you cannot love me. This, I have saved you from this day, and for that, you should be very grateful." With those words, she moved the container to a place of safety and left for the few minutes she daily needed to spend down on the shore of her sea. Sometimes she desired the sunshine to clear the cobwebs and confusion from her brain, and in her time alone that day, it did just that. Soon, a much more settled Innocetta made her way back to her grandmother's side.

INNOCETTA KNELT beside her grandmother and glanced up at Regge. It had been some days since his last visit. She often felt guilty at the demands on his old-man's time that this long summer was making of him, even though he'd repeatedly assured her he'd have it no other way. This had been his life given back to him, he'd told her, proudly showing her that he was no longer hiring a driver each time he traveled out to the inland sea. Only on his worst days did he no longer feel confident to make the trip alone, and on those days, he quickly reassured the questioning looks she gave him, letting Innocetta know he hadn't come alone, the hired man sometimes waiting in the transport while Regge did his business inside.

Today, he had a driver waiting. Innocetta took in the shaking in his hands, very pronounced today. Today's journey had been a long ride, he'd told her. He was very tired. However, he'd used this driver many times, and he'd feel at ease resting with his eyes closed on the return to the city. He tried to make his voice strong when he said those words to her, but Innocetta had spent too many heat-filled hours with her grandmother not to see the comparisons.

258

Even during the worst torment of the summer, the coolest of the caves deep within the mountain were still very comfortable, even too cool when wearing the light fabrics designed for the first blast of summer's heat, those worn until the beinning of winter's gripping cold. However, the moodiness of too much darkness could overcome the soul. In spite of the inner caves' residual coolness, the three resided in the hottest of the rocky rooms.

Bathing his neck against the heat, Regge watched as Innocetta rinsed her toweling and wiped vomit from Holcum's mouth. Each time the woman coughed, a small, additional amount leaked from her lips.

"Her color," Regge began. "Darker than before, it be. Pooling below the surface, could the blood possibly be?"

Innocetta looked up to see him standing with his hands firmly gripped at his waist. She knew he thought he was hiding the harshness of his day. The gripping of his hands tried to disguise the shaking she'd immediately noticed when he'd walked in. It pierced her heart that he felt he couldn't share that with her. How much must he be equating Holcum's deterioration with his own possible demise? It must, she knew, be the feeling of watching a prediction of his own not-too-distant future. How horrible it must make him feel, and yet he was refusing to shy away from his responsibility to the old woman and his visits to these caves.

It made her care for him all the more.

WHAT INNOCETTA didn't know was that he could have as easily remained in the city. He had other reasons for returning to the caves over and over. Her Uncle Regge was refusing to shy away from Holcum's beautiful granddaughter. The trips out to the sea, the feeling of being needed, had become a fountain of youth for an old man who had almost given up on any life outside the small motions of arising, dealing with that day's pains and discomforts, and retiring in the hopes of awaking to a new morn-

259

ing, even with the foreknowledge of just how preordained that new day would be.

Holcum had needed him her entire life on this world, and that hadn't proved to be a catalyst for the old man. For a time, he'd adored the small child he'd worshipped as his own, Arianna being the charm and goodness that had filled his nights and days. He had worshipped her beauty, but she was as a family member to him, and her beauty had been, was still, in truth, that of a treasured daughter for a father to take pride and joy in, not a beauty that might become an object of anything other than familial adoration.

This one, though, in which could be found the beauty of her mother as well as—and Regge had seen this in glimpses even in those early days of his associations with Holcum—the image of what her grandmother must have been in her youth, wasn't one he had seen grow through the stages of childhood, her developing beauty providing a backdrop of moments against which to compare just how far she had come in life, the familiar features providing the jolts of childhood memories that would remind him that she was still a little girl to him. He still saw Arianna that way. He saw her childhood scraped knees, the toothless grin of preadolescence, and the gawkiness of her teen years.

Innocetta had been thrown at him as a full-blown beauty. He'd recognized her mother in her, but she'd shown him so much more. From that first day when she'd tamed the old woman's wildness with a touch on her arm, he had known a twist in his heart that had told him this was the girl he should have met in his youth. All those years ago, this girl could have been the strength that in his time of need would have been a rock for him, that would have loved him with all the energy she had. When his own body failed him, she wouldn't have run from him, but would have loved him all the more.

She had hooked the old man's heart, and the months of summer had allowed her to reel him in. He knew the feelings were his only, and he understood the difference in the love she felt for him. He was certain it was love, too, the love of a niece for a treasured old father-figure who was there for her in her times of need, providing the emotional support that the old woman at her side wasn't giving, was, instead, draining from her daily.

That didn't stop the old-man's body he was forced to occupy from coursing those feeling and sensations through his blood, his muscles feeling younger and more alive, his heart beating stronger, and his brain coursing with whatever chemicals make love so satisfying to the truly infatuated youth just learning of how strong the love attraction can actually be. At times, it had been a shock to leave Innocetta's presence and walk up the transport, finding an old man in the reflections in the glassine windows surrounding the machine's well-loved and immaculately maintained interior. The first time he'd seen those reflections, he'd actually looked behind him, wondering just who else might be out there with him in this remote and desolate area, and with the looking, had known. It was him. He'd felt so young and alive when near the granddaughter; and actually forgetting the aged and mottled skin he couldn't see through his own eyes, he had moved taller and quicker, his very actions belying the old man he actually was. Then, as he'd walked up to the transport, he had seen the old man who had replaced his image of himself in that reflection, and by the time he'd returned to the city, he'd become that old man once again.

That had been hard, but harder still it had been to spend time away from his fountain of youth, so he returned to the sea again and again. He was helping Holcum, certainly, but he was really helping himself to that tiny sip of the draught of youth that love can give even the most aged of bodies. He knew what he was doing, and he knew it couldn't be more. He would take what he could get, because even this was better than withering and dying in those rooms in the city that had become his four-walled prison. This prison at least had the beauty of the grandmother bloomed again in the freshness of youth, and that he could appreciate, even if his reflection continually pricked him with the knowledge of his extended age.

Innocetta pierced the moment of silence that passed between them, only seeing the emotions of caring, love, and resignation flicker across the old face looking back at her, thinking he was feeling it for the dying woman under her care. "The delirium, Uncle Regge. When it comes and goes, she be like this for hours." As Holcum began to rest more easily, the coughing seeming to abate for a time, Innocetta sat back, resting her arms at her side. "I must have help, Uncle. In the city, you must find me someone who can carry part of the load around here."

Regge came to stand closer, and with some difficulty, knelt at her side. "Difficult, that may be, dear Innocetta. Have families, most will, and want to leave them, they won't."

"Uncle Regge, we have funds. We can pay credits, and the accounts won't even notice." She laughed a tired laugh. "Bring the families, if they must come. We can outfit a suite of rooms for them."

Standing, helping her old uncle to his feet, she motioned for him to follow her through several adjoining chambers. "I've already thought this through. These could be the rooms they'd occupy. They could be easily divided and suited to whatever needs might arise." Turning to Regge, she sighed deeply. "I be very tired. This heat, and the constant caring for my grandmother. The caring for her be all I can do, and I must have help to do the rest. You will do this for me, Uncle?"

She stepped to him and gripped his shoulders, her tiredness telling her to place her head against his chest just for the feeling of the strength of another person to buoy her own. As Regge placed his arms around her, his hands no longer shook, the touch of this woman he found so beautiful making him young again.

His voice lied to him, though, as he comforted her, agreeing to find someone no matter the price. His voice called him out as the old man he was, but he knew differently. With this beautiful woman, this love, in his arms, he was twenty-four again, and that cryo pod from so long ago that had shaken his life into the disarray it would become was just freshly landed. However, this time, Innocetta had stepped forth, and she was perfect and his; and the future he would live with her would be very different from the one he'd lived alone. He was not, *could* not be the one his voice claimed him to be. He held love in his arms.

THE INSTALLATION of Innocetta's help did drain Holcum's account by an amount that many people on this credit-strapped world would have considered significant, but not as far as margins counted. The dent in the balance was so insignificant as to be undetectable after only a few periods of interest credited back to the account. Innocetta certainly knew one thing. It would have been worth the cost, even if it had eaten all the funds MegaCorp had paid for the services her grandmother had given during the years she'd been under the auspices of their corporation.

The caves were transformed. Regge had known the help had to be given quickly, and he knew just how limitless the funds would seem on a planet where assets were exceptionally sparse. Calling on friends and pulling in favors, he ferreted old Ferrocement machines from storage facilities so long forgotten that the very warehouses they were in were no longer in the city's databases, only in the nearly forgotten written records from before the city's infrastructure was complete.

They were transported to the inland sea under the pretext of needing the storage facilities for the city's use, the caves around the sea available as free space for machines that were no longer needed by the city but too costly to replace to let them ruin. So, Innocetta had all the construction machines she could want. All she had to do was have rock, dirt, and water dumped into one end, and the other would emit the resulting "foam rock" with which to build her rooms. The bonus about this method was the machines' storage on site, available once more if they were ever again needed for additional construction.

One thing Regge insisted on, and for that, Innocetta was most glad, was to give the rooms she'd picked for the hired help to Holcum and Innocetta, using a series of caves farther down the sea front for the staff who were willing to come. They'd been happy as long as they were allowed to bring their families, and Regge had even agreed to the exorbitant wages they'd demanded. He'd promised Innocetta, and he didn't intend to let her down.

One thing he demanded of the people he hired, and he allowed no argument here, was for them to prove their commitment to their employer. He didn't phrase it quite that way, but it was what he'd done. He insisted they find their own way out to the sea, even if they had to walk. That also gave the construction team he put together some breathing space for having the living spaces ready.

The rooms were rough. The machines had been used to fill the cave recesses, squaring them up and building walls where walls were needed. Rudimentary plumbing and power lines were enclosed within the new construction, and even some rare and hard to come by solar panels and battery banks, unknown to Innocetta, were brought to the site. Doors wouldn't be possible at first, but the doorways were there as were the openings for later windows to be installed in the yawning holes where the caves abutted their view of the sea. Even the floors were leveled for proper walking and storage.

Innocetta was, at first, aghast at the amount of work and the extent of the rooms Regge was having transformed. She'd only wanted a few small spaces for a few hardy workers who were willing to share the hardships of the life she'd come to expect by the sea. Now, she had to admit, what he was giving her was much, much better. He explained to her that the cost of the work was mostly in the moving of the great machines and the men who were paid to do the work. Doing two rooms was little more than one, and doing twenty was little more than ten. Once the machines were up and running, the hired men just kept shoveling in the raw material found at the site, and the rooms kept being built.

Within days, the stored supplies from all the years of Regge's faithfulness were moved to deeper caves, and the spaces they had used daily had been made into real rooms. When Regge took her into the coolest of the caves sequestered in the dimness of the mountain, Innocetta admired the flatness of the floors and the smoothness of the walls, but what took her breath away was when he had her press her palm to the wall. Then he spoke to her the words he had most anticipated during the whole of the process of rebuilding the inside of the mountain retreat.

"Innocetta, for you, this be, so that to battle our world's heat again, except by your choice, you never need do. Your hand, move, and press down." Instantly, the room flashed into the brilliance of day. "Again, tap it, my dear." As she did, the light began to dim to a more usable level.

"Uncle Regge!" She turned to him, her face beaming her happiness. "How be this possible?"

"Keep a few secrets, I still can." He smiled broadly at the joy he had brought to this one he loved so. "Connections and credits. Credits and connections. Make the world go round, both can. Connections, I have. With your funds, made things happen, I did. Look. One more thing." Stepping through an opening, he showed her a simple bathing room with hygiene facilities, also with its own lighting system. "Cooling and heat beyond even my connections be. So sorry, I be, dear Innocetta. Light, I could give, and water, also. Pleased, you be?"

Innocetta grabbed him with both her arms. "Uncle, you don't know what you've given me. You be my healer and blessing."

"Wait! One more thing." Innocetta backed away, looking in wonderment at the man who had already given her more than she could have asked or even dreamed. "Tomorrow, furniture, Innocetta. A bed for you and one for your grandmother. Become a home, this will. Doors, later. Afterwards, to come, many things will. Be a home now, it shall."

There were some concessions for the hired help, but the extras had been done for Innocetta. That had been Regge's driving motivation. He would have broken heaven and Trasdrom'man to give her the things she needed to make her life better. Certainly, if she'd asked, he would have done the same for the other dwellings being laid into the mountain caves. As it was, the hired help were having the formed furniture they were accustomed to, the shaping planned into the walls as it had been done in Summer City so many years ago. The cushions to soften the Ferro-concrete would have to be the help's own. Only the wealthiest of Trasdrom'man's citizens had real furniture, and that was what Uncle Regge offered to his Innocetta.

His transformation of the primitive living quarters was a labor of love for him. He could never love her as his body wanted him to, but he could love her in this. From her smiles and exclamations of pleasure, he could tell that for all the things he had given her, small treats though they may be, she was very grateful. Would Holcum like them? He didn't care, because for the brief moments when Innocetta hugged him again in thanks, he was twenty-four, and during those few moments, Innocetta was all he cared about. Well, that and being twenty-four once again.

266

# —Chapter 11—

*The lightning ripped the sky asunder, and
the thunder screamed its revenge as the God of
the Sea rose out of the foaming waves.*

*"Command me," the voice of thunder rang
out, "but beware my wiles. What you ask for I
will give, but you may not get what you desire."*

—*From* Tales and Legends,
*Frank N. Stein,*
*c. 1822, old-Earth*

*UNDERGEN'L Ma'jene Holcum.*

Her hands gripped the cloth of her bedcoverings, and her body shook with the violence of her coughing. Holcum's body lay in the bed, but she wasn't there. She was on her great starship.

*The last Rejuvie will be mine.*

A moan of pain twisted itself from within her tortured throat. Even Holcum's remembered frustration at the words thrown at her so long ago still twisted in her gut. She *needed* to feel the thrill of the NeuroShok as it tormented the captives' flesh.

*Damn you, Bofsky, for taking what should be mine!*

Her body released its hold on her muscles as the old woman relaxed into the softness of the bed. Her bed. These coverings.

267

The old woman's eyes jerked open to see a room around her, not her well-known caves of safety. This was a room with walls, a ceiling, and furniture. Where was she?

Her breathing came faster, and she felt the things around her losing their focus, their crispness blurring into two of each thing. With a jerk of her head, she snapped the doubled things back into one, but it didn't hold. As she lay watching the ceiling above her, her vision blurred into the fuzziness that she seemed to recall more and more often from the past few days.

She remembered. This wasn't her ship, and this wasn't her cave. Not really her cave. The granddaughter had done something, but she wasn't sure just what. It had resulted in these rooms, though. The granddaughter had told her they were still in the caves, just that the caves had been transformed into real rooms.

Holcum had been too tired to argue with her. Caves. Rooms. What did it matter the names they were called? This bed was real, though. It had been so long since Holcum had slept on a real bed that she'd forgotten the sensation of softness underneath her. The first nights, it hadn't been pleasant, but her body had quickly come to crave this. The idea of returning to her pallet seemed reprehensible to her now. She tensed as she felt the tightening muscles of another round of coughing begin its slow descent on her frail frame.

"Grandmother! I thought I heard you in here. Be you all right?" Innocetta palmed the plate by the doorway, grateful to her Uncle Regge for his wisdom in providing for her grandmother. The lights came up to the low level Innocetta had preset for the night, knowing she might have to step in at any time, whether it was light or dark outside.

Between her fits of coughing, Holcum ground out, "Stupid child! *All right* is for youth and vapid dreamers. How can all right ever be given to this body again? Or is it yourself you are concerned about? Do you wish me to lie to you so you can return to your bed, content in the knowledge that you helped a poor old grandmother, that your very presence and concern eased her pain? If so, you're as dense as the rocks that make up these walls. You've done nothing but prolong my pain. I would have died months ago if you'd left me alone, and here I am, still suffering under your care. Let me die, girl. That's the only thing I have left to me, and you won't even allow me that. Get out of my sight, and let my lungs tear themselves from my body in peace. Go! And turn this blinding light out!"

Innocetta did as she was told, and she knew her heart would never become so hard as to take the fury of the old woman without it tearing at her, but she also knew that she was as stubborn as the grandmother, and that she would win any battles the old woman might want to pick with her. Tonight, Innocetta could do no good except to make sure the sad remains of the person on the bed was as comforted as possible, even if Holcum did wrestle her every step of the way. Innocetta was certain that if she were the one doing the fighting against the harshness of a life that had crushed her into nothingness, she would want to know someone was there to help hold the pieces together. That, Innocetta could do for her grandmother, and the old woman couldn't do anything about that, could she?

With a smile, she turned her own light off and crawled back into her private world of softness, thankful for the gift she had been given, the one from her precious Uncle Regge.

INNOCETTA HELD her grandmother's hand as the old woman's eyes widened, and her head rolled back and forth. She glanced at the hired help across the room, motioning with a nod that it was time for them to be gone. She had no idea what the old woman might say next, and she would just as soon be the one to hear it first.

"I can live again." The words cracked from the old woman's mouth as if sticks were being broken to build a fire. After a short pause, the sticks started up again. "I was there, girl, and I knew the stories, had seen them on the Vid." A hand lurched up to grab Innocetta's clothing at her neck, pulling the young woman closer to Holcum's face. "Are you understanding me? I have to swim in the water. I saw them do it."

"Swim, in the sea? You be ill, Grandmother." She would die if she went in the water. "A bath, we could provide that, perhaps."

"No! To swim! I must—" Holcum paused as she dragged a labored breath into her chest, gathering her strength as her hand held the younger woman's attention. "I tortured them for the answers, and they wouldn't tell me, not even when they died." She spat her final words, her hand just as quickly letting go of her granddaughter, the arm falling back to Holcum's side. She laughed a harsh cackle, and in her broken sticks voice continued, "So many of them died, and those I tortured did *not* return from the waters of the sea."

Holcum paused, her eyes looking from side-to-side as if attempting to locate an errant bit of information she had once known and then misplaced. Then, her eyes locked on her grand-daughter's. "One, we were told, had lived many lives. We were told they had found the proof of that one, and he died, too."

When coughing interrupted the grandmother's words, her granddaughter reached a hand to help. "Grandmother . . ."

Holcum swatted the offered hand away, hissing out her next words. "I guess he did die, although I didn't see it with my eyes. Bofsky claimed him for his own, and then the ship was gone. He couldn't have survived." Her eyes fluttered, her voice mumbling, "There was no way for him to survive."

Innocetta, not really understanding just what was being said, and even more, not wanting to believe the horror or how her grandmother could be saying these things, whispered, "Grandmother. No one walks from the sea after they are dead. The sea takes life, not gives it back." She watched her grandmother's face as the watery old eyes narrowed and then riveted Innocetta's own with an intensity that spoke of anger and betrayal.

"You weren't there, girl. Don't presume to tell me what I did and didn't see. The last living Rejuvie was on our battle cruiser, and still, we watched them walk from the sea for a year more, all new and fresh, the blush of youth upon their bodies. Each was taken, their answers demanded, and none would give them. For that, they died."

"Grandmother, where did this happen?" Innocetta had never heard of anything so horrific, and she didn't want her grandmother to continue in this way. Attempting to help her see reason, she questioned her knowledge of the facts. Surely her grandmother would see that this was all in her mind. No group, especially the well-respected organization that MegaCorp was reputed to be, would allow any of their employees to act in such an atrocious manner, and Innocetta had seen the proof that Mega-Corp had been the old woman's employer in the accounts that now bore her name.

"You doubt my word, girl?" For a moment, Holcum's retort was torn by a fit of coughing, and then more quietly, she let her slippery words peel from her lips. "You will see. Let me swim in our sea. Once again I will be the youthful beauty of so long ago." She held up one hand, her eyes resting on the old and weathered skin that held it there, and then reached to rub her granddaughter's hair between her fingers. "You have my youth and my beauty. You have taken what I didn't willingly give. It's time it was returned to me. The waters, they must be mine."

She turned her old, yellowed eyes back to Innocetta's, this time the anger gone, the quavering pleading of a desperately broken life in its place. "You must let me swim in the sea before I die. I will live again, my granddaughter. My youth will return, and I will be whole. I've paid my dues. I've lived this tortured existence without giving up. Now, I deserve my life back again. Take me to the water so that I can live."

Innocetta was broken inside by the tears falling from her grandmother's face. This she had never seen in her grandmother, the pleading and the desperate begging. If she thought it might really do any good, she'd relent and carry the old woman to the water, but reality was reality, and the wasted effort would no doubt do more harm than the help her grandmother thought it might provide her. There would be no sense in that. On this one day, even the change in the old woman's demeanor wouldn't shake Innocetta from what she knew was the best for the old woman.

As she stepped away, her grandmother's head resting on the pillow, Holcum's eyes finally closing in the restless sleep of the very old and infirm, Innocetta laughed softly to herself. *What stories they be, to go for a swim and be given youth all over again! Those be the makings of children's tales, and no one would find them believable except the most gullible of young minds.*

What Innocetta didn't laugh about was the talk of the torturing and killing. She had no doubt, at least she thought she was sure, that those things were the wild imaginings of an old mind creating memories that had never really happened. That was what she hoped. How horrible it would be to know that her own grandmother might have done such things!

At the thought of that, she laughed aloud, turning to be sure the grandmother lying amidst the softness of her bedclothes and finally sleeping was not disturbed.

*How silly of me. She be just an infirm old woman. Let her have her wild stories and imaginings if that makes her final days easier. I might also make my own past more exciting if I were lying on that same bed.*

However, she knew she would never make up such horrible tales about herself, and a small shiver ran up her spine. She attributed it to the coolness of her own chambers when she stepped back inside. Repeating aloud to herself what was becoming a daily mantra in the dullness of the ongoing summer heat, Innocetta looked around at the rooms that had been prepared especially for her and whispered, "Thank you, Uncle Regge. This has been the best of your gifts to me." As the sweat dried from her skin, she truly felt that way, and she knew that in this, she was indeed the luckiest woman on the planet.

INNOCETTA STOOD in one of the great window openings Regge's crew had left where the outside wall of the caves opened onto the cliff face. An enormous glassine window to be shipped in at enormous cost was planned for this location, but with the heat of the summer, it hadn't been immediately necessary for this time of the year. There were months ahead for the building of it, and besides, Innocetta enjoyed the unobstructed view. She also enjoyed the feeling of safety with having the built-up opening that provided her a place to sit as she enjoyed the protection of the thick Ferro-walls that now enclosed much of the cave's open side.

This time of day, the sun just now suggesting it would actually arise from its slumber to slash its broiling rays across the surface of this world humans dared to call home, was the time Innocetta could really enjoy this. Having stepped from the coolness of her room to this heated wind blowing from the sea made her want to soak up its warmth. She knew that as the day progressed, the heat would become oppressive, but she also had learned to take what each part of the day offered, especially when she knew it wouldn't last.

She turned, mildly annoyed, to see one of the hired town girls rushing in to get her attention. She stood, taking a deep breath at the frantic look on the girl's face, knowing there was rarely anything that anyone should be so excited about out here. Life at the sea, for Innocetta, didn't run at the pace of the city, and if something disagreeable happened, well, being keyed up about it didn't make it improve any faster. Not even the old woman's death, sure to come before summer ended, would be made any better by the hurrying.

"Yes, girl," she started, then remembered how she had felt less of a person when Holcum had called her that. She looked at the identifying tag the girl wore, the logging in and out each day at the reader Regge had provided verifying the girl's hours and pay. It also identified the girl with her picture and name. "Rhendona. What a pretty name! How can I help you?"

"Mos, the old woman, it be. Cursing everything, she be." The girl danced on her feet, revealing her frustration that Innocetta didn't feel her urgency, and Innocetta had to smile.

"Be she cursing you, Rhendona?"

"No, mos," the girl replied, "Everything else, but me, no." Then the girl relaxed a bit and gave a small grin. "Curse me, she might, if stick around, I did. Came for you, I did, instead."

"Thank you, Rhendona. That was the correct thing to do. I will go to her now." Coming to her was certainly not what Innocetta wished the girl had done. Old Holcum could have certainly cursed for a time longer without any ill effects, but this was Innocetta's responsibility. It wasn't what the city help were paid to do.

The old grandmother was sitting up on pillows when Innocetta stepped into the room, her disfigured face contorted with obvious dislike for the world at large. At least her voice was quiet when she arrived. That quickly changed with her granddaughter's presence. With something else to focus on, another person to hear her punctuated discourse, Holcum leaped into lively action, venting her frustration on her granddaughter.

"That child was mine! I felt her the moment she first moved inside of me, and I refused to have her taken out. They had no right to take her from me. I never harmed that child, and I would have cared for her. I would have.

"It was so hot that summer. I could barely move, but I gave her food. I paid attention to her when she really needed something. I never made her sleep outside, either. What if someone had come to take one of their children away? Would they have given it up without complaint, for reasons as flimsy as they gave for taking mine?

"They stole her life from me. They cannot return what's gone."

Innocetta placed her hands on Holcum's shoulders to quiet her. "Your daughter be not dead, my grandmother. She'll come to you, if I ask." Of that, Innocetta wasn't absolutely sure, but she did want to reassure the old woman, as well as let her know that the foolishness of her talk would not be taken at face value.

Holcum backhanded the younger woman's hands from her shoulders. "Are you as deaf as that girl who comes in here with her backwards speech? I didn't say she's dead. I know she's alive and living in the city. However, she doesn't know me, and I know well she wouldn't come to see me even if you asked. She's weak, and she deserves to be shamed. That's what I did to her those years ago. I shamed her, and I would do it again."

Innocetta stepped back, amazed that the old woman's mind could snap from crazy to lucid just like the flick of a seafly's wing. She would defend her mother, though.

"My mother has always supported me, and she be my best friend."

"Even better than that Regge? I see his eyes for you. You think he comes here just to help me. Bah! I see him as he is. He looks at you as a man looks at a woman. He seems to you just old flesh, but when you walk into his presence, he changes, and I can see the young man he was so long ago. He has love in his eyes for you."

"He comes because he cares, Grandmother. He's always cared for you, even before I was born. How can you paint him in that light?" Innocetta shook her head at her grandmother's accusations. "Uncle Regge be sweet, and he supports me even when you don't."

"Go find a man your own age, girl. They're out there for you. That old man just wants access to my accounts. I'm not dull. I remember how much I was given, and I know he used much of it to do all this I see around me. My accounts! How dare he spend my credits! He's probably even now taking a cut of my funds to cover his travels out here. If he hasn't earned it, he shouldn't spend it." Holcum's eyes narrowed as she paused to catch her breath, and then she continued, "You hear me, girl? Find you a real man instead of that old fossil."

Innocetta churned with distress at the old woman's accusations about Regge. She'd only seen him be proper and above-board with her, but the words hit home in one area. In spite of that, she responded in his defense, although with perhaps less enthusiasm than she might have otherwise.

"Uncle Regge spends only his own credits, Grandmother. All this, I authorized. Blame me. As far as a man, I have nothing to offer, and when you be gone, what be done with your accounts will be as you wish. I have no control over you there. I be here to help you because I *want* to."

"Bah! You *want* something from me. I have not yet settled exactly what. However, I want something from you. For what I want, I'll sign my accounts to you. How do you like that, girl? Will you negotiate a deal with me?"

The old woman had suddenly sharpened up, and Innocetta wondered just how much of her lunatic wanderings might be closer to the truth than she'd given her credit for. This, though,

276

this might be important. Could the old woman who hadn't spent a credit of the funds and was readying herself to die actually be trusted to do this? It would ensure her mother's future as well as anyone else who might be important to Innocetta, and that would include Regge, no matter how dark a shadow the old woman might try to paint across his intentions.

"Girl, will you deal?"

"Grandmother, what be the deal you wish? I've done all you've asked of me. What do you want that I would not have otherwise provided?"

"You have not done everything." Electric fire lashed from Holcum's eyes, and her words tore from her lips. "You think I don't know you do not intend to let me swim in the water? I know the stories. I was there, and I watched the youths step from the waters. The Vids didn't lie. I will swim. You will take me. That's my price. If I die anyway, you shall have all my funds." Holcum's look turned wicked as she continued in a tone that was cruel, a tone that sounded even crueler in the rasp of her old woman's deteriorated voice. "However, if I walk forth alive, I keep it all. Will you agree to that?" The grandmother grabbed her coverings, a sudden burst of coughing interrupting her question, contradicting the strength she was trying to show.

Innocetta stepped forward to dab the phlegm from the old woman's lips, and she spoke softly, "For something you want so much, I would do that for you without any credits in return. I thought your request only that of a twisted dream. Keep your accounts and your credit crystals, Grandmother. I'll not need them."

"Ha!" The grandmother pushed her hand away and tried to speak, coughing several times before her voice would form her words. "The deal is done. Besides, the credits are no good to me without life. If I die, they will be yours. Get that old lover of yours to prepare the contract. I'll honor my offer. Then, if I die, you'll have the means to attract a real man. Now, leave me to cough in peace. Go, girl!"

Once more, Innocetta was banished from Holcum's presence, but this time she didn't mind, and was in fact glad to be gone. This had been a time of revelations and understandings. Life with her grandmother was growing rougher by the day, and Innocetta was beginning to suspect it would get worse before it got any better.

"SHE REALLY wants this, Uncle Regge. We must do this for her." Innocetta was confident in her old uncle, but her grandmother's words were playing tricks in the back of her mind. Now, she could not help but wonder at every gentle touch and lingering look. Was there something more than an old man's actions, one who cared for others and wanted to honor an old responsibility? Innocetta didn't see it, but she was less relaxed around him, anyway.

"Dangerous, this be, Innocetta. Back to life, to bring her, the water cannot."

"We have help now, Uncle. A sling can be constructed for the hired workers to carry her in. She won't need to walk. She can be lowered into the water and brought back out again. This be very important to her."

"Very important to you, I see this also be." Regge looked at the beautiful young woman across from him,. He pulled out the legal instruments from the money house. All Holcum had to do was place her palm on it, and with her death, all the funds from MegaCorp would revert to her granddaughter. At least he'd been able to get this taken care of, if Holcum would follow through. He handed the sensor pad to Innocetta.

"To the sensor, have your grandmother press her palm while speaking her wishes. Carry it back, I can, to the money house in the city. A one-use instrument it be, and without another face-to-face confirmation, changed, it cannot be. Plan to be there when this, your grandmother does, to be sure she follows through."

"Thank you, Uncle Regge." Innocetta took the sensor pad, and for a moment, she readied her arms to hug him. Then, at the last instant, she stepped forward to plant a kiss on his cheek, wishing him farewell on his journey back to the city.

Later that day, the old woman did follow through on her promise to Innocetta, palming the sensor pad and saying the words she'd pledged. That did surprise her granddaughter, because she expected her to claim some errant glitch in her memory, the promise all but forgotten.

Innocetta also followed through. She had the sling prepared, and several of the hired help navigated, with their primary employer ensconced within the contrivance. Winding through the caves to the opening leading to the sea's rocky beach, they carried the withered form to the sea.

OVER HOLCUM'S head, lying with her eyes closed, the hired help from the city glanced at each other with knowing looks on their faces. In the bizarre ritual they were being forced to share, they saw confirmed what they'd been told all their lives. Rich people are different that the average person, and the very rich are very different. They'd suspected such when they'd learned of where their new employer lived. This visit to the sea just confirmed those suspicions.

They had only Holcum's croaked instructions on exactly what to do as they moved from the darkness of the caves to the brilliance of the afternoon sun. It would be easy for the old woman's skin, though yellowed and brown from her liver's failure, to be blistered from even a short exposure to the torturing rays of burning light, so special precautions were made. A large cloth was carried suspended over the sling. Each bearer wore thick fabric wrapped around his or her feet to ensure good traction, as a slip on the loose stones strewn over the beach could easily mean a fragile bone broken, never to heal.

The light shimmering on the waves as they bumped against each other caught the sun and threw it back in the group's eyes. The scene was intense and very beautiful. Even Innocetta was tempted to believe. What if this did allow the grandmother to regain her youth? After all, how many dying people actually went for a swim in the sea? None that Innocetta knew of had ever done this. Wouldn't her grandmother have the last laugh if this worked, and she was able to regain her youth and beauty?

The first problem was encountered when those carrying the sling initially stepped into the water. "Mos, very cold, the water be. This, to do, should we? Certain, you be?" They stopped with their feet in the water, holding Holcum in her sling, with her body suspended just above the top of the waves.

Innocetta leaned in to the old woman. "Grandmother? Be you ready? They say it be very cold."

Very tersely, Holcum squeezed her eyes shut and spit her words at her granddaughter. "I am dying. Put me in the water. I won't die from the cold. I will die from old age, and the longer you wait, the older I become. Do it, now."

The water was every bit as cold as they said. Even the heat of the world's extreme summers only warmed the top layers of the waters, the winds quickly stirring that with the colder layers underneath. If they'd been able to traverse the very deepest waters in the sea, they wouldn't have been able to tolerate the extremes of the temperatures found there, but no one on this world had the means or the desire to travel to those deep expanses, at least not and rise back to the surface again.

Holcum only traversed the very top layer, so the bitterness of the water was very cold but tolerable. She did choke with the suddenness of the temperature change when her body first dipped underneath the surface. At Innocetta's instructions, they carried her in until only her face showed, holding her there as long as the old woman could stand it.

Her limbs and body now numb, Holcum couldn't be sure if there was anything happening; however, she knew she must make sure. When she thought she would die if she didn't come out, and knowing she would die if she did, she barked a final instruction to her porters.

"Under the water. All of me." At a nod of Innocetta's head, that was what Holcum got. However, even a dying body will fight for its last breath, and the old woman's body that had gone under eagerly didn't stay under willingly. Fighting for the breath that had been stolen by the inrush of the sea's coldness, her limbs began to war against the age and sickness holding them down. Innocetta motioned for her hired hands to pull her grandmother from the sea, placing her by the lapping waves on the beach's sun-baked rocks.

Lying in the sun, the warmed stones at her back, Holcum drew in the heat of the furnace overhead to let it drive the chill of the sea from her skin. She didn't know how long this might take, if it worked at all. Calling out, she barked instructions to those around her. "A mirror. I must see if there's a change." Hearing footsteps running back into the mountain on a chase for the requested mirror, she reached up to touch skin that now gathered warmth from the fury of the sun. "How long until this skin starts to renew? Granddaughter, how long?"

"I don't know, Grandmother. I'll wait with you until you've made a determination. You mentioned waiting a year in your stories. Will it take, perhaps, that year? Maybe your body will heal from the inside out?"

"No!" Holcum spat the word. "It must be all at once. No one was found who was partially healed. This must be all at once."

Innocetta paused, not wanting to cross her grandmother in front of the help, but knowing she saw no progress at all. "From

281

inside, Grandmother, be the pain in your leg any less?"

"The mirror, where is it? I must see my face! Is that fool back with the mirror?"

That did have Innocetta worried. Her grandmother had refused to look in a mirror for many years, and her face hadn't retained any of its youth. First there had been the cording from the accident, then the ageing from all the years here on the sea. The yellowing turning to brown only made those conditions worse, and the grandmother wanted to see.

When the runner finally returned with the requested mirror, Innocetta cringed inside. She suspected how bad this might be, and there would be no way to separate the hired help from this tirade. Innocetta could see no improvement from the grandmother's time in the water, and if anything, she looked even worse for the chilling that the cold of the water had subjected her body to.

In the brightness of the sun, Holcum squinted as she raised a gnarled hand to motion the mirror over her face. Her breath quickening, she waved those away who were still trying to shade her from the rays of the sun.

"Let me see," she growled at them, grabbing the hand proffering the mirror.

As soon as she saw her face in the glass, she flung the arm aside with a howl of frustration, the mirror falling to the rocks, the resulting shards of glass scattering those who had carried the old woman from the sea. "This cannot be. They were given their youth from the sea. I saw it. I know it was real. I've hoped and waited, and there's no gift to me." She rolled to her side as if to stand, calling out to the sky, "I've lived crippled for more years than I could walk. No one has loved me in all those years. My body has not known the embrace of a man for so long as to no longer know how it feels." She quieted for a moment as she drooped in her exhaustion, her body shivering in the heat of the sun.

"Grandmother." Innocetta knelt to offer a supporting arm to the distraught woman on the stones.

"No!" Holcum waved her off. "I am a gen'l in the military, and I need no one's help. Stand aside. There are things I have done, and many things I haven't done, but I need no one's help to stand. If my body will not right itself with the help of this sea, then I will make my body do my bidding as it is." With an extreme effort in her withered limbs, Holcum flung herself to her feet, her furor-fueled muscles dragging her old frame erect. However, as soon as her nerve-damaged foot touched the stones, she could no longer keep up the pretense that she had the ability to gain control over a body that simply would not comply with her demands. Collapsing to the ground amidst howls of agony, the woman pounded at the hands that reached to offer her their help.

"I will drag myself into my home. I'll do this or die." All the others could do was stand aside and watch as Holcum did try to do just that, her old arms pulling her wreck of a body across the burning stones that blocked her way.

Finally, exhausting even her strident fury, the last of her stores of energy drained from her overworked muscles, Holcum lay on the stones, her face pressed against the heat of the rocks, and she held out her hand toward her granddaughter. "Innocetta, my granddaughter. Even this is taken from me. I beg you for your help."

Innocetta reached for her grandmother, and as she raised the limp form to her chest, she held her, Holcum's coughs too weak to even wrack her body, felt only in the closeness of the embrace. Innocetta watched as the bleary eyes on the old woman's face closed in defeat.

"Mos, to help you, let us, you must," several of the voices around her offered.

283

She waved them off. "This grandmother be mine, no matter how she tries to hurt and offend others. She be my burden this day, and I will be her support and strength. Please do not take that from me."

Innocetta was the strength her grandmother needed that day, and she did carry her back to her rooms in the upper caves. It wasn't easy, and several of the bruises her grandmother later developed were no doubt from the strength with which her granddaughter held the old woman.

Holcum should have been very grateful that she was held tightly and well. If she'd been aware of what Innocetta was doing for her, she might have felt that way. Grateful was the one thing Holcum could be. She couldn't love, but grateful was within her grasp. However, she passed out on her journey back to her chambers, and Innocetta's sacrifice went unnoticed by anyone except the help.

THERE WAS a different set of rooms than the ones Holcum and Innocetta retired to that night. Down the sea a bit, the rooms were a little rougher and a little less convenient, but they were home, too. These were the city folk who had been hired to help Innocetta with her grandmother. They were people, too, people with eyes and opinions and tongues. There were many interesting stories told that evening to entertain those who hadn't been present at the spectacle by the sea.

In one version, the listeners had laughed until they cried as the storyteller regaled them with his version of Holcum diving from the sling, so anxious was she to get into the water. He gestured with his hands as the story had her swimming like a fish, even growing gills and the fabled tail of the old-Earth mermaid, as beautiful in the sea as any woman had ever been on land. Then, with a whisper, he told of her siren song of longing to be back on the land, and the mighty sea god arising to tell her the youth she had been granted would be hers only as long as she stayed in the sea. More loudly, he laughed as he stood to give his version of Holcum's response, showing the way she had risen out of the water and cursed the sea god, telling him she had her youth again, and he couldn't take it from her. She wouldn't give it up. She had then dived deep, returning at a breathtaking speed to fly from the water and land upon the stones. All had watched then as her mighty fins had shriveled back into her withered leg, and her youth had once again become her wrinkled, aged skin. The listeners laughed at the tale, the old woman's meanness and obstinacy already legend.

There were other, quieter renditions that were kinder to the old woman and especially to the granddaughter who had carried her back to her room, refusing to give up her burden in spite of the weight and the climbing, even to the hands that were there and willing to take the burden from her. The granddaughter's tale was becoming legend, too, and it would be one that she would be glad to claim when her future became her present, and that was not far away.

# —Chapter 12—

*The devil dances*
*His mournful tune.*
*His minions sing*
*Under a waxy moon.*
*Watch out, my daughter,*
*He's coming for you.*

*-Witch's chant*

THE OLD WOMAN was still alive, and Innocetta didn't see how.

Among the help, the reason was clear. She was too obstinate to die, but they respected the young granddaughter, and they didn't let her hear their opinions. They had seen how she loved the grandmother even when the grandmother didn't love her back, and that was the backbone they saw in her. The yelling of the old woman, and the meanness she could show: *Weakness,* they whispered to each other. *Admire the strength of love, we do.*

Winter had crept up on the compound. With her hired help at her side, Innocetta no longer needed the regular boost of morale she had gotten all summer from her Uncle Regge. He'd come through with her windows and doors, and the compound for her and her grandmother was still warm from the heat the mountains had absorbed all summer. The windows that had been under construction back in the city during the summer were carried to the sea in the final days of summer's blast, and the workmen had scrambled to install them, sealing them tightly, the weather expected to turn at any time. When it had shifted, it had been with a blast of cold and freezing precipitation, and Innocetta couldn't imagine how her grandmother had survived all the years of solitude here. Even the smaller compound that had served the help all summer was snug and tight. Now, when the winds howled, and the ice pellets from the sky pounded the vast windows, Innocetta and her grandmother made their way to the warmest chambers deep in the mountain, those that never lost their heat, no matter how fiercely the cold attacked them. They were also grateful for the banks of batteries to power the interior lighting when the storms would blow for days at a time, obscuring the light of the sun. Innocetta considered herself very fortunate in this respect.

Now that the chambers were sealed against winter's fury, enough heat seeped through the Ferro-cement living quarters to make most of the rooms tolerable, if not really warm. Innocetta remembered about geothermals and how they could be adapted for heat, much as Winter City was. Perhaps, she considered, if the geothermals in one chamber could be redirected to provide heat for many chambers, the entire compound could receive the warmth of the innermost caves.

That was for later, though. She had other worries, now. Her grandmother wanted to return to the sea. To the *sea*. In *winter*. At this point, Innocetta didn't know who was the craziest, her grandmother for wanting this thing, or herself for actually considering it.

At least the old woman didn't want to get *in* the water this time. It seemed there was a ritual to be performed. Innocetta hadn't really concentrated on just what the ceremony was all about, only that the old woman had insisted. Innocetta hadn't been able to think of a way around this, either. She recalled how strongly her grandmother had wanted to go to the sea during the summer, and how she had manipulated the situation until Innocetta had arranged that awful scenario at the water's edge. Innocetta planned to be in control of any such events in the future, even if she did let her grandmother have her way.

Innocetta also thought of her dear Regge, and with that, the tears leaped forward, catching the beautiful young woman off guard. She'd never known the old grandmother in her youth, and she'd grown up with her mother's beauty as no more than the background of who her mother was. The idea of herself as beautiful was as foreign to her as the idea of herself as a groundie or as a wealthy young heiress. Yet, she was all three.

Regge had seen the beauty, and it had reenergized the old man he had become. Innocetta recognized the signs, now. He'd known his place, though, and he had respected the boundaries of propriety. His idea of responsibility was every bit as strong as Innocetta had imagined, his responsibility to her that of maintaining the correctness of an uncle-niece relationship.

It had broken his heart and his spirit to have her love withdrawn from him, and when her mother had sent word, Innocetta had railed at herself for ever doubting the old man. She hadn't even been given the opportunity to say her farewells. He'd been gone before news could be gotten to her, and Innocetta had been left to deal with her loss in whatever way she could. One thing had made her smile, though. His old red transport had been Uncle Regge's favorite possession, and he'd made sure it was hers.

Still, when the news had arrived, she had taken the next step, reaching a level of anger she'd never before approached with the old grandmother, no matter how abusive Holcum had been towards her. Innocetta had damned the old woman for taking the affection Innocetta and her Uncle Regge had shared, driving in a seed of doubt that had taken them from each other, and bringing the old man to his knees. Innocetta realized he had indeed loved her, perhaps as the old woman had said, but the harm had been in the young beauty's rejection of that love, and for that, the old woman was damned to whatever darkness occupied the deepest depths of her thoughts.

IN THE DARKNESS of her mind was exactly where Holcum dwelt, too, and she wanted the sea that had so cruelly rejected her to join her in those dark places. So, she was wrapped in many layers and laid in a waterproof sling. It was difficult preparing the old woman's body for the journey. Her old joints were drawing up, the kinking of her hands accelerating in a parody of a dance that couldn't be undanced. Just to work the layers of wrappings over the knee joints and twisted feet that no longer worked was to torment the old woman almost past her level of endurance.

*I will go,* she'd cried out to those around her. *Do this and let me scream in my pain. I'll have my revenge. The gods of these waters will suffer with me. They will be pulled with me into the depths of my misery as this body damns me to my final hell.*

The ice was frozen across the surface of the lake, but the precautions to keep the old woman dry as well as warm were in place, just in case. Many of the staff had grown to accept the old woman as warped and of no consequence, someone who would find strangeness to perform no matter what the situation. She was simply to be laughed at or ignored.

Others, though, were less kind, and as they helped prepare for the old woman's demands, they were not so very careful, at least not in doing the right thing. In their intentional carelessness, they were very vigilant to see that the old woman paid for her meanness of spirit and blackness of soul. Small wrappings were put on in such a way as to allow the whipping of the cold to reach in to burn exposed skin. Other layers had gaps that would cancel out the insulating properties of the cloth. The wind would be bitter, and the more protection they could appear to provide, the better the granddaughter would feel about this activity. The staff didn't want to offend the granddaughter and her goodness of heart. In spite of their feelings for the young woman who was sacrificing her life in the care of another, however, many of them did want the grandmother to suffer deeply.

That day, as Holcum was lifted and carried, the movements of her porter's arms were not careful at all, and they were roundly cursed on the way down the caves' paths to the shore of the sea. When they crossed the threshold of the thick door that had been placed to separate the lower living quarters from the final expanses of the caves that were open to the elements, the biting cold did reach in and nip at the places that had been so carefully contrived by the staff, leaving Holcum gasping as the knife pricks of razor-cold air stung her. The satisfied smiles of the porters, unseen within their own wrappings, warmed their hearts as they stepped outside. Once away from the protection of the enclosed spaces, the bitter cold overlaying the snow-covered stones of the beach brought additional cries of torment from the old woman.

"Grandmother," Innocetta cried, with the muffled voice of her own well-wrapped face. "It be too cold for this."

Though her body had betrayed her with its age, contorting once-young joints with permanent disfigurements she would have never dreamed possible, this day Holcum's mind was sharp and clear. On some days, she was betrayed by thoughts that wandered here and there, the world in which her mind existed not always the world in which her body endured, torn and twisted. However, on Holcum's good days, hardly good for those around her, the bad ones were wiped from her slate with the passing of the nights and the waking to the new dawn, so that every day Holcum actually remembered seemed to have been a good day. Her companions were not so fortunate. They remembered. Still, this was one of her best days in a long time, and she screamed against life.

"It will be too cold when my body is dead. This is how I know I still live. I must go to the water. Take me there."

ALTHOUGH HER grandmother could no longer actually raise her hand to indicate her wishes, Innocetta had learned to read the small signs. The twitching of a well-wrapped arm was all she needed to see, and in her own layers of clothing, she stepped forward, leading, the lake's frozen surface just ahead.

Innocetta remembered those first cold weeks out here on the water at the end of the previous winter, with Regge appalled that she would actually consider remaining with her grandmother. She smiled to remember just how obvious it had been that he was frightened of the old woman.

As she stepped aside to let the porters pass by, she offered a prayer of thanks to someone who could no longer hear her say it in person. *Uncle Regge, you were so kind-hearted that you could never stand against the torment this old woman allowed to boil over onto everyone near her. Yet, you cared for her in the only way you knew how. She was fortunate to have you, and in spite of all you did for her, she still allowed herself to destroy you in the end. Thank you, though, from the one who did love you, even if I did not show that to you when I could.* Her words to the man who had been so instrumental in all the changes that had happened to this place would surely be heard by him, Innocetta hoped.

"Step onto the ice," Innocetta instructed the men carrying her grandmother. "She was very specific about this." When they had done so, she stepped up to the litter and leaned in to the old woman. "What, now, Grandmother?"

"My mouth. I must have my mouth free. My lips. I will spit on these waters with the spit of my lips, and the gods of these waters will know my hatred. Now, girl."

Innocetta motioned, and the mouth was uncovered, the old lips working themselves as they prepared to fling their curse to the ice. Yet, when the lips opened and the old tongue pushed itself through those dry pieces of skin, no moisture appeared, for the tongue was as dry as the cold air around it.

"Water, girl. I must have water in my mouth. I must do this, even if I die here on this day, in this cold." Holcum's mouth continued to work itself, pulsing with her tongue's efforts to expel saliva, as if she could simply command the moisture to appear on her lips.

A small container of water was produced, the snowmelt warmed in a waterproof cloth held against someone's skin, deep in the folds of a protective wrapping. The water was quickly dribbled past the old woman's lips, the possibility of it refreezing in the process very real.

The old woman did manage a spit the second time, although to hear the stories told later in the lesser of the two compounds, it was less of a spit and more of a dribble, but to Holcum it was all she needed. Her old, worn body would do no more for her, and with the moisture, she threw her curse to the sea, her old mouth reduced to a mumbling torrent of motion and sounds punctuated with gasps of indrawn breath.

The old body lying on the litter started to shiver violently. Even her exposed skin was turning pale, no longer carrying the brownness that had become her color, the real color of her skin forgotten with the continued degradation of her illness. Innocetta knew the grandmother had been outside too long.

"Grandmother," she spoke, "we be going inside, now."

She hoped they weren't too late. As she watched the old face, it was apparent Holcum was somewhere other than with the granddaughter at that moment. Her eyes were glazed, and her lips were moving in a private conversation with no one but herself.

Innocetta looked away, certain no one else was going to be allowed inside whatever secretive world her grandmother was choosing to draw around herself.

THERE WAS a concealed world in which Holcum was immersed, but it was not the pleasant world of the fondly remembered past that young people like to think their no-longer-lucid elders slip into. This was a private world of hell and damnation. This was Holcum's curse, and it was leaking from her tired old lips, mostly unheard except in Holcum's world, as she threw her anger at all the things that had been a bane to her life.

Not everyone was ignoring the lips and the small sounds that were coming from them, though. As the old lips told of injustices done by the great corporation, MegaCorp, and as they cursed the military that had stolen her and made her their own, her words and sounds were marked. There were those on this world who dealt with the lack of medical care available on most of the more advanced planets. Blindness, deafness, and limb injuries easily corrected on other worlds were accepted as a part of life on Trasdrom'man, and the populace had learned old-fashioned ways of coping with those traumas. One of those was the reading of lips and the understanding of things only half said.

Later that evening, many of them would laugh as they were told of the epitaphs sent against the world on which they lived. They had, at times, spoken the very same words from their own lips, and those didn't surprise them. The heat, why, they had all cursed that during the hottest of the summer days, although several were already ready to admit that just a little warmth about now might be welcomed for a while, just long enough to warm bones already chilled to the marrow with the cold of this winter's winds.

It was the other words that brought them dismay. Why would anyone curse a world that was green and beautiful, where the seas were warm and ready for the inhabitants to swim? Where was this world where people lived among a forest of greenery and the abundance of growing food under a yellow sky?

Some of the stories told later that day would bring amusement. Maybe the old woman was cursing the yellow sky. Maybe the gods had peed on the world, and urine dripped across the clouds, scattered into the rains that fell across the lands, the water on the world forever the yellow of the gods' urine, the taste as nasty, and the world dying with the putridness of the gods' own yellow curse.

They would also remember the woman's words about swimming and rebirth, how she thought the sea of their world would return her to the beauty of her youth. Perhaps her yellow world wasn't real, just the stuff of children's dreams, the stories of pretend, doled out to lull small children to a restful night of dreams during cold winter nights when there was no warmth to be had.

Laughter would ring from the families in the lesser compound as they remembered the tale of the mermaid given the gift of youth, only to be arrogant, flinging herself back to the beach to wither again into the old woman she had been. Perhaps she really had seen the old sea god as he had risen to tell her of the conditions of her youth. Perhaps she knew him personally as a lover, or even as a sibling or child. One man had hooted his interjected opinion that she might have been all three at the same time.

Once the laughter from that version settled, others would comment that they had seen the old woman's body flail at the waters as she had demanded to be ducked underneath. She had certainly flung herself on the rocks as she had beat at them afterwards, trying to drag herself back to the safety of her caves. More laughter would echo throughout the lesser compound's rooms.

As the laughter from the stories quieted, a darker side of the old woman's mutterings was recognized. It was this world's seasons that dictated the cycle of life among the inhabitants of this planet, not the daughters or the parents or the grandchildren. This world's abusive seasons and harsh realities could be dammed by a curse, and all would understand that, but family was a different matter. Family, on Trasdrom'man, was all that made life something worth living, even something to treasure.

When the old woman began her curses of her family, blaming them for her life and its woes, many of those who could read lips had looked away. These were things that were sacred, and no one should know such things about such intimate family members. Those sitting around listening to the tales of the curses silently nodded their heads in agreement, knowing of their own mutterings they had at times made against their own families, and how, once they had made their peace with those same family members, they had been glad to forget those words, never having spoken them aloud.

Not all had looked away, though. More stories would be told in the lesser compound where the hired help resided, stories that would draw shock from the curses leveled at the granddaughter. These people had known of the grandmother throughout their entire lives, the stories telling of the old, insane warrior who lived out on the inland sea. For many years, she had been revered as a savior, her strength in the face of overwhelming odds driving scores of raiders from the face of the planet. However, that had been long before most of these people were born.

The stories these people had known of the old hermit were of the courage of a woman who had dared to brave the elements of a world without the manmade crutches of underground cities and water suits that the rest of the population used to prop up their inadequacies. What they had found when they arrived at the inland sea, though, had been a meanness of spirit in the old woman, and a granddaughter whose beauty could win many hearts if she wished, but who, instead, was dedicated to the good of the old woman.

To hear that this old woman had cursed their jewel of the sea had horrified them, because they knew just how much realness such a curse might have. Even if there were no gods to stir the curse into action, sometimes people did allow their minds to be swayed by the very ideas within the words of the curse.

They were satisfied with one thing the old woman had grasped as her own in her series of curses. She had nailed the new name of the sea on the head as she had railed her indignation at its refusal to honor her demands for renewed life, claiming the sea's refusal was this world's revenge for the anger she'd spewed against it during all her years here. The Sea of Revenge, she'd named it.

The hired help that staffed Holcum's mountain were content with the meaning of those words, knowing this sea had, indeed, taken its revenge on the old woman. They liked the name, and among themselves, they began using it. The inland sea it would be no longer. Now it was the Sea of Revenge, and in time, that name would eventually find its way onto the official maps of this world.

THOSE STORIES were yet to come, however, and this day, Holcum was still on her beach. The cold ate at her skin through the small openings her porters might have accurately called the Wrappings of Revenge. Before making back to the caves, Holcum had Innocetta back to her side, begging her to get the medic. The medic had painkillers. Please send for the medic.

Innocetta had agreed, even knowing the medic couldn't be summoned. Only the healer could come, and she'd already given all the help she could. A warm bed and a touch of the healer's paste would be all the painkiller the grandmother would get this night. It pained Innocetta, but the old woman had insisted on this, and the old woman would have to deal with this as best as she could. Her granddaughter would make it as easy on her as possible, but she couldn't take away what the grandmother had insisted on doing to herself.

THAT NIGHT, her withered form swathed in the comfort of her soft mattress and pasted with the healer's concoction, and her curses bled from her cancerous soul, Holcum slept. For those that watched over her, that night's sleep would be a good one, the hours filled with darkness, the soft snoring telling of rest, and the small sounds that a person makes during the night telling them of life still in the sleeping form.

Yet, the hollowness left by the curses only allowed memories to swell and bubble up to fill Holcum's dreams, and dream she did. These dreams should have been the pleasant fabrications of an old woman's life as it coped with unrealized hopes, yet Holcum's dreams that night might have been better classified as another variety, one that most people would place in the realm of nightmares. Yet, they were just the stuff of Holcum's life, the events that had happened to her world before her real existence of nightmares on this world had begun.

*The boy from the planet's surface cowered in the corner. He seemed to have no knowledge of why he was on her battleship, but Holcum knew better. He had stepped from the sea, that damned yellow sky overhead, and a team had grabbed him as the water had run from his naked limbs. These people thought they could fool her by sending their unclothed children into the sea. He was huddled there just as he had been found, naked.*

*He would know about what she asked, though. Even children knew more than they said. The last one had been a girl, and she'd screamed with a wild look in her eyes as she died, having told Holcum nothing. Holcum made sure this male was in the room* when she held the NeuroShok to the girl's body, the girl's nervous system frying itself from the inside out. Holcum had been satisfied to watch the boy pee himself as the girl's screams ignited a different kind of fire in Holcum.

When she'd been a child, Holcum had known her father. She remembered how he had read to her at night, and the warmth of his arm around her as his words slipped her further and further into the sleepiness that would carry her through the night. She'd worshipped him, and when the explosions had started, she'd known he would keep her safe. He died that day as she watched, and inside her soul, she had died along with him.

She had fought to hold her own against Bofsky. There had been secret meetings and even more secret understandings. Many crewmembers had seen their careers destroyed because they had gotten in Bofsky and Holcum's way.

Damn Bofsky! He refused to get rid of that fool Rezalton from her team. For Holcum's entire career, Rom'n Rezalton had been the scab that wouldn't heal. Even when that last downside mission had taken out several of her team, Rezalton couldn't manage to be in front to take the shell like the man he had never been.

Flowers. Her mother had liked flowers. Holcum had tried many times to forget that. Now, flowers made her angry, and she remembered why. Her mother had grown massive beds of flowers, cutting them and bringing them into the house, putting them into every room. Her father would come in and smell the flowers, and he would wrap his arms around her mother, lifting her from the floor, twirling her around while Holcum stood to the side, clapping and cheering. Sometimes, Holcum would pull a flower out and hand it to him as he swung her mother past, and he would put it in her mother's hair, burying his face next to it as he drew in the essence of the one he loved.

The soldiers who had killed her parents put their things down there. One after another, they crawled onto her, slapping her

298

*when she screamed with the pain. When her face and neck had begun to hurt more than what they were doing to her, she'd given up and accepted it as something that was now a part of her life. Soon, she didn't bother screaming anymore. There was no point.*

*She'd brought this on herself. When the raiders had gone, and she knew the second one she killed had impregnated her, she could have had it taken from her. She didn't, and that was her fault. For these handfuls of decades, she'd endured these daughters and granddaughters, and they had refused to leave her alone to be miserable and die in the peace of the loneliness of the caves.*

*She should have died on her ship. She only used the cryo pod to pull herself erect, to stand, her leg damaged in the suddenness of the attack. She'd never had any patience for those who ran from a battle, not matter how poor the odds. She always felt that people made their own odds, and that had always served her well in her military campaigns. The ship had buckled, though, and that had jarred her precarious balance. She hadn't intended to fall inside and wouldn't have if she could have stopped herself. The pod would have never closed, initiating its emergency escape process, if she'd been able to keep even one arm outside, an appendage to break the beam that signaled the all clear to the pod's escape controls.*

*She'd failed. She'd realized that the moment the pod opened onto this hellish world. There had been no difference in stepping inside and stepping outside. There had been no mental lag in the sensation of then and now, between there and here. It was one blink of the eyes, and then the next. It was the breath taken in one place, and the next taken fifty, one hundred, or even two hundred standard years and half a galaxy away. Her next breath had been on this world, Trasdrom'man, and that had been her curse. The waking had been slow and torturous, the damage to her body crawling over her like maggots on an infection, but the years in between had been gone in a moment without her permission.*

*Waking on this world was still her curse, and it would be with her until the day she died.*

With a minor shift, Holcum eased the pain in her leg, unaware that she had done so, the bed's softness absorbing the motion without a sound. Her snores continued, only occasionally breaking as one nightmare ended and another began, the darkness of the night drawing the events from the black recesses of her brain, events that had made the sweet girl of her childhood into the warped creature she had become.

She would forget these dreams, these nightmares, by the time she awakened in the morning, but for this night, she belonged to them, and they made her live her hellish life all over again. Too quiet to be heard were the whimpers that escaped Holcum's throat each time her snores broke just long enough to let her new nightmare begin. Those whimpers would have told anyone who listened with a sharp enough ear that Holcum didn't enjoy these memories, not one bit.

TRASDROM'MAN wasn't heavily populated, and its hit-and-miss communications infrastructure was centered around its one metropolitan center. Despite this primitive infrastructure, word did travel. Innocetta had the transport now, and within the caverns, there was plenty of room to store it. She found the occasional day when a list of important items was needed in town, or her mother's attention was desired to meet Innocetta's own suppressed cravings for affection and approval. Occasionally in the city she would meet a childhood friend, telling a neutered version of her grandmother's antics or a truncated tidbit of the staff's ineptitudes, the stories arranged to amuse rather than condemn.

One day in town that winter, her hired staff watching over the nearly bedfast grandmother while Innocetta gathered the things from town that she needed, in addition to the items requested by anyone out at the compound, she was with a friend in Winter City at an eating establishment in one of the warmer parts of the municipality. Letting her driver, one of the compound's staff, load the purchased items, Innocetta regaled her friend with several stories one of her hired girls had privately shared from those who'd lipread her grandmother's curses, especially sharing the curse renaming the great inland sea as the Sea of Revenge. Innocetta's friend had laughed at that one, agreeing that it was very funny.

Sitting in the booth next to the two women was another resident of Trasdrom'man who also enjoyed the story of the curse. His laughter was quiet and subdued, and he took the time to jot down the details of the events as Innocetta shared her story. He was a collector of tales that he offered as he traveled, using them as his social lubricant in selling items to people who didn't really need them.

He'd tell this story to people far and wide, and they would remember. Everyone on this world knew of the inland sea, and they also knew it had no name of its own. Other than the vast salt oceans that spread across the planet, giving rise to the massive winter storms that coated the land with snow, there was no other surface water source on Trasdrom'man. There'd been no reason to give it an identifier when it was the only one. It was not as if someone would, at some point, stop one's story, look around with an expression of mystified incomprehension, and then ask which inland sea was being referenced. It needed no other identification, but with this new name, people would feel ownership of the sea; and because that gave them a sense of belonging and power, they would buy what he had to sell. That was why he collected his stories. He was in the business of selling, and that's what the stories allowed him to do.

When he returned to his temporary domicile that evening, his wares packed to leave out the next morning, he slept well, his notes containing Innocetta's story tucked safely in his valise. He would have a good trip this time out, and people would relieve him of many of his wares, the realization that these things they bought took up precious space, had cost even more precious credits, and were hardly used at all, not coming to them until long after the traveling seller-of-goods was days gone.

What he didn't know was the push he would give in spreading old Holcum's curse, at least the part that gave the sea its name, to the far ends of Trasdrom'man. That didn't concern him. He was satisfied with having been in the right spot at just the right time to collect the words he had heard the beautiful young woman sitting behind him speak that day. The credits the story would help him earn were enough for him.

# —Chapter 13—

*4. Hold a mirrer [sic] in front of the deceased's mouth. It shoud [sic] not fog up.*
*5. If sure the deceased is dead, put a needel [sic] through a finger. If deceased does not wake, go to no. 6.*
*6. Nail coffen [sic] shut.*

*—Excerpt from a funeral director's manual dated 1823 AD*

NO MORE than a husk of a person, the woman who had been Ma'jene Holcum, the officer who had held a starstrike battle cruiser in the palm of her hand, who had been a girl with loving parents, and who had taken the life of a man as he took his pleasure in her, was dying. She knew this. She was trapped in her body, and only with the greatest of effort could she communicate. Her eyes, she could still move her eyes easily. Her eyelids, though. They were an entirely different matter. Only the greatest of effort would raise them, and then she had to work immeasurably hard to keep them pulled up to expose her eyes.

She'd seen the photo they'd brought to her. It was on the old ID card she'd kept during the years. She'd seen the face, the face that looked so familiar to her. She'd known the man's name would come to her. She just needed to think about it for a moment or two. She'd moved her eyes, her thoughts working their sluggish paths to come up with the memory she required. Their faces were so far away, those inquiring faces that wanted her to think so quickly. She would be able to think better, more quickly, if she could close her eyes. She wouldn't sleep this time, but the simple act of closing her eyes would take so much of the strain off, relieving her body to concentrate on the picture that had been on the card.

With the releasing of her muscles, the light from the outside world was gone, and the old woman could now think. Now, if she could remember what the card had looked like, the one they had held up for her to see. They'd be so disappointed if she couldn't tell them the answer they sought. She knew it was in her memory, somewhere. She had known him so long ago, and she thought she might have even loved him, but she wasn't sure of that, anymore.

He been a boy, that she knew, but he had been a man, also. She would place him, eventually. She just needed a few more moments.

When she opened her eyes again, the light in the room had changed. The faces with their questions were gone. It had only been a moment. She had simply needed to release her muscles' hold, so her thoughts could trace out the trail the memory of the picture had taken in her mind all those eternities ago. Then she would know the picture. She had it some of it now, but they'd not waited on her. Where were they?

*Rom'n.* She remembered. The word didn't mean much to her, just a name, but she would know the rest of it, eventually. She would have what they wanted to know. She would close her eyes just a moment more, and it would be there. She knew it would. She was good at remembering. That had always been one of her strongest strengths.

She didn't think he'd loved her. He couldn't have loved her. She'd never been loved, not in her whole life. Not even her parents. There were parents in her life. There had to have been. Every child has parents. She just couldn't remember hers.

She remembered flowers, though, and she remembered them in the sky. Even in her old woman's body, she cringed as she remembered seeing the flowers in the sky. They were big and red, and sometimes they changed to white with black leaves billowing out from them. One thing that was unforgettable to her, flowers were always loud, and they hurt her ears. The flowers had made her life go away.

She'd tried to be loved. She had really tried, but she was always, always . . . always . . . something. The words wouldn't come to her. She'd said them, once. A day late, she thought it might have been. A day late and something else. She'd seen the boy that first time. He'd been there, and she'd told him she was a credit short. That was it. She'd always been a day late and a credit short.

All the classes had been set, and their friendships had been in place. There'd been no room for the new recruit. Only the boy had wanted her, and she'd made the most of that. She thought he might have loved her that long-ago first year. He might have wanted her, if she'd only let him.

Maybe he did love her. She remembered a world that was so hot. It had been hot for three days, and then it had been hot for three nights. She'd burned with the heat, but then it had seemed to her it wasn't just the heat from the world. Her skin had been hot in places, and even hotter in others. Places that were already warm through the days became even hotter during the nights, something hot pressing against her skin, someone pressing against her skin, making her want her skin to be even hotter.

That boy, Rom'n. The boy who had become a man had done that to her. For those nights, he'd pressed himself against her.

305

She'd wanted him to, and when he'd stopped, his exhaustion pulling him from her, she'd pressed her skin to his even hotter skin, until they were entangled, and they'd moved together, the heat of the world not so great against the heat of their bodies.

On that last night, he'd almost said his hated words to her, had tried to say them to her. She'd stopped him from letting those words bleed over her, hadn't wanted to hear him say them. Now, all she wanted was to hear those words she had never listened to anyone say to her. Now, they never would, and the old woman knew this one thing for sure. She had never been loved, not even by the boy in the picture. He'd left her, just as her parents and lovers and everyone else had.

If the old woman hadn't been so old, and her mind not so twisted, she might have remembered one more thing. That boy that had grown into a man had loved that long ago girl very much, and the girl the old woman had been so long ago had driven him away, as willfully and as forcefully as she could.

She might also have known one more thing, if only her old, worn synapses had not already made the world of her memories into the world she would have it be. If her boy who had grown into that man were still alive out there somewhere in the vast reaches of space, and if his heart were waiting to beat once again on some distant plane of existence, there might still be an ember of that love glowing deep in his soul, waiting for the right moment to have it stoked back into existence. Perhaps, in some great game of chance, the boy's opportunities had been at least as great as Holcum's in getting off the doomed battle cruiser as it was decimated almost underneath her feet.

The old woman might have known that if she were not so wrapped up in her own version of her life; but then, that wouldn't have been the old woman's style, and she had certainly lived her entire life just the way she'd pleased, all for herself. There was no way she could change that now, not even if her ancient, worn brain could have pieced that option together for her.

She was Holcum, UnderGen'l Ma'jene Holcum, and Ma'jene Holcum didn't arrange her life's events around others. Those poor souls whose lives happened to intersect with Holcum's arranged the paltry events of their lives around her, and that pretty much explained why she found herself at the exact position in her life that she was in on that cold, winter day.

She was Holcum, and that was all she could ever become.

"SHE BE VERY old. Don't expect to like her, but she be my grandmother. For that, I claim her." Innocetta turned to the man next to her at the controls of her transport, Uncle Regge's once, but now belonging to her.

Innocetta had been told that her beauty would find her a man as quickly as an old-Earth flower finds a pollinating bee, but that had been one of someone's unfathomable old-Earth references. She'd laughed, telling the speaker that the phrase used such outlandishly arcane analogies when something more modern and understandable might have better suited the example. However, she did know she was very attracted to this man. She even liked to say his name. *Gregoirini*. It rolled from her tongue, and just imagining it made her smile.

Gregoirini threw his head back and laughed at the prospect of not liking this woman's grandmother. "Anyone so beautiful and charming, how could a beautiful old grandmother, you not have?" he whispered as he looked at Innocetta, the whiteness of the winter outside accentuating the dark-haired beauty with him. "In your old age, what you'll look like, get to see, I will. Excited, how can I not be?" He ran the back of his hand against her arm with a look of apprehension on his face. "Be warm, there, it will?"

"Warm enough," and Innocetta smiled at him, amused at his question. "Grandmother's chambers be the warmest in the mountains."

"A cave, it be, and sounds cold, it does. That be all." He turned to her and smiled. "Know, I do, what you said. Much like Winter City, it will be. Fine, I will find it, I be sure. Forgive me, you must, Innocetta, for all these questions I ask."

"No, I won't." He turned to look at her in surprise. Then his features relaxed, his relief clear on his face when he saw her smirk. She continued, "Your apology I will take when we get there, and in your surprise, you find it be even warmer and better than Winter City. I saw the warm clothing you put on, and the even heavier clothing you had out in your rooms. Even here," and she pointed to the back of the transport, "be more than you will need." She paused, then announced, "We will not even need to park outside."

Gregoirini looked at her, an eyebrow raised. "No? Drive in your house, then, you plan for me to do?"

She playfully slapped his arm. "Grow up, Gregoirini. These be the caverns that have been known here since the first days of our world's settlement. They be huge, and to park inside, we just drive up. It be cold inside the caves, but the walk be short, and we will be inside, away from the wind."

His eyes had a playful glint. He pressed her, "Discussed this before, we have, and to learn the truth, I haven't. Not the same be caverns and caves. Which be yours?"

"Ours be home, cavern or cave. Actually, ours be both, so we feel free to use the terms interchangeably. I know it be wrong, but they be ours, so, oh, well. People can laugh if they want. You already do, and I don't care."

"This transport does have more speed. We can get there before tomorrow, if you wish." Innocetta sat up, leaning against the door, in a good humor. She could see the rise of the mountains in the distance. She glanced at the slowness of the snow-covered landscape as it passed by outside, and she also remembered riding this trip with her Uncle Regge.

"A wreck, I'd have, and want me to do that, you would? Know me for a fool, your grandmother would, the moment she saw my face. Be careful, I will."

Innocetta knew it didn't make any difference what her grandmother knew. There wasn't much of a grandmother there, anymore, not as far as she could tell. That was the only reason she'd been willing to risk this trip out to the compound with her Gregoirini. She didn't want her grandmother to scare him off.

Innocetta hoped she was correct. The grandmother's mind never went very far. Her body might be failing her, but her mind was still very sharp, sharp enough to lash out hard. All she needed was to be pushed enough. A new grandson just might do that. Today would tell that tale just as soon as they arrived, and if Innocetta could get her Gregoirini to pull more speed from the old transport, it might even be today.

When they maneuvered up to the mountain, they stopped, the whiteout of the snow making it all look the same, and Gregoirini couldn't tell where to go. He glanced at Innocetta, and she turned her eyes to him, nodding her head forward, directing him to move the transport ahead.

"See it, I cannot, Innocetta. All seems white to me. Point somewhere, for me, you must, or drive into the sea, I might."

"That, you cannot do. You might drive into the mountain, and you will if you follow my directions, but the sea? It be on the other side of the mountains. Besides, it be frozen solid this time of the year. You could drive across it safely." She pointed to a place that seemed no more than white on white to Gregoirini. "There. The opening be there into our cave and our caverns. Your pick, the choice of words be yours. Just take us there."

"COMMANDED ME, you have." Gregoirini moved the old transport forward. His parents had a much newer one in the city, but this was a classic, and he was impressed it was so well maintained. Someone, he could tell, had loved this vehicle very much. What impressed him even more was the speed it could go. All transports he knew of, and certainly every other one he'd driven, moved at a snail's pace. They were designed for the city, both Summer City as well as Winter City. There was no room to go fast there. Transports were known for their pulling power, one of their primary uses. This one, though. This was a speed-loving machine. He'd had to learn to manage the speed. The power was much too much for most driving, and he was used to stomping on the juice just to get a small increase in speed in his parent's transport. Speed had to be learned to be safe.

His eyes finally made out the differences in color value that determined the white of the mountains against the white of the cave that opened into the recesses of the protecting rock Innocetta claimed as her home. The air biting them as they moved from the transport to the massive door granting entrance to Innocetta's family mountain compound was certainly cold, but not much more than the lesser streets in Winter City. Without his heaviest of wrappings to keep him warm, Gregoirini was very glad for that.

He was surprised to find real furniture beyond that door, and warmth, besides. The walls were much as in Winter City, or even Summer City, for that matter. The blown rock, the Ferro-rock, was as ubiquitous to Trasdrom'man as the heat in summer and the cold in winter, so that was background to him, and he quickly tuned it out. The space, though. These were not the caves he'd imagined when Innocetta had described her home to him. These were the caverns of explorers' dreams.

He wouldn't have known them for caverns, if he hadn't seen the mountains, and Innocetta hadn't told him as such. There were walls inside this mountain, and the rooms had flat ceilings. As Innocetta led him through, he compared the varying room sizes, the differing heights of the ceilings, and he tried to imagine the caverns that had been here for these enormous rooms to be constructed. He had great difficulty with that, because this *was* a home. It was a very large, and it was contained within a mountain, but it was a home, for all that.

Powered lighting. That was the second thing that took him by surprise. There should be no power in these mountains. There was no city power source that could stretch this far. That alone told him there must be more to this family's wealth than anyone in the city thought possible.

He turned to look at the simple beauty of the girl who had picked him from all the rest, and he gazed at her with a new appreciation. She'd never bragged, and with this, bragging, she could have certainly done.

What he really looked forward to was meeting her grandmother, the one who owned all this. Elegant, she must be, as well as eccentric and rich. The old, well-maintained transport for everyday use. This magnificent abode. He would guess their money had been in the family for a very long time, although people who had spoken to him about it said the family had come by it very recently.

Soon, hired servants greeted them. Innocetta turned to Gregoirini, telling him these were her grandmother's staff hired to maintain the compound and help with her grandmother's care. He took a deep breath, beginning to feel very out of his league. His family was certainly not poor and had one of the few private transports in the city. But this, this *space*, and hired *servants*. Even his family didn't have this. Innocetta hadn't boasted, wasn't doing so now, but rather, acted as if this was the way things should be, the manner in which people on the inland sea had always and should continue to live. He smiled to himself at the thought of living so well in such a remote spot. At the same time, he remembered the name the sea had been given by the local girls at the compound, and he smiled even broader. The Sea of Revenge, named by her grandmother. One of the staff turned to him, seeing his smile as an expression of greeting, and returned its warmth in kind.

LATER THAT evening in the secondary compound, warmed by cooking fires and the heat of many bodies, tales were told of the insanely handsome young fiancé who was so charming that he even smiled at the lowliest of the compound's help. The girls twittered with a vicarious thrill, and the adults smiled indulgently. It was nice to have a man in the house. In the main house, they meant, of course, for there were plenty of men in their house. The old grandmother and her beautiful granddaughter, though. A man would do them a world of good. There was a lot to smile about this night, and that was a cause for celebration.

There was another reason for a celebration, too. It was winter, and it was cold. On Trasdrom'man, it didn't take much of an excuse in winter to have a party, especially not when the pay was fair, the food was good, and the rooms were warm. Life on the Sea of Revenge had turned out to be very pleasant for those who had chosen to take the risk of the unknown wiles of living beyond the safety of the city.

Regge needn't have worried so much about the people he had found to work for the grandmother and her granddaughter. Not a one came who didn't realize just how much good fortune had been given to them, and they all stayed. Pretty soon, these families would know no other life, and they would no longer think of themselves as city dwellers. They were of the Holcum's compound, and their pride would begin to grow in that.

Tonight, though, there was a man in the house, and there was food and warmth. They had their celebration. This night deserved rejoicing, and that's what it got.

INNOCETTA PUT her hands on Gregoirini's chest, keeping him from walking through that door. Her heart was barely in her chest, anymore. Her throat choked on it, and her eyes were blinded with the dread of many months of memories, the harshest of which she wouldn't wish on her Gregoirini. All those memories were just through that door. While her grandmother was bedfast, and she'd hardly moved for days upon days, and hadn't spoken coherently in a full day, still, the dread was there. The worry that the old grandmother's bile-spiked personality would suddenly find this to be a good day to erupt couldn't be driven from her granddaughter's mind, no matter how much Innocetta tried to convince herself otherwise.

"Gregor, be you sure you want to do this?" Innocetta pleaded with her eyes, the barest of hopes still in her heart that he might change his mind, telling her he would love to return to Winter City to visit those gathering places where the young, the ones who were still willing to fight the season's cold to enjoy the life that not even winter's blast could take away, were gathered to share good company, and possibly even good food if someone with enough credits was part of the gathering. "She be very old and not so much like me as you might imagine." Innocetta dropped her head, her next words barely whispered. "At least that be what I hope."

Gregoirini reached his hand to cup her chin, raising it to look in her eyes. "So, Gregor, now, I be." He smiled. "For me to not do this, you want badly. Your grandmother, she be. What I find, no matter the woman behind those doors, be not you. You, coming to love, I be. Trust me, you must, Innocetta."

He put his arms around her and hugged her close.

HE *WAS* coming to love this woman, this beauty in his arms, and this, today, was one of the reasons. It was obvious to him she didn't want him to meet her grandmother, but still she refused to say why. Not one negative word had escaped her mouth, and that told him more than a mouthful of assurances, promises, or cover-ups ever could.

"Then, we will do this. Let me see if the staff be ready." She stepped to the door and knocked quietly, opening it just a bit. Leaning inside, she spoke softly, "Ah, Rhendona. It be you with my grandmother. How be she today?"

"Quiet, today, she be, just as for many days she has been. Speak, though, her eyes, they do. Never quiet, they be. Never quiet."

Innocetta moved aside, and the pretty local girl Gregoirini had earlier smiled at stepped through the door. He smiled again as she caught his eye, and she broke into a spat of giggles, sliding along the wall past him, then running until he could see her no more. He turned and caught Innocetta watching him with a smile on her face. He gave a big shrug, and she laughed.

"That be Rhendona. Don't let her bother you. Apparently, you've brought a crush on yourself by smiling at her last night. One of the girls was telling me so. She also told me you're now all the rage in the lesser compound."

"Lesser compound? Here in the mountain, there be another one of these places?"

Innocetta put her hand on his arm, readying herself for their entrance into the old woman's room. Leaning in to whisper, she told him, "We can thank my Uncle Regge for that. Only one compound was to be built, but he was the one with the foresight. He knew to build two." She looked into his eyes and finished in the most conspiratorial of tones, "Plus, we still have all the machines here whenever we decide to build more."

"More?" He laughed softly, just for Innocetta's ears. "For two people, all this be, and for more, already, you be planning?"

"Maybe," she laughed, just as softly. "I need help, though. With more people, you understand. More space can be hired to

314

be built. The more people, of course, they would be little ones."

Gregoirini turned red at the realization of what she was saying. As he cut his gaze to Innocetta's face, he was just in time to see her cut her eyes to the floor, her own embarrassment brightening her face as well.

He leaned in to speak into the freshness of the hair on her head, "Well, then, in, shall we go, the great-grandmother to meet?"

THAT WAS when Innocetta knew with confidence that her grandmother wouldn't drive this man away from her as she had her dear Uncle Regge, and that was also when she allowed herself to relax in his grasp, certain she'd finally found a strength that even she could lean on without fear of falling.

THAT GIRL, the hired one, was gone. Holcum hadn't given her permission to leave. Then the door, it was opening again. The girl should be returning, but this wasn't the same one. Holcum blinked her eyes at what she saw. This was herself from long ago, and the boy she'd known all those years past. This couldn't be real, and yet, there he was standing at her side. The old eyes in the unusable body Holcum now inhabited began to tear up. The pooling moisture caused the figures walking toward her to float, becoming sometimes one person, and sometimes four.

It *was* him. His hair wasn't quite as white, and his skin wasn't quite as pale, but it was his voice whispering to that other her as she stood there beside him. Those features. Her eyes blinked several times rapidly. She wished she could blink away these tears. She'd be able to see him better, then.

Rom'n was back, accompanying herself.

She didn't know how she could be here in this shell of a body and standing there, too, but it was true. It was happening. She was seeing it with her own eyes. She willed that other her to reach her arms to touch him, to run her hand along that beautiful face that looked so much as it had when they'd been young together. She willed herself to tell him what she should have told him when she had the chance all those years ago, those three nights they spent together.

That other her wasn't doing it. Why, Holcum didn't know. *How can I not control my own body? I'm standing there. I can see myself. I can see that boy, now a man, the one who tried to tell me he loved me so many years ago.* She began to rail at herself, her thoughts screaming at the other her standing just in front of her eyes. *Say it! Turn to him! Tell him those words! Tell him now before he goes away again! Now!* She began to shake with the intensity of her determination. She must listen to herself and not let him get away again. She couldn't relive this life over again. Not another lifetime of pain and agony.

She saw the other her reach out a hand, and when she felt a hand touch her face, that was when she knew. This other person wasn't her. She was having a waking nightmare, and this other woman, this *person,* had taken her boy, her *Rom'n,* and she'd carry him from her, love him, and leave Holcum twisted beneath these bedclothes, in this body, to continue to rot one day at a time.

She began to shake with rage. Of course, being so very old, her body so far gone, her furor only escaped to those watching as a small trembling of her muscles, almost as the tightly controlled laughter of one who had experienced a moment of purest joy.

Joy wasn't what Holcum was experiencing, however, and if anyone should see her and think that, they would be very mistaken.

GREGOIRINI TURNED to Innocetta as they exited the room, taking her elbow in his hand, just as Innocetta's eye caught Rhendona down the way. He paused as her hand motioned for the girl to take over her grandmother's care.

"See, so bad, that wasn't. Even liked me, I think she might have." He smiled as he teased her. "Of joy, those tears were. Saw laughter from her, I believe. That I look funny, you didn't say. More as the handsome man, I've seen myself." He puffed his chest out, only to release his lungful of air, and in that moment, laugh at his own humor.

She ran a hand slowly across his chest, the thick fabric of his clothing providing texture to her fingertips. She paused as if thinking, then lightly slapped him there and laughed. "Yes, Gregor, I think she must have liked you very much. I think she welcomed you into her home. I think she would want you to stay here and take care of me, if that be what you wish. She be like that, sometimes." She smiled at him, turning away quickly and not letting him see her smile fade away.

Innocetta had known one thing in there with her grand-mother. Those were not tears of joy that had fallen from those rheumy old eyes, and there was no liking of anyone in that heart. There was something else she knew, too. If that was indeed laughter Gregoirini had seen in the old woman, it wasn't the sort of laughter that made small children giggle with glee, wanting a grandparent to play yet another game to pass the day. Holcum didn't laugh those laughs, and Innocetta sometimes thought that perhaps she never had. When Holcum laughed, children had better be prepared to run. That was the Holcum Innocetta knew.

The old woman was her grandmother, and Innocetta would care for her until she no longer opened those old eyes, but when her grandmother laughed, Innocetta knew the great cooking pot nearby was boiling, and the oven was heated. A gingerbread house only looks tempting until the child realizes what's inside, and inside is death to the unwary visitor. When Gregoirini had said he thought he'd seen laughter, that had made Innocetta's blood run cold, and in the middle of this world's hellish winter, that was very cold, indeed.

317

GREGOIRINI PLACED the old identification cards he'd discovered into his pocket and ran his hands along the walls of the massive room, checking the varying temperatures. Some sections were downright hot, and he could feel exactly where the warmest spots were, too. In Winter City, his parents were full owners of their quarters. That meant the city no longer accepted any maintenance requests for that dwelling, making his family fully responsible. It was the price of knowing your quarters were yours and couldn't be reassigned to anyone else. If they ever wanted the city to pick up the maintenance costs in the future, ownership of the house would revert back to the city. When he'd been seventeen standards, he'd helped with a crew his parents had hired to extend the 'thermals from the warmest room in their Winter City house to his room on the far side of the residence. His parents had agreed to the massive cost as long as he helped on the crew to save on expenses. The geothermals in the city were straightforward. Pipes were run under and through the city walls, granting everyone access to the planet's internal heat, a warmth that was brought up by the water naturally surging from the core of their world to just under their feet. Lying on his sleeping mat at night, it had been comforting to hear the planet's lifeblood surging through his walls.

Not all places in the city were equally blessed, though. The lifeblood ran more hotly in some sections than in others, and with the high mineral content of the water, it wasn't unusual to have pipes clog or corrode, the repairs inciting a quick tear into a wall to replace a damaged flowpipe. The best places to live were those that had the highest water flow, often near the center, or perhaps towards the lowest parts of the city. The passageways and streets, for there were full-fledged streets in Winter City, were generally not lined with the warming flowpipe at all.

Gregoirini understood all that, and he knew this place must

have its own natural chambers within the rock allowing heated groundwater to share its warmth with Innocetta and her grandmother. If he could find the way to access it, this place could be infused with a level of comfort each winter that few other places on this planet could afford.

That wasn't his only idea, either. That same piping could have valves built in. This sea that these mountains abutted was certainly deep enough. In the city, as a student, he'd done a class exercise on the original surveys of Trasdrom'man. The inland sea, named by Innocetta's grandmother as the Sea of Revenge, was thought to be one of the deepest and coldest lakes ever discovered—second only to the vast salt seas that covered the bulk of the planet—with its mean temperature rising far slower each summer than the external temperatures would suggest. Those same flowpipes that carried heated geothermal water could as easily carry cooling seawater.

He glanced up from his musings. There was his Innocetta. He smiled at her, his excitement bleeding into his greeting.

"Innocetta. At these, look. See these, you must." He held the old ID cards and several memory crystals out to her. "Your grandmother's. From old MegaCorp, these be, correct? Visited the old MegaCorp cryo pod as a student, I did. Always interested, I was, and now holding these, I be. To get to one day touch them, I never thought I would. Much about them, do you know?"

TO INNOCETTA, the items were simply one more layer yet to be cleared from the rooms Regge had built for them. She'd known nothing of them until recently, when they'd been instrumental in providing the funds MegaCorp had given her grandmother. Innocetta had picked them up once afterwards, only to have her grandmother rail at her to put them back where she found them. She did point to one, though, showing an image of a slender yet striking young man with pale coloring and very light hair. His features were almost beautiful.

"My grandmother talks about him. Rom'n." She snorted a rueful laugh. "At least she used to talk about him. She doesn't talk about much, now." Her patience with the old woman had worn thin. Her love hadn't, but love and patience are two very different things.

"Perk her up, these may. To try, let me, will you?"

She pulled them from his hand. "Gregoirini, no. This one thing you should let go. Please. My grandmother be very old, and her health be very poor. Let her go in peace, please. You need not try to make her ending better with the likes of these."

"Innocetta," he continued. "All your life, yours, she's been . . ."

She looked at him quizzically, interrupting, "All my life? One summer, Gregor."

"One summer," he conceded. "Heard her speak, even once, I haven't. Please." He took the hand that held the cards and crystals, wrapping Innocetta's fingers around them, and his around hers. "This once? Another chance, never will I have."

Innocetta smiled at his reasoning and his enthusiasm. "Just this once, Gregor. Prepare yourself, though." Then she laughed. "My grandmother be a dragon gone to sleep, and you want to wake her. All the gods love a fool, and you the most of all. Go to your dragon, and I will go with you. The gods help us all, though. The gods may need to help us all."

The old grandmother did respond to the ID cards when they were shown to her. The first two she saw, touting pictures of people in old-fashioned military dress, triggered eye movements both frantic and unclear, the old lips trying to move, but no sound coming from them. Concerned, Gregoirini and Innocetta, standing across from the old woman, looked at each other, worried that their attempts to jar the old woman back into their world, to enable her to communicate with them, were overstimulating her system, and Innocetta laid the cards out of her sight on the bed-coverings.

Gregoirini whispered, "Just one more, Innocetta. One more, and put them away, we will." He pleaded with his eyes, his desire to communicate with the grandmother just once bleeding from him. Innocetta gave a reluctant nod, her mouth tightening with doubt, yet her love for the man standing across the bed from her telling her to allow what he was asking of her.

He picked up the final card, and he held it out to Innocetta's grandmother, who took it in her palsied hand.

THE THIRD ID card was the one with the picture the old woman had been shown so long ago, the one she'd had time to think about, the one she'd searched her mind for the information on, and this time, the name there on the tip of her tongue. She didn't have to think about this picture, to try to force her thick, cobwebbed-filled brain pull the story from the long-forgotten recesses of things stored away long ago, while at the same time, forming long-forgotten words with lips that refused to obey her commands. She could focus all her energies into making her chest push the air, her mouth and tongue form the resonating chamber, and her lips enunciate the sounds she had already strung together just for this event.

"Rom'n."

That was her first word, and the two puppeteers who held the strings, pulling the old woman along that path she had labored down so tediously, looked at each other, surprise dancing across their faces. They had to listen closely. The words weren't given the quick footsteps of youth, but they were spoken, one following another, stringing into sentences, and then into an unbelievable tale. The old woman told the story that went with the name, then another and another, some seeming to follow along with what her granddaughter had heard over the past year, and others connected in some way only the old women telling the stories would understand.

"From the first day at the academy," she began, as her hand, still holding the ID card, fell to rest on the bedding, "he loved me. But I never let myself love him back. I could have. I was orphaned as a child, and the soldiers used me for their toy. I wasn't old enough to understand, just the pain. That's why I couldn't love him. I had no love in me. The soldiers had taken it all. After our promotion, Rom'n held me, and we danced the nights away. He wanted me then, and I teased him. Later, I thought he could give me back the innocence I'd lost, and I tried to woo that from him for three days. At the end, it was just me, and I ran from him, leaving him alone.

"The ship took my leg from me. The floor was no longer there. I fell into the heat of summer, and I took that raider as he took me. Poor Arianna. I tried to love her, but I couldn't find the love inside of me. Only, in all my life, my granddaughter has loved me."

With those final words, Holcum's eyes locked on Innocetta's tear-filled ones, and her hand, gnarled and drawn up into itself, raised itself from where it lay beside her, reaching towards the granddaughter. Innocetta wrapped her hands around her grandmother's, one thumb resting against the ancient ID card, stroking it gently. The old crippled fingers moved, clawing, working free the ID card the granddaughter pressed into her hand.

"One hundred years." Holcum shook the card grasped in her twisted fingers.

"What, Grandmother? What about one hundred years?"

Almost choking, Holcum rasped out, "Dead. One hundred years, and he would have loved me." With her hand barely under her control, the shaking that of a palsied set of muscles too old and worn to care any longer just what the mind might tell them to do, she thrust the card at Innocetta, tapping it against her arm.

"Rom'n." Her body jerked itself in a violent fit of coughing, the pain coursing through her chest, as each cough ripped her muscles apart.

"Grandmother!" Innocetta looked up to Gregoirini, desperation on her face. "Gregor, what should I do?"

GREGOIRINI KNEW. He'd held his own grandmother when she'd died. Sometimes, that was all that could be done, and he knew that. Knowing they were held in love when they needed love the most was all that could be given. Understanding that, the tears of his own memories moistening his eyes, he gave his wisest advice to the old woman's most loyal protector.

"Love her, Innocetta. So she knows, hold her now."

Innocetta reached to place her arms around the old woman, the coughing shaking them both. Feeling the hand with the ID card moving between them, pressing them apart, Innocetta released the old woman to lie back against her bedding, reaching for the hand that needed her attention. The old hand in its quivering parody of a dance finally reached its destination, and Innocetta's open palm accepted the card that had ignited her grandmother this final time.

"He could have been mine."

Innocetta looked at Gregoirini with desperate eyes. He motioned for her to pay attention to the old woman. "Now, Innocetta, be the time. Listen now, you must."

She leaned over her grandmother, her ear close to her lips to pick up the words that were barely being said.

"He would have loved me. Now, he's yours."

Those were the last words anyone heard her grandmother speak. Rising to look at Gregoirini across her grandmother's bed, a sudden odor of urine permeated the room. A numbness came over them. When they looked down, they could tell.

The grandmother was dead.

# —Chapter 14—

*And the sins of the fathers and the mothers shall
be visited upon the children even unto the tenth
generation.*

*—Quote remembered from an
ancient and unknown holy book*

THERE WAS no real funeral.

In fact, there wasn't even a semblance of a funeral. What
would have been the point? Everyone who had cared about Holcum was either dead or in the room with her when she died.

There was grieving for the old woman. There was also rejoicing. In the stories told in the lesser compound, those voices and
renditions of the events that had made up the final year of the old
woman's life might have sounded as if some were rejoicing in
the death of a vile creature, the laughter at her odd behaviors
caricatured beyond all semblance of reality in order to entertain
friends and relatives. In their minds, rejoicing was exactly what
they would have thought they were doing. The wicked old witch
was dead!

However, to vilify someone, that person has to be known
intimately well. Otherwise, the person isn't truly vilified. He or
she is simply mocked. The Holcum from decades earlier had been

worshipped by some as a guardian hero for cleansing their world from the evils of the raiders who had returned to raid Trasdrom'man as the whim struck them, taking what they would, whether it be the virginity of children, hard-gained goods, or the casual human life, and then disappearing to let the hapless citizens pick up the pieces. What did it hurt if their hero chose to sequester herself far away from the blessed conveniences of civilized life as she lived out the role of cloistered holy woman?

To others, she was the wicked creature they used to threaten their children into doing what was right, to brush small teeth, wash behind the ears, and eat the small green things that parents always insist on adding to their children's mealtime plates.

She had been mocked more times in her life than most vile people ever are, but she had rarely been understood, and even more rarely had anyone taken the time to get to know her. The granddaughter had, and the granddaughter was the one who grieved, her right of letting go well earned.

Gregoirini grieved, also, but his grieving was for his idea of who the grandmother might have been. Those last few moments, however, had not truly been the grandmother. Perhaps the barbs of her personality had finally softened in those residual moments of existence, but that was not Holcum. He might as well have known the great old-Earth ostrich by the small, furred chick that preceded its violent adult nature. Gregoirini grieved for what he didn't know.

Only Innocetta knew the grandmother. That beautiful young woman was the one kindred spirit that the grandmother had been given on this world. When the grandmother had railed at the events of her life, and even at Innocetta, it had often been hard to take. However, when the railing was done and the grandmother once again allowed some measure of peace to permeate the relationship of grandmother and granddaughter, Innocetta found herself admitting each and every time that she would have reacted the exact same way had she been forced along the paths that had carried her grandmother to that particular junction in her life. When Innocetta grieved over the grandmother, her grief was the only one that counted.

When she rejoiced, it was also over the grandmother. For many months, Innocetta had forgotten the documents the grandmother had insisted on before she allowed herself to be taken to the sea, the dunking there hoped to return the vigor of youth to a body so badly abused as to be on the needle of death, the slightest sudden movement bringing driving pain that could pierce the life balanced there, letting the lowest underworld hell claim that person as its own.

The money house had not forgotten, though.

Within days of the news reaching Winter City, there was an envoy that traveled all the way to the caves surrounding the Sea of Revenge, and he was only slightly less impressed with the compound's living quarters than Gregoirini had been. He knew the balance in the accounts that had been transferred into Innocetta's name, and that had led him to expect something more than a modest cave complex. The good that old Regge had performed with his teams of workers and his foresight had been an endeavor that had outstripped almost anything on this world. While well-off and important society figures on other worlds might consider Innocetta's dwelling rough and even inadequately pretentious, there were no society figures from other worlds visiting Trasdrom'man, so their opinions were moot. For those who hailed from this globe, there was little to compare.

Innocetta lived in a palace, at least by the standards of Winter City and Summer City. When the envoy returned to the city complex later that day, he would describe the mysteries of what he'd seen, the rarely visited cave complex now a topic of city-wide conversation. Holcum had been the richest person on this world, even if she'd not realized just how much, in funds, she'd really

326

possessed in her accounts.

Now, that honor had been transferred, and when she was given the news, Innocetta found a place to sit to rest her newly staggered sense of her world. She'd seen the numbers before, and she'd known they were enormous. The pay accumulated, the interest, and all those years of Holcum's immersion in that pod had come back to Holcum that summer, to the one who had deserved it all. The numbers had stretched the imagination, but they hadn't been Innocetta's numbers. She'd let them slip from her thoughts so that she could deal with her grandmother, not with *what-ifs* in a credit crystal.

Now, the numbers were no longer what-ifs. They were hers, and the enormity of it astounded her. A lot, Innocetta had thought at the time, was used to build up the compound, with the solar panels and batteries to give them light even in the deepest chambers. Even with what had been spent, the interest on the accounts was so great, the money Regge spent had all come back to them, plus much, much more.

*It, you must spend*, the envoy from the money house encouraged her, *before tired of your novelty, people grow, and won't sell you anything.*

She couldn't spend all this, not in ten lifetimes. She looked at the man across the room, the one she would enjoy spending those ten lifetimes with, and smiled at him pleadingly.

"You'll help me, Gregor, won't you? Please tell me you'll be here to help me spend all these credits."

He walked to her, glancing at the amounts she'd received, his eyes opening wide, then he let his face break into a broad smile.

"Heat from your mountain's heart to warm your mountain rooms. Then, the cold of your sea to cool those same spaces. A good start, that will be? Maybe a bit of room for the little ones that will grow someday?"

"The heat for now, my love. It be winter, and cooling, we

don't need." Seeing his thoughts were already preoccupied as he walked from the room, the numbers and work crews already on his lips, she leaned back in her seat and laughed, speaking softly to herself. "Ah, Gregor. You be a man of action. You be suited for me, and I for you. Have pleasure with your funds, Gregor. After all, they never meant much to the old woman, and she lived just the life she pleased. Credits don't mean everything, and if you spend them all, we'll still have each other." She chuckled to herself. "Each other and a brood of children, if I get my way."

She also soon left the room, much richer than when she'd entered that morning. She was, she knew, the bona fide richest woman on this world, and she didn't even consider the credits as part of her riches. The credits were head knowledge to her. She would use them while she had them, but if they were gone some-day, her life would continue, and that was just the way she would want it. She was rich in love, and that was the way she wanted to live.

In this, following the dictates of her inner self, the grand-daughter's strength of character was certainly the kindred spirit to the grandmother. Holcum had always lived by her personal mandates, even if those mandates didn't quite agree with those she lashed out at. Innocetta's strength was found in love, and nothing would be allowed to sway her from that course, either.

In that, they both lived true to themselves, and as long as the granddaughter walked the face of Trasdrom'man, the grand-mother lived on.


GREGOIRINI JERKED away from the wall he'd been leaning against, momentarily startled. This wasn't the first time he'd heard rumbles in the Ferro-concrete. This time was different, though.

This time the wall had shaken.

Seismically, this world was very stable, and any fault lines there were ran along the trenches at the bottom of the salt oceans. No earthquakes had been recorded on land since the settlement of this world many years before. It didn't even occur to Gregoirini to suspect an earthquake. He had a much more practical thought in mind, that of the teenage engineer who had torn up his family's walls in Winter City to rearrange the piping that carried the lifeblood of the city. Gregoirini had heard the gurgling numerous times since being out here, but it was the shaking that got him to thinking.

He knew piping. He was very practical in those areas, his mind seeing the workings behind what covered the surfaces of walls and made them pretty. With people, he was perhaps not so capable, but walls and pipes he understood. Gurgling meant movement of the heated water in the rock behind the Ferroconcrete walls. That, he could use, because the water that moved behind the rock would also move through pipes and conduits to any location he chose. The shaking also meant something else: pressure, and pressure meant the liquid inside would *want* to find a way to go where he designed it to go.

Walking the perimeter of the rooms in the compound, paying attention to doorways, ceiling heights, and the varying temperatures of each space, he surveyed what might be done. In one room, he paused to dig through a container of items he'd brought with him and pulled out his old glass, the one his parents had splurged on when he'd been in school. Then, brushing his hand across it to activate its internal circuitry, he pulled and pushed his way to a program that showed geometries and volumes and forces. He'd spent time interfacing this on his glass during his years in his classes, and the use of this tool, one that might appear very difficult to someone unlearned in its use, was to Gregoirini the essence of clarity and ease.

Soon, he had the rooms, their sizes, and even the heating requirements for each in the range of degrees of desired increase or decrease entered, and the program took ever, configuring and refiguring the optimal placement of the flowpipes that might make these caverns the snuggest habitation on all Trasdrom'man. Within days, the hot water within the walls was being piped throughout the living areas of the compound, with the lesser compound receiving a secondary piping system that could keep their smaller quarters cozy and warm. Gregoirini explained to Innocetta that he could also set up a rudimentary set of valves in each room to adjust individual temperature preferences, but the time needed for that would be more intensive. She agreed that it was best to concentrate on heat for the time being; and valves as well as the cooling he'd spoken with her about could come later.

Innocetta was very pleased to have the warmth spread so evenly throughout the compound, no matter whether others might think more adjustments were necessary. As she admired the work, she joked with Gregor that he could perhaps siphon some of the water into a private bath for her relaxation. Somehow, she didn't seem surprised when he started to calculate just what would be needed to provide her request.

"Cap the pipes from the walls where it comes out, we could," he smiled, "and allow it to run for any length of time, draining directly into the lake. Continuous heat from the mountain's core, with an unending supply of water."

Innocetta laughed at his enthusiasm, taking his idea one step further. "Someone told me once this heat in the walls could be used to build a power plant. Perhaps when you finish my bath, you could go deep in the mountain and construct that power plant that was suggested to me so long ago."

Gregor had already thought of such a thing, not willing to suggest spending so much of her inheritance, but at her suggestion, he grabbed his glass and immediately started to move his hand across its surface. "Very possible, that be! Do this idea, I could. Funds, you have. Some of that, I would require, the machines with which to buy, but to plan, so easy, it would be!"

She took his arm, pulling the glass from his hands. She laid it aside, wrapping her arms around him, and laying her head on his chest. "There be time, Gregor. All your plans needn't be completed before winter be done." She pulled her head back to look into his face. "I love that about you. You jump in and get things done. Already we have the heat that makes this winter as if it were already over. Soon, you will make me think I cannot live without you."

He grabbed her, lifting her off her feet, and laughing with a joy he couldn't contain. "Already, to live without you, I cannot. To do these things, I'll continue, if have me, you will."

"Put me down!" Innocetta pressed her hands against his shoulders, laughing at his pleasure in her. More quietly, she continued, "I take satisfaction in these things you do for me. You've given me much joy. However, these things," she paused to look around her, her eyes resting on the flowpipes and the as-yet unfinished walls where they'd been installed. Then reaching a hand out to touch the glass she'd laid to the side, she went on. "These things be not what give me pleasure. Do none of these things, and I'll still find happiness in you. You say, *if* I will have you. Rather, you should say, if I'll give you up, because I won't. The old grandmother and I were the same in this, strong in our stubbornness. You've entered my life and made me need you. Now, I wouldn't give you up if you tried.

"I've come to love my home here on the sea. When I first came, I was appalled and only stayed for the grandmother. My dear Uncle Regge made this a house, and you be making it a home. If you'll stay, it will be a home for us both."

"In my mind, a home, already, it seems, and be at its center, you must." Gregoirini placed his hand on her head, running his palm over her hair, letting the strands draw themselves through his fingers, as he took in the smell of the woman who was allowing him to step into her life, hopefully to stay. As he let her scent overwhelm him, his body soon found his need of her was just as great as her need of him.

THAT NIGHT, they truly found one another. In the process, Gregor took Innocetta up on an earlier suggestion she'd offered him, one that was a natural result of loving this beautiful woman who was the pinnacle, the dóme, of this world here by the frozen sea. Before long, there would soon be many small ones running about, and Gregor would be pressed to come through with all the projects he dreamed of doing. Small ones take time, and soon he would have little of that. Funds to complete his projects might be seemingly unlimited, but the time to do them was another matter. They would eventually get done, however, and life would be good in the Holcum compound on the edge of the cursed Sea of Revenge. Innocetta's and Gregor's love for each other would see to that.

INNOCETTA TOUCHED the gray in Gregor's hair. She idly wondered when her own dark strands would reflect the years that were taking her by storm. She lay back, her head resting on the pillowing cushion, and her eyes found the ceiling above her head. There were rooms in this compound, she knew, that had no ceiling. Smiling in amusement to herself, she also knew that wasn't exactly correct. This mountainside was a complex system of caverns, and they all had ceilings.

Caverns. She'd finally come to follow Gregor's more technically correct terminology for these spaces in which she lived, and in which her grandmother had lived before she died. These *caverns* were often massive, and as Gregor had found the time to enlarge the compound, adding room after room, the volume of each original *cave*, she smiled again, had dictated the size of each finished room. At night, there were some rooms in which the ceilings were distant enough to fade into the darkness.

When the youngest of their children had grown enough to be independent, no longer needing the attentions of their mother during the night hours, Gregor had used Uncle Regge's old Ferro-cement machine to build a series of rooms just for the two of them. He hadn't understood at first why she didn't want to use one of the high-ceilinged chambers for their sleep time, but he had acquiesced. Even now, she wasn't sure he really understood, but it was like him to let her have her way in such matters. In this mountain of stone piled around and above them, it was somehow comforting for Innocetta to be able to look up from her bed at night and see where the darkness ended.

All but two of their children were now bonded, and some-times that still caught her by surprise, even with all the changes she'd seen in her life. Just the other day, she remembered, she'd been in the kitchens built in the old lesser compound, managing the menu the cooks were preparing for the coming gathering. She'd heard the sound of childish voices, those of the two youngest still with Gregor and her, and had smiled and turned, expecting them to run to her arms, their kisses hers, and her kisses expected in return. She'd been shocked to see two adults walk through the door, their animated conversation brightening their beautiful faces. She realized it had been a trick of the caverns and the bending of the sound waves as they wrapped themselves around the stone, sinuously undulating along the Ferro-concrete ceilings, and caressing the open doorways to tease Innocetta's ears with the reminders of how much time had passed unnoticed out here in these caverns that she'd called home for all these years. She had truly expected the small children those bodies had once been to step through that door.

As the light in the room changed ever so slightly, dawn soon on its way, Innocetta's breathing quickened as she remembered Gregor's arms around her just hours before, his skin touching hers, the movements of his body making hers one, her own gasping release causing her to melt against the man who could do that to her again and again without it ever getting old. They'd learned each other over the years. He had become her rock, making her strong when ill winds buffeted their family, and their family *had* been put to the test.

Many of their children, now bonded, lived in the distant city, returning home to family gatherings only when Gregor and Innocetta sent the transports for them. One, though. Innocetta turned her face so that the softness of her bedding soaked up her tears as she remembered the one that wouldn't be coming. She'd sent her away. Innocetta had done that, and it still broke her heart when she thought of it. She would do it again, and almost had with one of her boys. He'd allowed his will to be broken, though, and he and his mother had become good friends, his visits during the gatherings anticipated and enjoyed.

That other one, though. She'd bucked her parents, although she had really railed against her mother. Gregor had supported Innocetta in front of their daughter, but privately he'd fought to give the daughter her head, willing to let her go the way she wanted. Innocetta had stood firm, nonetheless. If the daughter wanted to bond with the older woman she'd brought into Innocetta's home, she would do it elsewhere. It would not happen here in the rooms of this mountain.

The son had listened to her. When he'd been a teenager and attending the live-away school in the city he had insisted on, he'd come home one summer holiday, his friend from his school traveling to the compound with him. Innocetta had entered his room early one morning, and she'd been very surprised to find his sleepover friend from school was much more than just a friend. Their sleeping forms were only partially covered by the light blankets needed even in summer in the cooled rooms of the Holcum compound. The dawning sun through the massive

334

glassine window mounted in the cliff face danced across their golden-skinned bodies, their limbs entwined in the remains of a very intimate embrace. She'd awakened both boys at once, sending the friend to a separate room until he could be returned to the city.

Her son had been furious, had brought up his sister and the death-thing she had done to herself when her mother had disowned her, and had threatened to do the same, to go with the boy and make theirs a life together, dead to the family, never returning to the compound ever again. He hadn't done so, however. He had finished his schooling, albeit with a tutor here in the compound. He *had* eventually gone to live with that boy. He had even brought the boy, a man by then, back with him on a long-ago visit, the two of them not really sure of their welcome. On that visit, Innocetta had admitted to her son, as well as the boy, that she had liked her son's friend then, and now, she liked the man he'd become, also. She even looked forward to him coming with her son to the gatherings. They took separate rooms, though, while they were in the compound. That was Innocetta's condition, and it was one she wouldn't give in on.

Innocetta turned her head to look through the door where she could see the morning's light filtering down the massive passageway that bore deep into the mountain. Not all the rooms could have sun directly from the cliff face. Many gained what light they could from the passageway through the massive window in the cliff face, with their wide doors angled sharply into the corridor. Innocetta's favorite time of day came when the morning light brightened the passageway outside her door, and at times she would rise to stand in front of the uncovered window, the sun streaming across her body, the passageway cooled in the hottest of the summers and warmed even in the coldest of the winters, the sun her friend at those stolen moments.

As much as she enjoyed lying next to her bonded man, that

predawn light, filtering in so very softly at this early hour, told her what she needed to do. Swinging her legs to the edge of her bed, she dropped them to the floor and sat up. It was time to greet the day. She crossed the room, and through the door, she found that which she needed to greet life this morning. The sun. She walked to the window as she had so many times in the past, its glassine stretching to the lofty heights of the cavern ceiling, and she basked. Her eyes looked outside at the waters of the sea, the winter winds already buffeting its surface, and her heart leaped to see the millions of fireflashes that danced across the tops of the frozen waves, the blinding pinpoints of reflected light softened by the self-tinting qualities of the window's matrix core.

Today, she hoped the upgrades to their small geothermal power plant would be completed. She'd convinced Gregor to install new, larger machines against his better judgment. He hadn't wanted to invest the enormous sums needed to bring the very best equipment onworld for this upgrade, but Innocetta had been convincing. With the most recent expansion of the compound, the original power plant he'd installed so long ago was barely adequate. She had promised him they could recoup much of the cost by encouraging other families to come to live on the sea. Of course, she had told him, they'd need to find the caverns for their own homes far across the other side of the water. He'd laughed. *The Sea of Revenge? Drive them away, the offer will. Best, it might be, a new name for the sea to have.*

Innocetta wouldn't hear of that, so she planned to find her own ways to make that quickly-stated promise to attract others from the city become real, even if they didn't yet know they wanted to come. She laughed to herself, remembering those words she'd spoken so confidently. She'd been much more convincing to Gregor than she now felt inside. Perhaps it was the changeover of the energy sources, as the upgrading process had caused repeated power cuts over the past few days. They had been irritating, and Innocetta wanted it to be finished before the upcoming family gathering.

She raised her arms and stretched into the brightness of the winter sun flashing off the sea's surface and smiled. Despite her momentary self-doubt, was she ever anything less than convincing? She thought more and more how like her the old grandmother might have been if she'd been given the opportunities of a loving family and the enormous funds to live really well. They had been two of a kind, and the old woman had never seen that. To tell the truth, Innocetta had caught it in glimpses, only, but time was painting the truth on the years. They had been soul mates, and in some way, they still were, wherever her grandmother was spending her afterlife, even if it was only in the heart of the one who had been willing to give that heart to the grandmother.

*The power plant,* she reminded herself. *It must be seen to.* Turning from her window, she walked to a storage area and pulled out clothing for the day. She'd need something warm for visiting the construction area. She wanted it completed before the rising sun left her world's sky, so to prod the workers, deep in the mountain she would go. If she were there, the workers would jump, her words keeping them busy. Why not? she wondered. After all, it be no more than I expect from myself.

As she pulled on the last of her clothing and exited the suite of chambers, she paused to watch her Gregor turn on the bed, his arm reaching for her.

*Gregor,* she mused. *Of all I have here, only you I couldn't live without. Would that I could spend the day in your arms.*

As she stepped into her day, she meant it, too. She just had a very busy schedule ahead of her, and Gregor would have to wait.

GIAN'A POKED her head in the doorway, an unusually heavy scarf wrapped around her neck. Innocetta looked up at her daughter and smiled. She was beautiful. She'd been so lucky to get her coloring from Gregor. No matter how long and hard the winters here on Trasdrom'man, Gian'a always had a beautiful freshness about her. Of course, Gian'i had those looks, also, and he was the equally beautiful twin to his sister, the pair of them two sides of a Trasdrom'man lyan, the most beautiful of coins on this world, he the head and she the tail. The coin, though, was rarely as beautiful as her children had grown to be.

"Gian'a, dear. Please come give your mother a kiss." Innocetta motioned with her hand, standing from her work surface to reach her arms to her daughter. As she placed her hands on Gian'a's shoulders, pulling their faces next to each other's, she chuckled and whispered to her, "And why be you dressed so warmly here in the compound? Have you just come from a pleasant walk outside, enjoying the shores of my grandmother's sea?" Innocetta smiled impishly with her questions.

Gian'a drew back, a look of horror on her face. "Mother! Outside? Have you been outside to endure the cold even once this winter?"

Innocetta laughed, returning to her seat, her work materials back in her hands. "Gian'a, dear. Don't be gauche. Outside? Seriously? I was teasing you. Why, this be the worst winter on record this world has known since the original settlers recorded the first one, and that one they were totally unprepared for. You can thank your Uncle Regge we have this warm mountain retreat to weather these storms."

Gian'a pulled her scarf more tightly to seal a place she seemed to feel was letting in too much overcool air. She sighed at a reference to someone she didn't even know, rolling her eyes to the ceiling. "Thank you, Uncle Regge, for these rooms in which we abide." She looked at her mother with a smirk. "Was that good enough for you, Mother?"

Her mother sat back, her materials held loosely in her hands,

338

and she let amusement play across her lips. "Thank you, Gian'a, for that eagerly stated rendition, and yes, it was good enough." Pursing her lips, she probed, "Be it really that cold in here to you?"

"Mother, you need to get up and walk the compound. Everyone, everywhere, be pulling out the warmest of clothing. May I get Gian'i to take me to my friend's in Winter City? In the transport?"

"Have you and your brother completed your schooling assignments for this week? I happen to know this friend of yours." Innocetta was already turning her attention back to her work in front of her, adjusting the eyepieces she'd recently been forced to wear for this close-up work. "This trip won't be a one-day event. Half a day just to get to the city, I know that. Have you made the necessary plans to stay, already?"

"Mother!" Gian'a turned to walk out the door. "I be not stupid. My friend will let me stay the night with her. Gia can come back to get me tomorrow." She walked through the door, and then she leaned her head back inside as if surprised her mother's answer hadn't already followed along after her. "Mother, can I?"

Innocetta looked up, in her thoughts her daughter's trip already a sure thing, the welcomed intrusion into her morning quick and uneventful. "Can you what, dear?"

"Mother! I asked you! The city?" Gian'a's look of exasperation made her mother smile in remembrance as she nodded her head and waved her daughter out the door.

*Truly cold in here, be it? I do feel a little chilled.* Innocetta pulled her lightweight robe around her, absently reaching to fasten it at her throat. Warmed a bit, she turned her focus back to the things she needed to do, those items in front of her on her work surface.

AROUND HER, the chambers *had* begun to cool. Currently, it was only a nagging thread of irritation to those who were dressed in the most lightweight of clothing, but soon, all would notice the permeating chill. Winter had come to the compound, and this season, it wouldn't stay outside, the thick rock of the mountain providing protection from nature's wrath.

Colder than the coldest winter previously recorded, it had certainly been, and the geothermals were beginning to freeze. Even this insular part of Trasdrom'man would know what the rest of the populace experienced each winter day, and that wasn't a pleasant thought. It was just that no one was thinking it, yet.

They would, though. Before this day was out, Trasdrom'man would see to that.

"GREGOR, IT BE freezing in here. Gian'a said so this morning, but this be extreme. I thought it was her imagination, but no more." Innocetta rubbed her arms with her hands. "Be it really that cold outside?" She walked over to pull closed the massive drapes that guarded the sides of the window where the wind had blown constantly all day, the swirling snow pelting the glassine when gusts reached down and thrashed the surface of the frozen sea.

"Than you know, even colder, it be, my dear. Checking with the power plant, I've been, and cooling faster than the deep underground can warm it, the water be. Rode back from the city with Gian'i and brought with us a city engineer. Suspected this, I did, although no way to know for sure, there was."

Gregoirini was already pulling on his warmest clothes, his next stop the underground power plant with the engineer. All the heated water for the massive Holcum compound was drawn from natural underground reservoirs far below where the water remained very hot, and after some of the heat was drawn from it to satisfy the plant's power production, the rest was pumped

340

throughout the flowpipe installed in the walls of the inhabited mountain chambers. Long gone were the days when there was enough pressure from the natural underground heating of the water alone to push the volumes of fluid needed to accommodate all the rooms the family wanted warmed.

"What be there to fix this? It can be fixed, can't it?" Innocetta put her head around that, the very idea filling her with shock and dread. The geothermals had become so ubiquitous with the caverns that she couldn't imagine the two as separate entities.

Gregoirini smiled at her, placing a hand on her shoulder and a kiss on her cheek. "To worry, there be no need. Have a solution, I thought the engineer might. Just wanted him here before the problem actually arose, I did. That, get, I didn't, and now, see the problem I've created, we can. Not so well did I do in planning ahead."

Innocetta wasn't satisfied with his answer and pushed him for more. "The plans, Gregor. What be they? A hundred transports all in a row, the power plants revved to the highest output known?"

Gregor smiled at the woman he loved, only now turning the mildest of gray, his own head nearly white. "Don't be petulant, my lovely one. Lining up the transports, we won't need. Draw the water faster, we will."

"Faster, Gregor?"

"Yes, Innocetta. The cooling of the exterior rock layers be causing the water inside to drop in temperature until, to keep warm, there be not enough for us." He seemed very pleased with himself. "The water, though. Pull enough, we can, although pumped offsite, the excess may need to be. To push the cooled water back into the ground helps us not at all."

Gregor's bonded one of many years stepped to him, sliding her hands into the interior of his opened coat, letting its excess girth wrap them both. "You be so warm. I be glad to see you've already worked this out." She stood against him for a few moments, and then questioned him. "Our pumps be not big enough to do this, be that the problem?"

Gregor enjoyed these moments when this soon-to-be grandmother took time for him, letting the rest of this compound's affairs mind themselves for a moment. However, he had to give credit where credit was due.

"Find the solution, the engineer did. Not the pumps, it be. Blasted out, the frozen water must be. Too cold, it be, to send back into the underground. Pull the water faster, yes, we must. But remember, also required, the water, offsite, must be sent." He grinned in anticipation, waiting for the response he knew would come.

Innocetta stepped back. "How? Rather, where? If it be so cold as you say, the water will freeze too quickly to carry far away."

That's when the man she loved so laughed at her lack of understanding. "Your idea, it all be, my good woman. Yours!"

"And the idea you be talking about? What be it?" She pursed her lips at him. "Whatever it be, be not mine. I had nothing to do with any of this until Gian'a told me of the chill she felt this morning."

"From many years ago, gave me this idea, you did."

Innocetta felt the beginnings of amusement. She again saw the boy of long ago in her aging man, his enthusiasm for projects sometimes overtaking his innate good sense. She didn't know what her idea had been, yet, but his enthusiasm already had her convinced it would get done.

"The power, we sell."

"Sell? Who will buy it?"

Gregor laughed. "Said that, you did, precious Innocetta. Now, we will."

"You have my attention, Gregor. How?"

Their conversation went on, Gregor telling Innocetta those things that explained just how the selling would work. It seemed the engineer felt the best way to handle the problem of the geo-thermals freezing was to draw them from the ground faster, not allowing the massive, water-filled cavities in the mountain's flanks to cool. Draw it much faster, he had said. He seemed to feel the underground chambers of water, superheated to massively high temperatures by Trasdrom'man's underground, fric-tion-driven furnaces, could not be impacted negatively, no matter how much water was drawn from them.

Gregor told Innocetta he had already worked up the contracts for caving exploration teams to explore around the mountains, and he was also putting together a list of items that would need to come from offworld. "When starts, the construction does," he told her, "want to come to live here, people will. Carve mansions for them in these caves, we will, built by the Ferro-cement machine, by blasting, and by the luxuries added to finish them out."

"We'll sell them these mansions? Summer and Winter City gives space to live almost for free."

"Not sell, Innocetta. Give." He grinned, and his eyes spar-kled.

"Gregor! I suggested this? I do not think so. What other woman did you treat as your bonded one to mix me up with her?" She drew away from him altogether, her impending laughter threatening to erupt and shatter his good opinion of himself.

"You did. Give the houses to them, we do, just to live in, but not to have. Sell the power, though, so to live in the houses, they can."

Innocetta caught on quickly. "I see, my bonded mate. We have the only source of warmth on this lake. Pump it around the mountains, and the warmth we've enjoyed will be the temptation they cannot resist."

Gregor jumped in with her. "And give them cooling in the summer, we can, when the summer sun beats down. Resist, no one will."

Innocetta was reminded once again of what a brilliant, hard-working man she'd lucked into when Gregor became hers. He'd taken her suggestion and made something magnificent of it. Was this outrageously glorious plan hers? Not really. It had come from someone else, someone who had cared about her very much.

She smiled, Gregor thinking it was for him, but she was remembering a man who had loved her long, long ago, and who had offered her an idea she'd pushed aside as worthless. Now, that long-ago man was giving his love back to her in this new and enormous project that could change the face of this world, or at least her part of it.

She looked upwards to the ceiling and breathed a thanks to the man whose love she wished she could have returned. *Thank you, Uncle Regge. Thank you for everything.*

IF THIS WORLD'S economy had afforded it the luxury of having the high-flying satellites that were commonplace in the skies of so many worlds, its people would soon have seen what was coming: the moving of the great Ferro-cement machines to new locations around the inland sea, the many trips into town to retrieve the expensive offworld goods, and the honeycombed rock surrounding the lake that was soon filled with finishing touches to draw the unknowing people still living in the city to this promised land. All these were predicting a new direction for Trasdrom'man's future.

Later, there would be a call to the Holcum clan to share what they had, the bounty of the unending supply of heat and cooling seawater keeping the mountain retreats comfortable year-round. For a time, some of the compounds were used in the summer only, the travel too rough to be made without the modified transports used by those of the Grandmothers' Compound. The winters were looked on as too much for anyone to bear out in the unconfined spaces of a windblown, frozen sea. All it took was for one family to stay, though, the enormous residences cooled and heated the year round regardless of the occupancy level, and soon, the news spread.

A method of pulling food from the sea was also found, the life within, until this time, unknown. Smaller creatures swam the waters close to the surface, and as those were fished, it was soon discovered that the smaller life was preyed upon by deeper creatures that were much larger. These were found to have a novel taste and to be quite an adventure to catch. Even a rudimentary ice-fishing complement eventually attracted its own share of enthusiasts.

Of course, not everyone on Trasdrom'man came to live in the compounds around the great inland sea, that enormous body of water so disappointing to Holcum that she had cursed it as her Sea of Revenge. Many were needed to remain in the city to service the port that maintained the trade Trasdrom'man depended on for its survival. Others were simply too poor.

Those that did come were eventually thought of by the city dwellers as aloof and exclusive. Many of the intrepid adventurers who now lived around the inland sea continued to maintain homes in the cities; most often these homes were used just a few times a year when business or pleasure called the mountain-dwelling folk into town. Many of those who were fortunate enough to join the sea's compounds did come to see themselves as the city dwellers viewed them, for they enjoyed the faraway luxuries found only in Holcum's mountain. What of it? They lived in massive homes, expandable with just a simple request to the Holcum Compound, the family that owned each of the dwellings, and besides, the city dwellers possessed nothing that compared, anyway. That, alone, set those in the compounds heads above those remaining in the city, if anything did, for all this that made the sea cliff dwellings so desirable was only given for a price, and it was a price only the most deserving of Trasdrom'man's inhabitants could afford.

With the turning of the years, the compounds grew more numerous, the mountains around the sea adequate to contain them all. As more and more time rolled by, the carelessness of those in the Holcum Compound with little to do except absorb the riches of others allowed the name of the compound to revert to an abbreviated form, those coming later calling it the Holc'm compound. One grandmother thought it sounded plain, and she decided it was the laHolc'm compound that controlled the inland sea.

The name of the sea never changed, though. The Sea of Revenge. It had been christened with the cursing spit of an old, crippled woman, and that name remained, even if only a few remembered just why.

Something didn't change, however. Around the mighty inland sea called the Sea of Revenge, the rich just kept getting richer, and they didn't mind that one bit.

# —Chapter 15—

*And in those days, great kings ruled the world, and they
had compassion on no one.*

—*Prelude to* Tales of the
Beginning of the World

AS WITH THE very rich on most worlds, when the demands of
food, housing, and catering to others who have power over him
or her no longer weigh on a person's psyche, the person becomes
very different from the rest of the world. So it was in the
laHolc'm Compound. Of course, to see them at the Winter
Renewing each midseason in the Winter City gathering room, a
laHolc'm would seem a finely dressed, richly fed, and very powerful person, one infused with charm and wit. That would often
be the case, too. Many of them did have charm and wit. Those
who didn't were never told, because they had power and financial
resources, exceedingly large financial resources.

Twins were not unusual at the laHolc'm Compound on the
Sea of Revenge. They might be kept together, or one cast aside
at the whim of whichever Grandmother happened to be currently
in charge, for the strength of the First Grandmother seemed to
find its way down the generational line. Those without it were
shunted aside by the currently sitting Grandmother, sometimes

with the best of intentions, and other times with the casual cruelty of the mean-at-heart.

The second set of twins was like that. Finances already sending its fingers of rot through the cavernous spaces of the mountain compound, the two, a boy and a girl, were as different as night and day. In fact, there were some who might have suggested—that is, if the Grandmother of the twins hadn't been so feared—that perhaps the ill-fated mother who bore these two, this hungry tiger and her hapless sheep of a brother, had, perhaps, had more than one partner the night when the twins were conceived. After all, it had been the first night of an unexpectedly quick blast of winter. The Educational Center's party in Summer City celebrating the end of the summer season was crushed by the sudden freezing winds, and the students who had not been able to rouse themselves from their partying ways were forced to huddle in an interior space, with only their body warmth and nighttime exertions to keep them warm.

When the mother of the twins, just a girl at the time, began to show signs of being with child, the whispers, too faint for the unborn child's Grandmother to hear, started.

*What a shame, and so young, too. I guess, going back to school, she won't be.*

Some whispers were not so kind.

*With that rich mother out there, expected this, I did. Find nothing to do, can that Holcum woman, except to meddle in her child's affairs.*

Some who'd seen their own loved ones die in the bite of an early winter blast showed more understanding in their remarks.

*Better than being dead, it be. Rather this, than freezing to death.*

Then, lo and behold, the child the girl carried turned out to be two.

The Grandmother saw the children as they were, even from

their infancy. Their mother, considered weak, was sent off to a distant settlement that would allow her no chance of return. She was bonded off to a scrabble farmer and forgotten.

The Grandmother allowed both children to stay in the compound, but she took interest only in the girl. Separated, the twins were raised in distant wings of the household. The girl, strong and willful, was given the treatment she demanded, among them the finest of clothes to be worn to the Grandmother's table, and the Grandmother liked what she saw.

The boy had the soft touch of an old soul, and an understanding spirit of empathy surrounded him. What he didn't have was the gift of subterfuge that would have allowed him to compete with his sister. His was the willingness to care about the people who cared about him. At fifteen years old, he and his sister had rarely met.

The Grandmother, her years piling behind her like water against a dam, refused to acknowledge that she might not live forever despite her most recent illness. The granddaughter was consumed with her desire for what the Grandmother had showered upon her. The richness of her life in the compound fed her determination not to lose or even share it. She was determined to have it all, refusing to share with her brother, the boy who lived quietly in the far wing of the compound, an unwelcome stranger she avoided when she could.

There was certainly enough to share. The compounds around the sea were vast and numerous, and all the income came to the laHolc'ms. However, sharing was not the way of the laHolc'm Grandmothers, and the granddaughter was very much as the old woman had been in her days of youth. A plan was needed. After much consideration, an idea came to her. She decided to befriend her brother.

As they neared their seventeenth birthday, she went to him over a course of weeks, carrying with her the very best of wiles a near seventeen-year-old can use to woo a sibling into a devious web of subversion. The brother was overjoyed. Here was a beautiful girl just his own age, one he had rarely seen, even though she lived in his own home. He knew she was his sister, but that was head knowledge alone. When he looked in a mirror, the face he saw, although similar in features, resembled nothing of the entrancing beauty that walked into his suite of rooms that early summer day.

He was mesmerized.

Nearing adulthood, for all his formative years, he'd been around no girls his age. His body came alive in her presence, and he could only follow in its wake, the sensation of needing to be near her seeming to him as natural as the sunrise following the night. He was falling in love, not with his sister, of course, but with the attraction to her beauty and charm that his body sent through his limbs, and each night, he could barely wait until he saw her again.

His sister intended the family fortune to fall to her, alone, and with no one to inherit other than she and her twin brother, she only had to find her opportunity. One day, her brother presented that to her.

"I've never explored any of the caves I can see from my suite," he murmured softly, as they stood next to each other in the deeply set glassine window that opened directly from his cliff-face chamber. He didn't really care about the cave openings he saw in the mountainside far above the sea's surface, but he did care about how his body tingled when he stood really close to his sister. When he whispered his words softly to her, he felt giddy pleasure in being so near to her, and that day, it could barely be said they weren't standing skin to skin. They were so close, he could smell the essence that seemed to be hers, alone. His head swam with the rush of blood to his temples, as well as to other parts of his youthful body. For this feeling, for this moment of sensation coursing through his flushed skin, he would have offered to climb the face of the cliff from his apartments directly to the cave opening he'd pointed out to her.

"Have you ever been cliff diving, brother?" His sister knew her chance had come. She turned to look at him, to find him literally nose to nose. She knew the answer to her question already, but this might be the opportunity to solve her problem, and to have her brother help her bring her solution to completion.

"Cliff diving?" His words were breathless. He didn't care about cliff diving, but he did care about standing close to this girl. "Can you show me?"

"I'll go with you, if you'd like. I have a thing I had shipped in from offworld." She laughed, her voice a tinkling bell in her brother's ears. "It be called a bathing suit, although that seems a silly name to me. It be not worn in the bath, but rather in the sea. I haven't put it on, not once, and I'd like to wear it for you. You may not like it, though. It be too skimpy for me to wear in front of just anyone. Anyone except you, of course. It only has a tiny strap to cover me here, and another tiny one to cover me down there." Her hand showed him the two places the suit would cover, and all he could think about were all the places that would be uncovered.

"I be sure I'd like it very much." The flush of his anticipation could be seen in the redness filling his neck.

"Will you dive with me?" She smiled her sweetest smile at him.

He didn't have to answer, because she could see it in the way his muscles twitched around the grin he couldn't take off his face. She reached up and put her fingertips on his chest, pushing him away, pleased with the ragged breath he drew in as he staggered, nearly stumbling over his own two feet. She walked to his clothing storage area and started rummaging through his things.

"What be you looking for?" Embarrassed she would see

things he considered private, he stepped to her to distract her. Except for his tutor, no one else entered his rooms, and in his spare time, the boy had managed to collect a number of things that might interest a maturing teen. He didn't want them found.

Undeterred, she continued to root through the items. "Something small and tight. Like this!" She pulled out a white piece of cloth, quite stretchy. "This will be perfect."

Turning a deeper shade of red under the neck of his shirt, the boy reached to grab it from her. "Perfect for what?" He managed to take the offending garment, wadding it in his hand and holding it securely as he crossed both arms over his chest.

"A bathing suit of your own, brother. For diving."

"This be not for swimming. This be for my physical activity training with my tutor, for under my outer clothing. It be for support, not for jumping into the sea." He smiled, relieved her reason for pulling out this very private garment that no one had ever seen him wear was something so simple.

His sister smiled her prettiest smile. "Just this once. If you still want to do this with me, of course. I cannot wear my new bathing suit if you don't have one, also. Please, brother." She reached under his arm and pulled the garment from his hand. "Put it on so I can see."

Truly embarrassed now, but unwilling to say no, he stepped around the corner and did just that. When she asked him to show her how it fit, he lifted his shirt just enough for her to see.

"It be for running and jumping exercises. I only wear it then." He dropped his shirt and turned away, his face matching his neck in color.

Not wanting to let this diving opportunity escape her, she begged him, "Leave it on, brother. If you do, I'll go immediately and return in my own. Together, we'll go find the caves you pointed out and see if they be good ones for diving." She stepped behind him, putting one hand on his shoulder, slipping the other under his shirt and running it around his stomach, letting her fingers toy with the waistband of his compression shorts. She leaned against him, her breasts firmly pressed against his back, and she pulled his buttocks against her.

There was no possibility that the boy's seventeen-year-old body could have turned her down that day, even if his mind had possessed the good sense to do so. When a boy is seventeen and has never had the chance to learn to manage his rampaging hormones in the presence of the opposite sex, he's helpless. That was why he died that day, jumping from the mouth of a cave dressed in simple white compression shorts. Yes, his body told him to go with his sister, her beauty inherited directly from the first Grandmother, but it was the look of surprise on his face as he fell to the rocks below that told why he really died. That, and the mysterious hand print on his back that couldn't be explained, not if he jumped of his own free will, as his sister claimed.

He was very dead, though, and soon, his sister knew, not even her sickly Grandmother would be in her way, not as long as she died before the last of the granddaughter's special bottles ran empty. That was coming along nicely, though, because the grand-daughter was of the Grandmother, and that was a terrible thing, indeed.

"BE I TRULY your favorite?" The laughter that followed the question echoed softly throughout the chamber. The Grand-mother, not so very old for a Grandmother, rustled her robes, the children in their playroom knowing her for a charming visitor who gave them treats and prizes when they charmed her in return.

Today, they gave the Grandmother their very best smiles, their tutors having instructed them on her attendance today, and the Grandmother was charmed. It was those days when she wasn't catered to or enamored of her grandchildren that fright-ened them. It was those days the children would smile their wary smiles. The boys would smell of urine, and the girls would have a tummy ache for the rest of the day.

They were glad this was a good day, and they laughed. *Yes, Grandmother. You be our favorite. We love to have you come to play with us. Your stories be the best. Would you please tell us one, now? Please, Grandmother. We want to hear the stories of the First Grandmother and how she swam in the sea so she could live forever.*

This was also a favorite story of the Grandmother, and when she told it, she always included her pet details, embellished those parts of the story she thought were weak, and did her best to frighten the children. It was the children's number one tale because it was the Grandmother's favorite, and they really liked to please her, even if it meant several of their group might stay up the nights after the Grandmother had her story times, their nightmares known by the screams that echoed through the halls of the compound.

The Grandmother always had her choice pets among those in the children's wing. Those under her special consideration were often allowed to sit closest to her, given special compliments to pay to the Grandmother, or even handed the freshest of imported fruits to shyly present to her as she entered the room.

This season, her favorites were two new children, a brother and sister. They had come with the Grandmother's newest consort. Occasionally, the consort showed up at the playroom with his lover. When they first arrived, the children would run to their father, showering him with the hugs and kisses they had always given and had returned to them whenever he came around. The Grandmother had been charmed by this the first time, but she soon found it wore thin. The consort wasn't there to snatch the Grandmother's attentive pettings and trained adorations from her most pliable audience. For a time after that, she came alone when she would visit, and after a rebuke to the tutors who had allowed the indiscretion, the consort's children learned to play the Grand-mother's games.

This group of children wasn't a static number. They would come and go, some family members falling into disfavor, their living quarters and their children moved offsite to accommodate the Grandmother's whims. The luckiest were allowed to go to the faraway city center of Trasdrom'man, whether Winter City or Summer City, depending on the season. The unlucky, those not in the Grandmother's favor, and certainly containing little or none of the Grandmother's internal drive or fortitude, often found themselves in the remotest of outposts, those with few water resources for surviving the brutal summers or even fewer geo-thermal resources for living through the coldest of the world's winters. After all, it was the Grandmother's responsibility to ensure that those who were most like her were the ones drawing power from her connections, resources from her accounts, and comfort from her compound. There was no sense in allowing bottom feeders to draw off the lifeblood of the laHolc'm Com-pound. Those who didn't support the one who controlled the purse strings of this jeweled life around the inland sea would have to find their sustenance elsewhere, and if those resources were inadequate for the continual propagation of life, so be it. They had made their choices.

The children in the playroom wanted to be of the Grand-mother. They wanted it very badly, even if it meant they had to lie, cheat, and steal the very approval that belonged to those who were more deserving. If a small child brought the Grandmother a special treat, and it was taken by an older one, the older child receiving the special smile of the Grandmother, that was the way things worked. If another young person could be sabotaged to give one or the other of them an advantage, then the attributes of the Grandmother must not be strong in the weakling who was dominated so easily.

It was only when the children grew older that these myriad jockeyings for position began to backfire on those who had once been successful in garnering the Grandmother's favor in the playroom. Anger from hard work undermined, well-deserved praise stolen, or punishments unjustly rendered built in the children. As they moved into puberty and beyond, the changes transforming their bodies and vaulting them into the emotional turmoil of adolescence, that rocket thrust of hormones slamming their teenage bodies through those hard years would sometimes erupt that bottled-up anger, ejaculating it in mad bursts of destruction across all those nearby.

For the young people versed in the intricacies of life in the Grandmothers' Compound, ways could be found to let that anger out. Tendrils of sweetness and offers of friendship would wrap themselves gently and securely around the one that had done the harm, perceived or otherwise, and just when trust offered an opportunity that was right, the anger would snap tight. Sadness would follow, or perhaps even darker events, if the motivation was strong enough.

Sorrow often accompanies death, and that wasn't unknown among the children of the laHolc'm Compound. It was sad, but it wasn't unknown. The children had learned from the best, and over the years, the Grandmothers had taught them well. After all, only the weak died, and when someone was weak, was a *groundie,* they didn't deserve to live.

It was by just such a method that the current Grandmother had come to inherit the title. While this Grandmother was a direct descendent of the original—as all the Grandmothers were— carrying both her physical features as well as the personality traits that would have clearly marked her to anyone who had known the First Grandmother before her arrival on Trasdrom'man, when this Grandmother had taken control of the compound, its inheritance falling to her within the legal strictures of this backward world, she had by no means been born first in line.

There had been a small gathering of the family to honor those who were the most deserving of the accolades they expected would be heaped upon them. Of course, in the rarified world of the Grandmothers' Compound, the most deserving were necessarily the most senior in line for ascension to the Grandmother's suite of rooms overlooking the much-maligned Sea of Revenge. To round out the attendees, key members of the highest planetary strata from outside the compound were also invited. As carefully prepared foods were set at each place, the participants were encouraged to indulge themselves in the culinary creations of the best food preparation experts on the planet. Only one person in the room was aware of the psychotropic chemicals that had been carefully embedded in certain of the servings laid out before those standing in the way of the one who was determined to be the next sitting Grandmother.

No lasting physical harm was done, thankfully, and by the time those who had imbibed the chemicals thought to have their bodily systems checked for invasive compounds, their bodies had purged the damning evidence from their bloodstreams. Physical harm hadn't been the intended consequence. The elite from Trasdrom'man had seen an eerily disquieting rendition of behaviors demonstrated that day that would exclude any of those affected from assuming power when it came time for the Grandmother to cede her place to another. Even worse, the Grandmother had been present at the celebration, and she had seen the debauchery from her potential successors. Those who might have been her heirs had sung loudly, been sexually amorous in polite company, and generally proven themselves as unsuited to be in the Grandmother's inner circle.

In the same manner that this Grandmother had taken control of her right to inherit, she had taken aim at the world around her.

Her consorts had been strategically chosen, kept at her side while they were useful to her, and cast away when their purpose was fulfilled. Her skills had given the laHolc'm Compound influence far beyond that of the inland sea's families who paid their tribute to the compound in the form of credits for the resources they still used to heat, cool, and power the palatial compounds ceded to them anew each planetary season.

It was the fourth consort that had given the city's highest-ranking offices to the Grandmother. He'd been in one of those offices, the very reason the Grandmother had chosen him, though he would never know that. His job parameters were that of dealing with direct access to the legal setup of the city's governing body, and the Grandmother had seen him as an opportunity.

When she'd come to him, her body still young, though not as young as with the first of her previous three consorts, he'd been swept off his feet. He knew there had been consorts before him, but he was confident he was the one who could keep the Grandmother. His charm, his high office, and the appeal of being connected with such a powerful woman all conspired to have him believe whatever the Grandmother might suggest.

At her prompting, he manipulated the fine print in the city records to allow her to appoint her consorts to any city office she wished, their tenure lasting until she chose to remove them or until their deaths. From time to time, there were those she felt unfaithful to the purpose that she required of them, and for those, tenure often ended in both.

Trasdrom'man's dual city, the one located above ground for summer and the second buried deeply within the rocky crust for winter, was the only real city on the planet's single continent. Having control of this twin grouping of buildings, the people occupying them immersed in the small details of their daily lives, mostly happy just to exist through the wildly erratic seasons regardless of who was in power, gave the Grandmother essential control of the planet. Resources were scarce on this tortured world, and if a new vein of some mineral or ore was located in some far section of the continent, the Grandmother's fist would be there to reward or crush, to have the final say in just who dealt with retrieving those resources, or even if they were retrieved at all. It wasn't always in the laHolc'm Compound's best interest for others to profit in exploring these new ventures.

Concessions were one good use of the Grandmother's powers in city government. As she gathered more people under her umbrella of influence, it became increasingly easier to let her whims become the dictates of the day. Vacate the compounds to attend the Winter Renewing in the city, even in the very worst of the season? Of course, if the Grandmother wished it. Limit access of certain goods through the city's spaceport? Those goods would instantly be transcribed on the city's list of prohibited items for import. Did a person who had offended her in some way still retain a high-paying job in the city? That person would find him- or herself with papers in hand for a transfer to the most remote of locations on the continent. This quickly became a world of the Grandmothers. This particular Grandmother was the pivotal power in ensuring it was set up in that manner, and also in making sure it remained so.

The more power she gathered under her dominion, the more the Grandmother felt she needed to reflect that in her home. She had the Ferro-cement machine operators frequently at work in the mountains as two rooms became one, the mountain overhead supported with the inherent tensile strength found in the rock mixture extruded into the vast spaces that made up the Grandmother's dreams. When she ran short of smaller rooms to combine, new rooms were blasted higher into the mountain recesses or dug out of the mountain's base.

To bring light into the complex warren of rooms, no expense was spared to bring the largest of glassine windows to Trasdrom'man, the man-made substance stronger than the stone in which it was installed. While the earlier Grandmothers had installed windows using the very costly substance, none had gone to the extreme of this Grandmother. The mountainside opened up after dark with the light sparkling from the compounds, the laHolc'm Compound the most impressive residence hanging over their Sea of Revenge.

It was the awe-inspiring landing bay blasted out directly over the sea that truly became the stuff of legend, the excess of it known even in the farthest reaches of Trasdrom'man, where the most destitute outcasts were forced to labor to survive the Grand-mother's displeasure. This new cavern was cut directly into the stone of the mountain, there being no chambers large enough to contain what the Grandmother had demanded to have there. Then, the great opening was fitted with a massive door that could be retracted whenever the grand transports—ones the Grand-mother intended to have built offworld—were taken in or out of the spacious landing bay.

She was the Grandmother, after all, and she could see no reason she should have to enter or exit her transports directly into the cold of the winter's wrath or the heat of the summer's fire-storm. Others in the city, or even around the sea, might have to do exactly that, but they were not of the Grandmother, and part of the concession they had to make as *groundies* was to put up with the little indignities that the Grandmother intended to made sure were no longer hers.

Those that catered to the Grandmother realized the benefits she demanded for herself would also be theirs, so they supported these changes without question, whether they were to the laws of the land, the construction of the compound, or to penalize those that they also began to consider as *groundies*. They paid the price, though. Luxury was theirs, and sometimes even the envy of those at the bottom of the social ladder. Yet, their souls were often heavy when they closed their eyes at night, and if from time to time, one or two of them might not wake to greet the next day, the Grandmother's ire removing them from her cache of followers, such was the price to be paid. As long as they weren't the ones paying the price, they could always point and blame some personal flaw for one or the other's permanent dismissal from life. That wouldn't *ever* happen to them. They were too careful. For many, their bodies continued to live in the luxury they demanded, even if the reaper had already claimed them inside.

When a later Grandmother used the massive compound's unwieldy size to coordinate her nefarious schemes for control and eventual domination of its resources and power, she realized others could also do the same. Her solution was a compound-wide collection of data banks and palm sensors that could control every aspect of her domain, including doors, lifts, and even whether a person was permitted to wander from room to room. In addition, all the actions that occurred with the walls of the compound were duly recorded and analyzed by the brain of the system.

This method of surveillance installed by the Grandmother had many good points, too. A hot bath could be piped directly from the geothermals boiling away under the lowest floor of the compound, one's cleansing water ready for use when that person arrived in his or her apartments. Or, just a word to the house, and the required lift would transport the passenger to where he or she needed to be. Was information desired about any subject, even those not directly related to compound security? The house voice could provide that with a whispered inquiry.

The most unexpected benefit of the house system wasn't the security it provided for both the Grandmother as well as the hangers-on that filled the compound, nor was it the hot baths enjoyed each night by many of those same hangers-on. It was the realization of just how similar the numerous shapes of the system's info reader slots were to the original Grandmother's memory crystals and ID cards. With a simple adapter, perhaps they could be read.

The items from the original Grandmother hadn't been forgotten. Rather, they had been placed in the large vault built for storing those things considered by the Grandmothers to be too valuable to throw away, but not necessary enough to keep close at hand. The original Grandmother's things were exactly that.

Retrieved and dropped into the adapters made to match, the currently sitting Grandmother was interested to see a download sequence initiate, the numerous files from the first Grandmother's things transferring into the house systems. There, for her ready access, were facts supporting many of the old stories that had been long told of the first Grandmother. The files revealed the military skills that had allowed her to fight back against the raiders when she had first come to Trasdrom'man, as well as her military rank that had brought in so many funds. One even belonged to the *Rom'n* of storied repute, the one the old Grandmother had wished she'd loved as she died by her beloved inland sea.

They knew she must have loved the sea, because some of those old stories also told how she visited it twice at the end of her life, just to swim its waters. Who would demand that of a place they hated?

That Grandmother had found it amusing to leave this *Rom'n* in the system. How quaint, she thought. Here the system was, set up to allow access to a man who had been dead hundreds of years, and there were many men alive today whom she'd locked out of the house controls simply because their presence was longer desired.

That amused her immensely.

"BRIEI'LA, IT BE very hot out here." The brother and sister

walked the shores of the Sea of Revenge, the old-fashioned water suits with their water bladders very cumbersome, as they normally rarely ventured outside during the summer heat. The light-darkening glare goggles sat strangely on their faces. Among those of the Fratenni laHolc'm Compound, to leave the palatial residence except during the rare pleasant spring and fall days, the compound's cooled and heated walls providing year-round comfort, was unthinkable. However, to do what this brother and sister were doing was also unthinkable, and even worse, could result in their deaths.

"Pump your bladder." At her brother's perplexed look, she laughed at him, reaching to point to the bulge at his chest. "There, you big baby. Press on it, and it'll cool your body. It works very well. Have you truly never worn one of these?"

Chia'ardo gave her an irritated look. "Have you truly never worn one of these," he spat, his derisive mocking intended to shame her into realizing the stupidity of asking him to meet with her this way. "We could have taken a transport if you wanted to speak of something forbidden. Then, at least we wouldn't be fighting off summer's heat." He pulled at his seldom-used glare goggles, more in irritation than in needing to adjust them.

Briei'la stopped and glared at the boy she sometimes didn't think could possibly be related to her. As he continued to walk forward, she wondered what made them different, those who were the members of the elite here on this world. The Holc'm family was the ruling class on Trasdrom'man, or at least at the top of the pyramid. Government in the city and over this world had become a convenience to those of the Fratenni laHolc'm clan. Well, Briei'la knew she had to correct herself, in that. It had become a convenience to the currently sitting Grandmother. She was the one who had all the power. It was her whims that were instantly translated into law. Briei'la saw her brother stop and turn to her.

363

"Sister, be you not coming? I haven't come to speak with myself in this heat."

Her steps were firm and her stride hard as she moved toward him. His eyes widened, seeing her disgruntled manner. "Chia, you were a child with me for many years. Now, you have forgotten all we learned in that time. We couldn't have the discussion I wish to have today in the transports where eyes could see us and ears could hear us even with no one else present. Do you not remember the tricks the tutors played to gain the Grandmother's favor? Even worse, the tricks we children had to be wary of, even among ourselves? We didn't understand it in those terms, that be true, but you and I did understand those we had to be wary of, and we were often frightened. Do you remember that at all, Chia, or be my brother now as soft as one who would be sent to work in distant lands to gather the resources our world needs to sell for food?"

"I haven't forgotten. You won't let me. I just wish to enjoy my days, my friends, and the knowledge that someday, some of this will be mine. I know it will, too." He smiled broadly.

"You know nothing. I must watch over my baby brother as if he were still a baby. Know this, brother, the old Grandmother be dying." She turned her eyes to him to catch the expression on his face. Surely, he had listened to at least some of the scuttlebutt going around the compound. Briei'la knew better than to believe all she heard, but this she had checked out for herself. It was true. From the look on Chia'ardo's face, it was obvious he was truly interested only in his friends and in his easy life, and that this news and its importance had passed him by completely.

Briei'la happened to know that this favorite brother of hers, one she would protect at all costs, was never to be part of the Grandmother's line. She also knew that was part of the reason he was still allowed to reside in the compound. Boys couldn't have babies with boys, and so she still had her baby brother.

That was also why she might be the one to assume the power that the Grandmother had wielded so ruthlessly over the years. If she could get this brother of hers to help her, she would soon receive what she felt was her due. Yes, she would show the pretense of sadness at the passing of a well-known and powerful family member, one who held queen-like power out here on the Sea of Revenge. However, the deed would be at her hand.

IF QUESTIONED, Briei'la and Chia'ardo would have no concept of what a queen was or how that applied to their world. Someone from the old-Earth past of many centuries before would have understood quite well, though. They also would have been aware that funerals aren't just about the proper appearance of sadness; and bereavement at the loss of a loved one does more than show the survivors' sorrow during their time of mourning. The truth would have been more than apparent to those long-ago royal hangers-on who had endured the often-capricious quirks of royal flightiness. The passing of a monarch was a time for the great wheels of power to shift, the royal alliances repositioning themselves in the light of which surviving members of the royal household could further the ends of those placed most highly in power, and also in deciding who needed to be eliminated from the inner circle.

Of the two on that day who walked the beach beside a cursed sea under the heat of a searing sun, while an old Grandmother lay near death, one, at least, understood the power plays of those long-ago royal courts. She was determined to make sure her alliances were the ones that gave her a step up the ladder to the top of the pyramid. Her brother? She knew he was clueless, but he was hers. With him at her side, she would entangle those who needed to be entangled, prop up those who were weak, and bring down those who were strong.

Briei'la would be the Grandmother, and she knew it didn't

take grandchildren to claim the position. The grandchildren could come later. Right now, it was the power that counted.

As she drew her brother to her, she began to explain her plans. When his eyes grew wide with understanding, she knew he would do as she asked. She would be the Grandmother, and her brother would help her. She wouldn't let it happen any other way.

BRIEI'LA REACHED to the wisp of hair trailing from under her headcovering. Rubbing it between her fingers, she was aware of the coarseness of those strands that were no longer the dark color they had been in her youth. "Oh, well," she murmured to herself. "It comes from so many years of children and grandchildren. Now, where be that brother of mine? Probably still with that new boy he's taken from the compound across the sea."

Briei'la stood, walked across the room to the great glassine window, and reached her hand to it. She remembered being told that this was one of the originals, the window installed at great expense before the massive expansions of the succeeding generations. She had chosen these chambers for that very reason. The previous Grandmother's chambers had been much larger, but they didn't have the character of this one, and that character, that sense of connection with the long-ago women whose strength had built this compound, this fortress, made her proud. She'd taken her share of consorts from the city, and each had been given a suite of rooms for his own use. Through the series of consorts over the many years, however, this was the only suite she had claimed for her own, with not even the consorts allowed residence here.

Chia'ardo had gone too far this time. He was almost as old as she, and now Briei'la had been forced to decide. That, she had done already, even as she stood looking out over the sea.

She walked to her private work area, and pressing the comm

pad, she spoke into it, her voice much calmer than she would be with Chia. "I be looking for my brother. Please check his chambers. By all means, be discreet."

She turned to the window stretching high to the top of the old cavern's ceiling, gazing out at the white-encrusted sea before her. One who explored no further than the principle chambers of the compound would ever know this for anything other than a palatial estate, the rooms of varying sizes and ceiling heights, although obviously very large and luxurious. Only those intrepid enough to explore past the farthest rooms would find the unfinished rock walls that told the true story of this vast complex. There one would find the great machines that drove the Fratenni laHolc'm family fortunes, pumping, heating, cooling, and sending power to the rest of the residents around the inland sea.

At a noise, she turned, her face blanching at what she saw. "You old fool! How dare you come to me like that! Could you not even rearrange your clothing from your tryst with that *boy* whom you've stolen from across the sea? The family and staff will see you." She turned back to the scene through the window, her anger at him barely calmed.

She heard him yawn as he spoke. "They know anyway, sister. What does it matter? Anyway, Rhono waits for me. I'll go to him again when you've said what you wish to say to me. I needed a break from our exertions, anyway. His youth wears out even me."

Briei'la turned back to the fool she still claimed as her blood. "Chia, you've put yourself in a very precarious position. Do you not see that? You have no sons, and so you can never be in line for this position I've wielded so well for these many years. For that very reason, you'll never know the status of a favored kinsman, protected by a series of Grandmothers who love you enough to allow you to stay under their care."

"What be your reason for speaking of this? All these things be well known. Get on with it. My boy awaits." He reached a finger to scratch his nose. "Besides, I have you."

She hissed at him, finally catching his attention. "You miss the point, and that boy *be* my point. When you were a youth, the others you took were laughed at as the fancy of an indulged adolescent. Now, these boys be seen as something much worse. They be seen as prey, tricked into your slavery by the promise of wealth and luxury. How old be this one, Chia? Need I even ask? He doesn't even shave."

Chia'ardo hung his head, his understanding of the seriousness of his sister's concerns seeming to filter through his engorged libido. His actions might actually be as bad this time as his sister suggested. The previous boy he had taken had upset his sister very much, and he had promised to be better, to choose his companions from those who were older. The words he hadn't said to his sister at the time were the ones in his thoughts. *Just not too much older.* However, this boy had been so beautiful. Chia had watched him from a small child, just waiting for him to mature enough to suit his needs.

He made his evasive reply to his sister. "He be old enough to do what I ask of him." He then snorted, suddenly tired of her accusations. "He could go, if he wanted. No one makes him stay."

"You once again miss the point, brother. It be the way it looks for one as old as you to prey on the boys of the families, no matter how pretty they look. I've been given an ultimatum." She walked up to him, unfastening his disheveled shirt and refastening it in a more orderly manner. "Trouble will come, if you remain." She flicked her eyes to his to gauge his response, only to find shock there.

Well able to read between his sister's words, the brother knew instantly what was to be done with him. "Sister? You'll send me away? You be the one they must give in to, not the other way around. Tell them no, sister."

Briei'la, the sister as well as the Grandmother, put her hands on either side of his face, and with her thumbs wiped the tears that had started to flow. "It be done, brother. The dwelling in Winter City be prepared for you as we speak. Take the boy with you, if you wish, but do not bring him back here to visit if you return." She took her hands away, turning back to the window where the wind was starting to whip up the snow, the sound of it as it buffeted the window very faint through the glassine. Loudly enough that he could hear her, she spoke once more to her brother, making sure her words were strong enough to be clearly understood. "Nor any of the new boys you take, either, Chia."

She stood there for a time until she was sure he was gone. That brother of her was becoming a nuisance, and though she'd sworn to protect him, he had gone too far too many times. She didn't care to see him again, not as long as he had one of those boys of his at his side, not under her roof.

"I SENT HIM away. Be that not what you wanted?" Briei'la stood, her eyes rimmed with red, refusing to let these *groundies* see her cry. She turned from them to face the window, remembering the last time she'd stood in front of this view, the sea through the glassine frozen in time, not wanting to deal with what was behind her. Then, her brother had been alive. Now, the heat of the sun's rays beat down on the waters below, the depths holding fast to winter's cold even in the brutal sun, providing the coolness that made the compound comfortable during the most trying of the summer's days. The sun, Briei'la knew, would take the life from the people of this world if it could. The sun, chased by the planet in its yearly transit, as close to being caught now as it ever would, was doing its best to wrest the cold from her sea, but the sea's depths were the Fratenni laHolc'm Compound's best revenge against that brutal monster hanging in the sky.

While these rooms were cool inside, Briei'la's heart was not. It wasn't love that burned within her. It was the hate for the death of her brother. These *men* had taken out their revenge on her poor Chia for what he couldn't help. Did he ask to be born kind-hearted toward those of his own gender? Did he ask to be drawn towards that sweetness in others?

These men claimed her brother had perverted their sons, taken them when they were impressionable, and forced them to want what was unnatural to them. That was a laugh! Could a creature of the sea that lapped the shores just outside this window be made to fly as the gliderhawk that soars through the summer's superheated thermal updrafts? Could her brother force a boy to be a girl, or a girl to be a boy? Perhaps her brother did choose to take these men's sons too early, but those boys had been what they were, not what Chia had made them.

Briei'la smiled at the reflection of herself she could see around the edges of her window, just where the heavy winter drapes shadowed the glassine. In the ghost of a self in her reflection, there were no tears, just the smile of a hollow-eyed demon. Her smile turned to a grimace as she thought of the men behind her. They would know this demon, too. Perhaps not today, but the future was not yet here, and she, the Grandmother, would make that future as she saw fit. Now though, she must deal with this day. The future she would make for these men was for another turn of this world's blazing sun, not this one that she must get through with them standing here, now, in her presence.

She turned. "Do not have the insincerity to pretend you grieve at Chia'ardo's death. He be gone, and at his own hand. You can be thankful for that. If I were to find any indication of your involvement, my wrath would know no ends."

"Mos. Briei'la, only the bearer of the news, we be. Truly, in our hearts, sadness for your loss, we feel." The men looked at the floor, which was wise. Their eyes would certainly tell the truth, and the Grandmother could not be allowed to see.

THEY WERE indeed glad the old man was dead, and they also knew it was the rough treatment he'd received in the city that had caused him to end his own life. He'd become an outcast, isolated and ignored, and that *was* at their hand. What was done was their fault, and they did fear they would pay. They just hoped the price would not be more than the satisfaction they'd felt at the news of the old man's body being found outside the city, his skin already baked red on one of the hottest of the summer's days.

The young man he'd taken in? Rhono *had* been beaten, and to the point his face was pretty no more. He'd taken his own life mere days before Chia'ardo had wandered forlorn into the desert sun.

While that lecherous old man was one they'd been glad to see the end of, they remembered others, also. Briei'la's brother may have deserved his death, but that was not true of everyone who had died. There had been other people sent from the Fratenni laHolc'm Compound before. Many. The men standing with their heads hanging in mock sympathy often knew the reasons, too.

Rarely, they felt, did those who were truly good remain at the compound. Those who had appeared in the city had often shown their true merit in the way they lived their lives, good lives many times, both men and women. That was why it was said around the city that lucky was the man who bonded with a laHolc'm beauty. Those from the compound who were interested in helping others, showing kindness and goodness of heart, and working hard to better their world, were not the sort of people wanted in the faraway compound on the Sea of Revenge.

However, goodness of heart did not necessarily ensure a long life for a member of the laHolc'm clan. The men standing in the presence of the Grandmother could easily come up between them with a handful of deaths they were sure had been arranged. There was that sweet laHolc'm girl who had bonded to the baker back when he'd been a young man, and that was years ago, now.

Nevertheless, the men in the room hadn't forgotten the out-of-control delivery transport the summer after her child was born. No one had ever been able to prove it intentional, but neither had anyone been able to locate the driver of the transport. It hadn't been the regular driver; that was for sure. He'd been home with his bonded one, sick in bed. Something he had eaten the night before had given him an illness in his stomach, and the local healer was with him when the tragedy occurred. Because the mother had been of the Fratenni laHolc'm Compound, the family had come and taken the baby, a girl child, from the baker, insisting they would raise her in the compound.

Then, there was that boy several years later who'd been sent away, rejected by the Grandmothers' Compound as unfit for whatever she seemed to demand of those she kept under her protection. There had been worries that he wouldn't survive. As a scrabble farmer, he'd faced a very hard life. The men in the room with the Grandmother couldn't think of anything more difficult than the life of a scrabble farmer, growing this world's meager food-producing crops during the heat of the summer, and tending the cave fungi in the winter. When he'd become old enough to bond with a girl, many of them thought he might make it, his distance from the Fratenni laHolc'm Compound providing him some protection from the wiles of the Grandmother and her clan. It was not to be so, though, and there had been a measure of sadness when they'd learned of his demise. Some of the city dwellers seemed to consider his death a simple farming accident, and had chalked it up to chance. Those who tracked the ones sent from the Fratenni laHolc'm compound sensed a different pattern, one of intrigue between siblings, as this one still had a sister in the compound, one that could easily become a Grandmother herself, if left unchecked.

The lone man who stood at the back of the group facing Briei'la had an especially fierce look on his face. For that reason, the others had refused to let him be at the head of the entourage. He had bonded many years ago to a Fratenni laHolc'm girl, one who had voluntarily left the compound. Thinking they were safe as adults, having learned to love each other outside of the laHolc'm family, they'd been reassured when their child hadn't been stolen as an infant. Surely she would be allowed to grow into a young adult who would be free of her family background. Such was not to be the case. Even as part of a family group, they hadn't been safe, and now, all this time later, if this man could find someone willing to take the risk of tangling with the Grand-mother's ire, he'd hire an assassin to let the Grandmother know just what it felt like when a person's life was considered worth-less by another, and that life was snuffed out without a second thought. Drowning had been the healer's pronouncement. Drowning in a pan of water, and two of them, his bonded woman and his daughter, drowning together.

There were those whose power in the city had allowed them to make alliances with those who dwelt out at the inland sea. Others with power or connections had managed at times to escape offworld on a ship of exports, their ride a long one across the blackness of space, their lives much longer than they would have been had they stayed. A few even managed to hide within family alliances, tucked away behind a name or even a wall, no longer seen by the Grandmother. Those were the victories won by people with long-term goals. There were advantages gained for some by this hiding, the playing of cards of knowledge, trad-ing favors to protect those hidden away or those running from Trasdrom'man. When the Grandmothers uncovered those plans, though, revenge was taken mercilessly, and tears flowed.

Even with all of these wiles, life on Trasdrom'man moved forward as relentlessly as its seasons. Through it all, the Grand-mothers became stronger, and that was what was important to them.

# —Chapter 16—

*"And the mountain was not just a mountain. If a careful observer looked at just the right angle, he or she could see the long, sloping tail along the backbone of the mountain, the mighty flanks in the foothills, and the great eye sockets in the shadowed caves. This mountain was the dragon, and the people of the village were afraid to wake the mighty creature. So, each generation, a maiden would be chosen for sacrifice . . ."*

*—Child's tale*

THE HISTRIONICS had no effect on the old Grandmother's decision. When the delegation had approached her about a possible liaison between her own holdings here around the inland sea, the First Grandmother's well-known Sea of Revenge, she had been surprised. No, angered was the correct word. Yes, angered.

Briei'la, in a well-worn voice, burst out, "I be not so old that such information slips by me unawares. This new place, this settlement on the far continent, has been purposefully hidden from me."

She looked around the room that she hardly left anymore. It was difficult for her to get around. Even her meals were brought to her. She reassured herself that it was her power that caused the meals to be brought to her rooms. It was because she *could* demand that her meals be brought to her that she no longer went to the dining hall to partake with the families residing under her largesse. However, deep inside her heart, on those days when her bones creaked and her joints were sore, she admitted the truth. She no longer went because it was too difficult. It was simply not worth the time and effort.

Looking to the door, the cushioned seat that sat there, she was startled. Where had that girl come from, she wondered, the one with the red eyes and the sobbing voice? Surely someone should tell her where to take herself and her misery.

Briei'la reached out a hand, quelling the shaking that surprised her, and touched the pad on the arm of her chair; soon, a different young girl bounded into the room, stopping suddenly as if interrupting something very intimate. Briei'la motioned to her before she could turn and make herself completely disappear.

"Girl," she whispered, as soon as the new girl got close enough to hear her without the whimpering mess by the door overhearing. "What be she doing here?" Briei'la pointed to the person across the room. "I was alone, and then suddenly she was here."

She looked furtively between the two youths, unsure how this could be happening. What was her life coming to? Would next, her day be overcome by an invading horde of wailing children?

THE HIRED serving girl at Briei'la's side had been given the responsibility to keep watch over the Grandmother's medicine, and with the old woman's question, she realized she'd been very lax. In the past months, the Grandmother's mind had begun to wander without the new medicines that came from offworld, and it was the serving girl's job to ensure that it was always taken on time. The Grandmother would remember this lapse once her mind was clear again, and the Grandmother would see that the girl paid. Covering was the best way to handle this, so she did what would enable her to avoid the penalty the Grandmother would give.

She lied.

"Grandmother, she snuck in without anyone knowing. I'll remove her. Then, I'll bring you a treat. I be so sorry, Grandmother. She will be punished." Her treat would be the medicine she should have given the Grandmother already this morning to keep her mind clear. She hoped she never got so old as this one, not even for all the power in the world. Although, she would admit to herself, to have this suite of rooms for her own would be very nice. Yet, what good would it do her if she didn't know who she was half the time?

REETIA TURNED to her mother, and she wailed the same mournful notes she'd used to grate on the old Grandmother's nerves earlier. "I don't want to live so far from you. Besides, I don't love this man. I don't even know him." At that, another wail escaped her throat. "He'll be old and withered. I just know it."

Her mother sat beside her and hugged Reetia closely as she ran her hand down the girl's hair. She also didn't want her daughter to be sent away to this new city, this new *settlement*. She didn't care for this way of bonding, this *political* matchmaking. It was nothing more than a way to bolster the old Grandmother's economic standing, and Reetia's mother had seen the old woman recently. She knew how bad she had gotten, her memory no longer hers without the medication she had to take every day. The old woman no longer knew what funds she did or didn't have. Her Reetia was just a girl, though. Her Reetia knew very well what was happening, and her Reetia would know the pain of suffering. That was unfair.

That boy her Reetia had been seeing would suffer, also. He was such a sweet boy, too. She remembered the last time he'd been to visit her daughter. He hoped to finish his schooling at the end of winter, and his father was helping him start a new business in the city. Reetia's mother didn't understand exactly what the new business was about, the financial side of things not something she was good at, but she did know the boy's family lived very well. They had a home in one of the compounds across the sea and also had a permanent residence in the city, two in fact, one in Winter City and another in Summer City. Her Reetia and the boy were to be given the residences as a bonding gift.

Now, this. Thank the gods above and below the sea that Reetia's father was no longer alive. He'd be livid if he still walked the surface of this world. The girl's mother held her as her daughter's sobs racked her body.

"Mother, I be already in love. I cannot love another." With a great series of sniffles, Reetia raised her head to look her mother in the eyes. "This, I cannot do."

Her mother just pulled Reetia's head back to her chest, knowing that in the Compound of the Grandmothers, choice was not in the cards for those whom the Grandmother chose to use as pawns in her games of power. Reetia would live with this. So would the boy. They had no choice. That might not make it easier, but it convinced Reetia's mother that it was no use to fight it. She wouldn't, either. To console her daughter was the best she could do, so that was just what she did. Even that was difficult enough.

In addition, after Reetia was calmed, her mother did one more thing. She looked up at the ceiling, and through her tears, she softly spoke the strongest words her daughter had ever heard her say.

"Damn you, Fratenni laHolc'm Compound. Damn you to the

depths of your cursed Sea of Revenge."

She meant it, too, every single word.

THERE WAS a purpose to the alliances that began to stretch across the surface of Trasdrom'man. Like spiderwebs of power, the alliances held the connections of the strongest families of this world intact. As far as Briei'la was concerned, at least on the days her hired girl remembered to give her the medicine that kept her mind clear, there was only one family on this world that mattered, and the rest just needed to be catered to until they came under her control. Then, they'd dance as she tugged the strings that bound them to her.

This morning, she sat, her world very narrow, the fog around her memories not yet cleared. She'd taken the medicine. She was pretty sure of that. She remembered the girl's fingers pressing to her lips, and something hard being forced into her throat.

The wind outside the expansive glassine window continued to blow, and Briei'la's eyes tracked the fingers of snow, the white explosions as the frozen flakes flung themselves against her window creating a pattern of crystalline dust that continually renewed itself. As of yet, however, these things barely registered.

When the clearing of her mind happened, it was a slow sharpening of her awareness, the warmth of the room that now comprised her small world coming into focus, the items around her taking on meaning. That bowl, sent to her from the city, a long-ago consort trying to curry her favor. A decoration on the wall, the once-treasured memento from a forgotten time spent with a friend. The dried flower on the table, one from her brother, the unfairness of his life lost while the Grandmother still grasped to hold the remnants of life left in her.

The slow dawning of returning memory was like new life, and after a time, the garnered memories of a too-long life surged through her brain. The events of her years clicked into focus for the Grandmother, such as the families around the sea who didn't want to pay the new prices for the power her compound provided to keep their homes warm throughout the cold season and cool beneath the summer's heat. Some of the families, and the Grandmother knew just who, too, were trying to gather support for extending the power to the city. This Grandmother would have none of that. Let that crumbling city work its own wiles to get the power it wanted. If they were unwilling to install the powerful machines to drive the superheated groundwater through the walls of their own wretched hovels, she had no interest in helping them. Besides, they had no sea. How could those places be cooled without overwhelming amounts of power? They were wasting their time. Those of her family who desired this just wanted to enjoy the comforts of her compound while spending their time far away from her

This other, though. This girl whom Briei'la had agreed to give for this alliance. This could be the coup of a lifetime. The bonding of this girl to that old man across the wastes of the plain, in itself, was of little concern to Briei'la, but the hired people who would transport her there would be much more than simple servants. They would be a reconnaissance team to report back on just how developed this new settlement really was.

The Grandmother knew how vital the world's one spaceport was to survival on this world, and there wasn't enough room in Trasdrom'man's economic structure for two of them. If that new settlement needed to die for her sphere of power to live, so be it. She would survive. The Fratenni laHolc'm Compound would survive. Girls might pay with their virginity. Boys might pay with lost loves snatched for schemes of power. Mothers might pay with the tears they shed for those they couldn't protect. However, it would be worth the cost. Those who wouldn't give up such small treasures were weak, anyway, and the weak were unimportant. They were groundies, and groundies were the bane of

Briei'la's world.

So, Reetia went. The old Grandmother, her plans drawn, took that which the girl didn't want to give, took it brusquely, and spent it wantonly. The knowledge she gained in the process told her little she couldn't have garnered merely by asking through more conventional means, but the Grandmother didn't enjoy trust as one of her more generous attributes. She brought disaster upon a young love simply to satisfy her own dark ends.

Had Briei'la achieved some sort of success with her manipulations, found a growing population center ready to overshadow the long-established city, that of summer and winter variety, some might have considered Reetia's sacrifice worth the gain to the Fratenni laHolc'm Compound. What the old Grandmother's minions found when they arrived at the new settlement was not a thriving intruder into the Grandmother's realm of rule, but rather a struggling enterprise hoping for a trading partner in order to survive.

The boy that Reetia had loved and who had loved her back had come to the Fratenni laHolc'm Compound, his search for his precious Reetia driving him to hope the news he'd received was in error. If he were to find the news was not in error, the poor boy had a contingency for that, also.

Arriving at the massive compound, the winter snows still whipping across the frozen soils, he had pressed his borrowed transport from Winter City through a day of hard driving, the slowness of it eating at his stomach, the idea that the *sluggishness* of this machine might be the doom for his Reetia's hand. He'd already been to the spaceport, his parents telling him of a chance he might still save his love from the fate being forced upon her. A ship was in, passage might be obtained, and freedom for the two of them found offworld. The value of the city holdings would be sent with him and his bonded one if he could save her in time.

The wind whipping his layers of clothing, his quick run to

the protected entrance of the landlocked side of the compound faster than the trip in the transport itself had been, the boy was admitted by a hired servant, and the mother was soon found. Her eyes told him the one he had come to find was gone, even before he could ask his questions of her or tell her of his already-made plans. With frantic eyes and a madness of manner, the boy begged the mother to tell him *where,* and he would chase her to the ends of the lands this world contained.

She was gone, the mother said, and she didn't know where. All she knew was that it took the fastest of the compound's transports two days there and two days back. Perhaps someone in the city could tell him more. She gave him a hug, and her eyes looked for a long time into his before she turned away. As he watched her walk down the long, elegant corridor lined with the refinement only excessive money could buy, he wasn't sure if he'd seen pity or wistfulness in those eyes that were so like his Reetia's.

He didn't return home that night. The next day, the borrowed transport was found at the entrance to the spaceport, left in the middle of the lane, blocking any others that might want to find their way there. The boy was gone, though, and so was the ship his parents had sent him to. He would find a new life off Trasdrom'man, and a better life, his parents hoped it would be.

THE CONSORTS couldn't leave, though. This world was theirs. Where would they go, anyway? Why would they go? Whether picked by the Grandmother for power or love, the life of one who would give his all to the Fratenni laHolc'm Compound could be fine, indeed.

Some of the consorts, however, thought the power was theirs when the Grandmother pulled them into her lair of intrigue. They would dress in their fine clothes, their faces trimmed and their earstuds sparkling, their sense of power flowing from the many minions who crowded around them to serve their needs. These newly powerful—and, in their minds, at least, they *were* powerful—would direct this one to there, or another one to move an item to that location, and expect the things to be done before the request was even completed. Many times the demands were indeed accomplished in just such a fashion, too.

If these consorts were especially adored by the Grandmother, or if the need of them was especially strident, they would sometimes be allowed to play the powermakers even in the gatherings of the elite, those groups of family members and trusted hired hands who would carry out the Grandmother's wishes, however dreadful they may seem. The consorts would be tolerated by the true powerbrokers, as they would attempt to steer the conversation, make a certain point, or campaign for something or the other that interested them.

At times, this could be taken too far. Rarely administered in public, the penalties were sometimes severe. In retribution for crossing some imaginary line the Grandmother might have made for herself, the consort might suffer something as simple as a look or a night spent outside the high lady's chambers. Depending on the amount of ire to be salved, he might have a favorite possession taken or miss a much-anticipated social event. For the most severe transgressions, revenge was the only word to describe the consequence meted out. Often banished to the city or a distant work camp, supposedly to supervise the Grandmother's interests, it was not unusual to find the death report of one of these before too many of Trasdrom'man's seasons had passed.

It was one of these consorts that caused the MegaCorp incident. In a power play over issues he felt he should be in charge of, the consort was certain he could gain control if he refused to attend one of the gatherings, embarrassing the Grandmother into ceding to his wishes. He wanted to be granted a controlling interest in the city's spaceport policies. The ships visiting Trasdrom'man should be subservient to the city's mores, the crew-members abiding by the rigid standards placed upon them by the rules of the world they were visiting. He, along with some of the Grandmother's previous consorts, those who had been the formerly favored ones of the laHolc'm Compound, hoped to trade these stringent rules for power in working advantageous deals with the shipping companies. After all, what crew wouldn't want to have the freedom to wander the city of a foreign world, let off a little steam, and know that the morning would bring anonymity with a lift-off to the stars above? For this privilege, the shipping company might offer to sweeten the deal financially, the extra credits lining some very empty pockets.

It might have worked, too, had the Grandmother not returned a day early from the yearly midseason gathering in Winter City to find her consort firmly wrapped in the arms of an unbonded girl. The wrath of the Grandmother didn't burn any more softly after her punishments were dealt to the pair, and when MegaCorp approached her shortly thereafter, she made the connections between the missed gathering, the subtle hints, and the timing of the meeting with the corporation. She placed her own restrictions on the ships that the great economic power could send to her world. When approaching the city's airspace, all ships must relinquish control to Trasdrom'man's remote guidance systems, and only a certain percentage, very small, could land with a crew. It was strongly stressed that drone landers would now become the preferred ships of choice. For the Grandmother, the cost to install the new guidance systems was prohibitive, but her anger still burned hot, and revenge was worth any price.

MegaCorp willingly adopted the restrictions, surprising many. Of course, by this time, MegaCorp no longer maintained any ships of its own. From its heyday, it had fallen far, but it remained a galaxy-wide power with a wide-reaching commercial influence through leasing cargo space on others' commercial ships to deliver its goods. These new restrictions for landing on Trasdrom'man were ones that actually saved credits for the shipping companies, making the crew's salaries much less a factor in the cost of the transportation, and the extra credits making this run more lucrative.

Reetia did eventually find love. It was not her boy, however, from long ago. She bonded as expected with the man who ruled the settlement far from the laHolc'm compound. She even bore him several children, none of which returned to the Grandmothers. She didn't find love with the old man, though. He was more of a father to her than a bonded mate.

When he died, his son by a previous bonding came to the settlement. The son was a much better manager of people and organizations. He ran the settlement well, and it began to prosper. For a long time, he avoided the woman his father had brought out for a lover and mother, feeling it would bring shame on the family. Still, she was beautiful, and he was certainly young enough for her, being only a handful of years her senior.

The old Grandmother's game of matchmaking, the one that had brought shame on her own compound, turned, its promise of misery broken. The two, the young girl torn from love and the old man's son, afraid of taking her love, danced around each other until the music brought them together. During one summer night, the coolest part of the darkness still hot with the sun's heat, the two tortured souls found release in each other, and love bloomed anew.

Far away in the Grandmothers' Compound, a secret was kept tightly sealed in a mother's heart. Her daughter had been reborn. When asked by others, she cast her eyes down, her tears a command performance. The Grandmother could never know. But when she was alone, that was the time she could allow her smile to shine. Her daughter, Reetia, had found her love after all, and the mother's world was right once again.

WHAT WORKED in tradeoffs of young girls to men old enough to be their fathers didn't always work in governments. For many years after Reetia finally found love, the world of the Grandmothers slipped quietly through time. The political workings of Trasdrom'man mirrored the changing guard of the old Grandmothers' Compound. The world she ruled she considered to be safely contained within her domain. The Grandmothers' confidence was an illusion, even if they didn't realize it, and illusions are easily shattered.

Reetia's newly bonded one was much better at managing the settlement that soon put down the roots of a city. It might never rival the Grandmothers' Compound around the Sea of Revenge, but it didn't contain the Grandmothers, and the people who lived there were satisfied with that.

One day Reetia had a choice to make.

"My sweet love, you be, dear Reetia." Bron'in wrapped his strong arm underneath her shoulders, her slightness not difficult for him to support. He laid his head back against the softness of the sleeping pad, its thickness that of the best-known pads in Far Town. He lay there a moment, breathing in the quiet of the summer night, the heat permeating the very air he drew into his lungs. Both the bodies lying together were flushed with the heightened senses of their recent exertions, and the breeze from the setting of the sun had long ago left the room. Bron'in rolled to his side, his free arm reaching to gently brush the tangled strands of hair from his love's face. He was careful to keep his skin from touching hers where possible. Their desires were already sated, and the night was too hot for heated skin to be in contact with heated skin.

"More, there be? Carry the weight of decision, your words do." Reetia's whisper was the thickness of honey in the night.

"Move, we must, or die, we will, sweet Reetia." He pulled the looseness of her hair to his face and breathed in her fragrance,

385

its heady aroma drawing him in, its attraction more the memory of love rather than the desire for mating their bodies once again. Reetia knew what he meant. This was their home, and it might continue to be, or it might not, but his words had nothing to do with the location of their domicile, or even Far Town.

The words had to do with the power balance of a world ruled by an autocratic authority structure centered in the often cruel and sometimes sadistic Fratenni laHolc'm Compound. The world of Bron'in and Reetia was growing, and on a resource-poor planet, there was little room for expansion. The old city and the new Far Town were like two hearts in one body, the first fully developed and beating wildly, its knowledge of its own superiority by default not allowing it to imagine another growing alongside it. The second heart, though, was young and determined to wrestle space for its own life from a landscape the old heart had already claimed as its own. It would have to force the larger, more powerful heart to give up room, to accept less, to coexist, no matter the tricks and wiles it had to employ. To do otherwise was to give up and die.

Far Town had no intention of dying. It had quietly dug deep roots into the economic and social substructure of this world, and it was sending tendrils of powerful connections toward Summer City and Winter City, building the nooses that would someday choke the power from the Grandmother's stronghold, the power base that itself would choke Far Town if left unchecked.

"Know, do I, my Bron'in, that you be my strength in the night, and my tower in the day. Whatever you wish, there, with you, I be."

Reetia closed her eyes and soaked in the nearness of his body, the smells of their union strong in the stillness of the air. Then she spoke the words she knew he wanted to hear. "Been there, I have, and know the twists and turns of the Grandmother's house, I do." She also knew she would have to excise this inverted syntax she'd allowed herself to adopt from the townfolk she now lived among. She'd need that if she were to blend into the Grand-mothers' Compound once again.

For Bron'in to be successful, for his plan to save the world Reetia had come to love, to even treasure, Far Town had to have a foothold in the old world, and it had been decided the best way to do that was to gain a deed to one of the compounds placed around the great inland sea. It had become widely known that permanent deeds to the compounds had, for years, been carefully handed out, guaranteeing that the inhabitants of the various manses huddled over the sea—that expanse frozen for half their year, and that kept them cooled the other half—would be forever bonded with the Grandmothers and the Fratenni laHolc'm Com-pound.

It was here that Bron'in planned to use his influence, Reetia's influence, really, to work the tendrils of his city's doings around those laws and those powerful people who could and would do damage to the inroads Far Town had made on this world. Reetia had told him how the bribes of the old city worked, the offices bought with the greasy credits slipped through even greasier accounts, many of those hidden away from the prying eyes of even the most astute account examiners. Bron'in's plan would, over time, change laws, the press of the newcomers forcing the Grandmothers to give them room, the power gained by the up-and-coming upstarts soon strong enough to make them the ones to be reckoned with. For this night, though, that future was there only in the dreams of those who could dream it.

Bron'in lay back on his bedding again, the ceiling and its rough texture drawing his eyes around the pattern of cracks and swirls he knew was there even though the darkness was complete in the room.

"Then," and Reetia smiled at the satisfaction she heard in his voice, "have the power taken from them, we will. Withhold it, we will, and come to us, they must. Then, own that power, we will, the very power they will need in order to make their laws, to command their mighty spaceport, and themselves to scratch, where even the lowliness of mammalian pets won't deign to lick." He turned his head to her, and together they laughed at the joke, one that was for them only, and shared with no one else.

IT WOULD take many years of maneuvering, of prices paid, and of small gains. Perhaps the both of them would be dead and gone before their ends would be attained, but they would have been there in the beginning. When Far Town was strong in the face of its opposition, the names of Bron'in and Reetia would be remembered as the ones who gave up their present to help the future become what it might be.

As the two planners grew old, so their plans did mature. A compound was gained from those around the great inland sea known as the Sea of Revenge. Funds did grease those slippery accounts, the votes shifting the rulings of committees just ever so slightly, the Compound of the Grandmothers not realizing just what had been lost. When the time came for the Fratenni laHolc'm Compound to engage a long-unused arm of the city's governing body to bring pressure against an opposing faction, they found it to be withered and dead, the power shifted elsewhere through once-trusted alliances that were now lost and laws that no longer favored the old order.

Far Town was successful in its machinations, because key players were willing to work beneath the notice of those who liked to parade their power. A strong foundation to protect themselves was built to ensure they wouldn't be swatted carelessly aside by those who had grown too used to unlimited power. Strength, not recognition, continued to be Far Town's goal.

The tendrils of these newly powerful people who worked for Far Town began to stretch far in infiltrating areas that the laHolc'ms had long claimed as their own. It was the power of Far Town that took the meager ruling that prevented MegaCorp personnel from making merry on the surface of this world, and used that ruling as a springboard to make to the laws that one day would wrestle a position of power for that once-struggling settlement that a long-dead Grandmother had dismissed as unimportant, not even worth the girl she had cruelly sacrificed to its invitations for a treaty. Under the indictment of the new underclass, an underclass that was willing to be the power beneath the power, more able to move easily, swiftly, and decisively without the strictures of observation hanging over them, Trasdrom'man became even more of what Trasdrom'man was.

To that end, they separated themselves from the rest of humanity, cutting off all possibility that the Fratenni laHolc'm Compound could undermine Far Town's inroads by contact with offworlders. Outside comm contact was severely limited, the communication between Trasdrom'man and the rest of humanity held in reserve for the powerful few. The port became even more restricted, the landing of ships by any company, corporation, or entity limited to the remote drones that MegaCorp had been forced to use. This way, the populace of this harsh world were virtual prisoners, and never could their best and brightest see better possibilities elsewhere.

Only one concession was wrestled from them. Pressure was applied from the trading companies, backed by threats of a shipping embargo. Ships in peril must be allowed access to whatever world was closest, not matter whether they were crewed or not. The condemnation that would come upon Trasdrom'man should they refuse to admit a ship whose peril might bring loss of life to its crew would bring retribution from all space-faring worlds. Give that concession, they were told, or the retribution they might receive if they failed to allow this would be dreaded and abhorrent. Trasdrom'man would be cut off from all shipping deliveries, and the world would die.

Even as Far Town touted the praises of the legendary first couple, the Grandmothers moved ahead also, soon forgetting that they had given up power to let another part of this world coexist along with them. The Fratenni laHolc'm Compound became known as the 'de Gaso-Fratenni laHolc'm Compound, as yet another shift in family politics added one more layer of a Grandmother's vanity to the rooms of the great caverns that the geological turmoil of Trasdrom'man's ancient history had carved into the interiors of the mountains that surrounded the great inland sea, the original Grandmother's famed Sea of Revenge.

# —Chapter 17—

*"Just as the mighty oak's seed must fall for the sapling to grow, so must the Son of Man die on the cross for Mankind to be born again. For the greatest of love is found in the man who would sacrifice his own life for another. So our Savior did show to us when he was stretched on the cross, his lifeblood running from his wounds. Do not fear death, for from death, our Savior promises us new life."*

*—Sermon excerpt, Chartres Cathedral, Paris, Earth, 1786 AD*

THERE WERE two ways he could know he was alive. He'd been told that once, had even learned it for himself. Yes, that had been a hard lesson. It was one he'd learned by himself.

Von'de. His sweet, sweet Von'de. His precious, loving sister was his no longer.

She'd protected him for years, teaching him the first of the two ways, the way telling him he was alive. She had kept him safe, and she'd loved him. Shel'rn had felt joy in his time with her, looking forward to her return each day she had to be away.

He'd known he was alive during that time. He had laughed at his sister's jokes, and he'd spent the days coming up with his own. She'd laughed at them, telling him he was precious to her.

When she sat with him at mealtimes, their shared food just for them alone, he never considered the care she had taken to fix the items just the way he wanted them, the years during which she paid attention to his likes and dislikes, watching the small looks he gave before taking bites of recipes newly experimented with, and the expressions he made, revealing his favorites after those first bites were taken. She remembered just for him, and he thought everyone lived with that level of love all the time.

He had loved his sister with all his heart, and it was a feeling that had flowed through him like electric fire, the lightning of love that made his heart race when he heard her footsteps outside the door and his eyes sleep when she kissed them a final good-night.

His life was the second way, now. He lived, and he knew he lived. He lived fast and hard, and life had thrashed him to within a fragment of his existence. Now he didn't wait for others to love him or think of him or want him to be important in their lives. He knew that would never come back to him.

Shel'rn had tried to run from all that had begun after his sister was gone. He ran hard, too. In the process, he let a few other people—those who tried to get close to him—know they lived, also. He taught them his lesson, the hard one. He found that most of them already knew the second lesson. He occasionally thought, just perhaps, they must know the first one, the better one, also, and had lost it as he had.

Not everyone had known the first lesson, though. He'd found that out. That was the surprise that had caught him off guard. At first, he thought the people who tried to get close to him under-stood him, knew his pain of reaching out, the love that had once been in his life and was no longer there. He soon found they hadn't understood, and with that knowledge, he'd felt even more alone. No, that wasn't right, not the right way to express just how he'd felt before the old woman had taken his credits, telling him her secrets in her dark room. He had *known* he was alone.

That had been the hardest thing, assuming that everyone had known the way of being loved, feeling protected, and then Shel'rn finding they didn't know at all. Yes, he'd learned the second way to know he was alive, and with that knowledge, he'd joined what other people already knew.

The old woman had told him her words, telling him she knew the great secret of the ages. *Love*, she'd shared in her darkened chambers, and even offered to show him. He'd paid her good credits out of his pocket to have her say those words to him. Then he'd laughed roughly as he left the small, dark room where she practiced her craft, thinking that he should be angry to have wasted credits he didn't have to spare. He wasn't, though. He'd not been angry at all.

The old woman had known his secret, and after leaving her, he knew that she knew. She told him of the first way, the one of being loved, the way he'd come to believe was surely his, alone. The sharing of the knowing had given a justification for his anger at the ones who had taken his sister from him. His knowledge was no longer his to live with alone. He no longer had to arise each morning knowing there were two ways to feel he was alive, that the first was the better way, and that no one else knew the better kind of love. The old woman had known.

Yet, when he'd lived it, he hadn't understood the treasure he'd held in his hands, and after it had been taken, he'd felt cheated at the precious thing that had been stolen from him. The old woman's words couldn't give that back to him, couldn't restore the past that had been ripped from him; but to know it was *real,* that it could be his again, was worth more than all the credits he could ever earn.

The second way. That was all he had now, and it tore at him inside. He leaned against the pole in a darkness that saturated the emptiness of the night. The darkness reached back to him, wrapping itself around him, protecting him as best as it could, its inky substance promising anonymity, drawing him out, wooing him to let his pain bleed from his broken heart and his dry eyes. The darkness promised it would take what he had to give, would hold him, and his world would be better, his *self* would be better, stronger, and he would no longer have to carry his pain.

He listened, and he hated himself for it. He felt the rising tide inside, the tears forming in his eyes, but he continued to hold his head high, his face looking into the darkness, and his eyes seeing nothing but the blackness. That was what he wanted to see, nothing. He refused to raise his hands to his face, refused to wipe the tears that fell from his eyes. His hands remained in his pockets, his shoulder against the pole, the darkness of the city around him, and when it was over, the hurt remained inside, as deep as ever.

Yes, he'd listened, and the darkness had lied. His sister had told him she'd never leave him, and she'd lied. One day, that last day, she'd come to him, her footsteps different from her usual light-hearted tap-tap-tap. He'd looked up to her as she'd come through the door, the joy in his heart suddenly unsure as he saw the look, the desperation on her face. She'd turned to him and then glanced away, putting her hand to her eyes, her fingers wiping at the redness there.

She hadn't brought her arms and her hugs to him that afternoon, her happiness in him making his day complete, the jokes he'd made up that day told to incite her laughter, the tears in her eyes ones of happiness and joy. That was the day, and he knew this only in hindsight, but on that day, his world had turned on the great pivot of that one moment, and it would never be the same.

Shel'rn hadn't understood then the great machinations of the

House of the Grandmothers, what the world knew as the 'de Gaso-Fratenni laHolc'm Compound. His sister did, though, and she knew what had been done. She'd become a pawn in the game, traded for business reasons, her bonding, this arranged match-matching, for no other reason than to bring additional power to the compound. Her brother, that one she loved so, was not to be part of the equation, and he would be sent away, far away, so there would be no temptation for him to be allowed to interfere in the Grandmother's plans.

He was sent, too. Before the evening was over, he'd been packed up and was no longer a part of his sister's life. He hadn't understood why she hadn't hugged him and laughed with him. Instead, she'd gone directly to his room and begun packing his things. When he pressed her for an answer, a reason for what she was doing, she brightened the look on her face and told him he was going on a trip, a sort of vacation where he would meet lots of new people.

He hadn't believed her. He'd seen the falseness in that bright smile, her eyes still red, and he'd known he didn't want to go on this trip, that he didn't want to leave his sister behind. When the men had shown up, intruding into their space, his and his sister's private world, he'd run to his sister, wrapping his arms around her, and refused to let go. His sister had wrapped her arms around him, hugging him tightly, but then she had let him go, let the men peel him from her, and hadn't stopped them as they pulled him kicking and screaming from the room.

As the men carried him down the hallway outside their door, he heard that voice he loved so one last time. She let out a wail of anguish that reached its long fingers of pain after him and had torn at his small heart. That's when he'd known, without really understanding, that he was never coming home again.

That had been the second way, the lesson he'd learned. Love lets a person know he or she is alive in the most joyous way possible. So, he had learned, does pain.

There was something else that had been part of the lesson. Pain wasn't quite so much fun.

FAR IS A WORD that has no real meaning to a small boy, one not yet into those years when a growing body and a growing interest in others' bodies have begun to fracture his focus on his family and his home. Far is in the next room where something cannot be seen without moving, without walking there in order to find or touch it. Far is the distance across the sea just outside the glassine windows where the distant cliff faces can be glimpsed, the mountains' sides there showing blank walls of stone in the day and covered with the sparking windows of the compounds at night. Far is tomorrow or the day after, a time that isn't today, a time for which one must wait, but not wait too long. Those places and times that are farther than that aren't real. They are words only, the meanings unclear, accepted because one has to just accept some things. However, accepting does not always mean understanding.

The men, and later, other men—and women, too—who took him away told him things he had to accept, but they were things he didn't understand. He was going far away, and they wouldn't arrive until many distant days. Those words had no meaning to Shel'rn. Far away was his sister's room. Really far away was where his sister went every day, the way to it lost in the confusion the few times he'd been there. Many days distant, to him, was after he slept, or maybe after he slept twice. However, before this trip he was forced to take was finally done, he slept many times more than twice, and he was much farther away than his sister's room. Much, much farther away.

The traveling was very hard on the small boy. It was still winter, and spring was many days away. The trip was also very hard on the adults, those men and women who were bundled up

396

in the slow-moving transports, some of whom endured the winter's biting wind whistling through broken windows. The group was a desperate lot, the men and women who were riding in the transports. Either they had acted poorly in the confines of the city or compounds, the consequences of which they were suffering now, or they had run out of options, and this was their last grab at any kind of life. They'd been told Shel'rn was an orphan with no living relatives, and that was the way he was treated. He was very frightened, and when he cried his tears of loneliness or whimpered his fear of the unknown, the men and the women, concerned with only their own small matters, spoke roughly to him, and then hit him if he didn't do as they asked.

By the time they reached the settlement, the passage of time in the transports allowed him to toughen up. He wanted away from the misery of the group he'd been subjected to. All through the trip, he hadn't known where he was going or what to expect when he got there. However, when he'd seen the buildings of the settlement, anticipation of the familiar world of people and warmth and food called to him, and he was away, lost in the settlement's desolate winter. He didn't miss the people in the transports and was glad to be gone from them. His dirty clothing, unchanged since leaving so many days ago, helped him blend in as one of the settlement's newest street urchins, and with their help, he did survive and, perhaps, even thrived in this new world of luck and opportunities.

Shel'rn certainly didn't see his new life as good luck or an opportunity, but he *was* still alive, and many others in the history of the Grandmothers' Compound were not. In that, he was very lucky, indeed.

THE WOMAN SAT, her hair limp around her face, and two small children played in the dirt at her feet. Shel'rn had seen her there before, and had also seen the children. He rubbed his face where his glare goggles pressed against his temples, puzzled at her as he walked past, turning his head to watch her, seeming to remember a third child playing there not so long ago. As he walked through the day's heat, he absently tapped his chest, the now familiar bladderpack pushing cooling water to the extremities of his body. He thought of the children in the dust, the shade their only protection from the blistering extremes of this world's summer days. They'd die without protection, and in fact, now that he thought about it, he was surprised they could have survived this long without some sort of shield from the day's heat.

*They must have a place of retreat for the middle of the day. Some room dug into the soil, the ground providing at least some cooling insulation from the sun's rays. Surely,* he thought, as he went on his way, soon to be late for his job if he didn't hurry.

It wasn't much of a job, he had to admit. If they fired him, and they *had* threatened, he wouldn't have lost much. Patrolling the town's ways, picking up the remains of other people's carelessness, was what he did. Shel'rn thought of all the years he'd spent in these very streets, the winter's cold forcing him to learn the narrow spots of warmth just where a heating vent might exit the side of a building, or a storeroom door might be carelessly left unlocked, the cold less inside than outside. He'd fought summer's heat the same way, burrowing into whatever low spot he could during the days, the marginally cooler nights used to live his life.

This bladderpack, this *water suit,* had been a godsend to him, and he maintained it with immaculate care. He smiled as he once again tapped his chest, the bladderpack hanging under his clothing. *Survival.* He knew about that. He'd be dead without his water suit, couldn't work this job or do anything outdoors without one of these.

He walked by a place he recognized, hidden, unless a person knew just where to look to find it easily, just a depression where the ground around a building's wall had been dug back many years ago. The reason for the digging was long forgotten, but the depression was still there, providing a cool place for a small body to spend the day in relative protection. No one occupied the recess today, but Shel'rn could see the forgotten remains from someone who had been staying there, the small body perhaps covered to be less easily seen.

*Yes,* he thought, *the forgotten remains of someone's carelessness sleeps here, just as I did many years ago.*

He also knew he'd have to mark this place in his memory. The trash there would have to be cleaned, or the street child who used the depression would be noticed and run off. Shel'rn had lived that life, and he felt an affinity for those who were downtrodden due to no fault of their own. He helped the homeless out in little ways like this when he could.

After a few moments, he came to the town complex where he checked in each morning. If he didn't check in, he wouldn't get credit for the hours he worked. No one was normally there when he scanned his identity into the machine. No one would check up to see if he'd shown up for work that day, but the reader would tell them if he was there, and also if he checked out after his assigned hours were completed. Only if he was seen loitering during the day, or if the trash started to accumulate around the buildings, would someone talk to him.

He gave a rueful smile as he stepped back into the heat, his day's pay now started. He did a very good job for the town, and he worked very quickly, too. His fast pace was what allowed him time to sit and visit with the people he came across during his duties. That sitting and visiting was also what had gotten him in trouble, the town leaders threatening him with the loss of his pay. He still held the position because no one else wanted it, and also, he knew, because he did what he was paid to do, to keep the streets clean.

This day, he decided, he would check on the woman and her children, if she was still there when his work took him that direction. However, for now, he had a real job to do, and that place by the building's wall where one of the town's urchins had slept was his first priority. He had to protect his own. He was all they had.

SHEL'RN NEARLY tripped over the shape lying in the dust. When he turned, he saw the woman from earlier, and she moved her head to look as he called out.

"Sorry, I be, mos. Leave this here, did you?" He watched her move her eyes to see what he was talking about, a slight frown rumpling the skin of her forehead before she looked away again.

Shel'rn looked down at the shape under his feet and realized it was one of the children he'd seen playing that morning. Concerned, he knelt to check the child, rolling it over onto its back. He watched, horrified, as the child convulsed, its eyes rolled back in its head, and it exhausted a long, final breath of air. Shel'rn looked up at the woman, who had turned to watch as he knelt by the now-dead form in his hands.

"Dead, he be, too?" Her mouth finally stirred. She turned her eyes to watch the one child still playing at her feet, its movements listless in the increasing heat of the day. Shel'rn looked at her, perplexed at how she could sit there when one of her children had just died. He arranged the dead child gently at his feet and stepped over to face the woman, kneeling to look her in the face. Gently taking her chin in his hand, he turned her face until her eyes locked on his.

*Shock,* he thought. *Shock and heat exhaustion. Also die, this woman will, if some help, she doesn't get.*

Unsure later why he did just what he did, only knowing he felt he had no other choice at the time, he stood and gathered the still living child in his arms. Reaching to take the woman's hand, he pulled her to her feet and began leading her with him. Glancing back, he hesitated for a moment, looking at the dead child and hating to leave it. Feeling the woman beginning to slump where she stood, he made the decision to help the living while they still lived, and the three of them moved on. Soon, he could see the door to his small set of rooms just ahead. It wasn't much. There was hardly space for him inside, but he couldn't let this woman and her final child die simply for the sake of a few handbreadths of space.

He led her down the steps, and with his foot, he nudged his door open, breathing in the welcome relief of the rooms sunk into the cool recesses of the banked soil, providing a redoubt from the rising heat outside. He stepped into the back of the two rooms and laid the child on his sleeping mat. When he turned again to the woman, she had dropped to the floor, wilted with no energy to stand.

Shel'rn stepped to his food preparation area, and he drew some water to cool her and the child. He now realized what he was doing, just what he had done in helping this woman and her child. He had made himself responsible for the both of them. He was supposed to be working outside right now. He'd signed in but hadn't signed out, and that wouldn't look good.

He sighed. It would make his life hard if he took on this new responsibility and lost his only source of income in the same stroke. However, that possibility he'd have to face when it came. Right now, he had to do what was necessary, and these two people needed his help. The best thing to do, he knew, would be what was right in front of him, and that's what he did.

Taking a clean cloth, he wiped the cooling water over the woman's face and arms, and as he did so, he noticed something he hadn't seen in the street as he passed her this day or on previous days. In a simple way, she was quite pretty. The son in the other room had the same look. His features would be as attractive once he was cleaned up. That, Shel'rn could already see, even through the dehydration and grime.

A touch of water to her lips, and she seemed to gain a bit of her energy back. She didn't move with the strength of a well person, but she was able to carry herself to the other room to lie with her boy. When Shel'rn knelt to tell her of the one they'd left by the side of the street, tears welled in her eyes, and she looked away.

*Knows, she does,* he told himself. *Broken her heart, it has.* When he told her he would go to retrieve the small body, the look of gratitude for the favor he offered twisted his heart. He was certain he couldn't know how she must feel, but he did know this woman's anguish tore at her deeply.

He didn't bring the boy to her, he told her later that day, as there was no place in his rooms to put him. The town had facilities for such as the boy's body, and she nodded her understanding, as she reached a slender arm to place her hand on his shoulder.

She sipped water continually that day, her color showing a gradual improvement, but the child at her side continued breathing rapidly and shallowly. When Shel'rn asked her name, she looked at him with a puzzled look on her face, then whispered softly, "Maisley. Yes, Maisley, my name be, I think." Then she closed her eyes and seemed to drift off to sleep.

Late that night as he lay on the seating bench in the front room, his mat given to the mother and her child, he stared at the ceiling over his head, and he breathed in deeply, his thoughts on the woman in the other room. He'd never had the responsibility for another person, and he knew he was barely able to manage taking care of himself. With those thoughts in his mind, he let himself drift off to sleep, never considering the sense of duty he shouldered daily for the current crop of street urchins who found a way to survive due to Shel'rn's diligent help.

LATER THAT NIGHT, something else happened that he never considered as a possibility. He found himself in a very intense dream with an unfamiliar woman he felt he seemed to know in some way. After some time of enjoying his dream, remembering the pull of such dreams years earlier as his manhood had come upon him, also remembering how as he had grown taller and stronger over the years, these dreams had been pleasurable from time to time, he allowed himself to wake, his body still full of the woman in his dream, desiring her, only to find the dream was alive and with him. Shocked at first, and then his body responding as it had in the dream, one that he only vaguely realized had been no dream, he gave himself over to it, the sensations drawing him in with an intensity he hadn't thought possible of his body.

When they were finished, Maisley, having met some need she'd been lacking, and Shel'rn, finding out more about a woman than he'd ever imagined, she returned to her boy, leaving Shel'rn to lie alone in wonderment at what had occurred.

SHEL'RN'S EYES locked with Maisley's, the coughing seemingly endless this time. Only when it quieted did they release their long-held breaths, the intensity of the moment tangible between them. The boy hadn't gotten better even after the healer had traveled to see him, and that had been all the way from Summer City.

Shel'rn let his eyes drop to the swelling at Maisley's waist, and he wondered how this had happened. No, he knew how this had happened. That first night he'd brought her home, the heat having taken her other son, and this one nearly gone, also, she'd come to him in the darkness. Whether in gratitude or in need, he'd never learned. She'd given him a quick look the next morning when she stepped from the back room, but other than that, she acted as if the incident had never happened.

Now, though, the incident happened again almost every

night. That hadn't started right away, of course. There had been nothing else between them until the woman's sickness. When she started getting sick in the mornings, she finally told him that this sickness was his, also. She offered to go have it removed—for a price, she knew a healer who would do so—but he'd been fascinated with the idea of a child. He'd protected so many others, others that hadn't known what he'd done for them, others that he never knew as he helped them nor had he been able to track what became of them. This one could be different. It could be his. That made his heart leap. He asked Maisley to let him think about it, and sometime after that, he went to her, asking her to keep the child for him. That had been their second night of intimacy.

He didn't know if he loved her. She was attractive enough, that was for certain. He knew now why she'd been there on the street all those days, and why she hadn't had a place to go. She told him all that and more during the many nights they'd been together since then.

Her husband had taken a sickness, and so had her oldest child. The family had come to the settlement from Summer City the previous year in hopes of a fresh start. It hadn't proven to be a good choice.

The husband started the coughing even before they arrived. He found work, taking the most menial of jobs, none of them lasting very long. When the coughing started, causing him to miss a day or two of work, there would always be someone who had taken his place when he returned.

When her husband died, there were no funds to pay for the rooms they were in. That was why she'd been on the street. Their things had been taken to pay the amount owed, and she and her three boys had been given the clothes they wore, not even a water suit left to them.

She had paused when she told him that, and then she'd

continued with a whisper that their boys had never had water suits. They'd been forced to remain inside every day during the heat. She'd reached her hand and placed it on Shel'rn's chest, laying her head on his shoulder as she continued, her voice barely loud enough for him to hear.

"Knew they were going to die, I did. To do, there was nothing. Gone, my Barr'e was. Then, after living in the open, our firstborn, also." She absently rubbed her fingers over the traces of hair on his chest as she shared the deepest part of her, that pain that would rip her in two if she didn't keep it carefully bottled up inside. Afterwards, she refused to speak of it again. "When started the cough, my next one did, taken from me, my life was. Emptied, I was, and to die, him, I couldn't watch. More than I could do, it was. Now, gone soon, my youngest will be. With him, my Barr'e dies a second time."

With those words, she turned onto her back and rubbed her stomach. As she spoke, Shel'rn heard a hint of a smile in her voice. "Here, inside, come back to me, life has. You, this little one be, Shel'rn. Saved me, you have."

He had reached to her, then, and together they had renewed that life once more. Today, though, the boy might die. He *would* die. Both Shel'rn and Maisley knew that. The coughing already had him, and he was far gone.

*Perhaps*, the healer had said, *if the heat, so much of his strength had not stolen from him, heal him, my medicines could. Help this small one, they will not, though.* The healer had shaken her head and turned from them.

Maisley leaned against Shel'rn's strength. He placed his chin on her head, moving his jaw back and forth as a way of acknowledging her presence. He felt the pressure of her belly against him, and even more to his body's liking, he felt the press of her breasts against his chest, the nipples already enlarged in preparation for the baby. They were to him points of fire, and as he felt that fire begin to surge through his body, he knew he was responding to the sensuality of the woman standing against him. His body couldn't help that, but even as he pulled her to the bed and let his body take the mother whose son was dying in the next room, tears ran down his face. He still didn't know if he loved her, and soon, the baby inside of her, the one he had put there, would greet him, and he knew what he was. He was just a boy. Then, even as he gasped in passion while his body wrenched the makings of life from him, the thought came to haunt him once again, the dark thought clouding his pleasure:

He still didn't know if he loved her.

MAISLEY SCREAMED again. "Gods! Hurt this much before, it never did!"

Shel'rn used a damp cloth to wipe the beads of sweat from her forehead, doing it just the way she'd told him. His heart pounded with the unsureness of what was about to happen. They couldn't afford to ask the healer to return. Maisley had said that with three sons already born to her, she probably knew as much as the healer, anyway. So, here he was with his damp cloth.

He was scared, though.

The pain came and went, and so did Maisley's screams, although they became more and more frequent. Finally, her knees high on the bed, she reached and grabbed them with her hands, yelling, "Now! Take it, now!"

Shel'rn jumped up, his eyes blinking rapidly as he realized what she wanted him to do. The baby was being born. She'd told him this would happen. He tried to think. A clean cloth. A sharp instrument. Yes, he had it all. As he moved to the foot of the bed, he looked, and there it was, a beautiful, ugly, wrinkled thing, and he reached for it.

"The cloth, Shel'rn. Reach with the cloth." Maisley, her exhaustion not so complete she couldn't be irritated, grabbed the clean towel at her side and threw it at him. "Be it a boy or a girl?"

Shel'rn seemed mystified at the question, seeing only the small limbs, the furred head, and the wrinkled skin. Then, reaching out, he wrapped the cloth around the small form between Maisley's legs and lifted it. He looked from the baby to Maisley. "Breathing already, it be, and shaking its arms."

Maisley repeated her question, needing badly to know the answer. "Boy or girl?"

Shel'rn paused. It was here. Wasn't that enough? Yet, he had the presence of mind to check between the baby's legs, whispering with a smile, "A girl, Maisley."

Maisley let out a deep sigh. "A girl. Thank the gods. Live, she might." Again reaching to her side, she grabbed the sharp instrument lying there and held it out to the baby's father. "From me, cut her. Then here, place her." She patted her stomach.

Shel'rn's eyes opened wide. "Cut her, Maisley?"

At that, she laughed. "Truly, fathered my child, a boy has. Attached, she be, Shel'rn. Set free, she must be. As I told you earlier, you must tie it, or bleed to death, she will. Cut fast and quick."

He did so, and the baby didn't bleed to death. He was very glad of that. When he placed the child, this girl baby, *his* girl baby on Maisley's stomach, he was amazed. He stood, his back straight, and tears started to run down his face.

*Maybe,* he thought. *Just maybe, love this woman, I do, after all.* There was one thing he did know without any hesitation. He did love his daughter. The instant he saw her, he knew that. He placed his hand on the small body on her mother's stomach. Maisley reached her hand and placed it on top of Shel'rn's. When he looked up at her, she was smiling at him.

He was surprised to think of something he'd never considered before. There was the chance this woman might love him, too. A smile opened up on his face, and he couldn't make it stop.

It was the most amazing thought. Perhaps she loved him, too.

SHEL'RN PICKED up the little girl in his arms and swung her around and around in the sunshine. He laughed with her as she giggled with the feeling of flying, safe in her daddy's arms.

"Remember this, little Relei'sene. This day, remember always. So many beautiful spring days all in a row, never in your life or mine have we had." He grabbed her to him, and they fell to the ground, the sun warming their winter-frosted bodies as they rolled around laughing in each other's arms.

At the end of their tumbling, Relei'sene sat on top of her daddy's chest. She reached down, leaning her face close to his, and she grabbed his ears. "More, Daddy. Spin me more, you must."

Shel'rn roared with false indignation, the little girl sitting on him howling with laughter at the meanness she knew was only part of the game, "Ask for more, you do? More? Get more, you will, little girl!" With one quick sweep of his arms, he rolled over, lifting her high in the air. Standing to his feet, he spun her around and around.

"Down, Daddy! Walk, let me!" Relei'sene beat on Shel'rn's arms until he slowed and set her on her feet. She giggled as she wandered from side to side, unable to control herself. "Look, Daddy. Silly, I be."

He ran to sweep her up once again, this time holding her tightly to him. "And love silly, I do, Relei'sene, so love you, I must." He kissed her on the cheek, and as she tried to wipe it off, he stuck out his tongue, running it over the spot she'd just brushed clean.

"Yuck, Daddy. Lick you, I will." She stuck out her tongue, giving Shel'rn no other option than to hug her too close for her to lick him.

"How your mommy be doing, let's go see, Relei'sene.

Maybe better, she be, and play with you, she will." She skipped beside him as he held her hand, and Shel'rn felt his heart wrenched with love for his daughter.

*Gods above and below, if any there be, a real prayer, this time, this be.* Tears came to Shel'rn's eyes as shook his head to clear them. He'd never really said a prayer before. He knew some people did, but he'd never thought of the gods as real. This, though, he really wanted, and it was worth a prayer to any gods who might be there. *Please, know a lifetime of days like this one, let my little girl. Please, Gods. The only thing from you I've ever asked for, this be. Take me, if that be the price I must pay, but to my little girl, be good.*

With those words, Shel'rn wiped his eyes with his free hand and looked at his daughter at his side. She sensed the turn of his head and looked up at the tall man holding her hand.

"Daddy, why you be crying? Be something wrong?"

He smiled. "No, baby. So in love with you, I be, that inside, keep it, I can't."

"Love you, too, I do, Daddy. Keep it inside, I can't, either. Going to tell everybody, I be." With that, she ran ahead, skipping along, singing, "Love my daddy, I do. Love my daddy, I do."

Shel'rn smiled as he watched her, listening to the words of her song as she sung them in her little girl's voice. *Love you, too, baby,* he thought. He looked up and sent his thanks to whoever had listened to his prayer. *Thank you.* He really meant it, too.

SHEL'RN LEANED and kissed Maisley on the forehead as the sound of Relei'sene's song filtered in from the other room.

"Beautiful it be outside, Maisley. Come to play in the sun with Relei'sene, will you? This day, no glare goggles be needed."

Maisley sat for a few minutes looking at nothing, then turned her head to the sound of her daughter singing, telling everyone her message about her daddy. Maisley gave a wan smile. "You,

409

so much she loves, Shel'rn. Wants everyone to know, she does."
She took his hand. "Love you, too, I do. Today, though." Her
eyes welled up as she choked out her next words. "Barr'e. The
boys. All of them. Love you, I do, Shel'rn. Trust that, you can.
Yet, comes back to me at times, the loss does. Outside again, take
her, you must. No good like this, I be. Go." She motioned with
her hand, leaning back and letting the tears flow.

Later that night, Relei'sene, exhausted from more outside
play than she'd ever known in one day, slept. Her parents didn't
sleep, though. For a very long time that night, Shel'rn soothed
the grief from Maisley's thoughts as he soothed her body with
his.

This man who had been a boy still when he'd rescued a
mother and her son from certain death in the heat of the summer
had grown up very quickly. Now, no longer that boy, he understood what this woman in her grief needed from him, and it was
something he wanted to give. Then, after a time, the soothing
stopped, and passion took over. At that point, what Shel'rn
wanted to give became something his body needed to give,
something his body could no longer resist giving to this woman
on this beautiful, cool, spring night. His passion also helped with
the grief Maisley had endured that day, and when their passions
were exhausted, both of them slept very well for the rest of the
night.

# —Chapter 18—

*. . . an eye for an eye and a tooth for a tooth. So,*
*the judgment was proclaimed throughout all the*
*land . . .*

—*From* Happy Endings Don't
Always Happen in Fairy Tales,
*author unknown*

THE OLD TRADER glanced at the ceiling above him. When he'd learned of the boy the old woman wanted to keep track of, he'd asked around, waiting for an opportunity to visit Far Town. He'd passed up contracts that would have paid him good credits, just to wait. Then, in a matter of days, there had been several contracts come to him, all to Far Town. He'd thought that strange, but it was no stranger than many other things he'd experienced in his life.

He found the boy in Far Town. He'd been unsure at first, knowing the old woman had wanted news of a *boy*. However, after checking thoroughly, he became convinced he'd found the one she was looking for.

What had thrown him off for a time was that the person the old trader had found wasn't a boy. Not by any means. The trader might have guessed him for a youth had he been alone, possibly, but this one had both a bonded one and a daughter. He was most certainly a man. Some people, the trader thought with no small amount of animosity, just stay young in their appearance longer than others. Lucky them. He scowled, recalling his own ragged visage from those times he deigned to peer into the occasional mirror.

He was still looking up at the ceiling when a door across the room opened. He couldn't tear himself away. It was too amazing. Who could have known there were actually real rooms in this mountain with ceilings that stretched so high as to actually seem to recede into the heavens? After moments more, the silence growing long, he turned his eyes to the person who had come through the door to stand in the room with him, and as he looked at her, he froze. It was her. The Grandmother. It chilled him to be in her presence.

"You bring me news?" The woman speaking to him was statuesque. She was no longer young, but her voice was strong, and her hair was dark. She pressed her lips together, obviously waiting for him to speak.

The old trader dropped his eyes to the floor. "Told I would get credits, I was." He flicked his eyes at her to see just how she responded.

"You'll get your credits. Now, the news you bring." She pressed her lips even tighter.

The trader hesitated, knowing it was sometimes easy to push the very rich too far, and obviously, this woman was very rich. He didn't want to give his information for nothing in return, though.

He continued, "Passed up many lucrative contracts, I did. Taken them, I could, but not and bring this news to you. Forgive me for being so forthright. Feed my mouth, these contracts do. Not free, food be." He dropped on one knee, that seeming an obvious move to him in this woman's presence, or perhaps, he considered, it was his bad knee, and it gave out at just that time. Later, he would give both versions of events to other traders he happened to share drinks with in various establishments.

Whatever the reason the man did what he did, the Grandmother seemed pleased. She reached into a pouch and took out a bag of coin credits, tossing them at the trader. "Will that satisfy your stomach? Will it fill it in its time of need? I think you will find yourself adequately compensated. Now, what be the news?"

The old trader caught the bag easily, his hunger perhaps not too far gone into the weakness of his supposed starvation. His hands shaking, he opened the top to see metal coins, the most substantial of credits, the Trasdrom'man lyans, nestled inside. He smiled before wiping it away, certain he'd already told the Grandmother that it was, perhaps, far more than enough. He looked at her, taking time to phrase his answer, not wanting his mistakes to cause him to have to give the bag back. "In the town, saw him, I did. Playing outside, he was."

The Grandmother's eyes narrowed. "Outside? He was playing outside?"

The trader's heart caught. He didn't know just what the woman wanted him to say, or what he needed to tell her to satisfy her curiosity. He tried again. "Spring, it was, and pretty, too, for several days in a row."

The woman snorted. "The weather be not a concern of mine. Do you have real news of the boy or not?"

The man jumped, his voice suddenly blurting out an answer, though not the one he would have probably given if the woman speaking to him hadn't startled him so. "Not a boy. A man. A grown man. Bonded."

"Bonded?" she snapped. "At his age?"

The old trader took a deep breath. She didn't believe him. However, there was no doubt he had the right boy. He dared to go on. "Bonded. With a child, even." He glanced up as the old woman froze, her expression telling the trader that the dance he was in with her had finally circled in the right direction. "Playing in the park with his child, he was, and laughing, they were."

"And?" The question was sharp.

He shrugged his shoulders. He didn't know what else she could want from him. He took a step back when she spoke next, her voice a hiss rather than a whisper.

"Male or female child, you fool!"

He let a smile ghost his face. Now he had reached the core of her desire. He replied with a slight bow, "Female, good mos."

Very faintly, he heard her say, "Thank you. Tell no one you talked with me. You may go." When he lifted his head, he was alone in the room.

DÓME ELUSSIE'SAN 'de Gaso-Fratenni laHolc'm walked the chamber in front of her glassine window, the summer heat already beating down on the world outside. She knew the sea would never warm, no matter how hot the sun grew as it tortured the waters, and the coolness of its depths coursing through the flowpipes in the walls around her provided the chill she felt in the air. She tugged her wrap tighter, knowing also, this coolness would be greatly appreciated as the tortuous summer wore on.

She stopped and spoke to the two men in the room with her, her elegance and refinement belying the intent in her words. "That Von'de has disappointed me, as always. Now, though, I have a granddaughter to take her place." She stepped closer to those whom she had called to her side to do this thing she needed done. "Von'de will be no more. Plans be already in motion. This one, though. This brother who has provided me with a girl child. This one we must deal with. Then, the girl child must be brought here to be raised in the compound."

The two men looked each other in the eyes, and then one of them turned to the Dóme and spoke. "Dóme Elussie'san, served you well, we always have. No different in this, it will be. Place your trust in us, you may."

After a pause and a throat cleared, the second man questioned, "Choose the method, may we?"

Dóme Elussie'san turned and walked to the window. When she had first wrested this compound from the previous Grandmother, duties like this had been hard. However, over the years, she had come to realize that to achieve her ends, there could be no soft spots. She remembered the boy. His older sister, too. They had been in her way from the time they were born, and that was why she'd washed her hands of them when they were young. Now, they were in her way again, and washing her hands of them was no longer good enough. This solution must be final, taking them from her for good. The girl, Von'de, her end was already arranged. With a word, her brother would be a problem no longer. With this daughter he'd provided, he'd served his purpose. She had no further use for him.

She turned to the two men. "You must be by his side until he breathes no more. Then bring the girl child to me."

"If a mother, there be?" The whisper came at her, another layer of maintenance to perform to keep this world of hers, this compound, at its best.

Turning from them, she cast her decision. "The mother be no concern of mine. Just the girl child." Hearing the men leave the chamber, she smiled as she thought out loud. "Those contracts to that old trader have played themselves out very well, indeed. It has been well worth the loss on those shipments."

With satisfaction on her face, she stood and watched the sun as it dropped behind the mountains, the darkness taking over the room. She didn't notice. After all, the rising darkness in the room was nothing compared to the darkness already deep within her heart.

AS THE SUN broke over the buildings in Far Town, Maisley stepped up behind Shel'rn, putting her arms around him, whispering into the bare skin of his back, "Be your nightmares so bad? All this night, you haven't slept. Share with me, can you not?"

Shel'rn drew a deep breath, holding it for a time before letting it slide from his body. With a breaking voice, he began, "Heavy on me, this news be, Maisley. My family be of the Grandmothers. For years, know that, I didn't. Now, sure of it, I be."

Maisley stepped around to stand in front of him. At first she didn't understand. "The Grandmothers? What? Unclear on this, I be." Everyone on their world knew tales of the Grandmothers, knew and feared to be noticed by them. His words chilled her to the core.

He looked her in the face as if searching, and then he turned back to the window to stare at the fierceness of the sun as it started to crawl into the sky. "Know of them, you do, my bonded. From the sea. laHolc'm."

"laHolc'm." Her voice broke. "Stories, they be, little children to frighten. Please tell me that. Stories, only, about the Grandmothers and the granddaughters."

"Nay." He hugged her tightly. "True, they be, and the Grandmother now in power be my mother." He laughed a sour laugh. "Though, only now do I know that." He paused and kissed her on the top of the head. "So sorry, I be, dear Maisley."

They stood for a time, and with her life fracturing about her, the stories heard both terrible and cruel, she asked, "To do, what can we? What should we?"

Shel'rn took a deep breath and smiled, his face not fooling his woman at all. "Far from the Sea of Revenge, we be. Perhaps here, safety will be ours."

She stepped back and slapped her hand sharply on the bare

skin of his chest. "Not from knowing we be safe did you, the night through, stand here. Lie to me, do not dare, Shel'rn. Take my daughter, and from you, run, I will." Tears broke from her as she wrapped her arms around herself and turned from him.

He stepped to her, wrapping her in his arms, and he whispered to her, "Best that might be. Safer, at least."

"No!" She whirled around, throwing his arms from her. "Suggest that, don't you even dare. Love you, I do." She paused as she heard her daughter shift on the sleeping bench that had been specially cushioned to allow her to rest safely outside of her parents' bed.

More quietly she went on, her eyes on her daughter. "Also loves you, your daughter does." At this, Maisley smiled, her eyes still stinging with her tears. "Even more than me, if possible, that be."

SHEL'RN LOOKED at his daughter with an affection that made his heart break. He knew she loved him. He knew they both did, and he also knew the danger they were in if the Grandmother ever learned of him. His sister, Von'de, was dead. Arriving at work some weeks past, he'd seen the report that had shown up on the town service Vids, the accident that had taken the beautiful, young Von'de to her death. With the set of facts in the report, he had determined just who he was, and he'd known what his mother would want from him. He knew one more thing, besides. He'd already lost in this battle with this woman and the child she'd given him. They would remain at his side.

He took a deep breath and whispered, "Then, be prepared, we must."

For the rest of the day, he told her the things they must do, and what must happen if certain other things should begin to occur. Relei'sene must be kept safe, he told her over and over. No matter what happens to me, Relei'sene must be kept safe. The things he worried about might never happen, he tried to reassure her, but if they did, at all costs, Relei'sene must be kept safe.

WHEN THE MEN grabbed Shel'rn's arms, he almost didn't believe it. He was at work. He was going about his business, his water suit on, and he was clearing a hollow in the soil where a waif had been sleeping. He had the debris in his hand, and then other hands had grabbed his arms. At first he thought only of the trash the hands had made him drop, his fingers automatically releasing the remains of the stolen food that had been consumed in this spot. He would need to bend down once again and pick it up all over. That irritated him, and he wanted to turn to ask what they were doing. Then, in that instant, he knew.

It was morning, yet, and Maisley wouldn't know he was missing until he didn't check out in the evening. She wouldn't know to run, to take Relei'sene and flee far away to keep his daughter from the clutches of the Grandmother. This was the Grandmother that was his mother, the mother who hadn't even acknowledged him when he'd lived at the compound all those years ago. His sister had been his mother. He called her his sister, but he'd known her as a mother.

Von'de hadn't been filled with the cruelty of the Grand-mother, one to fight and claw her way to the top. That was why she'd been sent away, used for a pawn in the economic power structure of the Grandmothers' Compound. She had borne no children, though. Whether through choice or design, Shel'rn would never know; but certainly out of spite, his mother had killed his sister.

He fought them when they held him outside the town, the baked dirt of the hills covering their deed from the view of those who might be looking from a town street or window. As the sun bore down on him, they pulled his clothing off his body, flinging his glare goggles to one side, ripping his water suit and his bladderpack from him. Then they held him to the ground, their hands on his feet and wrists, as the first few moments of burning soil against the bare skin of his back turned into hours baking his skin red and boiling the moisture from his body.

When they eventually stood, their own bladderpacks nearly depleted, Shel'rn didn't fight them any longer. He was struggling just to gather the strength to pull in another breath, trying to wait long enough to warn his Maisley to keep his daughter safe, to run with her.

The day nearing its end, he could finally hold out no longer, and his fight to breathe that next breath was lost. The men had promised their Dóme they would wait with him until he breathed his last, and they were men of their word.

As they walked away, ready to finish the next phase of their assignment, what they didn't know was that Shel'rn had found a way to warn his family. Not arriving home promptly from work, no matter the day or situation, was one of the triggers that Maisley and Relei'sene were to run. When the two men arrived at the rooms where they expected to find the daughter and a woman who was reputed to be quite attractive, there was no one home.

That was the pivotal point when they knew they were in hot water of their own, and they also knew, unlike the two they had let get away, they couldn't run. They would have to go back and face the Dóme, because if they didn't, she would come and find them. Neither option was very attractive, because both ways, they were already as dead as the sunbaked body they had held in their hands as its life had drained away.

Dead men walking. Dead man in the desert. This day, there was no difference. None at all.

# —Chapter 19—

Two things I saw
Across the dusty plain
Mixed among where
The war dead had lain.
One was the footsteps
As I followed you there.
The other was the tracks
Of your falling tears.

—Song sung in mourning
over the fallen

MAISLEY LOOKED at the packs and the goggles on the floor. *Said this might happen, Shel'rn did.* She took the two water suits that were still fresh in their wrappings and opened them. *Not to wait, I must. What he said, that be.* Slipping hers on, she filled the bladder with life-saving water. *If a false alarm this be, come find us, he will. Said so, he did.* She attached the bladderpack to her chest, its weight almost as heavy as the dread in her heart. *Take Relei'sene. Take her from the town.* Maisley opened the second water suit, her tears nearly overflowing as she looked at its child-sized proportions. *Who you be, tell no one. Barr'e's widow, you be.* She pulled her daughter to her, slipping the

420

unfamiliar water suit over her small body. *Find a family, you must. For a place to stay, offer them credits.* She pulled the pouch off the shelf, it containing inside all the credits Shel'rn had been able to get together. *Go quickly. Take nothing but yourselves, you must.*

With tears running down her face, she slipped both pairs of glare goggles over her neck and picked up her daughter. Looking around the room at what was left of the life she had come to love, she knew that once again, her world was being taken from her. As Relei'sene reached to play with the tears running down her mother's face, Maisley stepped through the door, and with that movement, her life as she had known it was no more.

*Come and find us, Shel'rn, my lover and my friend. Come and find us quickly. You, love and need, we do. You, love and need, I do. Come, and home again, bring us.*

She'd been here in her life once before with her Barr'e, and she knew her cry was a useless one. If Shel'rn were alive, he would have already come to her. Now, all she could do was protect the one in her arms, and against men and against Grand-mothers, that she would do to her death. That she swore before all the gods in the heavens.

She would, too. They could test her. To her death, she would protect this little one that was all she had left of her Shel'rn. That's what he would want her to do.

Relei'sene laughed at being outside in the heat of the evening, the fading rays of sunshine making her blink. "Going on a trip, we be, Mommy. Go to see Daddy, we can. Go with us, Daddy can, too."

Maisley hugged Relei'sene tightly to her so she wouldn't see the anguish sweeping across her face. Taking a breath to steady her voice, she whispered, "Wish he could, I do, baby. Wish he could, I certainly do."

The darkness soon covered them as they left the city far

behind. What was ahead, Maisley didn't know, but she hoped it was life.

With a new and unexpected sense of resolve, she straightened her back and quickened her pace. There was life, she knew, and she held it in her hands. She could do this, save herself and save this child. She marched into the desert's darkness for Shel'rn. She marched into the desert for Relei'sene. She marched forward for life.

# Glossary

| | |
|---|---|
| 40,000 known heavenly bodies . . . . . | cryo pods use these for triangulation |
| Aretne's Colony out on Rondeo World . . . . | healing colony |
| Arianna . . . . . . . . . . . | Holcum's daughter |
| Barr'e . . . . . . . . . . . . | Maisley's first husband |
| Briei'la . . . . . . . . . . . | sister to Chia'ardo |
| Bron'in . . . . . . . . . . . | Reetia's bonded one |
| captgen'l . . . . . . . . . . | rank in the MegaCorp military |
| Carli Fausti . . . . . . . . | gets signal; friend to Regge |
| Chariel . . . . . . . . . . . | Maggents' husband |
| Chia'ardo . . . . . . . . . | brother to Briei'la |
| Chrismast . . . . . . . . . | bastardization of the old-Earth holiday of Christmas |
| city's port and satellite division . . . . . . . . . . . | where Carli and Regge work |
| control manager . . . . . | from the spaceport remote guidance division |
| *coup de grâce* . . . . . . . | crowning moment |
| de facto . . . . . . . . . . . | in fact |
| death-thing . . . . . . . . . | to dissolve the bonds of blood, declaring oneself an outcast |
| Dóme Elussie'san 'de Gaso-Fratenni laHolc'm . . . . . . . . . . | grandmother to Relei'sene |
| downside . . . . . . . . . . | on a planet |
| dreamsense . . . . . . . . | ability to dream unrecognized knowledge into an explanation of the past or a prediction of the future |
| drivestick . . . . . . . . . | transport joystick |
| duty partner . . . . . . . | assigned to work together |
| ear pieces . . . . . . . . . | headphones |
| Far Town . . . . . . . . . | second major city established on Trasdrom'man |
| Ferro-cement . . . . . . . | spray concrete machines |
| fireflashes . . . . . . . . . | sun's reflection on the waves |

| | |
|---|---|
| Tommeoseo ........ | barber on Trasdrom'man |
| Trasdrom'man ...... | harsh planet with a highly elliptical orbit, resulting in wildly erratic seasons; very isolated with a poor economy |
| var'delk ........... | furred, four-legged mammal native to Trasdrom'man |
| viewscreen ......... | monitor |
| Von'de ........... | sister to Shel'rn |
| water suit ......... | personal tubular drip system that keeps clothing perpetually moist |
| water suit bladderpack | water reservoir for the water suit; also called a water bladder |
| wordVid .......... | electronic book |

Read all the books in this vibrant new series!

# The Se'Yan't Chronicles

Get Yours At:

www.ThreeSkilletPublishing.com